Audrey Corr is in her fifties and works as a buyer of props for films. This is her first novel, and she is currently working on her second. She lives in County Mayo, Ireland.

# Dead Organised

**Audrey Corr**

**POCKET BOOKS**

**TownHouse**

First published in Great Britain by Pocket/Townhouse, 2001
An imprint of Simon & Schuster UK Ltd, and TownHouse
and CountryHouse Ltd, Dublin

Simon & Schuster UK is a Viacom Company

1 3 5 7 9 10 8 6 4 2

Simon & Schuster UK Ltd
Africa House
64–78 Kingsway
London WC2B 6AH

Simon & Schuster Australia
Sydney

TownHouse and CountryHouse Ltd
Trinity House
Charleston Road
Ranelagh
Dublin 6
Ireland

A CIP catalogue record for this book is available
from the British Library

ISBN 1 903 65001 1

Typeset by SX Composing DTP, Rayleigh, Essex
Printed and bound in Great Britain by
Omnia Books Limited, Glasgow

For Murph

# Dead Organised

# Chapter One

I've been a poet and novelist for almost a week now and I am really getting the hang of it. Well. Since Carmel let me down so badly with the undertaking business, I had to do a complete stocktake, dig deep to discover my best qualities, and get on. You think you know people. She was all for it at first. Really excited about being Dublin's first firm of lady undertakers. Told everyone about it. You'd almost think it was her idea. Who did all the research? Visited the parlour homes, passing myself off as recently bereaved to get prices, checked out hearses, biers, graveyards, cars? She wouldn't even come with me. We had even got as far as getting a women's-enterprise, start-your-own-business grant from the EC, which we invested in lovely black clothes, shoes, and black edged business cards. But before you could say 'six feet under', she'd backed out. Said she wasn't cut out for undertaking. 'Who is?' I enquired. She couldn't answer.

It was Joe, of course, the friend. It would have been a different story if Joe had been involved. That was what this was all about. She wanted to bring Joe into it. She thought I didn't know. Everything goes back to Joe. Joe the Almighty. What she sees in him? She's one of those women who think they have to have a man, any man. Not me. Not this baby. We are not even speaking now. When I think what she called me. *Camel turd.* You don't have to be a genius to work out where that came from. It didn't touch me. Quite the opposite. I'll use the experience in one of my novels. Nothing is waste to the writer.

CARMEL: You can't use that sign, Shantell.
ME: Why not?
CARMEL: Read it, for God's sake. 'Don't let men put you down.' Not in our business.
ME: We haven't got a business yet.
CARMEL: And if you keep making signs like that we never will have a business.
ME: That's typical of you, Carmel. You are so negative. If it's not your idea—
CARMEL: You are acting like a spoilt child.
ME: Me? Well thank you Miss Nobody. You are the one who opted to go and live with socialist Joe. You spoiled everything. Don't come running to me when things go wrong.
CARMEL: At least Joe is trying to help people.
ME: And you think I'm not. Why do you think I am trying to start this business.

That was when she called me a camel turd but I won't put that in my dialogue.

It was exciting. A complete change. First I had to buy some bohemian clothes. Sort of flowing russets, with

2

holes and darns, because writers don't worry about that kind of thing. The nice lady in the charity shop was delighted, she hadn't been able to move those items since they were donated, and gave them to me for next to nothing. I tried a beret but it wasn't me. I decided to make do by letting the rinse grow out of my hair. Au naturel from now on. Another great writer thing. No big expensive outlay. One A4 pad, one Garda notebook, just to get me started, and one packet of Biros. I love the little notebook with its elastic, and the tiny brown bookie's pencils attached. The other tenants in my house said they hardly recognised me and Ann Murphy from flat four, who has such a thing about her hair, thought I didn't see her leaning over the banisters to look at my roots.

I feel so alert, so aware, so sensitised. The bird on the clothes-line, the evening shadows – I light candles all over the flat now – old people's smiles. And that after only three novelist days. I am so busy you wouldn't believe it. I joined the library, visited the Writers' Centre, had coffee in the Writers Museum, swept through the National Gallery and applied for a reader's ticket to Trinity Library. You'd wonder how I fit everything in but I do. The only interruption to my busy schedule was the odd call on my mobile from people, purporting to be bereaved, following up on the advertisement I placed in the *Buy and Sell*. So much for Carmel's input – 'No one in their right mind would book a funeral through the *Buy and Sell*'. She never had a clue.

I'm up like a lark at six thirty, to start my day writing a short poem. I like to start with a poem which, strangely enough, always rhymes better after a sleepless night. Breakfast next. A free-range egg, tea, and toast. By eight thirty I have tidied up, made my bed, and tended to other mundane domestic chores. At nine, I settle down to reread the book I got from the library, *Getting Started: The Essential Guide to Writing a Good Novel*, by Annabelle Titchmarch, resisting the temptation to go directly to Chapter 12, 'Getting a Publisher', and Chapter 13, 'Getting an Agent'.

Chapter 1, 'The First Steps. What is your story about? Who is your story about? First person, third person?' God. Boring boring boring. How can I flow if I have to think about that. 'Grammar.' We are a bit out of date, Miss Titchmarch, no one cares about grammar any more. 'Read samples of classic openings.' What is the point of that? You can't copy them. You would wonder about these writers of how-to-write books, wouldn't you? It's a bit like *How to Fly, the Technical Manual*. No matter how much you read it it's not going to get you up there. 'Layout and Spacing.' I ask you. I can do joined up writing, thank you very much, Miss Titch. 'Length and Title.' I don't know that yet, do I? I'll work that out as I go along. 'Take time to gather your thoughts.' Excellent advice. 'Writer's Block.' No problems there, thank God, quite the opposite. 'Discipline yourself to write something every day.' Gobbledegook might do for some people, Miss Titchmarch, but some of us are serious about our writing and 'something' is not a word we will accept into our creative psyche. 'Join a creative writing group.' *Nil desperandum* yet, Titch, will keep options open on that one. At last. Chapter 12, 'Getting a Publisher. Obtain copy of *Writers' & Artists' Yearbook*. Get to know your category and find publishers who specialise in your field. Remember, when you get discouraged, every publisher is on the lookout for the next best seller. It could be you. Perseverance should be your middle name. Don't be discouraged. Embrace your rejection slips as a learning experience. Overcome the hazards and success can be yours. And finally, always send a stamped addressed envelope.'

Hazards. Hazards? Like stab oneself to death with a Biro? Hang from the policeman's-notebook elastic?

'What do you mean I can't take this out?'

'*Writers and Artists* is a reference book. We don't let reference books out.'

'But I am a writer. I have to find a publisher.'

'I'm sorry, miss, but that's the rule. No reference books leave the library. We have a photocopier. You could copy the pages you want. It's only 10p a page for photocopies.'

'There are over 400 pages. That would cost me forty pounds. I could have *bought* the book, not to mention the bloody photocopier.'

'I'll have to ask you to leave the premises if you are going to take that tone.'

'What tone? You are a public servant. I am the public. My taxes pay your wages.'

'I thought you were a writer.'

'I am a writer.'

'Writers don't pay taxes in this country.'

'Do you know how much VAT there is on every Biro?'

'Doreen. Would you call Mr Scott, please.'

'All right. I give in. I will find myself a nook and try to categorise myself.'

Hazards, Miss Titchmarch. We know not the time nor the place.

Twenty chapters of 2,500 words, Miss Titchmarch says, would give a fair sized novel. You better get going, Shantell. That's a lot of words. Not a problem. No problemo. On your marks, get set, here goes . . .

Well would you credit that? The telephone. Hasn't rung for an age.

'Hello. Yes this is Shantell O'Doherty speaking. How can I help you?'

'It's my granny. She's dead.'

'Yes?'

'Is that Tranquil Interments?'

'Er?'

'Granny saw your advertisement in the paper and she told me to contact you.'

'That's very flattering but—'

'She said to tell you she was put down by men all her life and after Granda died, he's dead a good few years now, and my uncle Tommy, well he wasn't really my uncle but we used to call him uncle, she'd had enough of men putting her down, and no other man's hands were going to touch her. "Over my dead body," she always said.'

'My own sentiments entirely.'

'She wanted a decent send-off. She put two thousand pounds by for her funeral.'

'Two thousand pounds?'

'If that's not enough the rest of the family will chip in.'

'Can you give me a moment please?' Two thousand pounds. Could I do it? How difficult could it be? We were technically ready before. 'Sorry to keep you on hold, dear. Just checking our availability. There is a bit of a rush on at the moment.' Hearse, bier cars, lifters, say one grand. Extras, 400. That would give a profit of 600. 'When did you want the deceased done? I mean, put down?'

'Pardon?'

'Forgive me, dear. One of those undertaker's trade terms. When did you want the ceremony performed?'

'Saturday would be nice. Granny loved Saturdays.'

That's only two days. I'd never get it together in two days. 'I'm afraid we are fully booked for Saturday. The earliest I could give you is Monday. How would that suit?'

'I suppose we could wait until Monday.'

'Splendid. Is your granny down for any particular cemetery?'

'She had a space beside Granda but she said she wasted enough time lying beside him while he was alive. She wants to be cremated.'

'Great. I mean grave . . . brave decision, considering her age. You don't find many grannies being cremated.'

'So you can do it then?'

'Oh yes. We pride ourselves on our cremations. In fact, they are our speciality.' Well, Miss Titchmarch, what about that? Novel material falling into my lap. Steps one, two and six covered already. *Granny's Last Wish*. What a title. 'Could you give me some details please. Your granny's name?'

'Rose Deignan.'

'Age?'

'I think she was about eighty.'

'And your name?'

'I'm Rosie. Rosie Deignan. I was named after my

granny. I never knew her exact age. She always said she was twenty-one. Poor Granny. She never had much of a life.'

'Now don't go getting upset, Miss Deignan. We can get all the information from her death certificate.'

'I haven't got a death certificate.'

'The hospital will issue you with one. What hospital is she in?'

'She's not in hospital.'

'Where is she?'

'She is here beside me, in the flat. She wanted to die at home.'

'You are on the phone in a room beside a dead body?'

'That's why I am phoning you. She told me to phone you when she passed away. She said to phone you before I told anyone else.'

'Why?'

'I don't know why. She said, "Rosie, don't worry about anything. Those people will come over and take care of everything."'

'Exactly how long is your granny dead, Rosie?'

'About ten minutes.'

'You are quite sure she is dead?'

'I never saw a dead person before but she looks dead.'

'Oh my God.'

'Pardon?'

'A little prayer to God for your granny, Rosie. Rosie. Get a mirror and put it to your granny's mouth. See if she haws on it. We have to be absolutely sure.'

'Hold on.'

'I will. I will.' Be still oh racing heart. What a line. I must jot that down.

'She's not hawing, Miss O'Doherty. There's no breath coming at all.'

'Then we must presume she is dead and proceed accordingly.'

'Then you will come over?'

'As soon as I can, Rosie. What is the address? One-four-seven Tower Heights, Tower Road, Orchardstown. Right. Got that. And the phone number? 7640062.'

'You will come, won't you?'

'When I have made the necessary arrangements here I will be over. Sit still. Don't panic, and if your granny does breathe, ring me on the mobile.'

Calm yourself Shantell. Deep breaths. In, hold, out. In, hold, out. That's better. Notes. Find the notes on undertakers. Make a list. Ring Carmel. Lay out the black; what a godsend I got that black. So much to do. Steady, Shantell. One thing at a time. Shower and change. No. No time to shower. Use extra talc. Make-up. Pale, I think, would be appropriate, and perhaps a deeper shade of lipstick.

# Chapter Two

'I need some information on cremations, please.'

'Writing a whodunit are we?' The librarian smiled over at her assistant, Doreen.

'What? Oh I see, you remember me. No, actually. I'm wearing my other hat at the moment, or should I say, mantilla. I'm in the undertaking business.'

'I should have guessed.'

'I was very lucky. It was their last one. I popped into Winston's, on my way over here, to glance through their mourning section. Although I do have my own blacks it wouldn't do to be wearing the wrong styles, you understand. They didn't have a mourning department as such, the lady told me, but they did stock mantillas in the religious section. The moment I saw it I pounced on it.' Shantell paused, waiting for a reaction to her success.

'And you want information on . . .?'

'Crematoriums. Or should I say -toria? My Latin is a little rusty.'

'Could you handle this one, Doreen? I am still trying to trace *The Art of Feng Shui in Cold Climates*, for the rural gentleman over there. Doreen will help you, madam. Take a seat and she will call you.'

'I am in rather a hurry. I have a client waiting.'

'We will have to check our computer to see what we have on file. Please take a seat.'

'Should I get Mr Scott, Miss Conlon?' Doreen whispered to the librarian.

'No. She will only come back as something else. Look under Folklore. I'm sure we have something under "Funeral Rites and Wakes". Get it for her and get her out of here as quickly as you can.' Miss Conlon's whisper was perfectly audible. 'Sir,' she called out to the waiting rural gentleman. 'Yes you, sir. If you go to the section, Oriental Arts and Crafts, I think you might find what you are looking for, otherwise, I suggest you try a Japanese restaurant, they may be able to help you.' Miss Conlon's face adopted an expression of disapproval. 'Do I hear a phone ringing in the library?'

'Hello, Shantell O'Doherty here. How may I help you? Rosie, it's you. I can't talk at the moment. She's what? That's rigger's mortis setting in. Don't let her stiffen. Put the fire on. Keep her warm. I won't be much longer.'

'Here you go, miss. We have two books on funerals. That should keep you going. Do you want to check them out?'

'Yes. Oh. There is one more thing. Do you have one on rigger's mortis?'

'Rigor mortis. Miss Conlon.' Doreen's eyes never left Shantell. 'Miss Conlon. Would you know, offhand, if we have anything on rigor mortis?'

'One moment please, Doreen. Now, sir. If you turn left out the door, go down Henry Street to O'Connell

11

Street, you will find two restaurants, The Taisho and The Takamatsu, I am sure they will be able to help you. No trouble at all. Goodbye now. Did you need assistance, Doreen?'

'The lady wants—'

'I think I heard what the lady wants, Doreen.' Turning to Shantell, Miss Conlon raised her eyebrows. 'Correct me if I am wrong, but did I hear you requesting a book on rigor mortis?'

'It's very important.'

'Then may I suggest you go directly to the College of Surgeons? If you turn left out the door, down Henry Street to O'Connell Street, take a right and continue in that direction, you'll come to the college. I am sure they will do their best to help you.'

'Thank you. Thank you so much.'

'No trouble at all. If there is any justice,' Miss Conlon confided in another loud whisper to Doreen as they watched Shantell rush out through the library doors, 'they will accept her body as a donation to science.'

Shantell, following Miss Conlon's instructions, headed off down Henry Street. It was quite a walk to the College of Surgeons which would eat into her precious time. Was there any point in going at all? So long as Rosie kept her granny warm everything would be all right. If by any chance the granny did over-stiffen, there was bound to be a way to soften her. She would be better advised to sit somewhere quiet, have a coffee, and swot up on funeral procedures. It would save time in the long run. Gather your thoughts, Shantell. Remember what Miss Titchmarch advised. 'Take time to gather your thoughts. Time spent in preparation can save hours of heartache.' Pearls of wisdom there. No one could accuse Shantell O'Doherty of ignoring good advice. She spotted a nice looking pub down a side road off O'Connell Street and headed for it.

'A coffee please, barman, and a small brandy.'

'Coming right up, miss. Nothing like a hair of the dog. Take a seat and I'll bring it over to you.'

Shantell gave the barman a look of disapproval before sitting herself down in a corner. Ignore him Shantell. Cheek. Is there anything more annoying than a cheeky barman?

'There you go, miss. One Hennessy and one coffee. Doing a bit of reading then?'

'It's research, actually.'

You find a corner table in an empty public house and what happens? You get lumbered with a chatty barman.

'A fellow comes in here every night. He's a researcher.'

'That's very interesting.'

'Great man for the jokes. Always got a new one. Don't know how he does it. Me. I can never remember jokes. Always spoil them, give the punch-line away.'

'If you don't mind—'

'He told me a cracker last night. Woke the wife up to tell her when I got home and she nearly went barmy.'

'I'm not surprised if you woke her up.'

'It wasn't that. I was laughing so much I couldn't remember the punch-line—'

'Would you mind awfully. I must get on with this. I have an appointment in the College of Surgeons.'

13

'It never comes to you when you want it.'

'Morning, Matt.'

The barman's attention was diverted by the arrival of another customer.'

'Your usual, Mr O'Gorman?'

'You know me better than the missis.'

'Grand day, Mr O'Gorman.'

'Couldn't be better, Matt. Although they do say there is rain on the way.' Mr O'Gorman was surprised by Matt's cheeriness. On an average day, Matt's morning conversation usually ran to a series of grunts and 'Is that so?'s. 'Are you feeling all right Matt?'

'Why wouldn't I be?'

'Aha. I see it now.' Mr O'Gorman had spotted Shantell. 'This joviality is to impress the lady.'

'Customer–barman relations are very important in this trade, Mr O'Gorman.'

'You could have fooled me.'

That's it, Mr O'Gorman. Keep him up there with you. Some of us have work to do. Shantell rooted in her bag for her notebook and pen. Make a list of priorities.

Priorities. 1 Sift through funeral books. Extract relevant information.
2 Phone Carmel – She doesn't deserve it but I am not one to hold a grudge.
3 Apprise Rosie of information gleaned.

*Apprising Rosie.* Extraordinary. Everything that comes into my head is a novel in itself.

Extra priority. Write first two chapters of novel and send off to suitable publisher.

You know, when I come to think of it, if I had gone to the College of Surgeons I would have spent at least an hour between getting there and doing the research. So. If I'm the one who saved the hour then surely I should be able to have it for myself. I could get a lot done in an hour. I don't want to fall behind. 'Write something every day.' Again Miss Titchmarch's sound advice.

### Chapter 1 Paragraph 1 Page 1

Gillian Turner sighed deeply, crumbling the tissue in her hand, and looked out the window purposefully. She had watched for her Tom, her special Tom, for over a week now but to no avail. Her hand languished on the back of the sofa, her eyes filled up with tears, she dropped her tissue and leafed through his last long letter which she also dropped. Thinking of him, and him only, her hands went to her breasts, she felt a tingling between her legs and she knew what she must do. Tearing herself from the window view she slumped upstairs to her bedroom and threw herself upon the bed. She hated herself for this. For the low despicable figure she had become. But without Tom she was nothing. She stripped off her dressing gown, dived in between the sheets, and proceeded to masturbate.

What about that for an opening, Miss Titchmarch? I feel inspired. I feel I could go on and on.
'Another brandy please, barman.'
'Do you want a coffee with it, miss?'
'No. Just the brandy, thank you.'
If I'd wanted a coffee I would have asked for it.

Presumptuous as well as chatty. The two worst traits in a barman today. Where was I?

Gillian lay back, facing the ceiling, racked with guilt. What would Tom think of her? Would he ever trust her again?

'What's with Dracula's bride over there, Matt?' Mr O'Gorman nodded across in Shantell's direction.

'She's doing research for the College of Surgeons.'

'Dresses for the part, doesn't she.'

'You get all sorts in here, Mr O'Gorman, all sorts. The eyes of the world we barmen are.'

'Same again, Matt, at your convenience. It would make you think though wouldn't it.'

'What would?'

'A lady, on her own, drinking brandy at this hour of the day.'

'Heart-scalded I'd say. They do that you know, ladies. Get into black when they are stood up and pass themselves off as widows. I've seen it time and time again.'

'Is that a fact? Stood up.' Mr O'Gorman repeated. 'You know me, Matt, I'm not one of your chauvinists, but I could see a fellow getting cold feet. You'd be hard pushed to imagine throwing your leg over, if you get my drift.'

'Come now, Mr O'Gorman. You know what they say. Never look a gift-horse in the face. One man's meat and all that.'

'Mouth, Matt. Mouth. Never look a . . .' Mr O'Gorman was left talking to himself. Matt had left the bar.

'That'll be two pounds, twenty, miss.' Matt put the

brandy down on the table.

'*Oh*!' Shantell jumped. 'Sorry, you startled me, I was engrossed in my work.'

'More power to you, miss. Pity there's not more like you. Into the books like.'

'Why thank you. One's studiousness is not always appreciated. Oops. There goes my mobile phone. Would you excuse me. Shantell O'Doherty speaking. How can I— Rosie . . . Calm down, Rosie. I am working very hard on your behalf. Why at this very moment I am organising everything. I want to have all the facts and figures at my disposal when I come to see you. I shall be in touch within the hour. Make yourself tea, watch some television and you won't notice the time flying by.' Damn Granny, she muttered under her breath. Just as I was getting started. Think of the money Shantell. Every artiste has problems with money.

She got out the library books and looked at the titles. *Celtic Burials and Wakes* by Liam O'Malley and *Funeral Rites* by Jane Spottiswoode. Shantell put aside *Celtic Burials and Wakes*; that was out for a start, Granny wanted to be cremated. She opened up *Funeral Rites* by Jane Spottiswoode.

Isn't it amazing what you discover. You can't bury your nearest and dearest in the back garden in case you sell the house and the new owners dig the body up by mistake and, according to Ms Spottiswoode, you must be 170 feet from a well or borehole and 40 feet from running water. A borehole? We're not in darkest Africa . . .

'Shantell,' Matt confided to Mr O'Gorman. 'Shantell O'Doherty.'

'What sort of a name is that?'

. . . Cremations, page 43. Here we are. 'American and Asians traditionally used fire for their funeral services due, no doubt, to the extreme heat in their countries. When the practice first came to Britain, it was considered to be due to the lack of space, especially in cities.' This book is no use to me whatsoever. Who in their right mind would need this sort of information? Those librarians. Hopeless. More interested in their appearance than trying to help the public.

'Excuse me, barman. Do you have a Yellow Pages?'

'On the shelf over there, miss. Underneath the telephone.'

'Not bad legs all the same, Mr O'Gorman.' Mr O'Gorman and Matt watched Shantell as she went across the pub to get the telephone book.

'Steady, Matt. You stay behind that counter.'

'I was only making a comment.'

'And one comment leads on to another, and another, and the next thing you know, you're involved. That's the slope down which the human male slides.'

'I only said she had good legs. Where's the harm in that?'

'I'd like your wife to hear that. I suppose you get plenty of opportunities in a place like this. Close the front door. Stick up the Back in Five sign.'

'Mr O'Gorman.'

'I shan't tell if you don't tell, eh?' Mr O'Gorman winked towards Shantell.

That gentleman sitting up at the bar has not taken his eyes off me, thought Shantell. It is very distracting. Mind you, people always did say how well black suits me. Fast find. Coffins. *Cob*, *Cod*, *Coe*, *Cof*. Here we are. *Coffins and cabinet makers.* Brophy, Co. Donegal. O'Reilly, Ballyaughville, Co. Cork. Marvellous. Two coffin makers in the whole damn book and they are at opposite ends of the country. Try body bags. Body bags, body bags, there's *bodybuilding*, *vehicles*, *gyms*, nothing. Not a bloody body bag. There must be more than two coffin makers. Will you look at that. *Cold storage.* Right under *coffins*. Not exactly sensitive. *Rent-a-fridge.* Well, Granny, unless we find a carpenter fast we may have to do just that. Where's my pen? Okay.

List re funeral:
Coffin – carpenter
Transport – hearse and cars to follow

They will cost. They charge a fortune for those big black cars. It will eat into the money. The sensible thing to do would be to hire a Dormobile, get everyone into the one car.

Mourners – approx how many? Check with Rosie
Flowers and notice in paper

Dear oh dear. Things are mounting up. If we could get some sort of write-up beforehand then everyone would know about the funeral and we wouldn't need a notice. Add that to the list.

Publicity – write-up

That's about as far as I can go for now with the arrangements. Quite satisfactory. I don't know why I was so concerned. I think one more teeny weeny

19

brandy is called for before I brave the elements of Orchardstown. 'Barman. Oh barman,' Shantell sang across the room. 'Another brandy, please.'

'Jesus, Matt. She can fairly lorry down the juice.'

'I make it my business, Mr O'Gorman, not to count customers' drinks.'

'Now don't go getting uppity. I'll have the same again and throw in a small Jemmy. Take the lot out of that.' Mr O'Gorman handed over a twenty pound note. 'I like a woman with a thirst.'

'With the gentleman's compliments, miss.'

'My goodness, how very kind. Would you thank him for me?' Shantell raised her glass and mouthed a thank you to Mr O'Gorman. I knew he was interested in me. There is something about older men – they seem to find me irresistible. If I didn't have a corpse to worry about I would quite enjoy flirting with him. I'll give him one of my smiles. That should keep him going.

'You're welcome.' Mr O'Gorman waved back. 'I'm on to a good thing there, Matt. Did you see the smile. There's life in the old brittle bones yet.'

'I wouldn't bank on it, Mr O'Gorman. In my experience—' Matt broke off his conversation to attend to a young man who had come into the pub.

'Good day, sir. What can I get you?'

'I'm up from Kerry,' the man volunteered. 'For the day.'

'Well now, you're a long way from home. What will you have?'

'I'm looking for a place. I've been all over the city.'

'What place?' Mr O'Gorman asked.

'I have it written on a piece of paper.' The young man proceeded to search in his pockets. 'It's in here somewhere.' He turned out his overcoat pockets, his jacket pockets, his trouser pockets and, as Matt and Mr O'Gorman watched in fascination, an amazing array of paraphernalia piled up on the counter. When he started on his inside pockets Mr O'Gorman couldn't stand it any longer.

'Give the man a pint there, Matt, while he finds his piece of paper. We can't have our country cousins roaming the streets without sustenance. No, I insist.' Mr O'Gorman looked across to Shantell to make sure she was aware of his generosity. 'Haven't I roots in Kerry.'

You've really made a hit there, Shantell. He can't take his eyes off you. I'm sure he only bought that young man a drink to impress you. If he thinks I'm falling for that little game . . . I'll pretend not to notice. Always a sure fire way with men. There you go Shantell. Getting distracted again. What would Miss Titchmarch say? Concentrate. You have time for one more paragraph while you finish your brandy. Ignore him and the barman and the other one. I am sure I saw that other one before somewhere. *There were three men in a pub. A barman, a farmer and a . . .* stop. Stop Shantell. Your brain is too fertile for your own good. Ignore these men and their brute sexuality. *Brute sexuality, brute sexuality*. Let it flow Shantell. Feel the novelist sensation whelming up.

**Chapter 1 Paragraph 1 Page 1** (of second novel)
Felicity tore herself from the arms of the swarthy stranger and fled the cinema. She knew she must. The fiery passion he had aroused in her, which had lain dormant for so long, made her realise how much time she had waited for Jeremy. It had been so innocent. The afternoon matinée, £1.50 if you

went in before three o'clock, where she had whiled away so many lonely afternoons. He had been so kind. Helping her retrieve her messages when her bag burst and her shopping began to roll down through the cinema seats towards the screen. They had laughed together. Shared a bar of Fruit & Nut. Suddenly his tongue was in her mouth. His hand was opening her bra with the expertise of a computer component packer, and she was melting. She rushed home, put her messages away and went to her bedroom. Jeremy. Oh Jeremy. Not stopping to think she dived in between the sheets and began to masturbate.

'Miss, miss. Your mobile phone is ringing.'

'Jeremy. Jeremy.' Shantell's voice echoed round the bar and Matt, who was standing beside her, jumped with fright.

'It's been ringing for ages. We were nearly going to answer it for you. Everything all right, miss?'

'Forgive me, forgive me, barman. I get so utterly rapt it's hard for the average person to understand. No, don't be afraid. It's part of my work. We stray sometimes from the real world.'

'I'm not surprised,' Mr O'Gorman whispered to his new Kerry friend. 'That shower up in the College of Surgeons drink blood with their tea. That poor woman needs a drink. Do the honours there, Matt.' Mr O'Gorman turned round to Shantell. 'Madam, it would give me great pleasure if you could be persuaded to partake of another small one.'

'Not for me.' Shantell smiled at her benefactor. 'I must go. I have a client waiting.'

'I have to go as well,' the man from Kerry said. 'I

have to find the station and get my train.'

'And that from the man who took a pint to find a piece of paper in his pocket. It'll take you another three to find the station. Show us the piece of paper anyway so we see where you are trying to find.'

'I was looking for The Taisho, or The Takamatsu.'

'You're a bit wide of the mark, sir. I don't know where Taisho is but Takamatsu is a port on Shikoku in the Pacific Ocean.'

'But the librarian told me they were in O'Connell Street.'

I knew I'd seen that man before. It was the library. Intellectual I bet. Gentleman farmer – they always dress down. All the way up from Kerry to go to the library. He must be a poet. We probably have loads in common. 'Hello. I think we have met. I'm Shantell O'Doherty.'

'Doesn't that take the biscuit.' Mr O'Gorman smiled. 'You two knowing each other. Put your backside up here beside us, Shantell. I'm Tom. Tom O'Gorman. That there, polishing his glasses, is Matt, and your name, sir?'

'I'm Fionn. Fionn O'Fiachra.'

'What a beautifully poetic name.' Shantell beamed up at Fionn.

'*Quelle noblesse*,' Mr O'Gorman exclaimed. 'And were you named after our ancient warriors? Those noble Fianna whose feats and exploits were legendary the length and breadth of Ireland? Whose valour and courage gave voice to song and epic narratives which have been handed down from generation to generation, instilling pride and passion in all who hear them?'

'No,' Fionn said. 'I was named for my uncle Finbar.'

'What matter. We'll have a drink all round to commemorate our mighty ancestors. Same again, Matt, while we try to persuade this delicate little minx, Shantell here, to join us.'

'I never sit at the bar, Mr O'Gorman.'

'Well then, by the hokey, we will have to join you. This salubrious establishment does not lend itself to stand-offishness.'

*Je ne sais quoi.* There is no doubt about it Shantell O'Doherty. You definitely have it. Who would have thought that only last week things were so different? Look at you now. Two excellent opening paragraphs, one cremation, and two gentlemen desperate to join your company. *Camel turd* indeed. Eat your heart out now, Carmel. You should have stuck with me instead of clinging on to that Joe person. No faith, Carmel. No faith and no courage. Two paragraphs already. I wonder who I should get to launch my novel. It has to be someone well known.

'Here we go.' Mr O'Gorman and Fionn carried the drinks over to Shantell's corner table and sat down. 'Fionn here tells me he is interested in Feng Shui. What are your thoughts on that subject, Shantell?'

'I know exactly what my thoughts are on that subject, Mr O'Gorman. I never eat Chinese.'

# Chapter Three

'And she only died today, your granny?' Mr O'Gorman asked.

'The call came out of the blue. The voice on the other end of the line said, "It's my granny. She's dead." Why did she have to die?' Shantell sobbed into her mantilla.

'It's a hard fact of life, Shantell.' Mr O'Gorman patted Shantell's hand in a gesture of sympathy. 'Death comes to us all. I remember when my own granny died. I was devastated.'

'The telephone can be a terrible thing,' Fionn said.

'I must go to her. There are so many things to arrange.'

'Were you very close to her?'

'I never knew her, Mr O'Gorman.' Shantell sobbed even more.

'Dear woman, your forthright honesty astounds me.' Mr O'Gorman was moved. 'But which of us can say, I know this man, and really know the man?'

'Granny was a woman.'

'I am speaking metaphysically, my dear.'

'I am going to ring my granny tonight.' Fionn started to cry. 'I'm going to get to know her if it's the last thing I do.'

'Dear, sensitive Fionn. I feel I have known you all my life. I didn't mean to upset you with my little troubles. I know your poet's soul is aching. And you, Tom, dear friend. I must go now to Granny's house. I must leave no stone unturned in carrying out her last wishes.'

'Carrying out her last wishes,' Fionn wailed to Mr O'Gorman.

'They'll all be carried out in a minute,' Matt said to his regular, after-work crowd, when he heard Fionn's cry. 'They've been at it all day. You'd need the patience of a saint in this job. If the boss comes in now he will tell me to run them.'

'Did I hear the woman's granny died?'

'If you believe that you're worse than they are. Sure that's a story she made up to get a drink out of Mr O'Gorman.'

'Isn't it terrible the lengths some women will go to.'

'We don't know the half.'


'I never met anyone like you, Shantell. You are a wonderful woman.' Fionn fought hard to contain his emotions. 'Shantell.' He tore off his cap and threw himself down on his knees. 'I think I'm falling in love with you. Can I ask you something? I know it's the wrong time, the wrong place, but I have to speak my mind.'

'You can ask, Fionn. I could deny a fellow poet nothing.'

'Shantell. How would you like to be buried with my people?'

'What a thing to say, Fionn. I've never been to Kerry and I am certainly not going all the way there to be buried. And speaking of that, I have no plans to be buried at all in the next forty or even fifty years.'

'You don't understand, Shantell.' Mr O'Gorman laughed. 'It's a marriage proposal. A great honour in the country to be invited into a plot with someone else's people.'

'Would you excuse me a moment. I must jot that down. Miss Titchmarch says a true novelist misses nothing. Every nuance and every shade of human characteristic should be noted for future use. That would be a wonderful line for Felicity.'

'Felicity?' Fionn and Mr O'Gorman enquired together.

'Yes. Felicity. Felicity is in love with Jeremy.'

'Are they relatives?'

'No, not relatives but, like yourselves, they have become very new and dear friends. The more I write of them the more I will get to know them. Now I must powder my nose. No, don't get up.' Fionn, still on his knees shifted to let Shantell slide out from behind the table. 'We don't stand on ceremony.' She tottered unsteadily towards the Ladies.

'What was she talking about?' Fionn asked.

'It's the grief,' Mr O'Gorman said. 'It affects people in different ways. She must have been very close to her granny in spite of what she said.'

'The poor girl. Look at the books she has. Funerals and wakes and—'

'Put them down, Fionn. We don't want her thinking we are intruding into her belongings.'

\*

Shantell O'Doherty. Did you see yourself in that mirror. I know you never go below certain standards of appearance, but at the moment you have a glow the likes of which I haven't seen in you before. Dear, dear, man. *Shantell O'Fiachra. Mrs O'Fiachra, novelist and poet.* I know who I have to thank for this. First thing tomorrow I am going to phone Miss Titchmarch. When I think of all she has done for me. All that advice. Maybe I should send her flowers. Of course. It's so obvious. Why didn't I think of it before? I will ask her to launch my novels. Who better than Miss Titchmarch? *Thank you, thank you everyone. I know this applause is for me but I have to share this platform with Miss Titchmarch. Miss Annabelle Titchmarch. Without her I would never have reached my potential as a writer. I would have remained an undertaker.* Oh dear. Rosie and Granny. They went out of my head for a moment. I'll ring Carmel, see if she could pop over. It will be good to ring her anyway, get things sorted out. Wait till she hears my news. I think she thought I was jealous. Jealous because she had Joe. I mean you wouldn't even look at him on a dark night. I'll get on to her the minute I'm finished. Can't seem to finish. Your plumbing needs seeing to, my girl. You shouldn't be peeing this much after a few little drinks. Is that you peeing? Maybe if you stand up it will stop. Whoops. Slippery floor. The health authorities wold have something to say about this. Ouch, my head. How did you manage to fall off the toilet, Shantell? Get up. Get up at once. Are you still peeing? That's very funny. Imagine thinking the cistern filling up was you. On your feet, girl. Steady. Get the knickers up. Slowly. Slowly, careful now, you don't want to fall again. Did you wipe? Damn door. It seems to be jammed. 'Hello. Hello? Is anybody out there?'

'She's been in there an awfully long time, Mr O'Gorman. Do you think she is all right?'

'Ladies and their toiletries, Fionn, remain a mystery to the male.'

'But should we see?'

'You'd be a braver man than most, Fionn, if you were to penetrate that holy sanctuary.'

'It can't be right. No one takes that long.'

'Do you know the reason I come in here every morning? Well I'm going to tell you and I never told a living soul. To have a shite. Yes, that's the truth of it. A shite. And do you know why I am reduced to this painful situation, why I cannot get into the lavatory in my own home?'

'I don't see—'

'Women. That's why. The missis, the mother-in-law, the downstairs tenant, all women. I tell you the only hope for a man to get to do his business in his home is a return to that glorious institution, the outside privy.'

'Please, Mr O'Gorman, we have to do something. I'll go over to the door. See if I can hear anything.'

'No friend of mine is going to the front without someone to watch his back. Lead on, Fionn, leader of the Fianna, son of the bard Oisín, in whose name McPherson flourished. Find your Shantell and carry her away in your currach to Kerry.'

'What in the name of Christ are those two up to now?' Matt put down the glass he was polishing and, leaning as far as he could over the top of the counter, he watched as Fionn and Mr O'Gorman crept across the floor of the pub and crouched down in front of the door to the Ladies.

'Do you hear anything, Mr O'Gorman?'

'Nothing but the sound of running water, Fionn.'

'Will we try the door?'

'Nothing else for it. We'll have to go in.'

'Stop where you are.' Matt vaulted over the counter and charged for the door. 'Mr O'Gorman. What on earth do you think you are doing? You can't go in there.'

'Get outta there you perverts,' one of the other customers shouted down the bar. 'Do you need a hand there, Matt? We'll throw them out for you.'

'Get the guards, Matt,' came another shout from the back.

'It's okay,' Matt shouted over his shoulder. 'Everything is under control. Do you want to start a bloody riot, Mr O'Gorman? I am shocked. A man of your intelligence peering in through the keyhole of a ladies' toilet.'

'You don't understand, Matt. We are trying to rescue a lady in distress. My young friend here is concerned about his fiancée.'

'Fiancée? You'll have to do better than that. I know for a fact they only met this afternoon.'

'Youth and love move in mysterious ways.'

'Give over the nonsense now. Move out of the way. Miss. Miss? Are you in there?'

'Of course she's in there,' Fionn said. 'We saw her go in. That was ages ago. There is something wrong. Maybe she killed herself on account of her granny.'

'I don't know which of you is worse. Stand back there. I'll go in and get her. Neither of you is to move.' Matt went into the Ladies. 'Miss. This is Matt, the barman. Are you decent? I'm coming in.'

'Hey! Wyatt Earp! You forgot your horse.'

'Shut up you lot,' Matt called out to the crowd at the back. 'This isn't funny.' He entered the Ladies cautiously and closed the door behind him. Moments later he re-emerged. 'She's passed out behind the cubicle door.'

'What can we do?' Fionn said. 'We can't leave her in there.'

'There's nothing else for it. We'll have to take the door off the hinges.'

'Maybe we should call the fire brigade,' Mr O'Gorman said. 'They're always great men in an emergency.'

'I'm not having the fire brigade in my pub. She's not a bloody trapped cat. What do you think the boss would say if he came in? I could lose my job.'

'You can't think of yourself in a situation like this.'

'I'm warning you, Tom. You are on the brink. One more word out of you and you are barred for life. I think there's a screwdriver behind the bar. Don't move while I go and get it.'

'What's going on, Matt?' asked one of the punters.

'Nothing to worry about, lads. The lady is stuck behind the toilet door, that's all.'

'Where are you going with that screwdriver?'

'Where the bleeding hell do you think I'm going? I'll have to take the door off.'

'We'll give you a hand.'

'Stay where you are,' Matt shouted. 'The whole effing lot of you.'

'But, Matt. Stephen here works on the buildings. He'll have the door off for you in jig time.'

'Stand back. Stand back the lot of you.' Matt

brandished the screwdriver. 'The first man that so much as moves . . .' he waved it menacingly as he backed into the Ladies.

'We can't let him go in there alone. Come on men.'

Mr O'Gorman, Fionn, and the entire clientele, some with pints still in their hands, followed Matt, squeezing and shoving their way into the ladies' toilet.

'Listen,' Fionn said. 'Listen everyone.'

'A bit of hush there, if you please.' Mr O'Gorman addressed the crowd. 'Have some respect for the betrothed.'

'What is it?'

'She's crying her eyes out.'

'No she's not. She's singing. Listen.'

'Somebody loves me,' Shantell's voice came warbling over the top of the cubicle. 'I wonder who. I wonder who it can be . . .'

'Somebody loves her.' The gentlemen took up the song. 'She wonders who. Maybe it's you.'

# Chapter Four

'Hello, Rosie. It's me, Shantell, your undertaker. I know, dear, I know, but you're not going to believe what has happened to me since we last spoke. How is Granny? Rosie. You are shouting, dear. All the arrangements have been made and I am literally on my way to you. My fiancé is, as we speak, on the road hailing a taxi, and a dear friend, who you will meet shortly is in the takeaway. We did not want to present ourselves empty-handed. Rosie, have you got a measuring tape? God is already watching out for you, Rosie, there is no need to invoke him. Let me explain. A tiny contretemps with a lavatory door revealed the most useful information. It transpires that my fiancée has an extraordinary affinity to wood. Not only has he completed a three-year woodwork course in the Regional Technical College in Kerry, he has also acquired fame for chaining himself to certain endangered oaks and, but for heavy handed police brutality, my green warrior might still be in that forest. Mercifully he was on hand to rescue me when, locked in the interior of the ladies' loo, I thought all was lost. As I lay there, semi-conscious from a bad knock to my head, and while several other gentlemen sang a rousing chorus to keep my spirits up, he, Fionn, armed with only a screwdriver came to my aid. "Shantell, my love, it's me, Fionn," he said. "We are going to get you out." Then I said, "Oh Fionn." Then he said, "Don't worry, Shantell. I am a carpenter." Then I said, "Jesus was a carpenter." And that's when I knew, Rosie, that all was well. Fionn is going to make Granny's coffin . . . Rosie . . . Rosie . . . you are breaking up, Rosie. Don't bother to phone me back. We will be with you before you know it.'

'Hello. Hello, Carmel, it's Shantell. I have wonderful news. We have our first job and guess what? I am going to be buried in Kerry. Ring me as soon as you get this message.'

'Cooee, Mr O'Gorman, here I am. Stand in here beside me out of the rain.' Shantell was sheltering in a doorway watching out for Fionn. 'Did you get everything?'

'Two beef curries, one lamb curry, one vegetarian, two portions of chips, two naan breads, four poppadums, two bottles of wine, half a dozen Guinness, one bottle of Jameson, a half bottle of Hennessy, and an assortment of each man's poison by way of the deadly fag.'

'Splendid. Well done Mr O'Gorman. One cannot call to a house of bereavement empty-handed. Poor Fionn. He's going to get soaked.'

'Don't worry about that, my dear. Sure those fellows from the country never notice the rain.

They're born with an extra layer of waterproof skin.
It's evolution.'

'There he is. Fionn, Fionn! Over here.'

The taxi pulled up alongside Shantell and Mr
O'Gorman, and they bundled into the back beside
Fionn.

'I hope you know where you are going,' the driver
said. 'I couldn't make out a word that fellow was
saying. I was nearly going to throw him back out.'

'Tower Heights in Orchardstown please, driver.'

'Off to a party are we? There's a minimum fare on
Orchardstown, love. It's way out past the airport.'

'That's all right, driver, but we have to get there as
quickly as possible.'

'You'll get there when you get there, miss. This is a
taxi, not an express train.'

'Train. I should be on a train,' Fionn said. 'Do you
go anywhere near the station?'

'Which station?'

'I have to get to Kerry.'

'The only way you'll get to Kerry tonight is on
Shanks's mare. The last trains to the country are all
gone and there won't be another one out until eight
o'clock in the morning.'

'That means I'll have to stay in the station
overnight.'

'Fionn, Fionn.' Shantell interrupted. 'What are you
talking about? Mr O'Gorman and I are here to look
after you. Aren't we, Mr O'Gorman. And anyway,
after you've met Rosie and Granny and we have our
business sorted out you are coming back to stay the
night with me.'

'I've no pyjamas. I only came up for the day.'

'Up for the match, are we?' the driver asked,

grinning into his rear-view mirror.

'Sorry?'

'Don't mind that jackeen, Fionn,' Mr O'Gorman said. 'He's just trying to take the mickey out of you.'

'No offence, sir. Just making conversation.'

'As it happens,' Fionn said, leaning forward to talk to the driver, 'I might have been up for the match, if there had been one on, but the reason for my trip is very different. I saw a programme on Telefís na Gaeilge and I said to myself, Fionn boy, you have got to get more information on that, so I cycled to the village and got the bus to Killarney and the train to Dublin and went hell for leather to the big library down there off O'Connell Street but the woman there hadn't got the information I wanted so she directed me to take a left turn at the door and go down Henry Street but I think that's where I went wrong . . .'

'Why me, Lord?' the taxi driver said to himself. 'Why me? Always the last fare when you think you're on the home stretch.'

'. . . I think myself I might have taken a turn where I wasn't meant to so I went into a bar to ask directions and this woman got stuck in the toilets and I had to take the door off and then her granny died . . .'

'Have you enough room there, Shantell?' Mr O'Gorman asked, sliding his hand on to her knee. 'I hope you're not crushed between us.'

'Oh no, Mr O'Gorman. I'm fine, more than fine. In fact I feel quite oriental.'

'Eh?'

'Can't you feel it, Mr O'Gorman? The tropical rain, the aroma of exotic foods. Speeding through the city, mission-bent, on our errand of mercy.' Shantell sighed, and shifted a little towards Mr O'Gorman.

'That's the girl. Rest yourself there till we get to Orchardstown.' Mr O'Gorman closed his eyes and nodded off, his head on Shantell's shoulder.

'. . . And all the men in the pub started singing this beautiful song that I didn't know the words of and it was after that we, that's Mr O'Gorman and I, discovered it wasn't her granny, it was someone called Rosie's granny who had no one there with her to wake the body, so Mr O'Gorman decided we should come as well because you can't have a body in a house with no mourners and . . .'

Look at him, the darling. Able to chat away to the taxi driver like a true proletarian. Real artistes have no class thing. Not an ounce of snobbery in their bones. At last I am among my own people. Sit back Fionn. Sit back so that I can feel your wet thigh against mine. I can't get at my notebook without waking Mr O'Gorman. I will have to train myself to memorise everything.

## Chapter 1 Page 1

As she lay crushed between two men Germaine struggled valiantly to maintain her poise. How had it come to this? She loved them both. How could she choose? The one – mature, wealthy, wishing only to take care of her. Be a father to her. Something she had yearned for all her life. The other – young, handsome, full of reckless daring. Never a thought for tomorrow, living only for the moment. As she lay there, naked, beautiful, watching them sleep in all their manly glory, she wrestled under the weight of the decision she must make. Which of them would give her satisfaction? Deep fulfilling satisfaction.

Her hand slipped down between her legs and she began to etc., etc.

'. . . And I never found The Taisho or The Takamatsu in the end.'

'Not to cut you short, sir, but would you mind if I asked you what you were looking for in the first place?'

'I was seeking information from a book called *The Art of Feng Shui in Cold Climates*. It was mentioned on the television programme.'

'Feng Shui. Did you say Feng Shui?'

'Yes. Have you heard of it, driver?'

'Have I heard of it? You sir, have come to the right place. The wife had the whole house decked out in Feng Shui. To be honest, in the beginning, I was all for it, it was only when she dragged the wardrobe down from the bedroom and put it across the hall to stop the energy escaping out the back kitchen I felt it had gone too far. But that, as the man says, is neither here nor there.'

'Are we nearly there, driver?' Shantell opened her eyes, lifted her head up from Mr O'Gorman's lap, and peered out the taxi window. 'Why have we stopped? What is going on? There is nothing but black outside. Mr O'Gorman. Wake up, Mr O'Gorman. We have been abducted.'

'Huh?' Mr O'Gorman opened his eyes. 'Where are we? Where is Fionn?'

'I'm here.' Fionn and the driver turned round. 'In the front with Malachy.'

'Malachy?'

'Can you believe it, after all my searching, Malachy has been able to answer all my questions.'

'What the—' Mr O'Gorman rubbed at his eyes to make sure he wasn't dreaming, when he saw Fionn and the driver sharing a curry and washing it down with his Guinness.

'You shall be reported,' Shantell shouted.

'You don't understand, Shantell. I begged Malachy to tell me all he knew. He has been wonderful.'

'He is eating Rosie's curry.'

'It's my vegetarian one. We shared it.'

'How long have we been here?'

'Only about an hour.'

'An hour! What will I say to Rosie?'

'It's only round the corner, miss,' the driver said. 'We're almost there.'

'Driver . . .'

'Malachy. His name is Malachy,' Fionn said.

'. . . If you do not take us to Tower Heights immediately I am calling the guards.'

'If that doesn't beat everything,' Mr O'Gorman said. 'Throw us over a bottle of Guinness there, Fionn.'

'Mr O'Gorman!' Shantell was scandalised.

'Malachy is going to wait for us and take us back into town when we are finished with our visit, and tomorrow I am going to see his house in Finglas.'

'Do you know what I am going to tell you young Fionn? You country fellas could buy and sell us and that's the truth of it. Pass me over me beef curry.'

'No one is having anything else until we get to Rosie,' said Shantell. 'I gave her my word and I must keep it. There must be no more delays. It's vital to ensure she hasn't let the fire go out.'

# Chapter Five

'It's all very quiet. Are you sure this is the right block, Malachy?'

The taxi was pulled up outside the second block at Tower Heights and the three passengers were peering out through the misty windows.

'Yes I'm sure.'

'Every man for himself,' Mr O'Gorman shouted as they stumbled out of the taxi.

'Shush,' warned Shantell. 'A little decorum please. I don't want you looking like hooligans when we meet Rosie and her granny.'

'I thought granny was dead,' Fionn whispered.

'One-four-seven.' Malachy scanned the letter-boxes. 'There it is, fourth floor.'

'Typical,' Mr O'Gorman said. 'The bloody lift isn't working. We'll have to take the bloody stairs.'

'Language please, Mr O'Gorman.' Shantell waggled her finger at him. 'And keep your voice down, you'll wake the entire neighbourhood.'

'This is an OAP block,' Malachy said. 'They're probably all conked with their sleeping tablets.'

'Do keep up, Mr O'Gorman.'

'Jesus, we're only on the second floor. I'm humped – I'll have to take a breather.'

'Mr O'Gorman, get up. You can't sit there. Fionn, take those bags from him.'

'She is expecting us, isn't she, Shantell?' asked Fionn apprehensively.

'Of course she is expecting us. We wouldn't be here if she wasn't expecting us.'

'I'll tell you one thing for nothing, I'll be ready for the leaba by the time we reach the fourth floor. Anyone care to give me a bunt?' Mr O'Gorman begged.

'Quiet now. Line up. Fionn you stay beside me. Mr O'Gorman, Malachy, stay close behind. Tidy yourselves up a bit for goodness' sake. Fionn, take that cap off . . .'

'The next thing she will do is lick a hankie and wipe our faces,' Mr O'Gorman said to Malachy.

'Is everybody ready? I am going to ring the bell.'

'Surprise.' The three gents waved and grinned as the door of number 147 was tentatively opened and then swiftly slammed shut.

'Rosie. Rosie,' Shantell called in through the letter-box. 'It's me, Shantell. Shantell O'Doherty, your undertaker. Open up.'

'Shantell?' The voice was barely audible through the door.

'Don't be alarmed, dear. We have come at last. Open the door.'

Rosie stared at the letter-box of her granny's hall door, wondering what to do. The name was right. Shantell O'Doherty, not the sort of name you could forget. But who were those men with her? All she had to go on was a few phone calls. Still, Granny Deignan told her to ring and Granny was no one's fool. For the millionth time that day Rosie wished Granny had picked someone else. One of her brothers. Anyone. She'd have to open the door. They were making such a racket outside she'd have all the neighbours down on top of her and then they would find out about Granny being dead before she was ready with the arrangements. Undertakers do keep funny hours, she told herself. But then, people can die at *any* hour. Maybe it wasn't so strange that they had called at this hour of the night. Maybe they had had other bodies to take care of. Rosie went into the sitting room and picked up the poker from the grate. She crept back to the hall. 'Are you sure you are Shantell?' she called through the closed door.

'I am Shantell, Rosie. You can ring me on my mobile and then you'll know.'

'Who are those men with you?'

'I told you about them on the phone, dear. They have come to help. Be a sensible girl now and open the door. We can't organise your granny long distance.'

Rosie nervously pulled the door open.

'Rosie, we meet at last.' Shantell stepped into the hall and threw her arms around the startled girl. 'Let me introduce everyone. I'm Shantell. This is Fionn, our carpenter, Mr O'Gorman, our adviser, and Malachy, our transport captain. Everyone, this is Rosie.'

'Hi, Rosie.'

'Hello, Rosie.'

'Pleased to meet you, Rosie.'

'Hello.' Rosie, still clutching her poker, and unable to escape from Shantell's embrace, couldn't think of anything else to say.

'Inside everyone. Now Rosie, where do you want us?'

'You better come into the sitting room,' Rosie said, still afraid the noise might attract the neighbours.

'Grand little place you have here.'

'Very cosy.'

'Granny liked it.'

'Ah, Granny, mavourneen,' Mr O'Gorman said.

'I thought the granny was dead,' Fionn said.

'Oh poor granny.' Rosie burst into tears. 'Poor poor granny.'

'There there, Rosie.' Shantell comforted her. 'Fionn. How could you be so insensitive? Sit down, Rosie.' She steered Rosie to a chair by the fire. 'Sit down and let it all out, you are among friends now. Mr O'Gorman, get Rosie a drink.'

'Do you want to see her?' Rosie asked through her tears.

'Perhaps after we fortify ourselves with a little something. We wouldn't want you drinking alone now, would we. After all, what are friends for? Fionn, could you find some glasses? Mr O'Gorman, would you do the honours. Rosie. I bet you haven't eaten anything all day. You'll feel better when you've had something to eat. Malachy, get some plates. I'll be mother and dish out. You two don't need plates – you are only having chips.' Shantell addressed Fionn and Malachy. 'You've had your curry already. Now, Rosie. Doesn't that look nice. What will you have to drink dear?'

'I don't know,' Rosie sobbed.

'May I recommend a brandy to start? You can go on to wine after that. It's always better not to mix the grape with the grain.'

'Very wise,' Mr O'Gorman said. 'There's terrible danger in mixing grapes and grains.'

'I'll have a brandy when you're ready, Mr O'Gorman, to keep Rosie company. You gentlemen can help yourselves.'

'A feast fit for a High King,' Mr O'Gorman said. 'Fair dues to you, missis.'

'Why thank you, Mr O'Gorman.'

'Saving your presence ladies, but I will have to divest myself of my overcoat. Tell me, was it the curry, or is it inordinately hot in here?'

'Shantell told me to keep the place warm,' Rosie explained. 'I was only doing what she told me.'

'Don't snivel, Rosie. I did say to keep the place warm, Mr O'Gorman. Naturally I was afraid of rigger's mortis setting in, but there's no need to worry about that now. It's no longer a question of folding Granny into something suitable. We have Fionn who can assemble to our exact requirements.'

'What is she talking about?' Fionn slurred across to Malachy. 'Do you know what she is talking about? I don't understand what she is talking about.'

'You have me there, Fionn.'

'She's a wonderful woman. I'm going to marry her.'

'Good on you, Fionn. Always better to marry a woman you don't understand.'

'Shush.'

'What are you shushing me for? She can't hear me.' Fionn and Malachy had followed the others into Granny Deignan's bedroom and were standing at the foot of her bed.

'This is granny,' Rosie said.

'Hello, Gran. I'm Shantell.' Shantell smiled down at

Granny Deignan. 'I'm sorry we didn't meet while you were alive, but Rosie's told us all about you. Doesn't she look beautiful, so rested. Granny, we have come to fulfil your last requests. This is Mr O'Gorman, he will be doing the general organising . . . There is no need to shake Granny's hand Mr O'Gorman. This is Fionn, who will be building your coffin, and finally Malachy who will be in charge of transport.'

'What's this about transport?' Malachy shouted. 'I never said anything about transport.'

'A quiet word, Malachy.' Shantell jerked her head in the direction of the sitting room, signalling for Malachy to follow her.

'You don't mean to tell me that in the middle of someone else's tragedy,' she began, once they were out of earshot, 'you are selfish enough to renege on—'

'Renege? Renege on what? All I did was bring you out here in my cab. I never promised anything.'

'Am I to assume then, Malachy, that you allowed us to befriend you, you partook of our hospitality, our food, our drink, and when we ask for one little favour in return, you turn your back on us?'

'You don't understand.'

'I understand only too well.'

'I have to think of my job. It's not even my taxi.'

'Your job, Malachy. Your taxi. Have you any idea what I have deferred in order to help Rosie in her hour of need, her dire need? I, Malachy, am in the middle of an extremely important novel. Aha, I see from your expression that you are astonished. Yes, Malachy, I have sacrificed my precious time to help a friend. No matter publishers are waiting. No matter that my mentor, Miss Annabelle Titchmarch, wrote in no uncertain terms of the dangers of distractions. I could not live with myself if I didn't help—'

'Don't!' Malachy cried. 'When you put it like that, how could I refuse? Count me in. I won't let Rosie down.'

'I should also mention there would be a certain financial arrangement which would, I think, allay any fears you might have on the loss of a day's pay.'

'Hail Mary full of grace the Lord is with thee. And blessed is the fruit of thy womb Jesus.'

'I think you missed a bit, Mr O'Gorman,' Fionn whispered.

'I've been saying that prayer since I was knee-high to a grasshopper. No bloody culchie is going to tell me I don't know my prayers.'

'There's a bit about blessed among women.'

'That may be your Kerry culchie version but nobody knows his prayers as well as a Dublin man.'

'I know you Dublin men. The only time you ever pray is when you're waiting for a horse to come in, or you want the barman to give you another drink.'

'How dare you, you culchie craw-thumper. Put them up. Come on, put your fists where your mouth is.'

'If it's a fight you want,' said Fionn, pulling at the buttons on his coat, 'a fight you'll get.'

'Stop it. Stop it,' Rosie screamed.

'I'll take no insult from any man.' Mr O'Gorman danced around Granny's bed, his fists raised and clenched. 'Come on, ye cap-wearing crombie-coated culchie.'

'Mr O'Gorman. Fionn. Stop that at once.' Shantell ran back into the bedroom with Malachy close behind her. 'What do you think you are doing? Malachy, do something!'

'Lads, lads,' Malachy said, stepping in between the two of them. 'Take it easy. There's no need for this.'

Malachy's timing was bad. The intervention disastrous. At that precise moment both protagonists struck and, as two right fists landed hard on each side of his head, he fell prostrate on top of the motionless body of Rose Deignan.

'Malachy!' The ladies screamed in horror.

'Never in all my novelist, or undertaking, days have I seen such a spectacle. I can only hope you are both thoroughly ashamed of yourselves. Get up off Granny Deignan, Malachy. Get up at once.'

'I don't think he can, Shantell,' Rosie said. 'I think he is unconscious.'

# Chapter Six

Martin Duffy got his cocoa and sat down to watch *Thought for the Day*. He was confused. This couldn't be right. There was Father Brennan standing in a big field; the sun was shining, the cows were grazing, but Father Brennan seemed to be roaring his head off. Martin got up and banged the side of the television. Then he tried turning it off and on again but the interference was still there. Now Father Brennan was giving the blessing and he had missed the whole thing. He turned the television off in disgust. What the hell was going on? He could still hear the roaring. Puzzled, he sat back and tried to figure it out. The wireless was off, the gas was off. There was nothing else in the flat that could cause the commotion. Was it coming from outside? They had had trouble in the past with drug addicts but they had all been dealt with by the police. He jumped out of his skin with fright when the telephone rang.

'Martin. It's Ivy Simpson. Can you hear the noise?'

'I would have to be deaf not to, Ivy. What is it?'

'It's coming from Rose Deignan's. What should we do? Do you think we should ring the guards?'

'You know what Rose would do to you if you rang them.'

'But she could be being murdered in there. You'll have to do something.'

'What can I do?'

'You're a man aren't you?'

'Ivy. I am seventy-eight years old. What do you think I can do?'

'You were always the same, Martin Duffy. Young or old you never went out of your way for anyone.'

'If you're so smart, Ivy, you do something.'

'I will, Martin Duffy. And I'll know in future who I can call on when I'm being murdered or raped in my bed.'

'Listen to her. The last time a man looked at you, Ivy Simpson, was over fifty years ago—' He stopped as the roaring suddenly increased.

'Christ Almighty did you hear that?'

'You're right, Ivy. Even Rose on a good night wouldn't be making that sort of a noise. I'll ring the guards.'

'Martin. You'll have to go over and knock on the door.'

'What? Me?'

'Ring the guards and then go and knock on the door.'

'Are you out of your mind, Ivy?'

'She could be dead in there by the time the guards get here.'

'Yea. And I could be dead and all.'

'Martin Duffy. For once in your life do something decent.'

'There's no way I'm going in there on my own.'

'All right then, I'll come with you. They can't kill us all.'

Fionn and Mr O'Gorman half carried and half dragged the comatose Malachy into the sitting room while Rosie and Shantell reorganised Granny Deignan in the bed.

'Don't touch her,' Rosie said. 'Take your hands off her. Haven't you done enough?'

'I will ignore that, Rosie. I know bereavement can make people behave in a strange way. Say things they don't mean. Let's leave Granny to rest, shall we, while we go into the other room and go through the plans for tomorrow.'

'Tomorrow? I want to see the back of you all now, tonight.'

'Rosie, Rosie, Rosie. I can see why you were called after your granny. The pretty flush on your cheeks is a complete give-away. You probably had that as a baby. Some, not quite so literary as I, might call them hectic spots, but I can look beyond the obvious.'

'You're mad.' Rosie laughed hysterically. 'You're all completely mad.'

'Yes, dear. Now take my hand, Rosie, and come back into the sitting room. We will pretend this little fracas never happened. There is too much to be done for any more time to be wasted on tantrums.'

'Mad.' Rosie allowed herself to be led away. 'I am in the middle of a room full of mad people and I invited them.'

'No hard feelings, Malachy, eh.' Mr O'Gorman held a wet cloth to Malachy's head. 'A slight altercation, shouldn't have happened. Myself and Fionn here would like to apologise.'

'I am really sorry, Malachy. I don't know what came over me. I never fight with anyone. In fact, in Kerry, where my home is, I have the reputation of being among the mildest men in the parish. Only last week—'

'Shut him up,' Malachy groaned. 'Somebody shut him up.'

'There, you see, Rosie. All friends again. Make yourselves comfortable while I get out my notes. Mr O'Gorman, would you clear a bit of space at the table. Rosie, get some pens and paper so each person can jot down their duties as I call them out.'

'My head hurts,' Malachy said, 'and I can't see properly. I need a doctor.'

'Nonsense, Malachy. You'll be fine. Why, earlier today I had a bang on the head and look at me now.'

Rosie looked hard at Shantell when she heard this. Could that be the reason this woman was behaving so oddly? There had to be some explanation for it. The only undertakers Rosie had ever seen were outside a church, or a funeral home. Sombre men who wore dark clothes and solemn expressions and stood quietly and respectfully in the background. She couldn't imagine those men coming to your house with curry and chips and booze and fighting and falling over Granny.

'Rosie, dear, we are waiting.'

She would have to go along with them. It was her only chance to get them out of the flat.

'Rosie.'

If she could get to the telephone. She couldn't without being seen. Rosie handed out the pens and paper.

'If everyone is ready we can begin. The first thing to do is check Granny's will. We have to be sure to comply with all her final wishes. Have you got the will, Rosie?'

Rosie got up and walked over to her granny's sideboard. She had no choice. There were four of them and only one of her. God knew what they would do if she didn't do as they asked. Her hands were shaking as she got the will from the top drawer where Granny kept all her bills and her important papers. She had seen this sort of thing in the movies. Maybe they had guns. Rosie got out the will and sat down.

'Now, Mr O'Gorman, I think a little something all round is called for, while Rosie reads her granny's will. It will help us to relax. Could you repeat the honours? No. Rosie, I insist.' Rosie had tried to refuse her refill. 'It will do you all the good in the world. I promise you.'

Martin Duffy and Ivy Simpson stood on the balcony outside number 147.

'Can you hear anything?'

'No. Wait. I hear voices. They're just talking.'

'They must have killed her.'

'Leave off, woman.'

'I'm telling you, they've killed her.'

'If they'd killed her why would they be still there?'

'They're ransacking the place.'

'Oh yea, on tiptoe. Do you know what I think? It was the telly.'

'That was no telly I heard.'

'Did you have your hearing-aid in?'

'Of course I did. What do you take me for?'

'That's it then. You had it up too loud.'

'That was no telly. I keep telling you. I had my telly on and it wasn't making those noises.'

'Yea. But Rose has satellite hasn't she?'

'Satellite?'

'Sure I've been in there myself, watching all sorts of things.'

'What sort of things?'

'Not for the likes of your ears, Ivy Simpson. Do you think I want the whole clergy down on top of me? I know you auld ones. Running to the priest every time you hear the word *sex*.'

'Martin Duffy.'

'With your flower arranging, and your cleaning brasses, and your "yes father, no father, three bloody bags full father".'

'If you had a bit more religion Martin Duffy—'

'You can stand here all night if you want to but I'm going back to bed.'

'What about the police? You did ring them?'

'Don't open the door. If they don't hear anything they will go away again.'

'But they know your name.'

'You don't think I was stupid enough to give my name do you? There is nothing going on there, woman. I'm off.'

*Ding-dong, ding-dong, ding-dong.*

'Shush everyone, there's someone at the door. Rosie were you expecting anyone else?'

'No.'

'Did Granny ever have friends who called this late?'

'I don't know.'

'It could be someone trying to get at the will.'

'But nobody knows that Granny is dead.'

'Stay here, don't make a sound. I'll try and find out who it is.'

'I'll go, Shantell.' Rosie jumped up. This could be her chance. If she could get to the door she could get away. 'I'll probably know who it is. It could be one of the neighbours.'

'Stay where you are, Rosie. You are far too distraught to deal with sightseers.'

'Honestly, I'm fine.' Rosie sprang for the door.

'Fionn, sit Rosie down there beside you like a good chap. We don't want her being upset at the door.'

It's true, thought Rosie, panic-stricken. I am a captive. I will be found dead. Granny and I will be buried together.

*Ding-dong ding-dong ding-dong.* The rings were more insistent.

'Who is it?' Shantell put on a high and trembling voice. 'Who is there?'

'It's the police, ma'am. Garda Sean O'Rourke, and Garda Tim Hawkins.'

'What do you want with a little old lady like me?'

'We got a complaint down at the station, ma'am.'

'A complaint, Officer?'

'We had a call about strange noises coming from your flat. We are here to check them out. Ma'am. Ma'am? Are you still there? Is everything okay?'

'Yes, Officer. Everything is hunky-dory in here.'

'You're sure?'

'It is such a comfort,' Shantell continued to squeak, 'for us old people to know that you boys are on the ball, Officer.'

'Well, if you are sure.'

'Quite sure. Off you go now and find yourselves some villains and thieves. It is way past my bedtime.'

'Good night, ma'am.'

'Good night, Officers.'

Shantell bounced back into the sitting room.

'Nothing to worry about. It was only the police.'

The guards stood for a moment on the balcony before they moved on.

'Funny talk for an old lady.'

'You could never be up to them.'

'I'd love to get my hands on whoever made that hoax call. Wasting our time like this.'

Martin Duffy shrank behind his curtains, in number 148, where he had been crouched waiting for the guards. Bloody Ivy Simpson, he thought. I should have known better. I'm a fool to listen to that old biddy. I'm up the Swannee if they ever trace that call.

'You are all being so kind,' Rosie said. 'I have misjudged you. Please forgive me.' Rosie, tipsy now, and beginning to relax, had finished reading her granny's will.

'Granny seems to have covered all eventualities, Rosie. A very comprehensive will.'

'She gave everything away,' Rosie sobbed.

'Now, Rosie don't start. I am sure she wouldn't want to see you upset like this.'

'She remembered everyone. She even left ten pounds for the cats and dogs home.'

'A woman after my own heart,' Mr O'Gorman said, reaching into his pocket for his handkerchief.

'Did I tell you the first thing I am going to do when I get home to Kerry is ring my granny?' Fionn said.

'You did, Fionn. You did.'

'I never knew my granny,' Malachy said. 'She died

before I was born . . .' Fionn was moved and put his arm around Malachy's shoulder in a gesture of sympathy for his loss. '. . . I know I would have loved her.'

'I am sure you would have, Malachy,' Fionn said.

'Gentlemen, gentlemen, Rosie. What is this? Granny Deignan had the right idea.'

'What do you mean, Shantell?' Rosie asked.

'She knew what she wanted. If she were here among us, she would be the first to tell you, there are no pockets in a shroud.' Shantell was surprised when, after saying these words, there was a fresh outbreak of sobbing from her companions. 'Pull yourselves together. Enough tears. We have too much to do.'

# Chapter Seven

'Was everyone got their notes?' began Shantell. 'Let me recap. We did settle on Monday for the service. Fionn. Fionn! Wake up. You cannot go to sleep now.' Fionn jerked his head up and looked blearily about him. 'Once the details are sorted we can all get some rest.'

'But it's nearly morning, Shantell,' Fionn said groggily.

'All the more reason to fix the arrangements. A quick checklist and we can all rest for a few hours. We must have everything prepared. We cannot afford to allow the situation to reach a crisis level by not being prepared: Item 1. Fionn: you need wood, a hammer and nails. I myself think deal will do nicely. Oak is far too ostentatious.'

'Oaks,' Fionn sighed. 'I love oaks.'

'Not now, Fionn. Item 2. Mr O'Gorman: you are on, let me see, priest, invitations and—'

'Where is Fionn going to make the coffin, Shantell?' asked Rosie.

'Please don't interrupt. He can make it here.'

'There is no room in here.'

'We can move the furniture out to the balcony for a while.'

'What? We can't do that!'

'It won't take long. I mean, how long can it take to hammer a few planks together for goodness' sake? It might be nice, Fionn, if we could see some sketches of what you propose to do. We better add paper and pencils to your list.

'Item 3. Malachy: dormobile. I think we mentioned a dormobile as being the most economical. We probably need a ten-seater.'

'You don't get seats like that in a dormobile, Shantell.'

'Well get a minibus then. You are the expert on transport, Malachy. I can't think of everything.'

'What about the body? Are we having a hearse?'

'A good point, Malachy. A very good point. No. I think a hearse would be an unnecessary expense. I suggest we lay the coffin and the flowers across the back seat. That would leave room for about six people. The rest of the cortège will have to use their own transport.

'Item 4. Rosie: to inform family and friends of Granny's departure, prepare notice for the paper, get flowers and lay out suitable clothes for Granny to wear.

'Item 5. Shantell: ring Carmel. Visit crematorium. Organise paperwork, if any required, and generally oversee project. Also, try and find some time to continue with novel.'

'Novel?' Malachy wondered.

'I believe I did mention my work to you earlier, Malachy. I have, in fact, two works on the go at the moment and, hand on heart, I must confess I think they are going to be sensational.'

'I thought you were an undertaker.'

'I have many fiddles to my strings, Malachy.'

'So you are not an undertaker?'

'Technically, no. I had hung my hat up on the undertaking business. I resumed only to facilitate Rosie. Poor girl. She had no one else to turn to.'

'But if you are not an undertaker—'

'Malachy. There is too much to be done for you to indulge in taxi driver pedantry. If you wish to see my credentials I would be only too happy to supply—'

'I didn't mean anything. I was only asking.'

'If our government chooses to bestow an EC women's enterprise grant on myself and my partner then that surely is proof enough of the legitimacy of my capabilities in this matter.'

'I never doubted you. I was only asking. Sure I can tell by the way you are carrying on that you know what you are doing. Those lists and all.' Malachy's voice trailed off.

'Thank you, Malachy. I think that about covers everything. Has anyone else got any questions?'

Shantell turned to the others to find all three – Mr O'Gorman, Fionn and Rosie – curled up, fast asleep, on the sofa.

'I suppose we should hit the sack ourselves,' Malachy said. 'You and I should go into the spare bedroom.'

'Certainly not!'

'I didn't mean, you and I, together like, I only meant—'

'There seems to be a lot of things you don't mean,

Malachy. You cannot go in there. We must keep that room free for our artisan.'

'There's no doubt but you have a great way with words, Shantell.'

'That is because I am a novelist. You'll have to sleep there, where you are. I shall go into Granny Deignan's spare room and see about making space for the carpentry work.'


This room will do nicely. There's not too much in it to be shifted. I should make a note. Hold on, Shantell. What you should do is rest a minute, there will be plenty of time to organise things when the others wake up. Forty winks wouldn't do you any harm at all. The nerve of Malachy suggesting that we share a bed. I don't know what Fionn would say if he woke to find us together in a single bed. That other little incident earlier was unfortunate enough. Men. They must have their displays of National Geographic bravado. Males, puffing and blowing, staking claims on their territories. I think National Geographic should be made compulsory for men. It might put some sense into them. Some of those animals even pee about the place to make sure no one else gets their bit. It's flattering, of course, but so disruptive.

Those policemen. Now that could have turned into a tricky situation. However, I think I managed to handle things with a certain amount of aplomb. 'Courage', Miss Titchmarch said. 'Be sure of yourself.' If I had had any doubts I think today's events proved my capabilities. Who would have thought a group of people, thrown together by chance, could have become such a force? That bed does look cosy. I think, Shantell, you deserve a tiny rest. I'll lie back for a moment. Just a moment though. Mustn't sleep. Luckily I have trained myself to be able to wake on command so if I do drop off it won't matter. My ankles seem a little puffy. Strange that. Brandy always has that effect on my ankles. Doesn't seem to affect me anywhere else, just the ankles. It's good to stretch out. Poor Granny, stretched out next door. Still, we will have her all sorted by tomorrow afternoon. Carmel didn't call. She can't have got my message. I really do want to include her. I know she could do with the money and I am not one to forget a friend. She will be surprised when she discovers how much I have achieved. How I have covered every detail. 'The hallmark of a good writer is attention to detail,' Annabelle said on page 32. 'Leave nothing to chance.' I have left poor Gillian and Felicity, and you too Germaine. I will get back to you. You will have my undivided attention. You deserve my undivided attention. I wonder if I should get an agent before I approach a publisher. I must check that with Annabelle.

# Chapter Eight

Ivy Simpson put the kettle on and turned on the eight o'clock news. She hadn't slept well. She always felt cold when she hadn't slept well. She shivered and tightened the cord of her dressing gown. She was planning what she would say to that Rose Deignan. 'Keeping a body awake half the night. It isn't right.' She filled her teapot and, while the tea was brewing, went to the hall door to collect her milk. Ivy stepped out on to the balcony and stared, open-mouthed, at the entrance to number 147. There, all piled up, was a load of Rose's furniture. A bed, mattress, dressing table, chairs and boxes of her knick-knacks. Ivy recognised them. They came from Rose's spare room. She crept to the window to try and get a look in, but the curtains were drawn. She thought she could hear whistling coming from inside. Ivy scuttled past Rose's door and on to Martin Duffy in number 148.

'Martin,' she hissed, knocking lightly, afraid of being heard. 'Martin Duffy. It's Ivy. Open the door.' Martin didn't answer. 'Martin. For God's sake open the door.' The whistling from number 147 got louder.

'Oh my God. Someone's coming out.'

Ivy flattened herself against Martin's door, trying to make herself invisible. The door to Rose's flat opened and a woman she didn't recognise, armed with more boxes, appeared.

'Good morning,' the woman called out to Ivy. 'Lovely at this hour of the morning, isn't it.' She put down the boxes and disappeared back into the flat.

'Oh merciful hour,' Ivy cried. 'What's going on? Who was that?' She clung to Martin's door knocker as her knees began to give way. 'Are we all going to be evicted?' Ivy struggled to get back to her own flat. As she shouldered past Rose's home she heard the sound of the curtains being pulled back. She dropped to her knees, terrified of discovery, and crawled on all fours, into her own place. Ivy did not stand up until she reached her telephone.

Martin Duffy heard the door but didn't want to answer it in case it was the police. Who else would call at that hour of the morning? He wanted to have a decent story ready, if they did get him, and he wasn't always at his best first thing. Martin had his routine. Porridge on, scoot to the shop for the paper while the porridge was cooking, then a leisurely morning reading the news and checking out the horses. He hated having that routine interrupted. He was already out of sorts when the telephone rang.

'Hello.'

'Martin, it's Ivy. I was trying your door but you didn't answer.'

'Was that you at the bleeding door? Do you know what time it is? I thought you were the police.'

'I wish it was the police.'

'Don't start that again, woman. Look at the mess you could have got us into.'

'Martin. Rose is being evicted. They're putting her stuff out.'

'Don't be daft, Ivy. They don't evict old people from old people's flats.'

'I'm telling you, Martin. Look out the door if you don't believe me.'

'Ivy. Did you take your senility pills?'

'I'm not on senility pills.'

'That's what I'm trying to tell you. You should be.'

'Martin, I'm serious. If you don't believe me look out the door.'

'Give over, Ivy.'

'Martin. I swear to God, may I never ring you again if I am telling a word of a lie. Look out the door.'

'If you are acting the maggot, Ivy, I'll . . . Hold on.' Martin put the receiver down and went to his hall door. Moments later he was back on the telephone. 'Ivy. Ivy!' he shouted down the phone. 'Are you there?'

Ivy had gone to the front to watch for Martin. She heard him shouting but couldn't see him.

'I'm here, Martin. Where are you?' she roared back.

'Jesus, woman. I told you to wait on the phone.' He went back to the door.

Ivy and Martin, their heads poking out of 146 and 148 respectively, watched as the pile of furniture increased. Martin signalled to Ivy, putting his hand to his ear, for her to get back to the telephone.

'I told you, didn't I?' Ivy said. 'What are we going to do? Will we ring the police again?'

'Don't be daft, woman. If people are being evicted it's the police who do it.'

'We have to do something. We can't let her be thrown out.'

'We'll get everyone together.'

'Get everyone together?'

'It's the only way. We can't do anything unless the whole block stands together. You ring everyone on the first two floors, I'll do the rest. There's no time to organise anything else.'

'What will we do then, Martin?'

'We'll form a human barricade.'

'A human barricade?'

'Will you stop repeating everything I say and go and phone.'

Shantell whistled as she drew back the curtains in Granny Deignan's living room. She was pleased with her morning's work. It hadn't been easy, packing all that stuff and hauling it outside. She turned from the window and surveyed the scene in front of her. Malachy was folded into the arm chair. Fionn, Rosie, and Mr O'Gorman, sitting upright, as if they were watching television, were balanced against each other on the sofa, and all four of them, out for the count, were snoring and dribbling. Shantell went into the kitchen, put on the kettle and made herself a cup of tea. Five more minutes is all I'm giving them, she told herself. We did agree it was to be all hands to work as early as possible. I can't be expected to do everything myself. Shantell thought she heard a noise coming from outside. Probably that nice little old lady, she concluded. Very shy, the way she tried to hide herself away. Too much dignity to want anyone to see her in her dressing gown. I respect that. I know exactly how she feels. We all have our dignity. I must work a little old lady into my novel. She could be Gillian's great aunt, or maybe even Felicity's. Not Germaine's. Germaine would have to be an orphan for dramatic effect. A complete contrast to the others.

### Notes for Chapter 2
Great aunt, while on holidays with Gillian, finds her in bed with boyfriend. Great aunt has heart-attack. Gillian remorseful. Goes in ambulance to hospital where great aunt confides terrible secret. She too had a lover. Her family threw her out and she roamed the streets doing washing and other odd jobs. After years of searching her lover found her, but she had become old and worn and he didn't want her. Gillian, in tears, vows to look after great aunt for ever. Great aunt dies with smile on face.

Perfect. With a little work that could be two chapters put to bed, or maybe even three.

All of the pensioners from Block 2, Tower Heights, who could manage the stairs, had gathered on the balcony around Rose Deignan's flat. They carried an array of weapons, from egg slices and saucepans, to a coal-scuttle.

'What's going on, Martin?' the pensioner asked. 'What's the matter with Rose?'

'Shush,' Martin said. 'I'm trying to formulate a plan. Shush.'

'You tell us, Ivy.'

'It all started last night,' Ivy, standing beside Martin Duffy, gushed with importance. 'I heard this noise and I phoned Martin and he phoned the police and—'

'For Christ's sake, Ivy,' Martin said. 'They don't

need to know all that. What we do know is that Rose is being evicted and we are not going to stand by and let it happen.'

'Did she not pay her rent?'

'Rose always paid her rent.'

'Quiet. Quiet everyone. We want to take those bailiffs by surprise.'

'How do you know they're bailiffs?'

'Will you just look at poor Rose's furniture all piled up. Who else would do the likes of that?'

'Here's what we are going to do. I want all you men up here near the door. Women to the back.'

'Get out of it, Martin Duffy. Sure us girls are more able than you lot any day.'

'They'd never hit a lady, Martin,' said Lily from number 140.

'Don't be so sure, Lily,' Ivy said.

'Look. Who's leading this? You or me?'

'Sorry, Martin. You go ahead.'

'Lily's right, Martin,' one of the gentlemen put in. 'Put the ladies up front.'

'Listen to the ex-soldier. What do you think we are? Cannon fodder?'

'Make your bleeding minds up for Jesus' sake.'

'We'll do half and half.'

'Right. Get yourselves sorted out. Maeve Byrne. What do you think you are going to do with the coal-scuttle, burn them out?'

'There's no need to shout at me, Martin. Ivy told me on the phone to bring something heavy. It was the only thing I could find in a hurry. I didn't even wait to empty it and the weight of it is taking the arms out of me.'

'Why don't we blacken our faces? Like you see on the telly.'

'Rose is going to be halfway to the poor house by the time you lot shut up and listen to me,' said Martin. 'We have to take them by surprise. Get them out on the balcony. Once we have them out here, half of you get into the flat, and the other half drag that furniture across the front of the door. That way, the ones outside can supply food and other necessities in and out through the window.'

'That's a wonderful plan, Martin,' Ivy said. 'But how do we get them out?'

'Give me a minute will you. I can't formulate my thoughts with you jabbering in my ear.'

'We could rush the door,' said Tommy Doran, the ex-soldier. 'Overpower them, like.'

'Good idea, Tommy,' Martin said. 'But we don't have the men for it, if you get my meaning.' Martin jerked his head towards the ladies. 'We'll have to use surprise tactics. Work out a stratagem. Those fellows in there are as cunning as foxes.'

'What's he talking about, Lily?' Maeve Byrne asked.

'I haven't a notion, Maeve. But isn't he wonderful.'

'Gather round, everyone. I think I have a plan. We need someone on the ground floor to watch out for the van. They could send reinforcements and we have to be prepared. Mick. Get yourself downstairs as lookout. If you see anything phone Ivy's. Ivy. Stand by your phone. Huddle in everyone. We don't want them to hear anything. Surprise is our only weapon.'

John Doyle stopped his minibus outside Tower Heights, Orchardstown, and checked his book. It had been a busy night and he wasn't in the humour to do a funeral but, when Malachy phoned, he couldn't refuse. He owed him a favour and a mate is a mate. Must have been sudden, he thought. Malachy went off his shift early. Didn't even call in. That wasn't like him. John usually did the airport run, on account of having the minibus, so it wasn't too far off his track. He wasn't staying, he'd told Malachy. He'd get the people to the funeral home and then he was off again. He'd been on the job for twelve hours already. John saw Malachy's taxi parked outside one of the blocks and pulled in behind it. He's still here then, he thought. Some state he'll be in. Had to have been somene close for Malachy to stay all night. Glad I didn't let him down. John got out of his cab and looked up. He saw a large crowd, mainly elderly from what he could make out, gathered on the balcony, outside what he assumed must have been the flat. He hesitated, not sure whether to go up and find Malachy or stay where he was. He had just decided on going up when an old gent came out of the stairwell.

'Excuse me,' John began politely. 'I'm here for Rose Deignan's removal. Can you tell me if the remains have gone yet?'

'Vulture.' The old man shook his fist at John. 'What sort of people are you? You're not going to get away with it. Rose is not leaving here.'

'I'm sorry, mister. It must be very hard when your friends go.'

'She is not going anywhere. We've got a plan.'

'She has to go. You can't keep her up there. I'm looking for my friend, Malachy. Do you know if he is up in the flat?'

'He's up there, with the rest of your henchmen.'

'Thanks. You'll feel better, you know, when it's all over. The first few days are always the worst. The shock of it can be terrible. I felt the same when my own mother went.'

'You did it to your own mother?'

'We all have to go sometime.' John patted the old man's shoulder in a gesture of sympathy, and went on to the stairs. Poor old fellow, he thought. Taking it very bad.


'Ivy. It's Mick from downstairs. Get Martin on the phone for me quick . . . Martin. The van is here. There's only one man with it and he is on his way up.'

'Good man, Mick.'

'I had a look at the van. It's a class of a bus. They must be going to take Rose away with them. One of the men up there is called Malachy. The driver is gone up to meet him.'

'Don't worry, Mick. He won't get to meet him. We're ready for him. Did he leave the keys in it by any chance?'

'No. But I can scuttle it. I can let the air out of the tyres.'

'Wait a few minutes, so he doesn't see you over the balcony, then go for it.'

'Roger. Over and out.'

# Chapter Nine

Rosie opened her eyes, saw Shantell, and immediately closed them again. It had to have been a dream. A terrible, terrible dream. She waited a moment, counting. When she reached ten she slowly opened her eyes again and looked around the flat. She looked at Shantell, at the sleeping men, at the table laden with bottles and leftover food. As the memory of all the events since her granny's death came seeping back, she sank deep into the sofa, and buried her face in her hands.

'Rosie,' Shantell said sharply. 'We really have no time for sulking. Shake your bedfellows awake while I make some tea for everyone. Nothing like tea to give one a surge of energy. Look at me. One cup and I'm raring to go. I have a very good feeling about today. A positive tingle. You cannot beat a well planned campaign. When everyone knows their responsibilities it can work like clockwork.'

'Get out.' Rosie jumped to her feet, and started shouting at Shantell. 'Get out of here. Get your things together and go. Please go. You're mad,' she cried.

71

'You are completely mad. I don't know what I thought I was doing. I should have known the minute I saw you but I was upset about Granny. What am I going to do? What have I done? The family will kill me.'

Fionn, Malachy and Mr O'Gorman awoke in confusion when they heard the shouting, each of them trying to remember where they were, and how they had got there.

'This is a fine way to wake a body up,' Mr O'Gorman said. At this remark, Rosie let out a squeal. 'I am sorry, my dear, that wasn't very tactful of me.'

'You will all have to go,' Rosie shouted. 'Now. Immediately. Go before anyone sees you.'

'I don't remember coming,' Fionn said. 'I only came up on a day trip to go to the library. My ticket is only valid for the day.'

'She said you were the carpenter,' Rosie exclaimed, disbelief on her face. 'You were going to make a coffin for my granny.'

'She?'

'Your fiancée. Shantell.'

'I didn't know I had a fiancée. When did I get a fiancée?'

'In Hart's pub,' Mr O'Gorman said. 'In O'Connell Street.'

'I don't normally go into public houses.'

'Well you certainly changed that yesterday, me boy. You asked Shantell if she wanted to be buried with your people.'

'But I have an understanding, with a woman from the next parish, back home.'

'She better be very understanding.'

72

'This is a terrible state of affairs. I have to get home.'

'Speaking of affairs.' Malachy pulled himself up out of his chair. 'I better go and check my taxi. The boss is going to be livid over this. I didn't even ring in.'

'Sure when it comes to bereavement they can be very understanding,' Mr O'Gorman said. 'Once he hears about Granny he'll—'

'She's not your granny,' Rosie cried out. 'She's my granny. Get your own granny.' Rosie broke down in uncontrollable sobs.

'The girl's still hysterical,' whispered Mr O'Gorman. 'Poor wee lass. Do you think we should check next door, Malachy? Make sure everything is okay?'

'I'm not going in there. It wouldn't be right. I never even knew the woman.'

'You weren't a bit worried about that last night. You were all over her.'

'You pushed me over her. I remember now.'

'Stop it. Stop it the two of you,' said Fionn. 'Can't you see how upset Rosie is? Have some respect.'

'You're right, Fionn. I'm sorry. Maybe we better go.'

'We can't just walk out and leave her. Look at the state of the place.'

'*Cooee!*' Shantell walked in with a trayful of tea. 'Good morning everyone.'

Silence greeted Shantell as she bustled in. Fionn, Malachy and Mr O'Gorman could only gawp open-mouthed, while Rosie, still sobbing, shook her head from side to side in feeble protest.

'Jesus.' Malachy whistled through his teeth. 'What is it?'

'Tea.' Shantell beamed at everyone. 'I couldn't find any coffee. Who is for milk and sugar? Come along now. Don't let it get cold after all my trouble. Fionn, dear. What do you take?'

Fionn trembled as Shantell spoke to him. He felt his legs giving way. He looked at the woman who was calling him dear. The mascara embedded in the previous night's make-up had mingled with dust from her early morning activities. Highlights of cobwebs stuck to her hair and the freshly applied smear of bright red lipstick gave her face an appearance which seemed not of this world.

'Milk and sugar, Fionn? Or would you rather a little tot of something stronger?'

'Well, speak to your fiancée, Fionn.' Mr O'Gorman grinned. 'Don't be shy in front of us.'

Fionn's legs gave way. He landed on the sofa.

'It's all gone very quiet in there,' Ivy said.

'I can hear crying. Poor Rose. She's breaking her heart.'

'Are we all ready for action?' asked Martin. 'Does everyone know what to do? Wait until the body snatcher gets up the stairs. Let him knock on the door. As soon as it's opened, and he goes in, I want six of you to dive in after him. The rest of you move the furniture like we agreed. Don't say anything to your man. We don't want to put him on his guard. They have no hearts, those fellows. They're trained for this sort of work.' Martin looked over the balcony. He saw Mick at work on the minibus. 'Christ. He's taken the bloody wheels off. Good man, Mick.'

The pensioners all leaned over the balcony to have a look.

'Hooray!'

'Good on ye, Mick.'

'Shush,' Martin said. 'We don't want to give the game away.'

John Doyle paused on the third floor to catch his breath. He heard the shout. Giving the old dear the three cheers, he guessed. That's nice. Must have been popular. I hope there's not going to be too much fuss. You never know with old folks. Hard for them to accept the friends going. He reached the fourth floor and hesitated, surprised by the crowd assembled there. As he moved along the balcony he was aware that all eyes were on him. He started to sweat, unnerved by the silence.

'Not too bad this morning.' He nodded greetings and acknowledgements as he passed through the old folks. 'Sorry about your friend.' The crowd inched towards him. Christ, he muttered to himself. You'd think I was after killing her myself. He was about to turn and make a run for it.

'We know you are only doing your job, mister.' Martin came forward.

'That's right.'

'We don't hold it against you.'

'Good, fine then. Thanks.' John didn't know what to be saying. 'Is this the flat?'

'Yes. That's poor Rose's place.'

'They didn't take long to move her things. Making space for the mourners, eh? Excuse me.'

John knocked on the door of the flat. The designated six surged forward. Poised. Waiting. Ready to barge. No one answered. John turned round to the crowd.

'Are you sure this is the right number?'

The six jumped back.

'Give another knock,' Martin said. 'They're probably so busy going through Rose's things, they didn't hear you.'

John knocked again. 'Malachy. It's me, John Doyle. I'm here with the minibus.'

The occupants of number 147 had turned to Rosie when they heard the first knock.

'Do you know who that could be, Rosie?' Shantell asked. 'We are not nearly ready to receive guests.'

'It's probably Ivy. Granny's neighbour. What am I going to do? What am I going to tell her? She doesn't even know Granny is dead.'

'Answer the door, Rosie. Stall her. Tell her your granny is still in bed.'

'Too true,' Mr O'Gorman said. 'She is that all right.'

'I can't,' Rosie cried. 'I can't.'

'Tell her she can come back later.'

They heard the second knock and the voice outside asking for Malachy.

'For you, Malachy. A man with a bus for you?' Shantell asked, surprised. 'Why is there a man with a bus knocking on the door for you?'

'There's no need to jump down my throat, Shantell. You said last night you wanted a minibus. I got you a minibus. I phoned my mate when you all went to bed.'

'But not at this hour, Malachy. We are nowhere near to needing the minibus.'

'You didn't say a time.'

'Really, Malachy. Ordinary common sense would have told you we wouldn't need transport until later.'

'You said—'

'Stop it. Stop it,' Rosie cried out. 'Nobody is moving my granny into a bus. Don't let them put Granny in a bus.' Rosie appealed to Fionn and Mr O'Gorman.

'I am beginning to lose patience with you, Rosie. You, after all, were the one to call me. You must let me do my job and I cannot do it if you continue to behave like this. We do all understand how upset you are, but you must, for Granny's sake, pull your socks up. Malachy. You were absolutely right. We do need your minibus friend. We need to collect the materials for Fionn. I hadn't consulted my notes. Rosie's carrying-on threw me for a moment. Open the door, Malachy, while I get another teacup from the kitchen.'

Mr O'Gorman sat Rosie down beside him and put his arm around her. 'Don't fret, Rosie,' he said. 'We'll get all this mess sorted out. Malachy's friend can drive you to an undertaker's. They will take care of everything, make all the arrangements for you. While you are doing that, Fionn and I will get the flat cleaned up – by the time you get back, it will be spick and span and we will be gone. And don't worry, we will take Shantell with us, even if we have to carry her out. It will be all right, Rosie, I promise you. It was the drink. We all got a bit carried away. Sure I don't think young Fionn there had ever had a drink before in his life. Tell the undertaker you didn't realise your granny had died. You thought she was asleep. That's why you waited so long. You're a young girl, Rosie. They'll understand. And Rosie, one more thing. Don't mention anything to them about a lady undertaker. Don't say anything at all. Now, go and wash your face and tidy yourself up while she's in the kitchen. We don't want her to know our plans.'

The minibus was immobilised and Mick stood back admiring his handiwork. He had just removed the last wheel and sent it spinning off after the others when the squad car pulled up and two members of the Garda Síochána stepped out.

'What's going on here?' one of the Garda asked. 'Do you own that vehicle?'

'Who? Me? I do not, Officer. I was in my flat when I heard noises and I came out just as two young lads were running off up the road. Hooligans. That's what the youth of today are. Hooligans. You can have nothing. There's nothing sacred any more.'

'Do you know whose vehicle it is?'

'No, Officer. I can honestly say I don't.'

'Do you know how long it's been here?'

'Well it wasn't here last night, that's for sure. Probably stolen.'

'How do you know it was stolen?'

'I don't know if it was or not, Officer. I was only saying—'

'What's your name?'

'What do you want my name for, Officer? I only came out when I heard the noise. I was going to call you.'

'Name?'

'Mick O'Toole.'

'Address?'

'You're at it. Didn't I just tell you I came out of my flat.'

'Can you give me a description of the two youths you saw?'

'I would if I could, Officer, but, my eyes are not as good as they used to be.'

'Then how did you know it was two youths?'

'Skinheads. It's coming back to me now, Officer. Skinheads with black leather jackets, and jeans, and one of them had a wrench.'

'A wrench?'

'Yes, Officer. A great big one.'

'We'd better call this in,' Garda Troy said to his colleague.

'I'll be off so,' Mick said. 'I'll leave it to yourselves now.'

'Stay where you are, mister. We're not finished with you. We have a few more questions for you yet.'


Malachy opened the door of Granny Deignan's flat. 'John,' he said. 'Great to see you. Come on in.'

'What's going on, Malachy?'

'Come in. I'll explain inside.'

'*Charge*!' A great whoop went up and John and Malachy were swept aside as the six pensioners rushed the door.

'Jesus!' John fell against the door jamb.

'What the— Help!' Malachy hit the ground.

'Get them back inside, folks.' Martin said. 'We need them inside.'

Sinewy arms grabbed the two men and aimed them at the door.

'*Heave*!' Ivy screamed.

'Let me at them, Ivy. I haven't heaved a man in years,' cackled Peggy Moran from the first floor.

'Peggy Moran,' Ivy said. 'Leave that dirty tongue where it belongs and throw those men over to me.'

'Can we not keep them here, Martin? I can lock them in my flat.'

Malachy lifted his arm to try and defend himself.

'Hit an old lady, would you?' Maeve Byrne swung her coal-scuttle. 'Take that.' The coal scuttle landed on a sensitive part of Malachy's anatomy.

'Ow.' Malachy winced. 'Ow, ouch, ouch.'

'Careful, Maeve. You'll ruin his manhood.'

Maeve swung her coal-scuttle again. This time at John.

'Don't hit me, missis, please. I surrender.'

Martin was backed up against the door, holding it open. 'Throw them in. Hurry up. We're here, Rose,' he called into the flat. 'We won't let them take you.' When the two men were inside he pulled the door shut. 'Now, everyone. The barricade. Quick.'

Garda Troy was on the car radio to his super. He had reported the dismantled minibus and was waiting for confirmation of ownership.

'And, Sarge, could you get records to check out a Mick O'Toole? Yea. He was at the scene of the crime and I've got a gut feeling that he's involved. Yea. Description? Small, wiry, and bald on top. Wait. Hold on, Sarge. There's something going down here. All hell is breaking out on the top floor. You better send reinforcements. It sounds like a mob attack. Yes, Sarge. Send those reinforcements right away. We're going up.'

Garda Kellegher, holding Mick by the arm, had moved to the middle of the road. He was looking up at the top balcony trying to figure out what was happening.

'Eh. If you don't need me now, Officer,' Mick said. 'I'll be off.'

'Stay where you are. What do you know about this?'

'Who? Me? I don't know anything, Officer. I never saw those people before.'

'What people?'

'The ones who went upstairs.'

'Don't move. We'll deal with you later.'

The two gardaí, Troy and Kellegher, went into the block. Taking the stairs two at a time, they got to the top floor. They stopped when they saw the furniture stacked up outside number 147, not to mention the large group of pensioners, some of whom were sitting on the furniture, the rest squatting on the balcony.

'What's going on here? What do you think you are doing?'

'Nothing, Officer.'

'You call this nothing? What's that furniture doing on the landing?'

'Rose is redecorating.'

'If I don't get some information I'm taking you all down to the station.'

'On what charge, Officer?'

'Disturbing the peace for one.'

'We're the ones who live here. How could we be disturbing anyone?'

'We are protecting our homes, Officer.'

'From what?' Nobody spoke. 'Right.' Garda Troy took out his notebook. 'I'll have all your names.' He turned to Peggy Moran who was nearest him. 'Name?'

'Lillian Gish.' Peggy did a twirl. 'Thirty-six, twenty-four, thirty-eight.'

'If she's Lillian Gish,' Ivy said. 'I'm Veronica Lake.'

'That's enough, unless you want obstructing the

police in the course of their duty added to the charge. I'll ask you one more time. You can tell me here or you're all going down to the station.'

'*Martin*! *Martin*!' A voice screeched through the letter-box. 'They have young Rosie here as well. She's a hostage.'

Garda Troy heard the voice. 'Let me at that door. Get out of the way.' He bent over a dressing table and peered through the letter-box.

The six OAPs, panting and flushed from the charge, had collapsed into Rose Deignan's sitting room.

'It's the Gremlins,' Mr O'Gorman said. 'The Gremlins are coming.'

'Blackguards, scoundrels,' Kevin Clancy wheezed at Mr O'Gorman. 'That's right, sneer. Go ahead and sneer. Look at you. Feasting and drinking yourselves stupid while evicting poor Rose. Beasts. That's what you are. Fiends of the worst order.'

'Where is Rose?' Lily Murphy demanded. 'What have you done with her?'

They all heard Ivy shout 'heave', and jumped out of the way as John and Malachy came hurtling through the door. Rosie ran out of the bathroom and threw herself into Mr O'Gorman's arms. Fionn blessed himself and started a decade of the rosary, aloud, and Shantell, extra cup in hand, emerged from the kitchen.

'Who are these people, Rosie?' Shantell enquired. 'Rosie. You haven't invited them all for tea?'

'They have young Rosie,' Lily cried.

'Unhand that girl, you monster. Unhand her or we will call the guards.'

'Excuse me, sir,' Shantell said. 'Whoever you are. Kindly contain yourself. If anyone calls the guards it will be me. You are trespassing. Trespassing into a very delicate situation.'

'We know you. We know who you are.'

'I don't think I have had the pleasure.' Shantell smiled.

'We know your sort. Don't think you can soft-soap us.'

'Really, sir. I haven't the faintest notion what you are—'

'That's what they do. Get your guard down with soft soap and then pounce. Stand your ground men.'

'This is too ridiculous. Rosie. Kindly introduce us.'

'Don't say anything, Rosie. Don't let them intimidate you. We'll handle these creeps.'

'Perhaps I should introduce myself. My name is Shantell. Shantell O'Doherty. Novelist, poet and undertaker.'

'Undertaker?' the OAPs repeated in unison.

'Let me give you my card. Now, where did I put my bag? Malachy, I do believe it is under your foot. Could you oblige?'

Malachy handed over the bag. He nudged John, nodding towards the door, trying to think of a way to escape. As they moved forward, their way was blocked by Lily and, cowered by her age, they retreated and shrank back to sit beside Fionn on the sofa.

'An undertaker. They've gone and killed Rose.'

'Where is she? Where's Rose?' Alice Carmody from the second floor, who had been quiet up to now, darted into the bedroom. 'It's true. Rose is in there. She's stretched out on the bed. She's dead.'

'You see,' Shantell said. 'I told you. I'm an undertaker.' She handed out her black edged cards.

'Undertakers don't go round killing their clients, now do they?'

'So that's your game,' Kevin Clancy said to Fionn, John and Malachy, who were huddled on the sofa. 'Bring an undertaker with you on your evictions. Very neat. Get your cut out of it do you?' Kevin went to the front door and lifted the letter-box, and found he was staring straight into the eyes of Garda Troy. 'Tell Martin they've killed her. Rose Deignan is dead.'

Garda Troy pushed the furniture out of his way and hammered on the door.

'Open up. Open up in there. It's the police.' He turned to Garda Kellegher. 'Get on to the station. See what's happening to those reinforcements.'

His voice was drowned by a cacophony of sirens as two motorbikes, three squad cars, an ambulance and a unit of the fire brigade, all led by Sergeant Murphy, drove into Tower Heights. The cavalcade circled the block and stopped, surrounding Mick O'Toole who was still standing on the spot indicated to him by the Gardaí.

'Get out of the way, you idiot,' the sergeant said to Mick. 'Do you want to get run over? You are blocking the whole street.'

'He told me to stay where I was.'

'Well I am telling you to move. Pronto.'

Mick began to shuffle off.

'Stop,' said the sergeant. 'Who told you not to move?'

'The other Gardaí.'

'Which way did they go?'

'Up there.' Mick pointed to the top floor and shuffled off a little more.

'Where do you think you are going? Stay where you

are. I'll deal with you later.' Sergeant Murphy looked up. Two rows of heads faced him over the balcony. 'Get Troy and Kellegher on the walkie-talkie,' he said to one of his officers. 'Find out what the hell is going on.' He walked over to the fire brigade. 'Can you get me up there, Chief?'

'Sure thing, Sergeant. Pull over to the block, lads. The sergeant's going up.' Residents from the other blocks in Tower Heights came out of their flats to watch the excitement and a large group gathered under Block 2. Sergeant Murphy grabbed a megaphone from the squad car.

'Get back to your homes. There is nothing to see. This is police business.'

'What's going on, Officer?'

'Is it drugs?'

'Gun running,' came a voice from the crowd. 'They have guns up there.'

'Move back. Let the fire brigade through.'

'Sergeant. I have Garda Kellegher on the line.' Sergeant Murphy grabbed the phone.

'Kellegher here, Sarge. We have a hostage situation and a possible homicide. The culprits are inside. Maybe nine or ten of them. The flat is barricaded. No, Sarge, there's no sign of arms at present. I don't know, Sarge. It doesn't make any sense. And, Sarge. There's a gang of OAPs manning the barricades. No, Sarge. I don't know the ringleaders. I don't recognise any of them. Yes, Sarge. Right away.' Garda Kellegher turned to the group on the balcony. 'Right. All of you. Up against the wall and spread them.'

'Hey, Ivy,' Peggy Moran muttered. 'It's our lucky day. He's going to frisk us.'

*

'I'm sure I don't know what all the fuss is about,' Shantell said to the pensioners who were inside the flat. 'We have simply come to organise Mrs Rose Deignan's funeral which, I can assure you, will be a wonderful send-off. Fionn here is our carpenter. He is going to do us proud with a traditional Kerry coffin. Fionn . . .'

'The Third Sorrowful Mystery, Jesus was crowned with thorns.'

'. . . Oh do shut up, Fionn. I am aware it is a funeral but over-praying can be quite depressing. Mr O'Gorman is our florist and invitation specialist. He is also quite an expert on old Dublin wakes and rites and I am sure he will have some interesting, and unusual, touches to add to our service. Malachy is our transport man. All queries regarding transport should be directed to him. Sir. Yes, you sir.' Shantell addressed Kevin Clancy who was still over by the door. 'Would you mind stepping away from that letter-box. We don't want to attract unnecessary attention now, do we? I am sure there is something useful you could all do. Mr O'Gorman. Could you organise work parties? Nothing too strenuous for our elderly friends. We don't want any more deceased among us. It would be nice to touch up the paintwork, freshen up the flat for the viewing. There'll be oodles of time before Fionn has the coffin ready. Someone could light the fire and . . . Oh, I have just had a wonderful idea. Wouldn't it be nice to line the balcony with garlands?'

There was a loud thumping at the flat door.

'Open up. Open up in there. It's the police.'

'Now look what you've done,' Shantell said to Kevin. 'I did ask you to get away from the door.

Malachy, answer that please. Tell that policeman that everything is under control.'

'Open up or I will be forced to break down the door.'

'I'm not going to that door,' Malachy said.

'Must I do everything myself? What is the matter with you all? It can only be a routine call. Neighbourhood Watch or one of those things.'

'Neighbourhood Watch don't threaten to break down doors, Shantell,' Mr O'Gorman said.

'It's a raid. We're done for.'

'Nonsense, Malachy.'

'I've never done time,' Fionn said. 'I've only ever seen it on the telly.'

'Will you all stop it. Calm yourselves. Policemen are the public's friend. I shall open the door. Try and behave in a normal fashion. A policeman calling to the door should not throw you all into hysterics. Is everyone relaxed? Let me do the talking. I am perfectly capable of sending this gentleman on his way.'

Shantell opened the door with a flourish. Garda Troy, fist raised, about to hammer on the door again, brought his arm down hard, pounding the top of Shantell's head.

'Shantell O'Doherty, Officer. Novelist, poet and undertaker. How can I help you?' Shantell smiled and then passed out cold as Sergeant Murphy, megaphone in hand, loomed over the balcony in the fire brigade bucket.

# Chapter Ten

'Hello. Hello, Carmel. It's Shantell. When you get this message please call me at Orchardstown police station. I am only allowed one phone call so it is imperative you get back to me. I have so much to tell you I don't know where to begin. It's a bit difficult to talk as the station is chock-a-block but the two nice young policewomen who are looking after me found a quiet little corner. Just out of training college, they told me, and very keen to get on in the police world. They are keeping a really good eye on me and one of them gave me tea. You'd laugh if you saw me, Carmel. I'm not looking my best. Garda Troy accidentally knocked me out and one side of my face is purple but the doctor assured me it would fade and in a short time no one would notice the stitches. Hold on, Carmel. One of the police ladies is signalling to me. I think I wasn't supposed to mention the stitches, so ignore that – sorry Officeress. I didn't know – there was a tiny bit of a mix-up at Tower Heights but I expect it will all be sorted out soon. Granny can't wait for ever for her big day. By the way, Carmel, my mobile is down. Could you send me in a battery? I am absolutely lost without it and I may need a solicitor. Give my love to Joe. Look forward to hearing from you. Bye for now, Carmel. Oh. I just thought of something . . . What are you doing? Where are you taking me? I wasn't finished. I had something else to say to Carmel.'

'Officer. Excuse me, Officer. I wonder if I could trouble you for another Biro. This seems to be running out.'

'Preparing our defence, are we?'

'No, Officer. I am in the middle of an extremely important novel. I must make notes wherever I can. Do you think the sergeant will detain me much longer? It is rather difficult to concentrate in this little room. Perhaps you could move me to a larger one until things get sorted out.'

'This is a holding cell, miss. They don't come in different sizes.'

'I don't understand, Officer. I was merely doing my job. I know if I could talk to the sergeant I could straighten everything out.'

'Forget the sergeant, miss. It will be the district justice you'll be talking to.'

'But I must get out of here.'

'You are not going anywhere, Miss.'

### Notes for New Novel or Possible Poem

Alone in her cell Amy knew she would never betray Ralph. The long lonely hours only served to strengthen her resolve. No matter what the prison governor told her she would never believe he had been unfaithful to her. It was a trick to break her. To make her tell them where he was. Even when, night after night, she was ravished by her handsome guard she did not break. She thought only of Ralph. His kisses. His caresses. As her legs entwined Guard Constantine's she gave herself to him freely, imagining he was Ralph . . .

'It's no use,' Shantell told herself. 'The creative juices won't flow in this dreadful place. Guard. Get me out of here.'

The police station was packed. It was so packed that the crowd spilled over into the station yard and the car park.

'This is going to take all day,' the desk officer said to Sergeant Murphy. 'Did you have to bring them all in?'

'They are all implicated.'

'I can't take statements from them all.'

'We have the ringleaders downstairs. We're holding them for questioning. Get names from the rest of this lot, warn them they could be brought in as witnesses, then let them go.'

'What's the charge, Sergeant?'

'Barricading a flat. Malicious damage to a minibus. Obstructing the police and illegally holding a body.'

'She was definitely deceased then, Sarge?'

'Stiffer than a ramrod.'

'There'll be questions, Sarge. Detaining pensioners. Not good press.'

'Justice is justice, Officer. No matter what the age.'

'The ringleaders, Sarge? Have you got the list?'

'The three in holding cell one, O'Gorman, O'Fiachra and Malachy Conway. O'Doherty in cell two. Cell three, Rosie Deignan.'

'I thought she was dead?'

'She is dead. This is the granddaughter.'

'Did she know her granny was dead?'

'Of course she knew. Wasn't she the one responsible for all this.'

'But, Sarge—'

'Cell four. John Doyle, cab driver. Mick O'Toole, elderly delinquent. Cell five—'

'I don't understand, Sarge. If—'

'That's why you are a desk officer and likely to remain a desk officer. Cell five, three males discovered inside the flat, two outside, manning barricades, names as yet unregistered. Cell six—'

'Sarge?'

'What now?'

'We don't have six holding cells. We only have five.'

'Are you deliberately trying to thwart me? The officers' Rest and Recreation room has been commandeered by myself as a temporary holding cell, and will remain a holding cell until I say otherwise. Cell six contains six females. Two females discovered inside the flat in question, and four outside. Two of them were found to be carrying weapons, namely, a coal-scuttle and another device.'

'Device, Sarge?'

'An egg slice.' Sergeant Murphy slurred the words.

'What was that, Sarge?'

'An egg slice, dammit. You heard me.'

'Have I got this right, Sarge? An old lady snuffs it. Her granddaughter calls an undertaker. The undertaker gets drunk and moves all the furniture out on to the landing. The residents stage a protest. The police, fire brigade and ambulance services are called in. Garda Troy knocks the undertaker unconscious and we arrest everybody. Is that it, Sarge? Sarge. Where are you going?'

'Desk officer you are and that's where you'll stay.'

'Mr O'Gorman. Mr O'Gorman,' Rosie called through the window of her cell. 'Can you hear me Mr O'Gorman? I'm so frightened. What are they going to do to us?'

'Don't you fret, Rosie. We'll all be out in no time. Sure the judge will throw it out of court.'

'Judge? Court? What judge? I've never even been in a police station before, Mr O'Gorman, and now I'm locked up and nobody knows where I am.'

'My goodness, Rosie.' Shantell went to her window. 'We are all locked up. And I don't mind telling you a lot of the reason for this state of affairs lies on your head.'

'Steady on, Shantell,' Mr O'Gorman said. 'The girl did nothing.'

'Except whinge and cry, Mr O'Gorman, whinge and cry and attract the attention of the neighbours.'

'I think it was you, Shantell.' Fionn squeezed in beside Mr O'Gorman.

'Me what?'

'You attracted the neighbours when you put out the granny's furniture.'

'There's gratitude for you. You know well I was making space for you.'

'I don't know anything.'

'That is becoming very apparent, Fionn.'

'Mammy warned me about going to Dublin. She begged me not to go. She said they'd eat young country lads like me. I wouldn't listen to her, Mr O'Gorman. I had to find out about the Feng Shui didn't I. You'd have done the same. Now I'll never know. I'll be in jail for the rest of my life. I will, Mr O'Gorman, won't I?'

'Don't go upsetting yourself. They don't keep young people in for a first offence. How old are you, Fionn?'

'I'll be twenty-nine on my next birthday.'

'Twenty-nine?'

'That's all. That's why Mammy doesn't want me to see too much of Mary. You know the girl I was telling you about. The one I have an understanding with. Mammy thinks I am too young yet to settle down—'

'I can't hear what Fionn is saying, Mr O'Gorman. Is he all right? Should we call for a guard?'

'He's all right, Shantell. He'll be fine.'

'I've even asked Father Ignatious to have a word with Mammy about Mary but after this . . . Do you think they will get to hear? Father Ignatious is very strict about wrongdoing, he mightn't let me serve on the altar if he knew I was in prison and I don't know what Mammy or Mary will have to say about it, they thought I was mad when I told them about the Feng Shui—'

'Somebody switch him off,' Malachy implored. 'He is doing my head in.'

'Those Japanese,' Mr O'Gorman said. 'Isn't it amazing how their influence has spread throughout the country. With their bonsais and their little bridges, not to mention the electronics. They'll take over Georgian Ireland before we know where we are. The wife even calls her dressing gown a kimono now. "Pass my kimono, Tom," she says to me. Like some deranged geisha. You have to hand it to them though.'

'It's more than that, Mr O'Gorman,' Fionn said. 'It's their whole philosophy.'

'You won't catch me sitting around in a paper house. Philosophy or no philosophy. I'm a bricks and mortar man.'

'You see the reason I was so attracted to Feng Shui—'

'Mr O'Gorman.' Shantell pushed her mouth through the cell window bars. 'We are locked up in a prison cell. In Orchardstown. In a crisis situation. Don't you think you would be better served putting your mind to getting us out of here, than wasting time talking about the ins and outs of Japan?'

'China.' Malachy jumped up off the cell bed. 'It bloody well comes from China. Get him to shut up, Mr O'Gorman. If he says one more word about Feng Shui I won't be responsible for myself.'

'Responsible,' Shantell called out. 'You don't know the meaning of the word responsible. We got into your taxi in good faith expecting to be carried to our destination. Instead of that, we were hijacked on the side of the road. No wonder Rosie had time to get hysterical. She thought we weren't coming.'

'The worst fare of my life was picking up you lot.'

'Ah now, Malachy,' Mr O'Gorman said. 'Don't be like that.'

'You are paid to supply a service,' Shantell said.

'Paid. That's a laugh. I never got paid. I've probably lost my job and that's nothing compared with what the wife will do to me.'

'But your wife is a philosopher, Malachy,' Fionn said. 'You told me yourself she was a keen student of Feng Shui . . . Ow. Ouch. Stop, you're hurting me.'

'Let him go, Malachy. Let him go,' Mr O'Gorman said. 'You don't want violence added to the charge.'

'What's going on in there?' Shantell called out.

'Officer. Officer come quickly. You must open up the cell.'

'Stop it. All of you,' Rosie cried. 'We will never get out of here if you make trouble.'

'It's all right, Rosie. Don't cry.' Mr O'Gorman was holding Malachy down on the ground. 'We'll get you out of here.'

'This is all my fault. I only wanted to keep my promise to Granny. She'll never forgive me. We should be at her funeral now. I don't even know where she is.'

'Rosie,' said Shantell. 'As your undertaker I must insist you get a hold of yourself. I fully intend to lodge a severe protest. Why, even in darkest Africa, there is reverence for the dead, nothing is allowed to interfere with the rituals of mourning. We shall not be beaten by mere prison bars. Granny Deignan shall have her funeral.'

'She said I was her special grandchild. She was always buying me little treats, bringing me to the pictures. She said she could always rely on me.'

'I can see the headlines already. *Sacrilege at Orchardstown. Police incarcerate innocent victims.* This might not be such a bad thing, Rosie. It will certainly cut out the cost of obituary notices. Everyone will know about it. Crowds will attend. Granny Deignan will have the biggest send-off she could ever dream of. I am getting a good feeling about this, Rosie. It's quite exciting. Who'd have thought . . . Leave me to my thoughts, Rosie. I must prepare a press release.'

'Now, girls, watch what you say,' Ivy Simpson whispered, dunking her digestive biscuit into her tea. 'I'm sure this place is bugged.'

Ivy, Peggy Moran, Lily, Maeve and Dolores Watson sat in the officers' Rest and Recreation room, sipping tea and eating their digestives.

'I don't think so, Ivy,' soothed Dolores. 'That nice Garda wouldn't bug us. He said he was putting us in here for our own good. Keeping us away from hardened criminals I expect. He was very courteous. He said he wanted us to be comfortable.'

'That's right, Dolores. Comfortable enough to start talking.'

'How long do you think they'll keep us?'

'They can hold you for forty-eight hours.'

'I heard seven days.'

'Seven days? What about my cat?'

'You can get them to phone the NSPCA.'

'But they might put her down.'

'They'd do better to put you down, Lily. Will you give over about your cat. We have a lot more to worry about.'

'Seven days is for terrorists and drug barons. They'd never keep the likes of us for seven days.'

'I'm staying here as long as it takes to get those murderers behind bars,' Ivy said. 'To think of poor Rose. Dead in her bed all the time.'

'The policeman said that Rose had been dead a while, Ivy.'

'They were up in that flat for God knows how long. Martin and myself heard them the night before. We even called the police. I'll never forgive myself for not going in.'

'What could you have done, Ivy. If she was dead already?'

'We don't know that, do we. We don't know when she died.'

'They might have murdered you as well.'

'Why do you think they did it?'

'They were after her pension book. Rose had another ten good years left. That mounts up in pension money.'

'The things people will stoop to.'

'You can tell, just by looking at them, the sort they are. They'd shoot their own mother for a few bob.'

'What about young Rosie though, Ivy? Why was she there?'

'They had her drugged. Did you see her eyes? She was pumped full of drugs. They used her as a decoy to get into the flat.'

'The scoundrels.'

'I can think of a worse name than that, Lily. But I'm too much of a lady to say it.'

'Why do you think they let Alice Carmody go? She was in the flat same as me.'

'It was her pacemaker. It started to go wonky as soon as they put her in the Black Maria.'

'Typical. They didn't want a death in the station.'

'It wouldn't look good, I suppose, if she died in custody.'

'Another digestive, Maeve?'

'I don't mind if I do.'

'Shush. I think I can hear someone coming.'

'Well, ladies.' Garda Kellegher came into the room. 'I trust everyone is comfortable. You found the tea and biscuits.' All eyes looked to Garda Kellegher. The only sound was the munching of the digestives. 'Don't let me interrupt you. I wanted to make sure you had everything you wanted, that you were all comfortable. It's not often we have such an array of ladies in the station.' Garda Kellegher began to sweat under the steady glare of the pensioners. 'I'll be off then, if you are sure there's nothing—'

'Nothing, officer.' Ivy interrupted.

Garda Kellegher backed out the door.

'You see. I told you. Comfortable indeed. He heard us. How else would he know Dolores used the word "comfortable"? From now on, girls, mum's the word.'

John Doyle paced up and down the small cell he was sharing with Mick O'Toole. The old man, who hadn't recognised him, had been gleefully regaling him with the story of how he had removed the wheels of the minibus. John picked the old man up and was shaking him, beside himself with rage.

'Don't kill me, mister. I didn't mean any harm.'

'Didn't mean any harm? You took the four wheels off my minibus and you say you didn't mean any harm!'

'I was doing it for Rose.'

'How in the name of Christ could that help Rose?'

'We were trying to slow down the eviction. Honest, mister. That's all we were doing. Martin said to delay you. Till we had a plan of action.'

'The woman was dead. No action was going to change that.'

'We didn't know. We thought she was being evicted.'

'I've a good mind to . . .'

'Me teeth. You're after shaking out me teeth.'

'Jesus.'

'Put me down, you big galoot. Put me down or I'll call the cops.'

'Keep your hair on.' John lowered Mick to the ground.

'Is that supposed to be funny?'

'Sorry,' John said, looking at the bald pate. 'No offence. Though why I should be saying sorry to you . . .'

'Mind where you're walking. I have to find me teeth.'

'I didn't mean to hurt you.'

'Well you did, didn't you.'

'I have to think this out.' John sat on the edge of the bed. 'I answer a call to bring people to a funeral. I get arrested. And I end up sharing a cell in choky with the old codger who took the wheels off my bus.'

'Who are you calling an old codger?' Mick began. John started to get up off his seat. 'No. It's okay.' Mick backed away. 'Call me whatever you want. I don't mind.'

'It doesn't make any sense,' John said. 'Where does Malachy fit into all this?'

'Malachy?'

'My mate. The other driver. He's the one who called me.'

'They're all in it together.'

'In what?'

'Murder.'

Sergeant Murphy opened the door to cell five to find his prisoners squatting on the floor, smoking, and playing cards.

'Where the hell do you lot think you are? A holiday camp? This is a police station. Not some back-room bordello. Put out those cigarettes. Were these men not frisked?' he roared up to the desk officer.

'Give us a break, Sarge,' the desk officer shouted back. 'You saw what I had to deal with.'

'I want these men searched.'

'What's the matter, Sergeant?' Martin grinned up at him. 'Did the missis give you a hard time last night?'

'I'll have none of your lip. Turn out your pockets. Now.'

'What are you looking for, Sergeant?'

'Anything incriminating,' Tommy Doran suggested. 'They always do that in *Hill Street Blues*.'

'You're lucky this isn't the Bronx,' Sergeant Murphy said. 'I'd have been able to shoot the whole bloody lot of you. No questions asked.'

'That's not very clever, Sergeant,' Martin said. 'I could have you up for that. Threatening a prisoner.'

'Wise guy, eh? Let's see how smart you are tomorrow in front of the judge.'

'Tomorrow. We can't stay cooped up here until tomorrow. There's hardly room to swing a cat.'

'I want a solicitor.'

'Yea, Sergeant. We all want solicitors.'

'Who do you have in mind? Give the solicitors' names to the desk officer and he'll call them.'

'I don't know any solicitor, Martin,' Kevin said. 'And even if I did I couldn't afford him.'

'What'll we do, Martin?' Tommy said. 'None of us could afford a solicitor.'

'Not such the big boys any more, are we?' the sergeant said. 'The state will provide a solicitor where the plaintiff cannot afford legal aid. And God help him is all I have to say. You'll meet him in the morning.'

'Great. Thanks, Sergeant.'

'It's no thanks to me. It's written into the constitution and if I had my way it would be written out of the constitution. A waste of tax payers' money getting solicitors for the likes of you.' Sergeant Murphy went out into the hall. 'Desk officer. Get down here and confiscate every article not permitted in the cells. And I mean every article. Cigarettes, matches, shoelaces, neckties, penknives, keys.' His voice receded as he went down the hall. 'I want those trouser pockets empty. I want belts, string, nail-files.' His voice could no longer be heard.

'Quick,' Martin said. 'Hide the fags under the mattress, leave a few out for yer man to find, we can't go the whole night without a smoke.'

'There you go, Officer. I think you have the lot.'

'Thanks, lads. You've been a great help.'

'Hard day, Officer?'

'You don't know the half of it. It's going to take me all night to get enough transport to get everyone to the court tomorrow.'

'Sure we could walk, Officer.'

'Thanks again lads but Sarge wouldn't hear of it. Not with such a big case. He's hoping for promotion out of this. Good thing too. Maybe he'd be transferred back to his own county.'

'Tough one is he?'

'Hard as nails, lads. Hard as nails.'

'Where's he from anyway?'

'Kerry. He's from the Ring of Kerry.'

# Chapter Eleven

'All rise.'

Judge Moore entered the courtroom to a hushed silence. He checked the dossiers on his desk then signalled to his clerk, Mr Toner. The judge was in no mood for delays. He had no intention of missing the racing at Fairyhouse where his horse, Beaverbrook, was the favourite for the two thirty.

He studied the list: two drunken drivers, one wife beater, a couple of minor car misdemeanours and one case involving malicious damage with detention of a body and obstruction.

He made a swift calculation. Two hours. He instructed Mr Toner to begin proceedings and reminded him to order his car for twelve noon.

'Silence. Silence in court.'

As the judge studied the files the hushed whispers of the public had risen considerably. He was irritated to find that his courtroom was full. As a rule he took no notice of the public. Court followers, reporters, family members, he dismissed as an irksome nuisance. If he had his way they would all be barred from the proceedings. 'Court is no place for an audience,' he'd told his clerk on more than one occasion. 'Public galleries should stay in the theatre where they belong.'

'If it pleases your Lordship. Case number one. Alphonses Sweeney. Charged with ignoring a red light on the corner of Bachelor's Walk and Liffey Quay.'

'Call Alphonses Sweeney.'

Shantell sat in the long hall outside the courtroom. She had been driven to the court in a squad car, where she was dumped unceremoniously in the hall. Her Gardaí escort led her to a bench, spoke to the duty officer, and then left.

Smile Shantell. It's always a good policy to smile. Smiling radiates confidence and self-assurance. It's quite obvious you have been put in the wrong place. Where are the rest of my companions? Why is there no one to ask? No enquiry desk? That officer can't have realised who I am. He would never have put me here in this dreary hall, with all these shifty-looking people, if he had known who I am. It's a silly mistake. I'll find someone in authority.

There's bound to be an enquiry desk, or reception area, through those doors at the end of the corridor.

'Where do you think you are going, miss?'

'There has been a mistake, Officer.' Shantell smiled. 'Sit down.'

'You don't seem to understand, Officer. I have been brought to the wrong place. I don't belong here.'

'Sit down.'

'Let me go. Take your hands off me.'

'I am telling you for the last time, miss. If you don't sit down I'll have to cuff you.'

'Cuff me? You would dare to cuff a lady? You,

Officer, are employed to protect the public.'

'That's right, miss, and that's exactly what I am doing.'

'By threatening a tax-paying citizen with physical violence? I am telling you, you are making a terrible mistake. If you speak with your superiors you will . . . What are you doing? What are these things?'

'I warned you, miss.' The officer had produced his handcuffs.

'You can't do this.'

'Hey guard,' one of the other prisoners in line called out. 'I'm a tax payer. I shouldn't be here.'

'Neither should I, guard,' called another. 'There's been a mistake.'

'Help,' Shantell cried. 'Help. Police!'

'Listen to the woman,' one of the other prisoners laughed. 'Is she mad or what?'

'You're in the courts, missis. This *is* the police. *Help*. That's a good one. That's the best I've heard yet.'

'That's enough.' The Garda tried to restore order. 'Quiet. If you don't want rioting while in custody added to your charges.'

Smiling radiates confidence and self assurance. Shantell sat, staring straight ahead of her, handcuffed to the bench. A warm smile can break through all sorts of barriers. She turned to the gentlemen sitting next to her. 'Excuse me, sir. Are you a real criminal?'

'WhatdeyableedingmeanlasttimeIwashereIdonefuc kingnothinganhegavemetwelvebleedinmonths.'

'Pardon?'

'Yermanovertheregotatwohundredpoundfine.Anall hedonewasgivehismissisaslap.'

'Are you from foreign parts? An asylum seeker?'

'Areyoutakingthemickeyoutame?'

'I shouldn't be here, you know. There has been a misunderstanding.'

Judge Moore looked at his watch. The morning was going well. He was pleased with the way the cases had progressed. No shilly-shallying. The defendants before him had not created difficulties and he, in turn, had been more lenient than usual. He had one more case and then he would be off. He would lunch in the owners' marquee at the track. The judge allowed himself a smile. He began to picture it. Beaverbrook winning by a length. Himself in the winners' enclosure, accepting the plate, and congratulating the trainer and the jockey.

'Call Shantell O'Doherty. Thomas O'Gorman. Fionn O'Fiachra. Malachy Conway. Rosleen Deignan. John Doyle. Martin Duffy. Michael O'Toole. Ivy Simpson. Peggy Moran. Dolores Watson. Tommy Doran. Edward O'Neill. Lily Murphy. Maeve Byrne. Jack Nolan and Kevin Clancy.'

The clerk kept his back to the judge as the usher went to the hall and repeated the names.

'Mr Toner.' Judge Moore called his clerk to the desk. 'What the hell is going on? I was not informed of this – this charade.'

'The file is on your desk, Your Honour. I put it there myself.'

'You neglected to inform me of the nature of this case.'

'It's on the list for today, Your Honour. Perhaps you didn't see it as you were a little preoccupied.'

'Preoccupied?' the judge roared.

'Well, Your Honour, with the day that's in it.'
'Who is defending, Mr Toner?'
'Mr Shield-Knox, Your Honour.'

'. . . So you see Miss Titchmarch, my mentor, told me to use any and every situation. Nothing is waste to a writer. Why, this little episode alone is worth at least four or five pages. A writer must endure pain, you see. Imagination is all very well but nothing surpasses real actual pain. These handcuffs. How many other writers would have had the opportunity to wear handcuffs? Do you get my point? Do you see where Miss Titchmarch is coming from?'

'Wouldyaeverfuckoffanleavemealone.'

'You.' The guard pointed to Shantell's companion. 'You're in next.'

'Thanksbetobleedingchrist.Yourwomanhasmeblee dingdemented.'

At that moment, two familiar figures appeared in front of Shantell, accompanied by a Gardaí escort.

'Rosie, Mr O'Gorman. Thank goodness you have arrived. I didn't know what had become of you. The police officer would tell me nothing. Where are the others?'

'Shantell. What has happened? Why are you handcuffed?'

'Nothing to worry about, Rosie. An over zealousness on the part of the officer. Anyone would think I was some sort of villain.'

'The others should be here in a minute. We came in a police car but the rest of them were all loaded on to a bus.'

'We even had our own cavalcade,' Mr O'Gorman said proudly. 'Caused a great stir on the roads with motorbikes, hooting and blaring, all the way from Orchardstown.'

'Poor Shantell. You were here all alone.'

'Goodness, no. I had some very interesting people with me, particularly a foreign speaking gentleman. Very hard to make out what he was saying. He could understand me, but found it difficult to reply. Ah, Fionn, Malachy. You are here at last.'

Fionn and Malachy had been put off the coach first and were ushered into the hall.

'You'd think she was having a party,' Malachy said to Fionn. 'Have you any idea, Shantell, what it was like in that bus with all those pensioners treating us like murderers? A nightmare. That's what it was and it's not over yet. They can't wait to get their hands on you.'

'It will all be sorted out very soon, I promise you. When the judge hears the whole story the case will be thrown out of his court, and I have no doubt that the sergeant will be severely reprimanded. Judges hate their time being wasted.'

'You know about judges then, Shantell?'

'One does read, Malachy. One is aware of that sort of thing. Now. Don't look so cross. There is nothing to worry about.'

The pensioners stumbled out of the bus and into the hall. The first person they spied was Shantell. They made a run at her.

'There she is.'

'There's the murderess.'

'Hold me back,' Mick O'Toole said, making wild sparring gestures. 'Hold me back in case I do terrible damage.'

'What is going on here?' The police officer walked

down the hall. 'Sit down. All of you. There has been enough trouble here already. Garda Kelly,' he called over to a fellow officer. 'Get over here and take their names.'

'We already have the names.'

'Then take them again. I've enough to do with the rabble in the courtroom. Every pensioner from Orchardstown is out there. Judge Moore is not going to like this.'

'His horse is running today.'

'By the looks of this lot it will be running without him.'

Mr David Shield-Knox parked his red Mini outside the district court. He had been the only one in the office of McCann & Dudley solicitors – David made a point of always being early for work as it was his very first proper job since college and he was anxious to make a good impression – when a message came through from the local police station. Legal representation was urgently required for seventeen people, who had been detained overnight, and who were to appear before Judge Moore in connection with a hostage and possible homicide. A case of this magnitude should be handled by his superiors but he had been unable to contact anyone. He wasn't too concerned. He knew it was only a matter of an appearance and that the case would be put forward for trial at a later date. All he could do at this point was familiarise himself with the details and get copies of the statements. It was a big chance for him. A case like this was bound to attract media attention. If he handled the preliminaries well it could show him in a good light to his employers. He made his way to the corridor where the defendants waited to be called into court.

'Good morning, Officer. Mr David Shield-Knox. I am here to represent the accused. Would you be kind enough to direct me to my client.'

'They're all yours,' Garda Kelly said, with a sweep of his arm.

'Very amusing, officer, Now if you don't mind. Please announce me to my client.'

'Mr David Shield-Knox, solicitor. Here to represent the accused.'

The accused stampeded up the corridor and surrounded Mr Shield-Knox, backing him into a corner.

'All right there, Mr Knox,' Garda Kelly said. 'I'll leave you to it so.'

'Please. Please. One at a time. I can't hear you if you all shout at me. Perhaps I'd better start by taking your names.'

'More bloody names,' Martin said. 'We'll be in the Guinness Book of Records for names if this goes on.'

'How do you do, Mr Shellknock.' Shantell spoke over the din. 'Shantell O'Doherty. Delighted to meet you. Did my friend Carmel ask you to come?'

'Don't listen to her, sir.' Shantell was brushed out of the way by Ivy. 'She's the reason we are all here. Her and her cohorts. Murderers and thieves the lot of them.'

'Hold on, missis,' Malachy said. 'Who are you calling a murderer? You better watch your tongue.'

'Threaten an old lady would you?'

'Who are you calling old, Martin Duffy?'

'Please, please.' David began to despair. 'I must have your names. I cannot represent you in court if I don't have your names.'

'Oh, Mr O'Gorman,' Rosie whined. Rosie, Fionn and Mr O'Gorman were standing apart from the throng. 'This can't be happening. Can't you do something?'

'Look after her, Fionn,' said Mr O'Gorman. 'I'll get this sorted out. Garda Kelly. Give your list to the solicitor. Shantell, Malachy, John. Sit down over there.' He pointed to the bench on one side of the hall. 'The rest of you. Over there.'

'Who do you think you are?' Mick O'Toole said. 'You can't order us about.'

'I'm not ordering, I'm suggesting. I want to get out of here. I haven't missed Fairyhouse in thirty years and I don't intend missing it today.'

'He's very forceful,' Peggy Moran said to Ivy, sidling past Mr O'Gorman. 'I like a man who's forceful.'

'I'm married, missis.'

'Shame.'

'Thank you. Thank you everyone,' said David Shield-Knox gratefully as the noise settled down. 'I will try to get a moment with each one of you before we go into court. Mr Doyle?' He looked through the list. 'Perhaps we could make a start.'

'What do you fancy for the big race?' Martin Duffy sat down beside Mr O'Gorman. 'I hear Beaverbrook is in with a chance.'

'He's carrying too much weight. I'd go for Lightning Streak. He did well last time over hurdles.'

'Traitor,' Ivy Simpson hissed from her side of the hall. 'You were always a turncoat Martin Duffy.'

'Shut your trap, Ivy. You got me into this mess.'

'Women,' Mr O'Gorman muttered. 'They'd land a poor man in anything.'

'Too right,' Martin said. 'Too bloody right.'

\*

The usher stood in the hall beside the entrance to the courtroom, and read from his list. 'Call Shantell O'Doherty. Thomas O'Gorman. Fionn O'Fiachra. Malachy Conway. Rosleen Deignan. John Doyle. Martin Duffy. Michael O'Toole. Ivy Simpson. Peggy Moran. Dolores Watson. Tommy Doran. Edward O'Neill. Lily Murphy. Maeve Byrne. Jack Nolan and Kevin Clancy.'

'They are calling us,' Mr David Shield-Knox said. 'It's time to go in. Remember what I told you. Answer the judge's questions briefly. Don't elaborate. Simple, straightforward, direct. That's the key. If all goes well you will all get bail and be free to go until the trial.'

'Trial? What do you mean trial?' Martin asked.

'It's a serious charge.'

'We are not the ones on trial here,' Ivy said. 'That lot are.'

'The police do have charges against all of you.'

'When that judge hears the truth, how we tried to save Rose from eviction, he'll give us all medals.'

'Leave the talking to me.' Mr David Shield-Knox led his clients through the doors and into the courtroom.

'Will the accused take their seats,' the usher said, pointing to the vacant rows at the front of the court.

'Look,' Ivy said. 'There's Nora from number twenty-nine. Howya Nora.'

'The whole block is here. They've all turned out.'

'Silence. Silence in court.'

# Chapter Twelve

Garda Kellegher was in the witness stand reading laboriously from his notebook. 'On the morning of the sixteenth, Garda Troy and I were on duty in the Orchardstown area. We received a call from the station at approximately eight a.m. about a disturbance in Tower Heights. We proceeded to the place in question. On arrival in Tower Heights the first indication of trouble was a stationary minibus, registration number CSI 966, which had had all four wheels removed. The gentleman standing beside this vehicle was one Mick O'Toole. When questioned Mr O'Toole reported having seen two youths dismantling the minibus and running away. A wrench recovered near the scene was found to bear Mr O'Toole's fingerprints. At this point Garda Troy phoned the station to report the incident and ask for reinforcements. Having cautioned Mr O'Toole, Garda Troy and I then proceeded to the fourth floor in Tower Heights where a large crowd was gathered outside the door of number one-four-seven, occupied by Mrs Rose Deignan. Garda Troy and I observed a large amount of furniture stacked outside this apartment with several of the residents ensconced.'

'Could you get on with it, Officer,' Judge Moore said. 'We haven't got all day.'

'We, Garda Troy and myself, were alerted by a call from the letter-box.'

'What?'

'A call from the letter-box informing us that a hostage situation was taking place and later, from the same letter-box, that a body had been discovered in the bedroom.' Garda Kellegher searched through his notebook for the name. '"Tell Martin they've killed her. Rose Deignan is dead." The informant was later identified as Kevin Clancy. At this point Garda Troy proceeded to tear away the barricades in an attempt to enter the apartment.'

'Do I take it, Officer, that the barricades were on the outside?'

'Yes, Your Honour.'

'Silence.' A wave of laughter had ripped through the court. 'Silence in court. Proceed, Officer.'

'I was in radio contact with Sergeant Murphy, who had entered the complex with the reinforcements, and apprised him of the situation. I then attempted to take the names and addresses of the culprits who were manning the door. At this point Garda Troy had managed to gain entry to the apartment where he was greeted by the accused, Shantell O'Doherty.' Garda Kellegher closed his notebook and prepared to leave the stand.

'Your Honour.' Mr Shield-Knox stood up and addressed the judge. 'If it please the court, I have some questions for Garda Kellegher.'

'Is this going to take long, Mr Shield-Knox?'

'In the interests of justice, Your Honour. I feel I must—'

'Get on with it.'

'Thank you, Your Honour. May I ask, Garda Kellegher, why you discontinued your evidence?'

'That is all I have in my notebook.'

'Is it not true to say that an incident occurred when Garda Troy gained access to the apartment? That in fact Garda Troy struck my client such a blow as to warrant stitches?'

'That was an accident, Your Honour.'

'An accident, Garda?' Mr Shield-Knox addressed the court dramatically.

'Yes. Garda Troy was knocking on the door when it opened and he accidentally connected his fist to the accused.'

'May I suggest, Garda Kellegher, that you omitted the incident intentionally? That you and Garda Troy deliberately tried to cover up the attack?'

'I resent that, sir. Your Honour. This is an attempt to blacken the police force.'

'Mr Shield-Knox. Would you approach the bench.'

'Your Honour?'

'What are you playing at, Mr Shield-Knox? This is not a trial. This is a preliminary hearing. Garda Kellegher is not on trial here. Do you want to have the whole force down on our heads claiming unfair treatment from the judiciary?'

'But, Your Honour—'

'Carry on, Mr Shield-Knox.'

'Garda Kellegher. The matter of that serious assault will be deferred until a later date. You may step down. Your Honour. If it may please the court. As I am representing all seventeen of the accused it might be expedient to hear the statements of Sergeant Murphy and Garda Troy, and then adjourn for lunch. I would appreciate the opportunity to consult further with my clients.'

'No. Absolutely not. There will be no adjourning for lunch in my court.'

'I must protest, Your Honour.'

'The next witness,' Judge Moore said to the usher.

'Call Sergeant Eugene Murphy.'

Sergeant Murphy took the witness stand and slowly took out his notebook.

'Mr Toner. Would you approach the bench.' The judge leaned forward to his clerk. 'Has my car arrived?'

'Yes, Your Honour.'

'Tell my driver to get a traffic report. Tell him to work out an alternative route for Fairyhouse. The last thing I need is to be held up in traffic. How could you let this happen, Mr Toner?'

'What could I do, sir?'

'A decent loyal clerk would make sure this case was assigned to another district.'

'On the morning of the sixteenth I was on duty in Orchardstown when, at approximately eight twenty a.m., a call came through to the station. The call requested immediate reinforcements to assist in dealing with a suspected case of kidnap and possible homicide.'

Judge Moore groaned and buried his face in his hands.

'At approximately eight twenty-five a.m., I dispatched myself to Tower Heights in the company of three squad cars, two motorbikes, an ambulance and a unit of the fire brigade. On arrival in Tower Heights I was apprised, by telecommunication with Garda Troy, of the serious nature of the situation. I ascertained that a gentleman, who is here present, was involved and advised him to stay where he was. I then requested the chief fire officer, Mr James Scott, to assist. Mr Scott pulled his fire engine into position, under the balcony of the said apartment, and hoisted me to the fourth floor. Observing the scene at first hand, I ascertained a full riot was in place and proceeded, in accordance with section 428 of the Bill 78/23D "Rules for Riot Acts" as passed by Seanad Éireann, to take immediate action . . .'

'Sergeant Murphy.'

'. . . With your permission, Your Honour. I would like to present concrete evidence of the seriousness of the offence. Usher.'

The usher opened the double doors at the back of the courtroom and wheeled in a covered trolley. He steered the trolley down between the packed rows and parked it in front of Judge Moore.

'Why is there a body in my courtroom, Sergeant?'

'Evidence, Your Honour.' Sergeant Murphy prepared to pull away the sheet. 'The body is exhibit A.'

'Granny!' Rosie screamed and fainted away.

'Rose,' Ivy said. 'Look everyone. It's Rose.'

Uproar ensued as the crowd left their seats and started towards the body.

'Order.' The judge hammered on his desk. 'I will have order in the court. Get back to your seats.'

'What have they done to you Rose?'

'She's trussed up like a turkey.'

'I'm not having this,' Ivy said. 'Peggy, girls, come on. Let's get her out of here.'

'Protect the evidence,' Sergeant Murphy shouted. He jumped to the centre of the floor and, linking arms with the ushers, stood between the body and the crowd.

'Clear my court,' Judge Moore said. 'Mr Toner. Get the court officers. Arrest every one of these people.'

'They are under arrest, Your Honour.'

'This is a travesty,' Judge Moore roared. 'Mr Shield-Knox. I am holding you personally responsible for this. Mr Toner. Get me out of here.'

'Court is adjourned. All rise.' Mr Toner addressed himself to the few members of the public who had remained seated. They stood nervously as Judge Moore gathered up his papers and stormed out of the courtroom.

'Does this mean we can go, Martin?' Mick O'Toole said.

'I don't know. I don't know what we are supposed to do. Ivy has done it this time. Look at them. They'll end up behind bars.'

'Are you going to help us or not?' Ivy asked the menfolk as she clambered over the seats. 'Come on. Help us.'

The swarm of little old ladies was too much for Sergeant Murphy and his ushers. They were unable to hold their ground. Younger women wouldn't have been a problem but traditional respect for the elderly now rendered them helpless. Ivy and her cronies, who had been joined by the ladies of the public gallery, gathered around the body of their dead friend and, after a brief noisy consultation, started to wheel her back up through the courtroom.

'Grab the other end, one of you,' Ivy said, pushing the trolley. 'This thing has a life of its own. It won't steer properly.' The trolley banged and clattered into the benches. 'Push,' Ivy called. 'Faster. We have to get her out of here.'

The trolley took off, gathering momentum as it went.

'Look out, Peggy. Mrs Deignan's slipping off.'

'Get her legs back on to the trolley.'

'It's running away with us.'

With the ladies desperately hanging on, the trolley careered up the aisle and crashed out through the double doors.

'I think we better get out of here, Mick,' Martin said. 'Start moving towards the door. We can slip out one by one. Tell the rest of them to meet us in Clery's down the road. Kevin, Tommy, come on. We're going to make a run for it.'

Shock had temporarily immobilised Sergeant Murphy. Shock and disbelief. No one had ever stolen evidence from court before. They might attempt sabotage. Claim it had been tampered with. There was one appalling case where the evidence, wrongly labelled, had ended up in another court. But stolen from under the eyes of the judge, never.

'Stop those women.' Sergeant Murphy took out his walkie-talkie. 'Murphy here. There's been a robbery in District Court One. All units in the Orchardstown area to respond. Suspects seen leaving court wheeling tubular steel trolley covered by green hospital sheet. I repeat, all available units to respond. Approach suspects with caution they may be . . .'

'Armed and dangerous, Sergeant?' Mr Toner

suggested, watching the action from Judge Moore's desk.

'. . . out of control.'

Mr O'Gorman had carried Rosie out of the crush. He laid her down gently on the floor and cradled her head in his arms. 'Rosie. Rosie,' he said softly. 'It's all right, Rosie. You are going to be all right. Fionn. Come here. Stay with Rosie for a minute.'

'I'm all right now, Fionn,' Rosie said. 'I don't know what came over me. It was seeing Granny like that.'

'Hush. Hush, Rosie,' Fionn soothed. 'Don't try to say anything. Mr O'Gorman will find out what's happening and then we can take you home.'

'Not to Tower Heights. I never want to go there again. I never want to see it again.'

'I agree with you there, Rosie. It's a very strange place. I never saw anything like it in my life. Even Mammy would be surprised and she's been to England.'

'Help me up, Fionn. I feel silly lying on the floor like this.'

'Mr O'Gorman said we were to stay.'

'He didn't mean on the floor, Fionn. Help me up.'

Fionn took Rosie's arm and helped her to a bench. He sat beside her with his arm dangling over her shoulder. He didn't know how to hold her or what to say. He had never had much opportunity to talk to women. Even with Mary, the woman he had the understanding with back home, there was no talking. Mary had land adjoining his mother's. It was taken for granted they would eventually marry and combine the land. Mary was older than him. She would take up where his mother left off.

'You've never been in the city before, Fionn?'

'My first time.'

'You won't forget this visit in a hurry. Granny would turn in her grave . . .' Realising what she said, Rosie started to laugh. '. . . If she had a grave. If we knew where she'd gone. If she, if she . . . ha ha ha . . . hadn't been wheeled away with half the police force out looking for her.' Rosie couldn't stop the laughter. 'Oh, Fionn, were you really going to build a coffin in the spare room and then . . . ha ha ha . . . have all of us pile into a minibus?'

'I thought that was the way of the city. Shantell was the one who said—'

'Shantell. I must have been mad to listen to her. I'm sorry, Fionn. I forgot. Mr O'Gorman said she's your fiancée. Is she?'

'I don't think so. I never met her until the day before yesterday.'

'You didn't waste any time.'

'It was when she got stuck in the ladies' lavatory.' Fionn started laughing himself. 'I think I may have proposed to her.'

Rosie lost control. Clutching at Fionn, she screeched and hooted with laughter, while Fionn, who was delighted to have been the cause of such merriment, joined in. When Mr O'Gorman returned with Malachy he found the two of them, arms around each other, both talking and laughing at the same time.

'We might have a match here, Malachy.'

'Don't start that again, Mr O'Gorman. I think you've done enough matchmaking already. Well you two. What's so funny?' Malachy asked.

Rosie and Fionn tried to speak. Every word

dissolved them back to hysterics.

'I suppose you have to see the funny side of it,' Mr O'Gorman said. 'It's not every day a body is arrested and brought to court.'

'Granny Deignan wasn't arrested, Mr O'Gorman. We were.'

'I was speaking in the vernacular, Malachy. I meant us, you and me, body as a person like.'

'I think you're wrong there somehow. I don't know how but I know it's wrong.'

'Do you know, Malachy? You are beginning to sound like young Fionn here.'

'Do you blame me. I haven't heard one word of sense since I left the rank two nights ago. And speaking of two nights ago, what am I going to tell my missis?'

'I'm in the same boat, Malachy. If I tell her the truth she'll never believe me. Come to think of it, she never believes me anyway.'

'I've never kept secrets from my wife.'

'Well.' Mr O'Gorman looked across the courtroom at Shantell. 'You better start.'

'What do we do now?'

'The fellow over there, Mr Toner, said we should go. He said the judge wouldn't be back. Even if the police catch the old wans with the trolley he still won't be back.'

'They've a great life all the same, those judges. Money for old rope. And some money at that.'

'He has a horse running today at Fairyhouse.'

'Who. Yer man?'

'No. The judge.'

'What are we waiting for then? Let's get the hell out of here.'

'Come on you two songbirds,' Mr O'Gorman said to Fionn and Rosie. 'Time to go. I don't know about you, Malachy, but I could murder a pint. Do you fancy a quick one in Clery's?'

'Don't.'

'Just the one.'

'I have to get my cab. It's still outside Tower Heights.'

'I'll tell you what. We'll have the one and then get a taxi up to the flats. It's Rosie I'm thinking of. We can't all go off, just like that, and leave her. I hope you're not forgetting there is still a funeral to arrange. That is if they ever find the body.'

'Where do you think they went with the trolley?'

'They can't have got far. The police probably have them by now.'

'Did you ever see the likes of it?' Malachy began to smile. 'His Honour was horrified. And what about the sergeant? "Stop those women." And he afraid to do anything except gawp.'

'*All units to respond.*' Mr O'Gorman pretended to hold a megaphone to his mouth. '*This is an emergency. Transgressors to the pub. Follow your leader.*' They all started towards the door.

Malachy stopped. 'What about Shantell? Will you look at her. She's still sitting there, as if nothing had happened.'

'I think it would be best to leave her to herself for the moment,' said Mr O'Gorman. 'I dare say she has a lot on her mind right now.'

'It seems a bit mean,' Rosie said. 'To go off and leave her.'

'I spoke to her, Rosie,' Mr O'Gorman reassured her. 'She was talking about making notes. I don't think she will mind us going.'

'She probably won't even notice,' Malachy said.

'If it makes you feel better, Rosie, I'll tell her where we are going.'

'Where is my friend, John?' wondered Malachy. 'Did anybody see him?'

'Now you come to mention it, Malachy, I haven't seen him since the start of the trial.'

'I saw him,' Fionn said. 'He went out after the other older gentlemen. He said something about "finding that little fellow with the false teeth and wringing his neck". I wasn't sure what he meant.'

'There you go, Malachy. Nothing to worry about. He'll be in Clery's.'

David Shield-Knox forced a bright smile as he packed his few notes into his briefcase. He was ruined. His career was over. Blacklisted by Judge Moore, he had no doubt about it. It wasn't fair. No one told him about the evidence. He wasn't a mind-reader. They were supposed to tell you about evidence so you knew what you were up against. He couldn't go back to the office. He couldn't face the head of chambers, Mr Williamson, or any of the rest of them. David knew Mr Williamson had only taken him on because he knew his mother. Thinking of his mother, David quailed. He would have to emigrate. What would he do for money? He'd have to sell his Mini.

'Everything all right there, Mr Shield-Knox?' Mr Toner asked.

'Perfectly fine, thanks.' David's lower lip trembled.

'Don't take it to heart, son. Everybody blows their first case. I've seen some right do-lallys in my time.'

David sat down abruptly and began to cry.

'I'm finished, Mr Toner. Washed up and I haven't even started.'

'There there, Mr Shield-Knox. We can't have this. Pull yourself together. In a few days' time this will be all forgotten.'

'Do you think so, Mr Toner? Do you really think so?'

'I've seen it all before Mr Shield-Knox.'

'Thank you. Thank you, Mr Toner. I'm beginning to feel better already.'

Mr Toner strolled away. 'I've seen it all before all right,' he muttered to himself. 'But this takes the biscuit. Beaverbrook better win today or heads will roll. I've never seen His Honour in such a state. Sergeant Murphy had better look out for his stripes.'

Shantell lingered on in the courtroom. With everyone else gone, she planned to have a quiet word with Judge Moore.

I simply must interview that Judge. Such majesty. Such gesture. I would like to get him down pat for my novel. I could explain, quietly, how the terrible mix-up came about. Then, when he realises the true nature of my work, I dare say he will be enthralled and will agree to grant me an interview. What an understanding he must have of human frailty. What insights. Destiny. You were meant to be a writer Shantell. So many extraordinary situations falling into your lap. With so much material you might even have to employ a ghost-writer. A literary student perhaps. Someone, with a bit of grasp, who could organise the notes while you get on with the important creative bits. Remember Chapter 12. 'Every experience can help us become better writers.'

124

I expect I have had more experiences in the last few days than most writers would have in a lifetime. I must be true to them. Imbibe the atmosphere, Shantell. The apparatus of justice. What a wonderful title for my novel. I must put that into my notebook straight away. *The Apparatus of Justice. A novel by Shantell O'Doherty.*

'Excuse me, miss. You'll have to move along.'

'You don't understand. I must wait here for my friend Carmel. I am expecting her at any moment.'

'You can't wait here, miss. The usher is waiting to lock up. You'll have to wait outside.'

'You are His Lordship's clerk, aren't you?'

'That's right, miss.'

'What a stroke of luck. Could you, would you do me an enormous favour? I wish to interview the judge. I am a writer, you see, and it would be invaluable to my work to be able to chat to him face to face.'

'Face to face,' Mr Toner whispered under his breath incredulously. 'I dare say you will be meeting him face to face, eventually.' Aloud he said, 'His Honour has left the building.'

'You mean he won't be back today at all?'

'His Honour will not be sitting again until next week. Now if you don't mind.' Mr Toner gestured towards the door.

'Could I leave a message?'

'Please, miss.'

'I'm quite sure if he knew what it was about—'

'I have asked you nicely, miss.'

'I have no wish to undermine your abilities, sir, but this is a literary matter. A little outside your domain I should think.'

'Out.' Mr Toner could no longer contain himself.

His normal demeanour was being sorely tested. 'Out. That way.' He pointed to the exit.

'I'm not sure I like your attitude, sir. His Lordship would not be impressed if he heard how you were shouting at me.'

Mr Toner took Shantell by the arm and marched her up the courtroom.

'Let me go. You have no right to throw me out of court.'

Mr Toner slammed the door behind her.

# Chapter Thirteen

Clery's bar always did a brisk trade on court days. The bar had runs of snugs down each side, which afforded great privacy for meetings and consultations. The news from the courts was up to the minute. Every sentence and every fine handed down was discussed. The bar staff were experienced hands who, apart from their regular duties, administered advice, free of charge, to those unwilling or unable to trust the legal system. The snugs were used on a strict rota basis. Booking them in advance was not allowed. Sometimes the queue was so long, Mr Clery, the owner, threatened to charge rent. Even reporters, who were either too lazy or too bored to attend the court, knew that by sitting in Clery's they would get all the information they required to fill their columns. News of the debacle in Judge Moore's courtroom reached the bar before the pensioners had had time to get down the street. Mr Clery rubbed his hands in his apron, as he habitually did when he smelt his profits increasing.

'Get another barrel up from stores,' Mr Clery said

to his porter. 'And tell the kitchen to double up on the sandwiches.'

The gentlemen pensioners arrived at Clery's and were surprised when they were greeted personally by the owner.

'The first round is on the house, gentlemen,' Mr Clery beamed. 'What'll it be?'

'That's very good of you,' Martin said. 'What's the occasion?'

'You, gentlemen, are the occasion. Judge Moore is a very unpopular man in these parts. It's a pleasure to buy a drink for anyone who gives him a run for his money. Pints all round?' Mr Clery had already started pouring. 'I must tell you, gents, that a book has opened among the staff and clientele on your lady friends. The odds are four to one they get across the river with the body before Sergeant Murphy and his uniforms catch up with them. Any takers?'

'I'll take that,' Mick O'Toole said. 'They don't know Ivy. That auld wan could outfox a fox.'

'Take a seat, gentlemen. I believe we have a snug available. It would give me great pleasure to deliver your drinks personally.'

'This is the life, eh?' Mick said. 'Do you think he'd go a few fags as well?'

'Don't look now,' Martin said, 'but the opposition is here.'

'Wouldn't you think they'd have a bit of decency and go somewhere else.'

The opposition had arrived at Clery's. Rosie, Fionn, and Malachy settled themselves into a corner while Mr O'Gorman went up to the bar to order drinks.

'When you're ready, landlord.'

'I'll be with you in a moment, sir,' Mr Clery said.

'Do you hear him.' Mick was leaning out of the snug watching Mr O'Gorman. '*Landlord*. Where does he think he is, the colonies?'

'Ignore them. Pretend they're not there. Let's just enjoy our drinks, for Christ's sake. We've had enough trouble for one day.'

'There you go, gentlemen,' Mr Clery said, putting the pints down on the table. 'Would that be the other party?' he asked.

'That's them all right.'

'Work away, gentlemen. I'll be back to have our chat in a jiffy.'

'Bloody vulture,' Martin said. 'Look at him. He couldn't wait to get over to them. Bloody voyeur.'

'He gave us free drinks though,' Mick said. 'He can't be all bad.'

'Buying information. That's what this is. I've a good mind to throw it back at him.'

'Steady on, Martin. Wait till we've had a sup before you get hasty.'

'Yea, Martin. You said to ignore them.'

Mr Clery took his time walking back to the bar. He wanted to get a good look at the trio in the corner, to size them up for future reference.

'Now then. What can I get you?' he asked Mr O'Gorman.

'Two pints and two lemonades please.'

'Do you mind me asking, sir?' Mr Clery played ignorant. 'Would that be the young girl who lost her granny?'

'What have those old codgers been saying?'

'Not a thing, sir.'

'What do you know about it?'

'Only bar talk, sir.'

'I'll thank you to keep your bar talk behind the counter. That young girl is upset enough as it is. I won't have her being bandied around as the topic for today.'

'We get them all in here you know.' Mr Clery wiped the counter. 'They all come in to Clery's. The winners and the losers. Now if you take my advice—'

'The only thing I want from you is a drink. Are you going to serve me or not?'

'Certainly sir. No offence. Only trying to make conversation. Take a seat, sir. I'll have them sent over to you.' Mr Clery signalled to one of his staff to take Mr O'Gorman's order while he rejoined the pensioners.

'I've had a chat with your friends over there. Very touchy. That doesn't go down well in court. I've seen it over and over again. The touchy ones always lose. If you want my opinion you lot are on a winner. Especially with Judge Moore. He hates touchy ones.'

'All we want is justice.'

'To do right by Rose Deignan. That's what we want. That's what we're here for.'

'In the opinion of this bar,' Mr Clery said, 'and we very seldom get it wrong, you can't fail. Now, gents, I'm sure you are nearly ready for a refill.' He called over to his staff. 'Same again here please. Another round for this snug.' Mr Clery walked back behind the counter and opened a large black ledger. 'Pass the word around,' he said to his head barman. 'I'm taking odds on the pensioners.'

Both parties sat in their separate sections of the bar, mulling over the events of the morning. Mick

O'Toole, who couldn't resist popping his head out of the snug every few minutes, reported back to his companions any snatches of conversation he managed to overhear. Mr Clery, making a show of collecting glasses and emptying ashtrays, nipped back and forth between them picking up titbits with which to regale his regular customers and his staff.

'That fellow is getting on my nerves,' Mr O'Gorman said, referring to Mr Clery after one of his sorties. 'He's back and forth like a yo-yo. Wouldn't you think he'd have something better to do.'

'I think he's only trying to be friendly,' Fionn said. 'They're like that at home.'

'Me arse, Fionn. There's friendly, and then there's sheer bloody nosy. Yer man is in the latter category.'

'You are very quiet, Rosie,' Malachy said. 'You've hardly said a word since we came in. Is it because of that lot over there?'

'I should go over and talk to them,' Rosie said. 'They were Granny's friends.'

'Go ahead if you want to, Rosie. We'll be here if they give you any stick.'

Mick, dangling out of his booth, caught sight of Rosie as she got up to leave the table. 'It's young Rosie,' he said. 'I think she's leaving. Hold on, wait. She's coming this way. By the hokey, I think she's coming over to us.'

'Hello, Martin. It's me, Rosie.'

'What can we do for you, Rosie?' Martin said.

'We don't associate with traitors, do we lads.'

'Shut up, Mick. Give the girl a chance. She is Rose's granddaughter.'

'Thanks, Martin. I wanted . . . I wanted to come over because you are Granny's friends and I . . .' Rosie couldn't continue. Tears began to well up in her eyes. 'It's all dreadful and instead of being at Granny's funeral we are here and . . . and we don't even know where she is . . . and I don't know what to do . . .'

'It's those drug pushers,' Mick said. 'I know the way they operate. They get you all confused and the next thing, wham, you're hooked.'

'What?' Rosie looked confused. 'What is he saying? I don't know what he is talking about.'

'Give over, Mick.'

'We thought they had you doped,' Martin said. 'Ivy said she could tell you were drugged by the look of your eyes.'

Mr Clery, who had been hovering nearby, nearly fell into the snug.

'Don't be ridiculous,' Rosie said.

'Well if you weren't drugged what were you doing with those evictors?'

'You've got it all wrong. No one was evicting anyone.'

'We all saw the furniture out on the balcony.'

'And the van waiting to sneak Rose away after they killed her.'

'No. No,' Rosie said. 'You don't understand. Granny had died and I was trying to carry out her last wishes.'

'Her last wishes? To have all her things put out on the street and to be taken away in a van? Come on, Rosie. Pull the other one. You don't expect us to believe that.'

'If you would only let me explain.'

'Explain,' Mick shouted. 'Explain. How could anyone explain? You should be ashamed of yourself, Rosie. After all your granny did for you.'

'Stop it. Leave me alone,' Rosie cried. 'You don't know what happened. You won't let me tell you.'

'Is everything all right, Rosie?' Mr O'Gorman had walked over to the snug and was standing behind Rosie. 'Are these gentlemen upsetting you?'

'*Us* upsetting *her*?' Mick jumped up. 'That's a good one.'

'I was trying to explain everything, Mr O'Gorman, but they won't listen to me.'

'They are going to listen, now, whether they like it or not. Malachy, Fionn,' Mr O'Gorman called over to the corner. 'Come over here, and bring your drinks with you. This could take some time. We are all going to sit down like civilised human beings and get this put right. And you.' Mr O'Gorman spoke to Mr Clery who had pulled a stool up and was about to join the company. 'You can skedaddle.'

Shantell stood outside the courthouse. The street was deserted. 'That stupid, stupid man,' she said aloud. 'He has made me lose everyone.' She started to walk away and then stopped, abruptly. 'My goodness. I nearly forgot.' She banged on the courthouse door. 'Hello. Hello in there. Could you open up. There was something else I wanted to ask you. *Hello.*'

Mr Toner, who was still standing behind the door, couldn't make up his mind whether to answer or not. If he did answer she would probably keep him there all day. If he didn't, she was bound to cause a disturbance on the street and there had been enough disturbances for one day. Mr Toner didn't have much option. There was the dignity of his office to preserve. He opened the door cautiously.

'Yes?'

'I forgot to ask you. When the police catch up with Granny Deignan, do you think they could give me a ring on my mobile. My number is 088 608276. It is down at the moment but my friend, Carmel, is going to arrive with a battery. You see, I still have to make the arrangements for Granny's funeral. There is still so much to do. So many things to organise. I'm lost without my mobile. How did we ever manage before? I must contact Rosie and Mr O'Gorman and the others. They may have gone back to the flat. Do you think I could come in and use your phone? I won't be long. I need to find out where the police will take Granny. Rosie is very attached to her granny. She will be so pleased to get her back.'

As she spoke Shantell pushed hard against the door and Mr Toner, who had kept his foot firmly against the bottom of it, was barely able to hold her at bay.

'The court is locked, miss,' he said. 'No one is allowed in.'

'One teeny phone call. That's all I ask.'

'I'm sorry, miss. Orders are orders.'

'No one will know.'

'I will know.'

'But I must make my phone call.'

'If you are looking for your co-offenders they are all down in Clery's bar.'

'For goodness' sake. Why didn't you tell me that before?'

'Because you didn't give me a . . .' Mr Toner was talking to himself. Shantell had scurried off down the road.

You could hear a pin drop in Clery's as Mr O'Gorman told his story. The entire bar sat riveted to their seats. He began by describing his first meeting with Shantell in the bar off O'Connell Street. How they got talking when he, mistakenly, thought she was a researcher for the College of Surgeons whose grandmother had just died. Mr O'Gorman spoke gravely and without hesitation. He didn't elaborate. He didn't have to. The facts of the story held his audience enthralled. Fionn's appearance in the bar, lost on his first trip to the capital, brought with it a wave of sympathy from the crowd. Was there anything worse than being lost in a big city? Mr O'Gorman let a moment pass before carrying on. The lavatory door. The sing-song. The engagement. Mr O'Gorman left out nothing.

'Another round here please, barman. I'm dry as a desert.'

Nobody said a word until the drinks were rushed over and the barman, anxious not to miss a word, resumed his place quietly among the audience.

'Go on.' A voice came from the neighbouring snug. 'We want to hear the rest.'

Mr O'Gorman took his time. He took three long swallows of his pint before he resumed.

The taxi, the takeaway meal and the carry-outs were next. Gasps were heard as the details of the menu and the off-licence order were relayed. The delay in getting to their destination. When he, Mr O'Gorman, and Shantell slept in the back of the cab while Fionn and the driver, Malachy, struck up a rapport due to a shared interest in the mystical arts of Feng Shui. And finally, the arrival at Tower Heights where Rosie was waiting, entirely innocent as to the nature of her saviours, to be given instructions on the matter of her granny's funeral arrangements.

'And that's about the size of it, gentlemen,' Mr O'Gorman said. 'The rest of the story you know yourselves. We had the best of intentions but, as a fair amount of alcohol was consumed during the course of the day, our judgement got slightly blurred. I take my fair share of blame, and I am sure I can speak for the others when I tell you how sorry I am for the upset we caused you. Not to mention what young Rosie here has had to put up with.'

'Oh yes,' Fionn said. 'You can certainly speak for me.'

'That's quite a story,' Martin said. 'It's so unbelievable it's bound to be true.'

'Isn't the drink a terrible man,' Mick O'Toole said, lifting his pint to his mouth. 'He has an awful lot to answer for.'

'I would appreciate it, gentlemen,' Mr O'Gorman said, 'if you would allow me to buy you a drink. Bury the hatchet so to speak. If we put our heads together we are bound to come up with a resolution to this dilemma. What do you say?'

'Take the drink,' came cries from the adjoining snugs. 'Bury the hatchet.'

'I'll take that as a yes,' Mr O'Gorman said, as there was no response from the Tower Heights residents. 'Barman. Set up a round for my friends here.'

A cheer from the crowd lifted the roof. Everyone started talking. The ins and outs of the story were dissected and analysed from every angle. The barman went to pour the drinks while Mr Clery retrieved his ledger from behind the counter, and changed the entry.

'What will happen now?' Rosie asked. 'What about the judge? And what about Granny?'

'First things first, Rosie love,' Mr O'Gorman said. 'Let me get this organised and then we'll make a plan.'

'I don't like the sound of this,' Malachy said. 'I feel I've heard this before.'

'Martin. Where do you think your lady-friends have gone with Mrs Deignan?'

'Knowing Ivy, Mr O'Gorman, it could be anywhere.'

'Right. The first thing to do is find Ivy, get the body back, and give that woman a decent burial.'

'Will the judge allow it?'

'He has to allow it. Saving your presence Rosie, no offence, but he can't leave her hanging round for ever. We won't be called back for a while – these things always take an age, and if the funeral is over, and all parties are reconciled, he will be only too delighted to drop the charges. I've seen it time and time again. He'll be as happy to see the end of it as we will.'

'What about Shantell? What will we do about Shantell?' asked Rosie.

Mr O'Gorman stopped in his tracks. He had momentarily forgotten about Shantell. 'Come to think of it. Where is she?'

'She stayed behind in the court.'

'I hope they don't lock her up again.'

'She meant well,' Rosie said. 'I know she did. And I did ask her. I am going to go and look for her. We can't leave her out of this.'

'I'll come with you, Rosie,' said Fionn. 'We won't be long Mr O'Gorman. We'll find her and bring her back.'

Rosie and Fionn were on their way out when the doors were thrown open and John Doyle burst into the bar.

'Where is he? Where is that little git? I've been looking all over for him. He's going to pay for my wheels.'

'Jesus, save me,' Mick said. 'He's after me.'

'Calm down, John,' Malachy said. 'He didn't mean any harm.'

'Didn't mean any harm? Did you see the state of my cab?'

'We'll all give you a hand to get the wheels back on. Sit down and relax. Have a drink. We are trying to get this mess cleared up and then we can all go home.'

'I'm sorry, mister. We thought you were with the bailiffs.'

'Don't go into that, Mick. Let's leave well enough alone.'


'Hello, everyone. Look who I found on the doorstep.' Shantell entered the bar pulling Fionn and Rosie back in with her. 'Isn't this nice, everyone together. What an attractive pub. I do so love the old-fashioned kind. There is always such a friendly atmosphere when you walk in the door. Let me squeeze in there beside you, Mr O'Gorman, I won't take up much room, and you can introduce me to the company. Courts are such an unfortunate way to meet people. Oh dear. Did I interrupt? Please. Do carry on. Pretend I'm not here. I'll be quiet as a little mouse. Rosie, Fionn. Have you somewhere to sit? John, hello there. Come and sit beside me. We had so little time to talk yesterday. Now let me see if I have the names right. Martin and Mick and Kevin and Tommy. I hope I haven't got you mixed up. Dearie me. I seem to be the only one without a drink. Barman!'

Conversation had stopped dead as the entire clientele

of Clery's pub had turned towards Shantell. Even Mr Clery, who was never at a loss for words, didn't respond. He was so mesmerised by her that, for the first time in his bar career, he didn't think of his profits.

'Barman. If you please.'

Mr Clery snapped out of his reverie when he heard the second call.

'Yes, madam. What can I get you?'

'Pale dry sherry please. In a large glass.' Shantell turned back to the circle. 'Where were we? I want you to fill me in on every detail. I am a stickler for details because of my profession. I am a writer, you know, as I'm sure my companions have already told you.' Shantell took her notebook out of her bag. 'You won't mind if I jot down a few notes as we chat. It's invaluable to my work. Miss Titchmarch, my guide and mentor, says you should listen to the people around you. Eavesdropping is the surest way to get one's dialogue right. You would all absolutely love Miss Titchmarch if you knew her. You may speak freely. I give you my word I will never reveal any of your names in my novel.'

Mr Clery delivered Shantell's sherry and, as she graciously allowed Mr O'Gorman to settle the bill, she did a wide sweep of the bar. 'But where are the ladies? I thought they would be here. What have you done with them?'

Ivy and her league of elderly friends, still clutching on to the trolley bearing Rose Deignan's body, hurtled down the corridor, and crashed out through the doors, to the Garda car park.

'Whoa, whoa,' Ivy cried, as the pensioners struggled, desperately, to gain control. Two of the ladies, hanging on to the back of the trolley, had had to let go. Gasping and out of breath, they couldn't keep up with the pace.

The trolley finally slowed, thanks to a sharp brush with a stationary police car, spun twice, and came to an abrupt halt. The impact caused Rose, still wrapped in her green hospital sheet, to slide off the trolley and drop gracefully to the ground, where she landed propped up against the back wheels.

'Quick,' hissed Ivy. 'Get her out of sight. The police will be here any minute.'

'Where, Ivy? There's nowhere to put her.'

Ivy looked around. The bus that had brought them to the courthouse was parked close to the wall at one side of the car park. The driver was over by the gates talking to the security guard. They were too far away to hear the commotion.

'On the bus. Get her on the bus.'

'We'll never lift her.'

'We have to. There's enough of us to do it. Get two on each arm and two on each leg. When I say heave, lift her up. Peggy and I will get down and give her a bunt from underneath.'

'She's stiff as a board, Ivy.'

'Of course she is. She's dead isn't she. Now, on the count of three. One. Two. Three. Heave. Steady. Steady. Hold on, hold on. Peggy, get under her. Under her Peggy. Dolores Watson, keep your end up. You have her tilted. Get her straight now. That's it. We have it. Keep that sheet around her. Don't let it slip off. She's starkers underneath.'

The ladies aimed the rigid body at the bus and hobbled across the car park.

'Make for the door everyone. Head for the door.'

'I can't hold her Ivy. She's slipping.'

'We're nearly there. Make for the door. No, no, stop. We won't make it. I can hear the guards coming. Get round the back of the bus. They won't see us there.'

Ivy and her gang had barely made it out of sight when several uniformed Gardaí came running out of the building into the car park. The officers spotted the trolley sitting in the middle of the car park beside the damaged police car, and immediately surrounded it. They stood there, staring at it, trying to figure out where the body could have got to. The ladies, trembling behind the bus, could hear their shouts. 'They've taken the body . . . spread out . . . cover the car park, they can't have got far . . . check the gates, maybe they had a getaway car.' The ladies heard them calling to the security guard. 'Did a gang of old ladies, carrying a body, go out the gate?'

'No officer,' came the reply.

'They must have doubled back and be hiding in the building. Get inside, search the courthouse.'

The ladies took advantage of the officers' disappearance. They shuffled round to the front of the bus and, after some manoeuvring, got the body on board.

'Her legs won't bend. How will we get her into a seat?'

'Bring her down the back. There's more legroom.'

The green hospital sheet was the next problem. It was lucky that Lily Murphy was wearing two cardigans, and Maeve Byrne had a skirt on over her trousers. 'I'm susceptible to draughts', she'd explained, when Ivy expressed surprise. They dressed Rose as best they could and placed her at the window, beside the emergency exit. She looked for all the world as if she were going on a trip.

'You will sit in beside her, Lily. Lean against her. As if you're falling asleep on her shoulder. Has anyone got any lipstick?' asked Ivy.

'I have,' Maeve Byrne volunteered. 'Give me a minute.' She rooted in her handbag. 'Here it is. African Sky. Is that all right?'

'Where is she going with her African Sky?'

'If you don't want it—'

'Give it to me,' Ivy said, snatching the lipstick. She put some on Rose's mouth and rubbed a little on to her cheeks. 'There. That's better. She looks a bit more cheerful. Now, are we all ready? Dolores. You go over to that hut and tell the driver we are ready to go home.'

'Why me?'

'You always wanted to be an actress. Now's your big chance.'

'What will I say to him?'

'Tell him the case is over and we can all go home. Make it good now. We don't want him getting suspicious.'

The driver smiled when he looked in his rear-view mirror. His passengers were having a great time. They sang one song after another, all the old favourites, and could they belt them out. Sad really. Even a trip to the court was an outing for them. He must do something about organising a proper day-trip. Take them off somewhere for the day. He could get his boss to donate the bus one Sunday, when things were slack. Decent of that judge to let the ladies go and only keep the menfolk. Dragging pensioners into court like that.

It wasn't right. That poor old dear seemed a bit upset when she was telling him about it. Dolores, she called herself. You don't hear the old names any more.

'Approaching Tower Heights, ladies,' the driver said. 'All passengers get ready to disembark.' He chuckled, pleased with himself.

'Dolores. When the bus stops, tell him the steps are too high and you can't get off by yourself.'

The driver turned into Tower Heights and pulled up beside the pensioners' block.

'Home sweet home, ladies. Take your time now. There's no rush getting off. We don't want any accidents, do we.'

Dolores gave her best performance. She twisted and turned at the door, blocking the driver's view of the back of the bus, and gave little cries of fright.

'Could you help me, driver? I'm very nervous of stairs.'

'Hold on there, missis. Let me out first and then take my arm.'

'Get ready,' Ivy said.

While the driver was off the bus, helping Dolores down the steps, she opened the emergency door and let Rose slide out.

One by one the ladies bustled off the bus. They made a great show of thanking the driver and waving him off. They waited until the bus had driven out of sight before they turned to Rose. There she was. Lying on the kerb. Her legs stuck out in front of her and slightly raised, her arms rigid down by her sides.

'We did it,' Ivy said. 'We got her home.' The ladies danced on the pavement cheering and crying. 'Come on, girls. We have a funeral to arrange.'

*

The defendants in Clery's bar started to drift away. Those with spouses waiting for them synchronised their stories. Wrongful arrest and mistaken identity were the most plausible of the excuses offered up for discussion, to explain the two-night absence. Some elected to tell the truth. Malachy was sure his wife would understand, but the advice from the older contingent was to keep mum. 'Never tell them anything. That way you can't be wrong-footed,' was the general consensus.

The majority were returning to Tower Heights. John and Malachy had to collect their vehicles, and some of the pensioners, who couldn't remember if they had locked up or not, were worried about their homes. Shantell had drifted away from the company and was involved in a deep conversation with Mr Toner, who had slipped in for a pint after his shift. Mr O'Gorman and Martin Duffy set off briskly in search of a bookie's. They had had a couple of hot tips for Fairyhouse and didn't want to miss the remainder of the meeting. Rosie and Fionn remained in the booth. When Fionn shyly slipped his hand through hers, she didn't pull away. They sat together quietly, not saying a word.

# Chapter Fourteen

Cell Block J.
Parnell Jail.
Co. Laois.

Dear Miss Titchmarch, or may I say, Annabelle,
  What can I say. We have done it, you and I.
One of my works, the first of my hexad, is almost
complete, and I am writing to you, through your
agent, in gratitude and admiration. I want you to
know that without your words of encouragement,
and practical advice, I would never have gotten
through. Your book, *Getting Started*, has been my
bible. I carry a copy with me at all times. One of
the girls in the print shop kindly shrank a copy of
it to pocket size. There were times, Miss
Titchmarch, when even I had moments of doubt.
When, due to a small contretemps with the law I
found myself residing at the above address, I felt I
could not continue.
  It was, at first, difficult to adjust. But, after the
initial settling in period, I found the routine and

discipline conducive to my work. So much so, in fact, I was able to skip your chapter on 'Finding the Time'. To celebrate my achievement, the other residents threw a little party. No vino, of course, but a wonderful concoction brewed by Tanya, my cellmate, put us all in floating form. Tanya the tigress they call her, due to the fact she is doing time for attempting to devour a certain piece of her husband's anatomy. I have to tell you that she has a wonderful turn of phrase and her insights into married life have been a revelation.

They seem to think the world of me in here. They call me 'a ticket' which, in the jargon of this establishment, is quite a compliment I can tell you. Between ourselves I think they are a little afraid of me. Forgive me. I am getting away from the point.

I am seeking permission to dedicate my work to you. It seems only right as you were the one to inspire me. I have taken the liberty of assuming you will say yes and included your name for the dedication. I must tell you now, there is one other name so far, my friend Carmel. Carmel recently got involved with her boyfriend, Joe, and it's a bit tricky. I don't want his name on my first book but you know how sensitive new lovers are. Carmel was my first business partner, well, sleeping partner really as she didn't do anything, but one must be loyal. There may be other names added to my dedication list as I go along but yours will definitely be the first. As for the rest, I shall let myself be guided by my publisher in this matter, when the time comes.

Watching for the post is both a joy and a sorrow. The joy, knowing a reply is imminent, and

I will shortly see my name in print. The sorrow
will come when the thrill of anticipation is gone. I
will no longer be an anonymous writer, struggling
alone in my garret, living on my wits. Rest
assured, Miss Titchmarch, I will never change. In
the face of fame, I will always remember my time
of struggle and the people who stood by me.

Until we meet,
Yours sincerely
Shantell O'Doherty

'Lights out. Lights out in five.' The dull voice went
down the corridor.

Shantell hated lights out. She had always been a
night owl and would never get used to the regime of
lights out at nine thirty in the evening. It was one of
those 'things' with Carmel when they shared a flat
together. Carmel had always been an early to bed sort
of girl.

Shantell sealed her letter to Miss Titchmarch and
hastily wrote the address. There were moments,
especially at night, when Shantell felt very angry with
Judge Moore. But she couldn't stay angry. If it hadn't
been for Judge Moore and his sentence, she might
never have finished her novel. She had written several
'thank you' letters to him, care of the court, but as yet
had had no reply. It was a great comfort, she told him,
how her friends had rallied round when he
pronounced his verdict. When that nice Mr David
Shield-Knox vowed he would appeal, she had felt
quite the star. She wanted to let Judge Moore know
that she owed that feeling to him.

Shantell sat on the edge of her bed, closed her eyes,
and prepared her thoughts. She smiled as she saw all

the faces. Rosie, Mr O'Gorman, Malachy, Fionn. Dear Fionn. Rosie had written that she and Fionn were dating and she was going to Kerry to meet Fionn's mother. And poor Granny Deignan. Such a pity she hadn't been able to make it to her funeral. The photographs were very good but it wasn't the same as being there.

Rosie's brothers had taken over the funeral arrangements. They had been very angry at first, Rosie said. Accusing Rosie of all sorts of things. They calmed down when they discovered that Granny Deignan had left nothing but the price of her funeral. The state would have eaten any inheritance, they explained to Rosie. It probably would have cost them money if she had left anything. Rosie confided that, although Jenkins & Sons, Funeral Directors, did her proud, the ceremony lacked the intimacy she knew her granny would have wanted. Shantell smiled as she read, 'how pleased Granny Deignan would have been that all the pensioners from Tower Heights had attended and had thrown a big farewell party for Rose on the fourth floor after the service.'

The cell went black. Shantell was plunged into darkness.

Mr Clery had spent the week prior to the trial in preparation. 'TOWER HEIGHTS – THE RETRIAL' posters were displayed in the pub windows, and a sandwich board, placed prominently on the pavement outside the pub, read 'PRE-TRIAL BREAKFAST SPECIAL'. When he contacted the newspapers he was in a position to relate all of the events leading up to the trial and, having remained in close contact with the accused – he had taken a keen interest in the funeral arrangements of Mrs Rose Deignan, sending to the church a tasteful wreath and mass card signed by all the members of his staff – he was able to bring them up to date on the current situation. Mr Clery sent a typed report of the details to the various editors:

The ladies, who had absconded with the deceased, had been apprehended by the police on the ground floor of Tower Heights. Unable to carry their burden they had telephoned to the Samaritans claiming that the deceased was about to die and could only be resuscitated in her own flat, number 147 Tower Heights. They requested that The Samaritans 'send a few strong men to assist in getting her up the stairs'. The names of these ladies were put on file and their fingerprints were taken.

Ms Shantell O'Doherty was rearrested on the evening of the first trial. She had become obstreperous, having consumed two bottles of dry sherry, and had verbally attacked a Mr Colm Toner, clerk to Justice Moore. The Gardaí were called to the scene and Ms O'Doherty was arrested for attempting to interrogate them with a view to an exposé she hoped to sell to the National Enquirer, entitled, 'Focus on the Force'. Her theme, she said, was corruption, cover-ups, and coercion. The Gardaí did not take kindly to this and, in view of Sergeant Murphy's instructions to keep Ms O'Doherty under surveillance, thought it advisable to bring her in. She was remanded in custody until the retrial of the first trial.

The funeral of Mrs Rose Deignan took place at the Church of the Assumpta in Orchardstown. After the service her body was removed to Glasnevin Cemetery for cremation where a moving eulogy was read by her granddaughter. Accompanying the mourners was a detachment of Gardaí from Orchardstown police station. Prominent in attendance were Mr Joe Cullen of Civil Liberties, Ireland, Ms Maeve Peterson of Greenpeace, and Mr Noel O'Brian of Amnesty International. There was also a representative from The Samaritans.

Mrs Deignan's grandsons were said to have been surprised by such a noteworthy gathering. They admitted that they had had no idea that their grandmother had been involved with any political groups of organisations. They were reassured by a Mrs Ivy Simpson that Mrs Deignan wasn't involved, but that Mrs Simpson, along with her associates, had invited the noteworthy guests for protection. The funeral party then adjourned to Tower Heights where they continued their festivities well into the night.

Mr Clery was very pleased with this report. An appetiser. He knew his reporters and what would get them interested.

On the morning of the retrial, Clery's bar opened early. Although not officially an early house, Mr

Clery had taken the liberty. He felt sure that this small breach of the licensing laws would be overlooked on this one occasion. He had invited all of the accused to his breakfast special and was gratified that most of them had taken up his offer. Mr Clery was on hand to brief the reporters on their arrival. He introduced them, individually, and took time to pose for photographs with some of the accused. Two of his snugs had been set aside for exclusive interviews, and a member of the bar staff was assigned to attend to the needs of interviewers and interviewees alike. Mr Clery was delighted with himself. 'Let them keep their literary pubs and their singing pubs,' he said to his staff. 'I can see it now. "Clery's. The Jurisprudence pub of Ireland." This will put us on the map as a major tourist attraction.'

There were two distinct camps within the pub: the gentlemen collected at the bar counter discussing world affairs; the ladies, sitting together in a dignified circle, studiously avoiding the reporters and photographers and concentrating on their breakfast.

'Will you look at them,' Martin Duffy said, nodding over towards the ladies. 'You'd think butter wouldn't melt in their mouths. Wait till the judge gets hold of you lot,' he called over. 'He'll probably give you life.'

'That's more than you've ever had, Martin Duffy,' Ivy shouted back to him.

'Ignore him, Ivy. He's just trying to get a rise out of you. He's showing off for those reporters.'

The two groups had hardly spoken since Rose Deignan's funeral. Ivy and her ladies had vowed they would never forgive the men for not helping, on the day of the trial, with their efforts to rescue Rose. The gentlemen, for their part, had accused the ladies of being bats. Snatching a body from a court of law and thinking they could get away with it. When the solicitor, Mr David Shield-Knox, entered the pub, both sides vyed for his attention, claiming priority.

David Shield-Knox had been touched, and not a little surprised, when his employer, Mr Williamson, had allowed him to continue with the case. He was not to know that the senior solicitors declined to take it on. They were all acquainted with Judge Moore and had no wish to damage their future careers. 'It will be a good experience for you, David,' Mr Williamson had said. 'Get you used to being in the public eye.'

He swelled with pride when he entered Clery's bar and saw his clients waiting for him. They greeted him like old friends, waving, and calling his name. He was especially touched when Mr Clery himself, the owner of the establishment, ushered him to a booth and, despite his protests, served him a full Irish breakfast. He wasn't used to preferential treatment, especially from publicans and restaurateurs. He vowed to do his best. He wouldn't let them down. When he finished his breakfast he took out his briefcase, checked his notes, and called over his clients, one by one, for consultation.

'Not guilty, Your Honour,' David coached. 'That's all you have to say. Leave the rest of the talking to me. I have been trained for this sort of thing.'

'That's right,' Mr Clery said. 'You listen to Mr Knox . . .'

'It's *Shield*-Knox, Mr Clery.'

'. . . He knows what he is talking about. Tea? Coffee? Can I tempt anyone to another rasher?'

'No thank you, Mr Clery. Have I talked to everyone?' David looked down the list. 'I seem to be missing a few people. Rosie and Fionn. Malachy and John Doyle.'

'Malachy and John are probably at work,' Mr O'Gorman said.

'But they are coming, Mr O'Gorman? They do realise they must turn up for the trial? If they don't appear the police will issue a warrant.'

'Don't worry. They'll be here. Cab drivers have to be of exemplary character. They couldn't afford a blot on their copybook. That's why they are so few and far between.'

'And Fionn and Rosie?'

'You have me there Mr Shield-Knox, I don't know. I haven't seen them. What about Shantell? Is she not on your list?'

'Shantell will be arriving by police escort and delivered directly to the courtroom. I will get some time with her inside before the case starts.'

'It's not right you know. They shouldn't have kept her in.'

'I did my best to get her released on bail,' David said. 'But the judge refused my petition. I really did try.'

'There there now, no need to get upset. We all know you did your best. Don't we, everybody.' A unanimous *yes* echoed round the bar. 'You need all your energy for the trial.'

The queue for the public gallery outside court number two was halfway down the street. The crowd, who had arrived early in the hopes of getting a seat, were being entertained by a busker whose usual patch was outside the cinema. His repertoire, he said, consisted of 'songs from shows with a soft shoe shuffle as the climax'. He didn't have much by way of courtroom lyrics. To the dismay of the queue he had no time to display his talent. He had only unpacked his guitar when he was moved on.

'On your way, mister. This is a court of law, not a damn three-ring circus.'

The crowd booed and hissed as the ushers escorted him away.

Mr Toner stood in the lobby appraising the scene. 'His Lordship is not going to like this,' he muttered to the porter. 'He is not going to like this at all.'

A police van drove up the street and stopped in front of the main entrance. The crowd surged forward, anxious to see who was inside. Shantell, flanked by two Ban Gardaí, stepped out of the back.

'It's her. It's her. It's Shantell, the undertaker,' the crowd screamed, jostling to get nearer.

'Get back. All of you, get back now.'

'My goodness. Have they all come to see me?' Shantell asked the Ban Gardaí. 'Hello. Hello, everyone.' Shantell waved to the crowd. 'How kind of you. I am positively touched.'

Mr Toner threw his eyes up to heaven. He knew exactly how touched Shantell was. 'The undertaker. You'd think she was some sort of Mafia hitman the way they're carrying on.'

'Move on, Shantell.' The Ban Gardaí took Shantell's arm. 'Into the court.'

'Officer. Do you think I could pop into Clery's to see my friends? I'm sure they are all in there. It won't take a minute.'

'You are in custody, Shantell. You can't go popping anywhere.'

'Let her. Let her. Let her.' A chant went up from the crowd.

'Get her inside,' Mr Toner said. 'Quickly. Before this gets out of hand. There's reporters in Clery's. All we need is for them to get wind of this. There's been too much publicity about this case already.'

'Did you see the papers, Mr Toner?' Shantell asked. 'I thought they were very good myself, especially the headline that read "Corpse Lifted from Court". That really was a winner with the inmates. Although, personally, I don't think the photograph did the ladies any justice at all. What did you think, Mr Toner?'

Shantell was bundled into the courtroom and Mr Toner closed the doors.

# Chapter Fifteen

There was a buzz of expectation from the gallery as the defendants entered the courtroom. Extra officials had been drafted in and were standing, strategically, around the room. They had been given strict instructions. At the first hint of lawlessness, action was to be taken. The dignity of the court must be upheld. There must be no opportunity for anarchy. The whole legal system had been affected by the ludicrous events of the previous trial, and worse, Judge Moore had been the butt of several jokes in the Law Library.

Mr David Shield-Knox waited until his clients were settled and then strode to his position at the front of the court. He turned to face the audience with a gracious bow of acknowledgement. Sergeant Murphy, standing to one side of the court with his officers, stiffened with disapproval and made a note in his book. Mr Shield-Knox had a lot to learn. He'd soon find out whose bread it was better to butter.

Malachy and John Doyle slipped in quietly. They found a place beside Mr O'Gorman.

'You were cutting it a bit fine.'

'We thought we weren't going to make it.'

'Did you see any sign of Fionn or Rosie? It will look very bad if they are late.'

'Oy, John. How's it going?' Mick roared across the seats. 'No more trouble with your wheels?'

'Have you no respect, Mick O'Toole. Where do you think you are?'

'Respect. Will you listen to Ivy Simpson. Dracula's little helper. Any more bodies to snatch, Ivy?'

The ushers stepped in quickly. As they spoke to Mick he shrank visibly in his seat. Ivy, watching the exchange with satisfaction, nodded to her companions. 'That'll teach him, him and his big trap.' Ivy stopped smiling as the ushers made their way over to her.

'Have you anything you wish to say, madam?'

She looked up at the two ushers who were towering over her and shook her head.

David Shield-Knox swept over to Malachy and John. 'Plead not guilty. Whatever happens. Whatever is said. Remember. Not guilty.' He shook each of their hands and rushed back to resume his place.

'Not guilty of what?' Malachy said. 'We're not guilty of anything. It's already been established that the old lady died of natural causes. We shouldn't be here at all.'

'Speaking of natural causes, Malachy, how's the wife?'

'Don't even ask, Mr O'Gorman. Don't even ask.'

The young couple came galloping in at the last minute. 'Rosie. Fionn. Over here,' called Mr O'Gorman. 'We were all worried. Where have you been?'

Mr O'Gorman didn't hear the reply. The side door of the courtroom had opened and Shantell emerged from the corridor. The crowd cheered. The pensioners, unsure what to do, sat stoically watching her entrance. Shantell gave a little dash forward and, before the Gardaí pulled her away, managed to embrace her companions.

'Rosie. Fionn. Mr O'Gorman. I've been so looking forward to seeing you. Malachy!' Shantell threw her arms around him. He edged away. 'What, no hug for me?' Malachy's wife had threatened to attend the public gallery. 'We will have a proper get together after the case. I have so much to tell you.'

'Ms O'Doherty.' Shantell was walked to her seat.

'All rise.'

Judge Moore had but one thought on his mind as he entered his court and gazed on the accused. Fairyhouse. Beaverbrook had romped home at twenty to one and he had not been there to witness it. He had not even made it to the presentation. The whole celebration was over before he arrived and these people were responsible. He had discussed the case, in private, with his clerk and had assured him that this would have no bearing on the case and that he would be as impartial with this case as any other. After a stern warning to the accused that any repeat of the previous occasion would result in prison sentences, the case got under way.

Garda Kellegher went to the witness box to be sworn in.

'Mr Toner,' Judge Moore called to his clerk. 'In view of the fact that there are so many present, I want them all sworn in together.'

'Your Honour?'

'Get them all sworn in together. I won't have the court's time wasted.'

'But Your Honour?'

'Do it now, Mr Toner.'

'All rise.' The entire court, including public gallery, got to their feet. 'Raise your right hands . . .' Every arm went up, with some, in the gallery, going as far as to make a dubious military gesture. '. . . And repeat after me. We swear . . .'

'We swear.' The courtroom echoed to the voices.

'. . . to tell the truth . . .'

'To tell the truth,' the crowd roared.

'. . . the whole truth . . .'

'The whole truth.'

'. . . and nothing but the truth.'

'And nothing but the truth.'

'. . . so help us God.'

'So help us God.'

'All sit.'

'All sit.' The crowd, carried away with the momentum of the chant, continued the response.

'Mr Toner.' Judge Moore banged on his desk.

Mr Toner, confused for a moment, began gesturing for them to sit down.

'Order. Order in court.'

'I must protest, Your Honour.' David Shield-Knox stayed on his feet. 'This procedure is highly irregular.'

'Are you questioning my decision, Mr Shield-Knox?' There was a dangerous edge to Judge Moore's voice.

'Certainly not, Your Honour . . . I would never question . . . er, no.' David faltered under the harsh gaze of the judge.

'Then kindly sit down and let us proceed. Garda

Kellegher. Have you anything to add to your previous testimony?'

Garda Kellegher flicked through his notebook and then looked to Sergeant Murphy. The Sergeant shook his head.

'No, Your Honour.'

'Then we will take it as read. Call the next witness.'

'That's not fair, Your Honour,' came a call from the gallery. 'We want to hear it. We've been queuing for hours.'

'Silence. Silence or the court will be cleared. Call the next witness.'

Sergeant Murphy took the stand.

'I trust, Sergeant, that there will be no controversial evidence this time.'

'No, Your Honour. The evidence in question is now buried.'

'It was a beautiful burial, Your Worship,' Ivy said from her seat in the second row. 'You should have been there. You would have loved it. He would have loved it.' She turned to the other ladies for confirmation. 'Wouldn't he, girls.'

'Your flowers, Dolores. I still can't get over them. Dolores has a wonderful way with flower arranging, Your Honour. It's a gift.'

'Don't be daft, Peggy. Yours were just as nice.'

'That priest gave a lovely sermon, I could feel the tears running down my cheeks.'

'Enough. I will not have this in my court. Mr Toner, will you get order.'

'If there is any more of this disturbance you will all be removed.'

'There's no need to get on your high horse. We were only telling His Worship about the funeral.'

Mr Toner shrugged. He was helpless. His threats had no effect whatsoever. He knew if he sent them all out he would only have to bring them in again. All he could do was hurry the case along. 'Sergeant Murphy. Could you continue with your evidence.'

'Certainly, Mr Toner. His Honour was asking about the evidence—'

'It's buried,' roared the gallery.

'This is intolerable,' Judge Moore said. 'I am going to ad—'

Mr Toner leapt to his feet before Judge Moore could finish his sentence. He knew what the judge was going to say. He had to stop him saying it. He approached the bench and whispered to the judge. 'With all due respect, Your Honour, if you adjourn the case there will be questions asked. The cost to the tax payer, two retrials, all on free legal aid. It wouldn't do and Your Honour would be forced to have to deal with these people all over again. The press would have a field day.'

The judge addressed the court. 'I shall make one more attempt to hold this trial in a proper and respectful way. If there is one more interruption, and I mean one more, I shall adjourn and you will all come back before me. If this happens I promise you you will regret it. Sergeant Murphy.'

'Thank you, Your Honour. On the morning of the sixteenth I was on duty in Orchardstown, when at approximately eight twenty a.m., a call came through to the station. The call requested immediate reinforcements to assist in dealing with a suspected case of kidnap and possible homicide—'

'Sergeant Murphy.'

'Your Honour?'

'It has come to our attention that there was no kidnap and there was no murder. Could you get on with the charges that are in front of us or do you intend to waste the entire morning reading irrelevant material from your notebook?'

'If it please the court.' David stood up. 'Perhaps the sergeant could read out the charges. I think, Your Honour, you will find that the accusations laid against my clients are without foundation. I intend to prove that my clients are entirely innocent.'

'No one in this court is innocent unless I say they are innocent. Now, Mr David Shield-Knox, do you intend to question Sergeant Murphy or may he step down?'

'I haven't finished my testimony, Your Honour.'

'I think you have, Sergeant. Unless you want to mention how you let a group of elderly ladies steal evidence from under your nose. Evidence that should never have been produced in court in the first place.'

'The cheek of him,' Peggy said under her breath. 'He's older than we are.'

'They're always old, Peggy, by the time they get to be judges. I wouldn't be surprised if this one's a bit senile.'

'If you would let me continue, Your Honour.'

'Sergeant Murphy. We do not have time to listen to your novelette. Get to the point.'

'May I protest, Your Honour.' David was not exactly sure what he was protesting about, but there was something wrong. Surely he should be the one to dispute the evidence. How could he if the judge wouldn't allow it to be read. None of his textbooks had mentioned the possibility of the judge not allowing the police to read their evidence.

'I protest as well.' Every head turned towards Shantell as her voice rang out across the room. 'It's very unkind of you, Your Honour, not to allow the sergeant to read from his notes. I take notes all the time you see, for my novel, so I know how important they are. My goodness, if someone was to take my notes from me I would feel positively naked. If you like, Your Honour, after the trial I could show you some of my ideas from my notebook. I am building up quite a collection on murder mysteries and your help would be invaluable. With all your experiences . . .'

'Here we go.' Mr O'Gorman leant across to Malachy and Fionn. 'His Honour won't know what hit him.'

'Silence!' Judge Moore hammered on his desk. 'Mr David Shield-Knox, control your clients or I will have them physically restrained. Sergeant Murphy, read the charges.'

Sergeant Murphy dithered with his notebook. He didn't want to antagonise the judge further but, unless he referred to his notes, he was afraid he might be incorrect with some of the details or the dates. The whole thing could be thrown out if he made a mistake and these people would get off scot-free.

'The charges before the court are . . .' Sergeant Murphy hesitated a moment. He wanted time to gather his thoughts.

'Let him read his notes,' Ivy Simpson called out. 'Sure what harm can it do? Anyone can see he's lost without them.'

'Mrs Simpson. Please.' David turned round to face Ivy. 'You must not speak out of turn.'

'We have a right to our say.'

'Yes, Mrs Simpson, but only when you are called

upon, and not before that. May I apologise Your Honour . . .' As David turned back the judge was leaving the room.

'Court will recess for fifteen minutes,' Mr Toner announced. 'All rise.'

'Your Honour. You can't go, Your Honour, not yet. We've only got started. Please come back.'

There was bedlam in the courtroom. The public, shouting down from the gallery, threw suggestions and expertise to anyone who would listen to them, while the reporters, who had attended the trial, dashed out to phone their newspapers. As David Shield-Knox gathered his defendants together and began to shepherd them back to the corridor for consultations, the Ban Gardaí each held Shantell by an arm, restraining her.

'Not you, my girl. You're coming with us.'

'I want to stay with my friends,' Shantell protested. 'Why can't I stay with my friends? Mr Shield-Knox, David, can't you do something?'

The Gardaí led Shantell away through a door behind the judge's desk, while one of the porters, who was on a small retainer from Mr Clery for up-to-the-minute court news, made a beeline for the pub.

Mr Toner, Sergeant Murphy and officers Troy and Kellegher stood watching the scene.

'I'll have to go to his nibs,' Mr Toner said. 'I don't know what got into him. I never saw him like that before. I'm sure when he recovers himself, Sergeant, he will apologise to you.'

'Seventeen years I'm in the force, seventeen years. In all that time I have never witnessed a spectacle like this.'

'I'm sorry, Sergeant.' Mr Toner left the courtroom.

'I think that went quite well.' David spoke confidently to his defendants who were, once again, lined up on each side of the corridor. 'The judge did get a little rattled, but that's probably a good sign. It means he is not being complacent. He refused to listen to the police evidence, which seems to infer he's on our side.'

'He walked off, Mr Shield-Knox. How can you say it's going well when he walked off? I've never seen a judge do that before.'

'You should know, Martin Duffy. You were before the courts often enough in your time.'

'Minor infringements, Ivy. I was never charged.'

'You have experience, Mr Duffy. That's wonderful. I will pick your brains if I may. Perhaps you could tell me what happens now. When we resume, do we get sworn in again, or does our oath still stand? I'm a little unsure of some of the finer details.'

The defendants stared at David in amazement. How come he didn't know? Mr O'Gorman swore under his breath and whispered something to Malachy. The Tower Heights residents looked at each other, uneasy for the first time since arriving at court. No one said a word.

'Do we take it, Mr Shield-Knox,' said Mr O'Gorman slowly after some minutes of silence, 'that this is your first trial?'

'Yes, Mr O'Gorman. I'm cutting my teeth, so to speak, today. Rest assured I will leave no stone unturned in proving your innocence and getting an acquittal for all of you. My employers have every confidence in me. They felt that this trial needed fresh blood. "Not a trial for the jaded palate," if I may quote Mr Williamson, our head of chambers. Perhaps you might like to see my certificates . . .' David opened his bag, took out a sheaf of papers, and passed them around '. . . which I happen to have in my briefcase. Take your time, I'm sure you will all enjoy looking through them—'

'Mr Shield-Knox.' Malachy jumped up from his seat. 'We have a judge who is frothing at the mouth. We have three policemen who are out to get us. We are looking at time, if we don't get our act together, and you want us to look at your bloody certificates.'

'Calm down, Malachy. This is getting us nowhere.'

'I know where it is going to get us. It's all very well for you lot, but John and I have jobs. We have families to support.'

'I have to support my mother.' Fionn broke in on the conversation. 'She doesn't even know where I am. I could have rung the post office in the village and asked them to give her a message but I didn't know what to say. I couldn't tell her I was waiting for a trial. She would have got the priest.' Fionn broke down.

'Jesus,' Malachy roared. 'I'm in a madhouse.'

'It's all right, Fionn.' Rosie put her arm around Fionn. 'I'm here to take care of you. We'll see this through together.'

'I love you, Rosie,' Fionn blurted out.

'Isn't that lovely,' Ivy said. 'He loves her.'

'I thought he was with the other one.'

'No, Peggy. The other one was just trying to get her claws in him. You could see that a mile away.'

'He's a lovely fellah, Rosie. Your granny would be proud of you. She always said, didn't she, Dolores, she would love to see you settled with a nice fellah.'

'They're off again,' Mr O'Gorman said. 'Is there no way of gagging them short of a firing squad?'

'Now you know what I have to live with,' Martin said. 'I have that morning, noon, and night. If they're not banging on the door, they're on the phone.'

'Please. Please, everyone.' David tried to restore order. 'We must get on with our defence. When we go back into court, ladies I beg you, you must not speak. You must not say a word. You will be called when, and if, you are required. I have prepared a speech which I am confident will remove the necessity of any of you being asked to take the stand. As soon as the first opportunity arises I shall deliver that speech and the whole case against you will fall apart. Trust me. I do know what I am doing. You have all seen my certificates.'

'Mr Shield-Knox.' A female officer – one of those who had taken Shantell away – called from the end of the corridor. 'Miss O'Doherty would like to see you.'

'Of course, Officer. I will come right away.' David smiled at his clients, a broad beaming smile. 'Remember. Trust me. I will see you all back in court.'

David found Shantell sitting in a small windowless room, at the back of the courtroom. The officer, who had escorted him down the hallway, showed him to the room and then left, closing the door behind her. David was nervous. He wished he had asked the policewoman to stay. He was a little in awe of Shantell. He had never come across anyone so bohemian. A writer, no less. All sorts of things flashed through his mind. He would have to be on his guard. Sharp and witty, yes. But she should be able to see the real him, the man behind the mask, the man with the keen intellect and deep sensitivity.

'Hello, Miss O'Doherty.'

'My knight in shining armour. At last we are alone. But it's Shantell, please, and I shall call you David. Only when we are alone, of course. It wouldn't do in court. You have come here to defend me. To get me out of this terrible situation. You must know how grateful I am. I confess to you, David, I am a trifle nervous. I am sure you find that hard to believe. You deal with this sort of thing every day. But you will appreciate I have never been in court before. I have never been in prison before so I am entirely at your mercy. Tell me what I must do.'

'There is absolutely nothing to be nervous about,' said David. 'I have prepared a defence that is flawless. As I told your companions moments ago, you will all leave this court exonerated. In fact I would go as far as to expect a public apology from all your accusers at the end of my speech.'

'I feel better already. I knew I could count on you, David. We shall all celebrate with champagne as soon as it is over.'

'Time's up, Mr Shield-Knox.' The officer opened the door. 'His Honour is ready to resume.'

'I'll see you in court, Shantell.' Shield-Knox left feeling very pleased with himself.

As soon as David had left the corridor the defendants had their own consultation. They all agreed that, whatever their chances were, they would be better off without him. The ladies felt sorry for him, but the general consensus was that they were not going to be the guinea pigs for his first teeth. He could represent

Shantell, if that's what she wanted, but they would defend themselves. Two of them would speak for all. Martin Duffy would represent the Tower Heights residents and Mr O'Gorman would speak for the others. That way the judge wouldn't get upset.

'I don't see why it has to be Martin,' Peggy had protested. 'Ivy or Dolores or any of us can talk as well as him.'

'Do you want us getting life?'

'You better watch it, Mick O'Toole. It was you took them wheels off.'

'Ladies, ladies,' Mr O'Gorman said. 'I have no doubts about your capabilities, but you must remember the judge is of the old school. Look at it from his point of view. He has no idea how to cope with modern women like yourselves.'

'He's right you know,' Peggy said. 'A lot of men feel threatened by intelligent, articulate women.'

'That's settled then,' Martin said. 'Thank God for that.'

'We will put you in the stand, Rosie,' Mr O'Gorman said. 'Tell the judge what your granny asked you to do. Tell him exactly what happened. I will explain how Fionn and Malachy and myself got involved. He's a man who takes a drink, he'll understand. Martin can take up the story from there. Why he called the police. The mix-up about the furniture. You, Mick, will have to have a good story for the minibus wheels. Play on your age. Tell him you got confused. The truth is we were all confused. We really did think Shantell was an undertaker.'

'Do you think it will work, Martin?'

'I'm sure it will. We'll have as much chance by ourselves as we would have with Mr Shield-Knox. If we all stick to the truth, no elaborating, and no butting in.' Mr O'Gorman looked directly at the ladies. 'When the judge hears our side of things he is bound to let us all go home. Judges are reasonable men, and anyway, they would have nowhere to put us if he sent us down. The jails are chock-a-block as it is.'

'Thank God for small mercies,' Ivy said.

# Chapter Sixteen

'All rise.'

'Do you know I am sick of all this bobbing up and down,' Ivy said. 'It's worse than mass.'

'Ivy,' Mr O'Gorman hissed over at her. 'Remember what we said.'

All eyes were on Judge Moore as he re-entered the courtroom and sat behind his desk. After a long hard look at the assembled crowd, the judge slowly and methodically laid out his papers before nodding to Mr Toner.

'Be seated,' Mr Toner called. Mr Toner had no need to ask for silence. There wasn't a sound in the courtroom.

'Proceed, Mr Toner.'

'Mr Shield-Knox?' Mr Toner said.

'If it please the court,' Martin and Mr O'Gorman said together, jumping to their feet, 'we would like to represent ourselves.'

'Do I take it you are dismissing counsel?'

'Yes, Your Honour.'

'You do not want legal representation?'

'No, Your Honour.'

'Very well.' The judge made a note on his papers.

'I would like to call Rosie Deignan,' Mr O'Gorman said.

'One moment please, Your Honour.' David walked over to Martin and Mr O'Gorman. 'Mr O'Gorman. Do you think this is wise?'

'Don't worry, Mr Shield-Knox. We know what we are doing all right. You have enough on your plate with Shantell.'

'But I am willing to represent everyone.'

'I'm sure you are, Mr Shield-Knox. But we would prefer to do it ourselves. It'll leave you more time to concentrate on the main issue.'

'May I approach the bench, Your Honour?'

'No you may not, Mr Shield-Knox. Kindly sit down.'

'Rosie Deignan to the stand.'

Rosie and Fionn stood up, hand in hand, and moved towards the stand.

'Not you, Fionn,' Mr O'Gorman said.

'I'm not letting Rosie go up there on her own. Where she goes, I go.'

'Very admirable, Fionn. But she must go on the stand alone.'

'I can't go on,' Rosie cried.

'You must go on,' Mr O'Gorman said.

'She can't go on,' a voice called from the gallery. 'Why doesn't he leave the poor girl alone? Anyone can see she's terrified.'

'Oh yes she can. She must,' Mr O'Gorman said. 'You'll be fine, Rosie. I'm here to help you.'

'Oh no she can't,' roared the public gallery.

'Order. Order.' The judge banged on his desk. 'I

will not have my court turned into a rehearsal room for some pantomime.'

'Oops, he's going to regret saying that,' Mr Toner muttered to himself.

'Mr Toner. What are the charges against this young woman?'

'She is not charged with anything, Your Honour. She is here as a witness for the defendants.'

'Does the sergeant have her statement?'

Sergeant Murphy stood forward. 'If it please Your Honour, I can take one now.'

'Sergeant Murphy. There are long queues of criminals waiting for my attention. Criminals with histories of crimes including theft, arson, GBH, not to mention murder, rape, fraud . . . Do I need to go on?'

'You must go on,' roared the gallery.

'Enough. Every spectator, and every person who is not working in this courtroom, is fined one hundred pounds for contempt. One hundred pounds or one week's imprisonment.'

'But, Your Honour, you can't do that,' said Mr Toner.

'Oh yes I can.'

'Oh no you can't.'

'Mr Toner. Are you taking the mickey out of me?'

'What? Me, Your Honour? How could you think that?'

'I don't think much of a judge who uses bad language,' Ivy sniffed.

'For God's sake, Ivy. Doesn't it make him more human.'

'It's like a priest swearing from the pulpit, Dolores. You just don't expect it.'

'Your Honour.' Shantell stood up and tried to make

herself heard above the clamour that had broken out all over the courtroom. 'Your Honour, members of the public. If I may be so bold.' She took a few steps forward towards the judge, hesitated a moment and then collected her chair which she placed in the centre of the floor between the judge and the public. Standing on the chair she flung her arms out dramatically, 'Listen to me,' she called. 'I am the one you want. Let these people go.' The judge, the ushers, the police, the solicitors and the public were momentarily stunned into silence. 'Do what you want with me but do not send innocent people to prison.'

'Hooray. Hooray for Shantell,' the public gallery sang. 'For she's a jolly good fellow . . .'

'You're all on probation,' Judge Moore roared, hammering away on his desk. 'Sergeant, I want all their names.'

'. . . for she's a jolly good fellow . . .'

'Silence.' His Honour's words fell on singing ears.

'Thank you. Thank you all.' Shantell beamed from her chair. 'This is a wonderful moment for me. It came to me in a flash while I was detained for His Honour's pleasure . . .'

'Wowwee judge.' The shouts poured down from the gallery. 'Go for it, Shantell, we want to hear all about it.'

'I thought she was a bit of a dipstick before,' Malachy said. 'But I was wrong. She's stark staring loony.'

'. . . This is my destiny. My destiny as a writer . . .'

'She'll have a destiny all right. I think I know what it might be.'

'Officers. Restrain that woman. Have her taken into custody.'

'She is in custody, Your Honour.'

'Well chain her. Lock her up. Don't just stand there. Do something.'

'Could you step down, miss? Here, take my arm. Come on now.'

'Usher. You are not trying to get a pussy-cat down from a tree. Grab a hold of her man. Get her down.'

'May I try, Your Honour?' David Shield-Knox crept up to the bench. 'I'm sure I could persuade her.'

'Feel free, Mr Shield-Knox. You might as well join in, in this, this appalling spectacle. Never, in all my years in the judiciary, have I been subjected to such outrageous behaviour.'

'Shantell. It's David. David your counsel.'

'. . . All writers down through the centuries, have suffered for their work . . .'

'Shantell. I think we need a teeny weeny little chat. Would you like me to join you up there or would you be more comfortable if you came and sat down beside me? I would be more comfortable if you sat down. I don't have any head for heights. Not since Nanny dropped me from my pram. I am getting treatment. I'm seeing a vertigoligist, but I don't think I am quite ready yet.'

'Jesus, Dolores,' Ivy said. 'There's two of them at it. One's as bad as the other.'

'That's where you're wrong, Ivy. What he's doing is applying psychology.'

'What would you know about psychology, Martin Duffy?'

'More than you think. I live beside you don't I? I've had plenty of practice.'

'My poor David.' Shantell looked down at him. 'I shall come to you.' She held out her arm to the usher.

'If you would be so kind.' She stepped off her chair, and allowed herself to be led back to her place.

The court fell silent. All eyes were on Judge Moore. One or two members of the public let out a nervous laugh but quickly suppressed it. What would he do now? What action would he take? The seconds ticked by. Lily, who hadn't said a word up to this point, leaned across and whispered to Martin. 'I haven't got a hundred pounds, Martin. I only get seventy-nine pounds a week on the pension. Does that mean I'm going to jail?'

'Don't worry, Lily. We're all in the same boat.'

'I wish he'd do something. Me nerves are in bits.'

'Shush.'

Another long silence ensued.

'Mr Toner.' The entire court jumped with surprise as Judge Moore bellowed out the name.

'Your Honour?' Mr Toner went to the bench in response to the judge's beckoning finger.

The crowd leaned forward trying to make out the hushed conversation between the judge and his clerk.

'Sergeant Murphy. Would you approach the bench?'

'It's a conspiracy,' Ivy said. 'They're ganging up on us.'

'Shut up, Ivy. We're trying to listen.'

'Mr Shield-Knox. To the bench if you please.'

David patted Shantell's hand, smiled encouragingly to the other defendants, and joined the group gathered around the judge.

Muffled whispers started from the public gallery, the seasoned court followers giving their opinions to anyone who would listen, offering precedents, and citing other cases they had attended, while the friends and relatives of the pensioners talked about benefit concerts and raffles to raise money if the contempt fine was upheld. After a few moments Mr Toner addressed the court. 'All rise . . .' Judge Moore stood up and walked out of the courtroom. '. . . Ladies and gentlemen. Please remain seated . . .'

'He's only after asking us to rise,' Dolores said. 'No consideration for anyone's arthritis.'

'. . . His Honour has retired to his chambers where he will hold a short consultation with Mr Shield-Knox, Sergeant Murphy and myself.' The trio swept out of the courtroom after the judge.

'I don't like the looks of this, Mr O'G,' Malachy said. 'I don't have much experience of courts but this I do not like.'

'Will you listen to him,' Ivy said. '"This I do not like." All this is your fault. You and that fellah beside you and that weirdo from the country. Not even to mention her lunaticness over there who came down with the last shower. You're the ones who came into our respectable estate with your carry-outs and your curries. Fooling that poor girl there into thinking that you were undertakers and her granny just dead in her bed. You should all get ten years for what you put us through. Amin't I right girls.'

'You never said a truer word, Ivy,' Dolores said.

'Preying on pensioners and getting them in court,' Lily joined in. 'You should be ashamed of yourselves.'

'Ladies, ladies. It won't do for us to fall out. We are all in the same boat here.'

'Who are you calling a lady, Mr Mighty-Mouth-O'Gorman. If you are so good with words how come you haven't talked us out of this? A loquacious oscillator, that's all you are. Yackety-yacking in pubs all day long. That's all you're good for.'

'Where'd you get that one, Ivy? Loqua . . . what was it?'

'I read it in a book. Good isn't it.'

'What does it mean?'

'I don't really know, Dolores, but it seemed to stop him in his tracks.'

Mr Toner, Sergeant Murphy and Mr David Shield-Knox sat opposite Judge Moore in his chambers. It was a most unusual strategy, considering it was still a preliminary hearing, for a judge to assemble people in his rooms. Sergeant Murphy, ill at ease, sat on the edge of his chair clutching his notebook. David, who didn't know it was unusual, and had never been in judge's chambers before, was tense and nervous, convinced there was something he had done wrong.

'Gentlemen,' began the judge. 'I think you will agree the situation in my court is intolerable. The only recourse against this mob element would be to try each individual separately. This, as I am sure you are aware, could run into years and cost the state thousands of pounds. It appears to me that any case against these pensioners would be thrown out of court, on sympathetic grounds, due to their age. A prison sentence would send up a tirade of protest. A fine would be uncollectible due to their limited financial resources. I am aware, Sergeant Murphy, of the flagrant misuse of your men, and that of the fire brigade services, but it seems to me no crime, as such, was actually committed.' Judge Moore checked through his notes. 'Four wheels were removed from a minibus but, as I understand it, they have been replaced. I suggest we discuss the case against the pensioners on humanitarian grounds. Put them on probation with the proviso that if they ever appear in court again, for any reason, these misdemeanours will be taken into account.' The judge paused and looked at David. 'Now to your client, Mr Shield-Knox. It is my belief, having witnessed the spectacle in court, that Miss O'Doherty is in need of psychiatric help. I recommend she receive treatment over a period of six months and, based on the results of assessments by the state psychiatrist, I will decide if she is fit for trial. Impersonating an undertaker, inciting a riot and withholding a body. These are serious charges and not ones I take lightly.' The judge paused for a few moments, allowing time for his words to sink in. 'Do you, Sergeant Murphy, have any objections to my findings?'

'Under the circumstances, Your Honour, I'm inclined to agree with you. At least decent criminals know how to behave, they know their place, not like this lot. It's been my understanding you can never trust the non-criminal type in court, if you get my meaning.'

'Absolutely, Sergeant Murphy. Mr Shield-Knox?'

'It seems a trifle unorthodox, Your Honour. Not that I am questioning your judgement. Oh goodness me no. Wheels of justice and all that. I have to admit I am a little disappointed. I was looking forward to a rip-roaring trial. Everyone acquitted and so forth.'

'Technically they are acquitted, Mr Shield-Knox.'

'But I wanted to be the one to get them off, Your Honour.'

'Don't pout, Mr Shield-Knox. It's unbecoming in our profession. Mr Toner, have you anything to add?'

'Not me, Your Honour.'

'Then please note the agreement of the Sergeant and

Mr Shield-Knox for the record. If you are ready gentlemen. Mr Toner.'

Mr Toner opened the doors of the chambers and led the way back into the court.

'All rise.'

The judge, Sergeant Murphy and Mr Shield-Knox duly took their places.

'Be seated.'

'Oh for Jesus's sake,' Dolores cried. 'I didn't even have time to get up.'

The judge cleared his throat, waiting for the subdued whispers to cease. He gave three light knocks on his desk before commencing.

'Will the accused please rise,' Mr Toner said solemnly.

'After consultation with your legal representative, Mr David Shield-Knox, and the member of the Garda Síochána involved in the incidents, Sergeant Murphy, it is the opinion of this court that the accused, namely: Thomas O'Gorman, Fionn O'Fiachra, Malachy Conway, Rosleen, alias Rosie, Deignan, John Doyle, Martin Duffy, Michael O'Toole, Ivy Simpson, Peggy Moran, Dolores Watson, Tommy Doran, Edward O'Neill, Lily Murphy, Maeve Byrne, Jack Nolan and Kevin Clancy, shall be given the probation act. In effect they are acquitted of the charges hereupon but their names shall remain on record. It shall be noted, if there are any breaches of the peace, however trivial, the charges will be reapplied. In the matter of Miss Shantell O'Doherty. It is the opinion of this court that she shall undergo, for a minimum period of six months under Bill/98/29A, as amended in the Select Committee on Health, a series of psychiatric assessments. The result of the assessments will determine whether or not the charges held against her will proceed. Case dismissed.'

'All rise.'

Judge Moore gathered his papers and prepared to leave the court.

'Your Honour, Your Honour,' Shantell called out before anyone had a chance to stand. 'May I speak? May I say a few words before you go?'

The judge paused and looked at Shantell.

'I would like to thank you, Your Honour,' she went on, 'to thank you from the bottom of my heart. This means so much to me. I will have the opportunity to gain so much experience and material for my writing. I must tell you, Your Honour, the moment you passed sentence on me an idea for a new work popped into my head. You may like to jot it down; I always find it imperative to jot, then if I need your advice on the legal end of things, you will have a note of it. I see it as a murder mystery with a touch of romance. A judge falls for a murderess but he can't condemn her even though he knows she is guilty. It would be a whole new genre for me. What do you think?' Shantell waited a moment before going on. 'I can see you are astounded, Your Honour. Don't be. It may take some time, I do have several other projects on the go, but I intend to dedicate this work to you. It's the very least that I can do.'

Judge Moore stared at Shantell. Was she sending him up? He looked across to Mr Toner for assistance.

'How soon can I begin, Your Honour? I am itching to start my assessments.'

'A word, Mr Toner,' Judge Moore said.

'It will all be arranged, Shantell.' David Shield-

Knox stepped in and spoke quietly to Shantell. 'His Honour doesn't make the arrangements himself. Mr Toner will tell us what the procedure is.'

'Thank you, David.' Shantell smiled at him. 'And thank you everyone.' She made a sweeping gesture to the court. 'I would like to invite you all to celebrate, to share a little drink with me, before we go our separate ways.'

'Mr Toner. Get me out of here.'

'All rise.'

The judge left the courtroom.

'You are invited as well, Your Honour,' Shantell shouted to the slam of the chambers door.

'Well I've heard everything now,' muttered Dolores. 'Inviting the judge for a drink, what does she think she is doing? She'll get us all sent to prison. We're on probation as it is.'

'What does that mean, on probation? Does anyone know what it means? Can we just go, walk out, as if nothing had happened?'

'I think it means your name is on his nibs's books.'

'Look at them,' Ivy said, nodding across to the gentlemen who were shaking hands and slapping each other on the back. 'Schoolboys. They'd be happy in prison. Everything taken care of. Card-playing and telly. What more could they want? Suit them down to the ground.'

'Lily. You've the best speaking voice. Go over there and ask the man can we go.'

'I couldn't, Dolores.'

'Don't be daft. He's not going to eat you.'

Lily made a movement towards Mr Toner but scuttled back when she heard Shantell shout, 'Don't be absurd. You can't take me away.' One of the ushers held Shantell by the arm. 'I'm going to the pub to celebrate with my friends. David. What's going on?'

'I'm sorry, Shantell. You have to remain in custody until the arrangements are made. It won't be for long I promise you. A day or two at the most.'

'But I don't want to go now. I don't want to go today at all. I have to contact my friend Carmel. You haven't met my friend Carmel. We're very close. We go back a long way. Something very important must have cropped up or she would have been here. I must tell her about my assessments—'

'Come along now, miss.' The usher pulled gently at Shantell's arm.

'Don't worry, Shantell, I'll come and see you tomorrow, as soon as I've found out some details.'

'Oh Shantell.' Rosie ran over to her. 'I'm really sorry. Fionn and I will come and visit as soon as we can and I'm sure the others will too.' Rosie looked at Mr O'Gorman and Malachy and the residents of Tower Heights. 'We will, won't we. We'll all come and visit.'

Coughs and stutters came from the gentlemen while the ladies were momentarily silent.

'Of course we will.' Lily, who had a very soft side to her, was almost in tears. 'We'll come as often as we can.'

'Speak for yourself, woman,' Malachy muttered.

'I think that's a wonderful idea, Rosie,' Fionn said. 'We can take turns. I can get up from Kerry at least once a month.'

'She's only going to be kept for about two days for God's sake. Anyone would think she was getting life.'

'You have to go now, miss.'

'We'll keep in touch, Shantell. Don't worry. I have your mobile number. I'll call you.'

'Goodbye.' Shantell paused and looked around before she was led through the door. 'Goodbye for now, everyone. David, would you come with me as far as my transportation?'

'I bet you Joan of Arc wasn't so dramatic and she was being burned at the stake.'

'Martin Duffy. How could you? And the poor girl gone off to prison.'

'You've changed your tune, Dolores. Not that that surprises me.'

'I didn't think she'd go to prison. I mean, when all's said and done.'

'Give over, Dolores. You don't know what you mean and I don't know what you mean, but I've a lip on me for a drink that would stop a child's pout.'

'Lead on, Mr O'Gorman,' Martin said. 'Are you coming, Malachy?'

'Not me. You can count me out.'

'Sure can't you come for the one? The wife's going to kill you anyway. Half an hour is not going to make any difference.'

'Come on, Malachy.'

'The wife will understand. After the morning we've been through.'

'You need something sustaining, Malachy. We all do.' The rest of the gentlemen nodded in agreement.

'Just the one mind.'

'Scout's honour.'

The men headed off through the main court doors.

'What are you girls doing?' Ivy asked.

'If that lot are going to the pub, I'm going too. I want to make sure they're not bad-mouthing us behind our backs.'

\*

184

'Let them through please. Let them through.' The public had cleared the court and were outside Clery's pub trying to catch a glimpse of the defendants. The landlord was making a passageway to the door.

'I feel like royalty,' Dolores said.

'This way. You're all very welcome.' Mr Clery had roped off a section of the pub for the celebration. 'Congratulations to one and all. Now, folks, the first drink is on the house and after that you are on your own.'

'And very generous of you too,' Mr O'Gorman said.

'We try to do our best.' Mr Clery omitted to explain that the backhanders he'd had from the media for interviews with the defendants would more than cover one round of drinks. 'There are a few people here who would like to talk to you when you've had a chance to settle yourselves.'

'Ten minutes of fame, what?'

'Do you know, Mick, there's people who'd kill for that.'

'As far as I'm concerned,' Malachy said, 'I want to forget about the whole thing. A bloody nightmare from beginning to end.'

The hubbub in Clery's was beginning to settle down. The reporters, well satisfied with their interviews, were gone. The court followers, already discussing the chances of a known felon due before the judge at ten a.m. the following morning, had drifted away.

'You'd have to feel sorry for her all the same.' Ivy, on her third glass of stout, was talking to her lady-friends about Shantell. 'She's like a Cyclops. Leaving a trail of disaster behind her.'

'I think you mean a cyclone, Ivy.'

'I know what I mean, thank you very much, and they do too, Mr Know-it-all, and if you weren't eavesdropping, as usual, Martin Duffy, you wouldn't be called upon to have to interpret what you think I mean.'

'I don't think she's the full shilling, God bless her.' The ladies nodded agreement into their respective glasses.

'I hate to see anyone taken away like that in a car.'

'Don't worry, Lily. They're not coming for you yet.'

'Can anyone tell me where we are in relation to Hueston Station?'

'Jesus, Fionn. I forgot all about you you were so quiet.'

'I can walk you to the station, Fionn,' Rosie said. 'It's not far from here.'

'Love-birds. Will you look at the pair of them. Isn't it amazing where love will flourish.'

'Dolores!' Rosie went bright red.

'He's a lovely innocent fellah, Rosie,' Ivy said. 'You could do things with a fellah like that.'

# Chapter Seventeen

'Hello. Hello, Carmel. If you are there could you pick up. Carmel it's me, Shantell. I hope you are not away somewhere, Carmel, and missed the news. You could have knocked me down with a feather when I saw myself on the TV. Twice in one day, Carmel, the one o'clock and the six o'clock. There was no warning. I had no time to do anything with myself. We left the court by a side door but those reporters got wind of it and I faced a barrage of cameras and microphones. The moment was slightly spoiled when David, David Shield-Knox my solicitor, I don't know what came over him, but he tried to throw his cloak-thing over my head. Somehow I managed to catch it and drape it over my shoulders. The reporters were all shouting and flashing lights. "No comment," David kept saying. "Miss O'Doherty has nothing to say." A little bit cheeky, I thought – he never asked me, but on reflection he was probably right. I had no speech prepared and it is always better, with the press, to be mysterious. They followed me right down to the

waiting Mercedes and even chased us down the road
a bit after we drove off. You wouldn't realise,
Carmel, how easy it is to become famous. Don't
worry if you missed it. I have ordered several copies
of the tape and I'll send one on to you. Call me as
soon as you get this message. I am on the mobile at
all times . . . Carmel, is that you? Have you just
come in? I was leaving you a message. It's so long
since we actually spoke. You did see me on
television? That's wonderful. Tell me, honestly,
how did I look? Was my hair a mess? Can you, hold
on a moment, Carmel, the nice screwess is waving at
me. What? . . . Sorry, Carmel, not you. She says my
time is up and I have to hand in my mobile. Well
really, it's a bit much. I've been hanging around for
hours waiting to be admitted, and as soon as I get on
to you, she says my time is up . . . Give that back to
me. You've no right . . .'

'David. You've come.'

'I hardly recognise you, Shantell. You look so –
different.'

Shantell was sitting alone at one of the long trestle
tables in the visitors' room. She was wearing a bright,
semi-transparent, yellow blouse, brown trousers, and
a pair of sneakers. Her hair was brushed back and
tucked into a yellow Alice band while her face, devoid
of any make-up, was scrubbed squeaky clean. She
waved him to a seat opposite her.

'Come sit by me.'

David stared. He had only ever seen her in black.
Black from head to toe. He was wary of this
transformation.

'Do I, David? Do I really look different? That's

wonderful because, I must tell you, I feel different. I have always had the ability to adapt, to blend in, with any surroundings. Now David, don't keep me in suspense, tell me what you know. What has been decided? What is my future?' Shantell stretched forward and took his hands in hers.

David struggled to keep his eyes from the yellow dunes that were heaving up and down in front of him. 'It's very good news, Shantell. The staff here are convinced you should not remain as an inmate. They are happy to run your assessments as an outpatient. However, they do agree that continuous monitoring is essential. You will be released immediately, provided you undertake to attend the clinic on a daily basis to start with. These sessions will be scaled down depending on your progress. I am sure that at the end of your six months, at which time you are due before Judge Moore, we need have no qualms about the outcome. Shantell, are you listening to me? Is there something wrong, Shantell?'

'David. You don't seem to understand. I don't want to leave. I want to stay here. You have no idea how much I have learned since yesterday. Why, it would take months, years even, on the outside to get such insight into the human psyche. And I am getting on so well with everyone. Look at me. Look how I've changed.' The yellow dunes were trembling individually, David broke out in a sweat. 'Ask Dr Walpole or Dr Pilkerton. I bet they will tell you how well I am getting on.'

'It was Dr Walpole and Dr Pilkerton I spoke to, Shantell. They both recommended your immediate discharge. In fact they urged me to organise it.'

'I can't believe you, David. I can't believe you are trying to spoil things for me.'

'Spoil things? I am getting you released. You should be overjoyed. You will be going home tomorrow.'

'I thought there was a bit more to you than the usual solicitor type. I thought you had more imagination. I stuck by you when my co-accused gave you up. Is this how you repay me? Is it? Am I just another notch in your freedom belt?'

'What are you talking about, Shantell?'

'Leave me.'

'But—'

'Leave me.'

'If that's what you want. I have to check in with my office, I could—'

'Go. Check in. Tell them how you let me down.'

'But I got you out, Shantell.'

'Precisely.'


Shantell sat on her bed in the dormitory waiting to be called. Her release papers were signed, a taxi had been booked and she was all ready to go. She placed the carefully folded yellow blouse and hairband on the bed next to hers with a little note of thanks. Doris, the lady who occupied the bed, had given them to her but she couldn't keep them. She had come with nothing but her handbag and she would leave the same way. She picked up her notebook, the only thing she had been allowed to keep with her, and flicked through the entries. Notes for novels. Notes for poems. Cremation details, facts and costs. 'So much material.' She spoke sadly to her notebook. So much material. What was she worried for? She could encapsulate this experience, this atmosphere, with a few notes and work on it later. One look at her notes and everything would come back to her.

**Notes for Novel or Long Poem Entitled 'Doris Doing Life'.**

1: Doris was doing life. A crime of passion, her lawyer pleaded, not premeditated. Normally she, Doris, couldn't hurt a fly. There wasn't a vicious bone in her body. It was a misfortune that the axe had been to hand and her husband's back was turned.

2: In that split second, instead of splitting the briquettes, which is what she normally used the axe for, she accidentally split his head. Her remorse knew no bounds. She loved her husband and in fact had planned a holiday abroad for both of them.

3: She only did what any loyal wife would do when her husband told her he wanted a divorce. Tried to prevent him from leaving.

4: Roused by her husband's indifference to her she tried to gain his attention.

5: She only meant to wound him as he had wounded her.

The judge showed no mercy. This had been her third attempt. The one that proved fatal.

'Your taxi is here. You can collect your things at the front door when you sign out.'

'Thank you, screwess.'

'Call me that one more time and you won't live to see another day.'

'Oh dear. I seem to have upset you. We never really got a chance to get to know each other. I did want to stay but both Dr Walpole and Dr Pilkerton felt I should remain at liberty. I'll be dropping in of course, every now and then, so if there is anything you need . . . It must be frustrating for you in here all the time. We could help each other. I am a novelist you see, and I could put you in my book—'

'Out.'

'Let me give you my mobile number in case you change your mind.'

'Go.'

'I'd like to say goodbye to Doris.'

'You can't.'

'Why not? There is something I need to ask her. It's very important. It's for my research.'

'Take yourself and your notebook and get going.'

'I don't know why you are being like this. I could tell the press. I'm sure there are reporters waiting out there for me.'

'Well you better get going then, hadn't you. You can't keep your public waiting.'

'You are so right. I hadn't thought of that. Tell Doris I will write to her.'

The warden escorted Shantell out of the dormitory and down the stairs to the main entrance.

'She's all yours,' she said, as she handed her over at the front desk. 'Get her out of here.'

Shantell, armed with her handbag and her mobile phone, hastily brushed her hair and checked her face before she stepped out into the street. The big door closed behind her. 'Where is everyone,' she wondered aloud as she looked up and down the road. 'This is ridiculous. There must have been a mix-up with the time.' She banged on the prison doors. 'Open up. Open up in there. I think there's been a mistake.' A small sliding grille opened from inside. 'Was the press informed of the time of my release?' The grille slammed shut.

'Where to, miss?' the taxi driver asked.

'Did you see that, driver? I've been locked out.'

'You're a first there, miss. I never heard anyone complaining about being locked *out* of a prison before.'

'Into town please, driver. I will direct you from there. Do you have a cigarette lighter in your car?'

'No smoking allowed, miss.'

'I do not wish to smoke, driver. I must charge my mobile.'

'Been in a while then, have we?'

'Please. It is vital that I charge.' Shantell hung over the front passenger seat and handed the charger to the bemused taxi driver. Staying in that position, she made her calls.

'Hello. Hello operator. Could you put me through to the newsroom . . . I don't know. If I knew I would hardly be ringing you now, would I. I want to talk to people who do the news on television. I was on the telly, you probably saw me. Shantell. Shantell O'Doherty . . . no, I don't want her number, I am her. I have just been released and I wish to inform the press . . . if you do not get me the number I shall report you to your superiors. Hello. Hello.' Shantell jabbed the off-key and dialled another number. 'Rosie. It's Shantell, your undertaker. Rosie, I need you to get some telephone numbers for me. I'm in a taxi and cannot get them myself. I shall meet you in town later and you can give them to me. The first one is the editor's desk in RTÉ . . .'

# Chapter Eighteen

'It was an extraordinary chain of events, Matt.' Mr O'Gorman sat, propped up on his usual stool, in Hart's pub. 'If you read it in a book you'd hardly credit it.'

'I'm not sure now, Mr O'Gorman, that you didn't bring a little bit of it on yourself and sure didn't it make a celebrity out of you.'

'I'm not the better of it yet. And Mrs O'Gorman is still giving me the cold shoulder.'

'You're out, all the same. She didn't keep you under house arrest for long. I thought we wouldn't see you for months.'

'Sure I had to come out. We've arranged a meeting.'

'Who's arranged a meeting?'

'The group. It's for the stress. To help us through our trauma.'

'No offence, Mr O'G, but you don't appear to me to be a man suffering from stress.'

'It took years off my life, that's what it did, the worry of it.'

'And where is this taking place? Oh no.' Matt saw

Mr O'Gorman's expression. 'Oh no you don't. You're not meeting here?'

'And why not? You can be an honourable chairman.'

'You can't be serious, Mr O'G. You haven't arranged to meet those old age hooligans here. I don't want my place swarming with police.'

'Where's the harm, Matt? It's the handiest place we could think of for young Fionn to find when he comes up from Kerry. He only knows the library, the old folks' flats, the police station, the court and that pub, Clery's, and none of us wanted to go back there. Making money out of other people's miseries. Clean up, they do, on the residue of justice.'

'When is this taking place?'

'Today. At three o'clock. That's why I am in so early, to give you a bit of warning. I told them you might rustle up a few sambos and maybe a bit of soup.'

'What do you think I am running here, meals on wheels?'

'It's always quiet here on Mondays. Think of the extra few bob in the till.'

So much to do. Shantell bustled about her room sorting things out. Anyone with five novels on the go knows exactly how that feels. Up earlier than the larks, eat breakfast, freshen room, shower, then check through notebooks and follow up on novels. Midday appointments with Drs Walpole and Pilkerton then back to the flat for a light lunch and a bit of a rest. Dr Walpole was astonished and amazed when she heard about the novels. She often asked how the plots didn't get mixed up. It was so simple, Shantell explained. She had a notebook for each novel. Dr Walpole knew nothing about Shantell's mentor, Miss Titchmarch, or *The Essential Guide to Writing a Good Novel*. If she did, she would know how important this was.

*Notebook 1*. Gillian Turner. Well poor Gillian was still waiting for her Tom. Things had progressed a little. She had heard from him and she was receiving medical treatment for her little problem, i.e., the masturbating. She was going from strength to strength with her levels of will-power and, in fact, soon she might not need Tom at all.

*Notebook 2*. Felicity knew it was all up with Jeremy. He was married and had no intention of ever leaving his wife. She returned to the cinema day after day in the hopes of finding her swarthy stranger and when she realised she had seen the movie, *The Day The Earth Caught Fire*, so often that the management gave her a signed photograph of the main star, and complimentary popcorn, she took her courage in her hands and placed an advertisement in the *Buy and Sell* free newspaper for a companion and was currently awaiting replies.

*Notebook 3*. Germaine. Now Germaine is a different kettle of fish. A bit selfish is our Germaine. Causing problems. If things don't move on she might have to be shelved or perhaps placed in another setting.

*Notebook 4*. Amy from block 10. This one going fine. Amy served her sentence and was reunited with her Ralph. In fact they were about to marry but it might bring the book to a close too fast. On the other hand he was a revolutionary and anything could happen with that. He could die and, as his wife, she could take over as squad commander. Or, they could marry and she would influence him to give up his ways and get a job. On the other hand she could confess, on the eve of their wedding when they swore to have no secrets from each other, that she had had it off with Guard Constantine, explaining to Ralph that she was thinking of him all the time and begging for his forgiveness. It was a pin job really.

*Notebook 5*. Doris on Death Row. No reply to letters to Doris so this one waiting for a little bit more research. A trip to the library is needed for Doris. The bones of it there, but it lacks a little bit of teeth. If David Shield-Knox had not interfered Doris would be much further along.

One of the things Shantell didn't tell Dr Walpole or Dr Pilkerton about was that each time she returned from one of her assessment sessions, she felt a whole surge of creativity. For some reason Shantell thought it prudent to keep that to herself.

Today was to be even busier than usual. The reunion was taking place. Shantell was thrilled when Rosie phoned. She had almost begun to think that her mobile must be on the blink, it had been so quiet. A social afternoon. How wonderful. A meeting of friends. All because of you Shantell. She smiled to herself in the mirror as she got her face ready to go out. You, my girl, have a way with you and no doubt about it.

'I don't know what we are doing this for, Ivy. Really

I don't,' Dolores said, struggling to get her going-in-to-town coat on. 'I'd have been just as happy at the bingo.'

'Remember what that stress counsellor said. She told us not to bottle up our emotions. She said we were to talk about our ordeal. If we didn't, it could lead to pent-up fears.'

'Give over, Ivy, it's me you're talking to. I've lived through seventy-six years of pent-up fears, and being told otherwise by some young one straight out of nerve school isn't going to change anything.'

'She was doing her best, Dolores. Are you ready? We don't want to be late. We've to meet the others at the bus-stop at half-two.'

'Have you heard anything about what's happening to Mrs Deignan's flat?'

'No. Not a thing.'

'Does it go back to the council?'

'I don't know, Ivy. Maybe young Rosie will move in. It would be nice to have some young blood around the place.'

'I can't see it. They keep those flats for sheltered accommodation. You have to be on the pension or the disability to be entitled.'

'They won't keep it idle for long.'

Rosie sat over a cup of tea in the station buffet watching the train times on the huge announcement board, and asking herself, for the umpteenth time, what she was doing there. There had been nothing said between herself and Fionn. She had called the number in Kerry and left a garbled message. She didn't know what to say. She didn't want to make things awkward for Fionn. His neighbours might know nothing about his trip to Dublin. It was stupid being there when she didn't know if he would be on the train. Maybe he didn't get the message at all and she was wasting her time. Rosie would have preferred not to attend the meeting herself but she didn't want to let her gran's friends down. She felt responsible for the whole mess. All those pensioners on probation. Most of them had never even been in a court before. They had been so good to her. Not one of them had accused her, or blamed her, for what had happened.

She should go. Jump on a bus and go into town. No one would know she had made an idiot of herself going to meet him. He'd probably forgotten all about her. With his life in Kerry, what would he want with a Dublin girl? All of a sudden she couldn't remember what he looked like. Rosie jumped when a loud announcement came over the tannoy. The Kerry train had arrived at Platform 7. She'd stay in the buffet, watch from there, but there were too many people around and she might miss him. She went to the counter to pay for her tea, fumbling in her bag to get the money out. She wished she hadn't come. She wanted to get away as fast as she could.

'Tea, please.'

'Mug or cup?'

'No. I had it already. I want to pay.'

'Eighty pence please.'

The money spilt out over the counter and on to the floor.

'I'm sorry.'

'It's all right, love. Take your time.'

Rosie scrambled about picking up her change. She paid for her tea and fled the café.

'Rosie. I knew you would be here.'

'Hello, Fionn.'

'Here you all are now. No trouble finding the place I hope?' Mr O'Gorman stood at the door of the pub greeting his guests. 'Martin, Mr O'Toole, ladies. You're all very welcome. A grand spot this. So central and yet so quiet. This way folks. This gentleman behind the counter here, philosopher, psychoanalyst and bartender extraordinaire, is Matt, our host for the afternoon. Matt, I'd like you to meet the residents of Tower Heights. Triumphant battlers of the balcony. You read about them in the newspapers, now meet them in the flesh. Matt has set up a nook for ourselves down the back where we won't be disturbed. Sit down, sit down everyone, make yourselves comfortable. The soup and the sambos are on the house.' Mr O'Gorman gestured across the counter to Matt, giving him no chance to protest as the *oohs* and *aahs* of appreciation came from the crowd. 'Might I suggest, before we get settled, some sort of a pool for the liquid refreshments? Say five pounds a man, or woman, to start.'

'Hold on there, mister,' Ivy said. 'Most of us ladies drink glasses. We're not subsidising your pints.'

'Quite right. Shall we say ten pounds per man and a fiver for the ladies? Does that suit everyone?'

'I only want tea,' Lily said. 'Do we have to pay for the tea?'

'We are missing a few of our little group yet. We'll give them a few minutes before we begin. What do you say we order a round while we wait?'

'I hope you didn't ask the sergeant, Mr O'Gorman. Or the judge.'

'Very droll missis. Matt. I think you could set up a

few pints. Are we a bit shy in the kitty there, folks?'
Mr O'Gorman started to count the money.

'Excuse me, mister,' Ivy said. 'Who died and made
you our leader? Dolores. Take charge of that money.'

'We'll hand it over to Matt,' Mr O'Gorman said.
'He can let us know how we are going with it.'

'We will not,' Ivy sniffed. 'Every publican was once
a barman. I'm not contributing to his fund.'

'Ivy. Will you leave it out,' Martin said. 'You
wouldn't trust an angel if he came down to lead you
to Heaven.'

'I only want tea,' Lily tried again. 'Do we have to
pay for tea?'

Matt steadied himself, gripping on to his pumps.
'Do you want these pints pulled or not?'

'Pull away, Matt. There'll be plenty of takers.'

David Shield-Knox packed some papers into his
briefcase and prepared to leave the office. He had
been surprised to get the phone call from Shantell. His
first contact with her since that ridiculous day when
she was so annoyed at being released. He was in two
minds whether to attend the get-together. Strictly
speaking, as a solicitor, he should remain uninvolved,
but it had been his first case and, he had to admit,
things had been deathly dull in the office since then.
What harm could it do? He could drop in, say hello to
everyone, and be back in the office before anyone
even noticed he was gone. Not that anyone took any
notice of him anyway. He had expected to be praised,
fêted even, for the way he had handled the case. No
one else in the firm had ever been in the news. 'A
damn publicity stunt,' his employer had shouted at
him. 'No one in this firm will court publicity unless I

say they court it.' He had brushed David's explanations aside, with mutterings of 'if it wasn't for your mother . . .' leaving a veiled threat in his wake. As he walked into town, he had been careful to leave the red Mini parked outside the office so that they would assume he was around somewhere. He felt like a truant schoolboy. The get-together wasn't in an area of the city he knew well and he was enjoying the anonymity of it. He might not go back to the office at all. He might take the whole afternoon off. That would make them sit up and notice him. He spotted Malachy ahead of him and ran to catch him up. 'Malachy. Wait up, Malachy. Is that you?'

'David.'

'What a stroke of luck. Heading for the rendezvous? I am so glad I met you. We can go together. Tell you the truth I'm a bit nervous. Not quite sure . . . you know what I mean. Do you know where it is? I'm not too familiar with this area. But of course you do. You're a taxi driver. Stupid of me. I must say it will be strange meeting everyone again.'

'I didn't expect to see you, David.'

'I didn't make up my mind to come till the last minute. Work and all that. Actually, I sort of snuck out, did a runner, so to speak. Felt I had to meet the gang.'

'How did you know about it?'

'Shantell phoned me.'

'Shantell?'

'I've only got the one pair of hands, missis. You'll have to wait for your tea.'

'Have you not got it on tap?'

'Missis. We have Guinness, Harp, Heineken,

Murphy's, Bulmers, you name it, on tap. Tea we don't have on tap. Tea we boil a kettle for.'

'Would you like me to put the kettle on for you?'

'Lily. Would you ever sit down and leave the man alone. Here. Here's a small port. Put sugar in it and it'll be the same as having tea.'

'Egg and onion, anyone?' Peggy Moran was passing round the sandwiches. 'Or a nice bit of ham. I have to say they do do a lovely sandwich.'

'Onions give me heartburn.'

'Have some, Dolores. There's nothing else going to burn your heart at your age. Mick O'Toole, take those sandwiches out of your pocket.'

'They're for me pigeons.'

'Will you look what the cat dragged in.'

'It's Malachy. And your man the solicitor.'

'Who asked you?'

'In you come, gentlemen.' Mr O'Gorman got up from his seat. 'Grab a chair there. You're very welcome. What'll it be?'

'I'll have a pint, Tom.'

'Good man yourself, Malachy. And you, Mr Shield-Knox?'

'Please. Call me David.'

'What's your poison, David?'

'A glass of shandy, thank you very much.'

'Matt. A pint for my friend here and a glass of shandy.'

'Shandy, tea, sandwiches,' Matt muttered to himself. 'I might as well close the pub and open up a café.'

'Now then. If everyone's got something in front of them,' Mr O'Gorman said, 'we could begin.'

'Rosie's not here. We should wait for Rosie.'

'And while we're waiting, those two can put their money in the kitty.'

'Ever vigilant as usual, Ivy. What would we do without you?'

'I'll have another one of those ports, Mr O'Gorman,' said Lily. 'You are right. It does taste a little bit like tea.'

'You're supposed to sip it, Lily. Not swallow it down like medicine.'

Two more figures appeared in the pub.

'Here she is. Here's Rosie. Hello Rosie, love. Come and sit down beside us. We were waiting for you to start the meeting. Who's that behind you? I should have guessed. Fionn, the man from Kerry.'

'How are you Rosie? We were only saying you never come to see us.'

'I couldn't, Dolores. All this has been my fault. If it hadn't been for me none of this would have happened.'

'If it hadn't been for you?' Ivy said. 'Do you not realise that that granny of yours had a lot to do with it? What was she thinking? A lady undertaker indeed. Could she not be buried like every other decent citizen? Oh no. Not Rose Deignan. No offence now, Rosie, but you have to admit she was going to extremes. Did she tell the other members of the family? Did she say anything to us, her friends and neighbours? She knew we'd laugh her out of it. *Lady undertaker.*'

'I don't see what's wrong with that.'

'That's because you're young, Rosie. You don't know that undertaking runs in families. Do you ever see a job advertised in the newspapers or in the job centres for undertakers? Of course you don't. And why? Because no one could look the part unless they were born into it. Stop blaming yourself. Isn't that what the counselling is all about. To help us to stop blaming ourselves, to exonerate . . .'

'To get rid of our pent-up feelings,' Dolores said, butting in. 'That's what you told me when you dragged me along. I wanted to go to the bingo.'

'. . . ourselves from blame,' continued Ivy.

'Listen to them,' Martin said. 'Group dynamics. She never heard the word "exonerate" before she had counselling.'

'Order. Order.' Mr O'Gorman banged his pint glass on the table. 'All of us here, with the exception of Mr Shield-Knox, are on probation. In the eyes of the law we are offenders, we have a record. We must present ourselves at the police station and surrender to counselling at the discretion of our probation officers. I don't know how this counselling has affected your lives but, for myself, I can tell you that Mr O'Gorman is not pleased. I have, in my sessions, only just reached the age of twelve and if this goes on I will be dead and buried before I arrive at my teenage years. Mrs O'Gorman, quite rightly, feels that not a lot is being achieved through these sessions. She also fears that she may be coerced into becoming involved and, if I do drop dead, a possibility she had cited extensively of late, she will find herself continuing my sentence. A sort of suttee-in-law, so to speak. She has a theory that once these people get their hands on you . . .' Mr O'Gorman raised his hands implying that he need not continue.

'I haven't got a counsellor,' Fionn said, looking at Rosie. 'But I wish I had.'

'How come, Fionn? You were just as involved as us.'

'I was exempted because we live in the country and there are no counsellors in the area. Mammy had a word with our sergeant and she told him she wasn't driving me forty miles to Tralee every week and forty miles back again and that if there was any counselling to be done she would do it.'

'Isn't that terrible. And all that madness in the country.'

'Lily.'

'I wanted to go, Mrs Murphy. I really did.'

'Don't worry, lad,' Ivy said. 'We can fill you in, can't we girls. We've been every week . . .'

'Ladies, ladies. We must continue. My purpose in inviting you all here today is to find a way to prove, without a doubt, that we are in no way a danger to society and therefore these counselling sessions should be allowed to cease.'

'. . . The first thing he said to me was about not bottling up my feelings . . .'

'I wanted to get the counselling, Mrs Murphy, so I could get the courage to tell Mammy about Rosie.'

'That's beautiful, Fionn.' A tear dropped into Lily's port.

'. . . I told him there was no danger of that. I was always a one to speak my mind.'

Mr O'Gorman looked to the other gentlemen. They were getting nowhere. Was there no stopping the ladies?

'Lily, Ivy, Dolores, Peggy, the rest of you. Would you for the love of Jesus shut up and let the man get on with it.'

'I beg your pardon, Martin Duffy,' Maeve Byrne butted in. 'Neither myself nor Peggy Moran have opened our mouths.'

'Except to guzzle down the drinks, Maeve. The pair of you have been up and down to that bar like yo-yos. You're supposed to be taking this seriously.'

'Thank you, Martin,' Mr O'Gorman said. 'If we all could settle down and approach the problem systematically I'm sure we can come up with a solution.'

'May I interject?' David asked.

'Feel free. Everyone else does.'

'I was wondering. You don't all attend the same counsellor?'

'No,' Mr O'Gorman said. 'That's the trouble. We're all on different approaches.'

'My fellow's gorgeous,' Peggy said. 'You could spend hours listening to him.'

'For God's sake Peggy.'

'What? A minute ago you were giving out because I didn't say anything.'

'How did you get a man, Peggy? Dolores and I have a woman.'

'The one I got keeps asking me about rubber,' Mick O'Toole said. 'I don't know what he's on about. I only let down a few tyres.'

'Order. Order. Go on, David. What are you trying to get at?'

'From an outside point of view,' said David, standing up, 'what you need is one counsellor. One voice to speak for you. One voice who can tell the court that in his, or her, opinion, you are sound, sane members of the community who were led, by some quirk of fate and against your will, to perpetuate acts that normally would be abhorrent to your natures. I, for one, would endorse that opinion to any court in the land should you honour me with that task.'

David's voice trembled with emotion. 'For any service I can render to this effect, I am humbly at your disposal—' He broke off and sat down abruptly.

A stunned silence came over the group followed by a small ripple of applause.

'Very noble. Very noble indeed,' Mr O'Gorman said.

'Encore, encore,' Maeve cried out. 'You wouldn't get such a speech in the Abbey.'

Lily sobbed openly.

'I think we should all take a moment to collect ourselves.' Mr O'Gorman moved over to the counter and spoke to Matt. 'Did you put anything in that shandy?'

'Who, me? You know better than anyone, Mr O'G, there's days a person could drink their loaf off to no effect, and other days when they only have to get the aroma of a drink to be on their ear. This must be one of his aroma days.'

Shantell threw a final glance of approval at herself in the mirror before she left the flat. She felt she had achieved the look she sought: sombre, yet lightly intellectual. No need to overpower her friends with an ensemble unsuited to the occasion. She allowed plenty of time to do a little food shopping, pop into the library and be interestingly late. A tiny morsel in a bag and a few books always created a certain impression. She had observed that intellectuals never carried round vulgar bags of shopping. They gave off an aura of living on pearls of food, a hint of veg, a wisp of meat, and definitely never pudding. She toyed with the idea of ringing Carmel and inviting her along to meet everyone, but decided against it. If she came she would probably bring the dreaded Joe with her and the day would be spoiled. Carmel would expect everyone to make a fuss of Joe so he wouldn't feel out of things. It was too much really. Shantell would be torn. Better to meet all her new friends alone. She could phone Carmel later and tell her all about it.

Shantell made straight for the information desk in the library. She didn't want to waste time browsing. She had dithered for so long in the cheese shop, she was running late.

'Excuse me.' She bent over the desk and spoke to the top of Doreen's head.

'Yes,' Doreen said, not taking her eyes off her computer. 'How can I help you?'

'I am a regular library user and I need some information immediately.'

'On what?' Doreen still didn't look up.

'Death row.'

Doreen's head jerked up. Immediately she recognised Shantell. 'You're the woman . . . Miss Conlon,' she said in a strangled voice. 'Could you come here a moment please.'

'What is it, Doreen?'

'I'm in rather a hurry,' Shantell explained. 'If you could point out the section.'

'You are the woman—'

'Yes. I am she. I must tell you I never expect to be recognised. It's amazing, once you've been on the telly, how many people recognise one.'

'Miss Conlon. I have a lady here requesting information on death row.'

'Direct her to the Law Library.' Miss Conlon, busy with her files, answered automatically. 'What did you say?' Miss Conlon, suddenly realising what had been requested, rushed across to Doreen.

'Hello.' Shantell smiled at Miss Conlon. 'Shantell, Shantell O'Doherty. Novelist and poet, yes.' Shantell encouraged Miss Conlon's memory. 'You were extremely helpful to me recently with regard to obtaining information on crematoriums. Ah, I see you have placed me now. I need anything you have on death row. You mentioned the Law Library. Unfortunately I don't have time to go to the Law Library. I'm on my way to a meeting actually, and really, the sort of research I need at the moment is more on the biographical side of things rather than the legal. *Last words*, *My Last Week Alive*, you know the type of thing I mean. I need to get down to the nitty-gritty feelings of the condemned person. Perhaps something from Texas. They do still have the death penalty there I believe.'

Doreen put her hand to her mouth and hissed through her fingers, 'What will we do, Miss Conlon?'

'Would you care to take a seat, miss. I'll have Doreen look something up for you.'

'I don't have much time.'

'It won't take any time at all. Doreen, follow me please.' Miss Conlon led Doreen through a door at the back of the information desk. 'Get Mr Scott. Tell him to phone the police straight away. I'll try to stall her. We saw what happened after the last time she was here. An old lady's body was stolen. The Lord only knows what she has in mind this time.'

'Hel-loo,' Shantell shouted in through the open door. 'I'm afraid I don't have time to wait. I'll be late for my meeting. I'll pop in tomorrow and collect whatever you have managed to gather.' She left the library and headed for O'Connell Street.

Shantell couldn't find Hart's pub. She knew it was the place she had first met Mr O'Gorman and Fionn, but where was it now? How could she forget? Fionn had proposed to her in that pub. Dear sweet Fionn. It would be so good to see him again. Her carpenter and, in a strange way, her saviour. Fionn had been a sort of catalyst for her. She had been on her way to the College of Surgeons, though why she was going there she couldn't remember offhand, something to do with the library. Oh dear, this wasn't happening. She was over an hour late. What would they think of her? Shantell darted up and down the side streets hoping to recognise something, anything. Thank heavens. There it is. She stepped into a doorway beside the pub and took out her mobile phone.

'Hello. Hello. Is that the *Irish Times* office? Could you please put me through to the newsdesk? I wish to make an anonymous call.' Shantell spoke briefly, disguising her voice, trying to sound as mysterious as possible. She hung up and dialled another number. 'Hello. Hello. Is that the *Independent Newspaper*? I wish to speak to your newsdesk . . .'

The meeting was in full swing. The kitty of tenners and fivers had been replenished several times and Matt was hard pushed to serve the flow of drinks.

'Do you know what I'm going to tell you, Davo?' Martin, a little worse for wear, had his arm around David's shoulder and was slurring in his ear. 'I'm reelly reelly sorry about that business in court. Firing you and all. It wasn't right, was it folks,' he addressed the members of the group.

'We didn't want to, you know,' Lily said. 'The powers that be thought they knew better.'

'I understand,' David said. 'I'd have probably done the same thing.'

'You're a gentleman, Davo. No doubt about it. No hard feelings then?'

'None whatsoever.'

'You have to admit though, looking back, if it wasn't for all the trouble and all, the whole thing was funny. I mean there we were, minding our own business, and the next thing, wham, we're in the middle of a siege. Wham again and we're in court. As for that lot. Running away with the corpse.'

'We were only thinking of Rose.'

'I'm glad you find it funny,' Malachy said. 'I nearly lost my job, not to mention my wife.'

'Lighten up, Malachy. You were up to your neck in it by the time we got involved.'

'If I ever meet that woman again I won't be responsible for my actions.'

'When you think about it, Malachy,' began Martin, 'if it hadn't been for her we might never have met, and look at us now, a group representing the whole strata of society. Here we have the law, represented by Davo here. Our rural brother, Fionn, and Rosie, the epitomy of the aspirations of our youthful nation, and lastly ourselves, senators of life, dispensing wisdom and knowledge to all concerned. Not to mention a hostelry, which I have not attended myself before, whose warmth and friendliness is unsurpassed, thanks to our new comrade, Matt. And do you know something else I'm going to tell you, Malachy? I will never ever get into another taxi, unless it is yours. That's how strongly I feel.' Martin attempted to rise.

'You could never hold your drink, Martin Duffy.'

'I would like to propose a toast. To undertakers everywhere so long as they're not here.'

'Hear, hear.' The pensioners applauded.

'Now then,' Mr O'Gorman said, looking at Fionn and Rosie. 'What are you two whispering about in the corner there?'

'I've asked Rosie to marry me.'

'What?' Mr O'Gorman nearly choked on his pint. 'She's not going to the toilet I hope?'

'Mr O'Gorman!' Ivy was scandalised.

'It's a long story, Ivy.'

'I think that's beautiful,' Lily sobbed.

'I swear to God, Lily, if they were ever looking for a replacement for Powerscourt Waterfall, you should apply. I never saw such waterworks out of anyone.'

'Leave her alone. You're the one who put her on the port.'

'Well if she doesn't stop her crying I'll be the first one to *de*port her!'

'Very good, Mr O'Gorman.'

'That's a good one, Tom.'

'Men. You're all the same. Anything for a laugh especially at the expense of us poor women.'

'Shut up the lot of you. I want to hear about Fionn and Rosie.'

'I've asked her to marry me.'

'And what did she say?'

'Stop talking about the girl as if she wasn't here. Rosie?'

Rosie burst into tears.

'Now look what you've done. Don't mind them, love. You can tell your Aunty Ivy.'

'I wish my granny was here.'

'Of course you do, love. It wouldn't be natural if you didn't.'

'I want to tell her I said "yes".'

Cheers and shouts went up as everyone gathered round to hug the couple.

'That's wonderful, Rosie. That's the best yet.'

'Well would you credit it.'

'Champagne, Matt. Champagne for the happy couple.'

'If you want to tell your granny, Rosie,' Lily said through her sobs. 'I know a lady who can bring you over to the other side.'

'But of what, Lily,' Mick O'Toole asked. 'Of what?'

'Isn't this a great day,' Dolores said. 'And to think I was going to go to the bingo.'

'Love at first sight. It's a miracle.'

'Glasses, Matt. Glasses for the champagne and one for yourself. We all have to celebrate this great occasion. Stand up there now, the pair of you, till we get a look at you. In the middle here, that's it. Ready everybody. Glasses raised—'

The pub doors opened.

'Hello. Hello, everyone. I'm so sorry I'm late. I hope I haven't held things up. I got quite lost. My goodness, what's this? Champagne? You shouldn't have, you naughty things. I have done nothing to deserve it. Mr O'Gorman. I am sure you were the instigator. You must have had someone stationed outside watching for my approach. I am overwhelmed. Let me give you a kiss. For me?' Shantell swept the glass from Mr O'Gorman's hand. 'This is truly wonderful.'

The pub doors opened again.

'Come in, come in,' Shantell called out. 'Here we are. Smile everyone. Oops.' As Shantell planted a big kiss on Mr O'Gorman's cheek, cameras flashed, and a crowd of reporters rushed to the bar.

'Oy!' Matt came out from behind the bar. 'This is a private party. You have no right barging into my premises like that and taking photographs. Sit down and order a drink and behave like normal customers, or I'll be forced to call the Gardaí.'

'No, Matt. Not the Gardaí!' The pensioners all started shouting at once. 'Keep the Gardaí out of it.'

Mick O'Toole ran forward to the reporters. 'We'll tell you everything you want to know. We're all on probation, we are not allowed to get into trouble. Don't force him to tell the Gardaí. I'm too old to go down.'

'Easy, Mick, easy. None of us are going anywhere. What do you want?' Malachy asked the reporters.

'We got a tip-off that something big was being planned here today.'

'Something big *is* planned. That's what the champagne is for. Something that you have spoiled.'

'Another siege?'

'A body-snatch?'

'An engagement. These two young people have got engaged. That's what we are celebrating and if you have nothing better to do than barge in here and spoil their day I feel sorry for you.'

The reporters looked around the pub. It was obvious nothing was happening. Nothing newsworthy. No story. They started to back away.

'Yea, back off you pack of pizza-pushers.' Mick put up his fists and started to dance around. 'Come on.'

'What did you call us, Granddad?'

'Nothing,' Mr O'Gorman said. 'He didn't say anything.'

'There's nothing here, boys. It's a leg-pull.'

'Yea,' Mick said hiding behind Mr O'Gorman. 'Shove off.'

'Shut up, Mick.'

'I am more than happy to grant you an interview.' Shantell walked after the retreating reporters. 'I could tell you all about my progress. I'm sure your readers would find it interesting.' She followed them out on to the street.

'What the hell was all that about?'

'Harassment,' Mr O'Gorman said. 'Pure and simple.'

'The question is, how did they know we were here?'

'How did *she* know we were here?' Ivy asked. 'Who told her?'

'It was me,' Rosie said. 'I told her.'

'Why, Rosie?'

'I felt sorry for her. We were all meeting and I didn't think she should be left out. She didn't mean any harm.'

'She may not have meant it but by Christ she certainly caused it.'

'You're too kind-hearted for your own good, Rosie.'

'I'll tell you one thing,' Mr O'Gorman said. 'If they print that photograph I can never go home again.'

'Come on now, Mr O'G. It probably won't come out.'

'It'll be a blur. You know what newspaper photos are like.'

'Thanks for those words of comfort. It's all very well for you lot, but I'm telling you, I'm done for if it appears.'

'We could get after them,' Mick said, 'and grab the camera.'

'I know what *I'll* grab Mick O'Toole. What was all that about pizza-pushers?'

'That's what they call them in foreign countries.'

'Paparazzi, you idiot. Paparazzi.'

Shantell breezed back into the pub. 'Alone at last. Isn't this nice. What has everyone been doing? Do fill me in, I'm dying to hear. David, Malachy, Mr O'Gorman? I've been having the most marvellous time with my doctors. I'm really beginning to know myself. Have you been seeing doctors? I'm sure I could arrange for you all to come with me to visit Dr Walpole and Dr Pilkerton. I know they would be tickled to meet you. I go to them most mornings which is why I was a little late arriving. I had to pop into the library after my visit. That's where I met you, Fionn. Remember? Are you still interested in Chinese food? They are doing the most wonderful cookery programmes on the television; I could tape them for you. It would be no trouble at all.' Fionn had begin to protest. 'Yes, cookery and origami programmes. I do origami at my sessions. If anyone had some paper I could show you. My elephants are the best in the group. Barman, do you have some coloured paper, or a menu?'

'Time's up folks. The bar is closing.'

'What do you mean,' Martin said. 'It's only five o'clock in the afternoon.'

'I don't care what the time is. You'll all have to drink up. The bar is closing.'

'What's going on, Matt?' Mr O'Gorman called Matt over to the side of the bar. 'What are you doing?'

'You know what's going on, Mr O'G. I want her out of here. It's all going to start again. You know what happened the last time. My after-work regulars will be coming in shortly and I don't want them doing a runner. They're still talking about her as it is. I'm sorry, Mr O'Gorman. Either you get her out or you'll all have to go.'

'. . . It takes absolutely no time. You ladies will love it. You can decorate your homes with all kinds of things. It doesn't have to be elephants.'

The ladies sat open-mouthed as Shantell talked to them.

'Am I losing it or am I hearing what I think I'm hearing?' Ivy said, leaning over to whisper to Dolores. 'What is she talking about?'

'Well, you *are* losing it, Ivy, but so are we all. The woman is mad, stark staring mad.'

'That's not very nice, Dolores,' Rosie said. 'She's not mad. She just lives in a world of her own. My gran used to say that people who were like that were special.'

'I'd like to be special,' Lily said.

'Oh you are, Lily, love. You are,' Dolores said.

Mr O'Gorman was in a huddle with the men. 'What are we going to do? We can't ask her to go. We've got to think of something or we are all out on our ear. David. Can you think of something legal?'

'Yes, Davo, think of a law she could have broken.'

'I'm afraid she hasn't done anything. To be barred from a public place you have to have done something undesirable or unsociable and she hasn't done either.'

'What about driving other people bananas?' Malachy suggested. 'Surely there's a law about that.'

'Hold on,' Mr O'Gorman said. 'I think I have something. I think I know how to get rid of her. Back me up. Whatever I say, back me up. Eh, Shantell. Did anyone ever tell you you have a great way with words? The lads and myself here were only saying it. Weren't we lads.' The men all nodded in agreement. 'It's a great gift that.'

'Why yes, Mr O'Gorman. As a matter of fact they did. My friends are always remarking on it. How flattering of you to mention it.'

'We were thinking you would make a great reporter yourself. Listening to you now, and seeing those lads who came into the pub, sort of put it in our minds.'

'Do you think so? Do you really think so? It's the writer in me, words seem to pop out willy-nilly.'

'Oh yes. You could have a career in that line. Great money to be made in the reporting business. Pity you didn't have a word with those newsmen. They could have given you a few pointers. Are they gone far?'

'I don't know, Mr O'Gorman.'

'It would be worth your while to talk to them about it. You could catch them up in no time. I'd say they would be only too delighted. They're always looking for new blood in the reporting world.'

'That's a wonderful idea, Mr O'Gorman, I think I might do that. I do have a lot of material I am sure would be of great interest to the public. Would you all forgive me if I dashed off?' Shantell addressed the ladies. 'Something important has cropped up that I must attend to.'

'Not at all, love. You work away. Don't let us keep you.'

'You are all so kind. We'll meet again very soon I promise. Goodbye everyone. Goodbye. Must fly.'

As soon as the door closed behind her everyone breathed a sigh of relief.

'A stroke of genius, Mr O'G. Well done.'

'Very well done, Mr O'Gorman,' said Matt, 'but you are all leaving now anyway. You've had enough. I am not going to be responsible for pensioners getting pissed on my premises. Finish up now.'

'Jesus, Matt. After all that.'

'Carmel, it's Shantell. I was hoping to catch you in this time. You seem to be as busy as I am these days. I have had a wonderful day and I wanted to share it with you. I have been visited by the most amazing revelation and naturally I want you to be among the first to know. It means putting a few things on hold for the moment, but it feels so right, so destiny. Don't think I am mad but I have discovered my true kismet. "Slow down, Shantell. Start at the beginning," I can hear you saying. I know you Carmel. You are the one person who understands me. It's such a comfort to know I can always rely on you. You were the one who always had your feet planted firmly on the ground.

'I attended a little afternoon soirée with some close friends – champagne, finger food, you know the sort of thing. I was only there moments when a swarm of reporters descended on us. Questions, photographs, they were insatiable, they couldn't seem to get enough of me. Matt, our host, finally managed to get rid of them and eventually we were able to settle down. My friends were a little disconcerted at first, and for a moment thought that in some way I was responsible. I ask you, Carmel, is it my fault? Do I, or have I, ever courted fame? Anyway, it came to me in a flash as I talked with the reporters, I should write for the newspapers. I could turn my novels into weekly serials. People would buy the paper if only to be able to follow the adventures of my heroines. I would concentrate on one novel, send it off chapter by chapter, and then start a letters page inviting readers to write in and guess what was going to happen next. It would leave great scope to branch out into all sorts of areas. Do ring and tell me what you think. You know how I value your opinion.'

# Chapter Nineteen

'But Dr Walpole. I'm not ready to leave. I haven't told you everything.'

'I think we are quite up to date, Shantell. There is nothing further we need to know. We shall send our report to your solicitor and a copy will be forwarded to the clerk of court in time for your next appearance.'

'I can't be finished, Dr Walpole, I was getting so much from my sessions. I shall tell you the truth, doctor. I have the outline of a serious novel based on my mornings here. I need – in fact I *must* – continue.'

'We do have a lot of other patients to attend to, Shantell.'

'What if Judge Moore doesn't agree with your findings. Would I be able to stay on?'

'I think you'll find he will agree with our assessment.'

'May I see it?'

'That is impossible. Our files are confidential.'

'But not to me, Dr Walpole. Surely not to me. After all, I am the subject of those files.'

'That is our policy, Shantell.'

'Dr Walpole. If I don't see my file I shall have no recourse but to lodge a complaint. It is vital that I continue my sessions. Miss Titchmarch, my mentor – I haven't told you about Miss Titchmarch yet – she expressly states the importance of persistence. Persistence and perseverance. The two Ps imperative to the writer.'

'With all the novels you have on the go already, Shantell, I'm sure you don't need to start another one.'

'You obviously know nothing about the creative mind, Dr Walpole. I know if I was to give you a brief synopsis of my outline it would help to change your mind.'

'No. I'm afraid it wouldn't, Shantell.'

'I could jot it down for you.'

'No, Shantell.'

'Dr Pilkerton?'

'Dr Pilkerton feels exactly the same as I do. The court ordered six months' assessments and that time is now up. I'm sorry, Shantell, it's time to go. I have a waiting room full of patients. Patients who need my attention.'

'I regret having to say this, Doctor, but you shall be hearing from my solicitor.'


'Hello, David, it's Shantell. David, I must meet with you urgently. I need you to take a case for me. I wish to sue the Eastern Health Board. Please call me back the moment you get this message. I shall be at home all afternoon working on my novels, but do not be afraid to disturb me.'


'This is most unsatisfactory, David. First you tell me I

cannot sue Dr Walpole, though your reasoning is very suspect. I do not believe it would cost thousands of pounds or that I wouldn't have a chance of winning, and now you say I cannot come into court with you. Why can't I come with you?'

David Shield-Knox and Shantell were sitting in a small coffee-shop beside the courthouse. It was ten fifteen a.m. and Shantell's appearance in court was scheduled for ten forty-five. David had exhausted himself trying to explain to Shantell why he had refused to take her case against Dr Walpole. He had ignored her phone calls, presuming it was either a whim or perhaps she had had a little too much to drink, foolishly thinking she would forget about it, and that she would realise that suing a government health board was not something to be taken on lightly. Now he had a headache and he was anxious to get away.

'I don't understand. It's my appearance.'

'It's a private hearing, Shantell. You don't physically appear. As your legal representative I shall be there for you. The judge will have a copy of your assessments and will make a decision whether you stand trial for impersonation or not. I have read the file and I feel confident he will throw the case out of court.'

'But I was looking forward to it. I wanted to report myself for the newspapers. I won't interfere.'

'I'm afraid it's not possible, Shantell.' David did not tell her about the letter from Mr Toner, Judge Moore's clerk, requesting, in the strongest terms, that Shantell did not appear. He had no intention of exasperating the situation. His employer had issued words on the subject. 'Say nothing. Accept the judge's

224

decision and get out of there as quickly as possible. Your career in this office rests on this, David. One hint of publicity and you may pack your briefcase. I have seen this woman's assessments – the judge is not going to take this to trial. In and out, David.'

'It doesn't seem fair, David.'

'Don't worry, try to relax, it won't take long. I must go, Shantell, it wouldn't do to be late.'

'You will be sure to tell the judge I wish to continue with my assessments?' David busied himself with his briefcase. 'David?'

'I'll do all I can.'

'I shall wait here for you, David. I shan't leave this spot until I know my fate.'


'Hello, Rosie. It's Shantell. I'm phoning from a café. I'm waiting for David. . . . Yes, David. Today is the big day. I have my court appearance . . . No, I don't actually appear which seems very strange. David appears for me, he's gone in there now . . . Yes. I am on my own. I thought everyone would be here, the whole gang . . . Don't worry, dear, I'm fine. It is a bit nerve-racking but I have my notebooks with me and I am sure the time will fly . . . Would you, Rosie, that would be wonderful. It's called The Quill's Rest, yes, on the river beside the courthouse. I'll see you shortly then.'


'Another coffee please, waitress. I am waiting for a friend. I should really be in court but my solicitor didn't want to put me through the stress. He is wonderful like that. So thoughtful and sensitive. David Shield-Knox. You probably know him. You must get a lot of solicitors in here being beside the court. You couldn't miss him. He is very distinguished.'

'Will that be all, miss?'

'Nothing else thanks.'

'One pound twenty please.'

'It's a very nice place you have here, so near the river. Quite inspirational. One could feel a muse coming on.'

'Could you pay me, miss? I haven't got all day. I do have other customers.'

'I can see how busy you are, don't let me detain you. I worked as a waitress once. I know what it's like with chatty customers when you want to get on. It wasn't nearly as attractive as here though. Our chef was temperamental, very difficult to work with. He and I didn't click. A personality conflict you might say. Do you get on with your chef? Please don't think I'm being nosy. I am a novelist you see. A novelist and poet, so naturally I am interested in talking to everyone I meet. Getting background information is material, so to speak.'

'Mr O'Donoven, you better get out here. There's a woman putting us in a book.'

'Nothing of the sort. I am not putting you in my book, I'm merely saying . . . What do you mean you are not serving me? I must wait here. I'm expecting a friend any minute. There is really no need to take that attitude. I am entitled to have my coffee. I have paid for it. My solicitor will be returning shortly and I am sure he knows the legalities of paying for coffee and not being allowed to drink it . . . No I do not want it in a takeaway cup. I insist on having it in here.'

'Rosie. Rosie, here I am.'

'Shantell, what are you doing sitting on the wall with your coffee? I thought you were going to wait for me in The Quill's Rest.'

'It is so beautiful by the river I couldn't bear sitting in there any longer.'

'Let's go back inside. It's freezing out here.'

'We'll find somewhere else, Rosie. Somewhere we can chat in private.'

'I thought you had to wait for David?'

'We can leave a message for him at the court telling him where we've gone.' Shantell linked Rosie's arm. 'Now then, I want all your news. How are the gang? How is Fionn? You can tell me as we walk along.'

Mr Toner stopped short when he saw Shantell at the doorway of the courthouse. He had stepped out of the courtroom only moments before to give some papers to the porter. A split second later and she might have appeared in front of Judge Moore. That idiot Shield-Knox had been told to make sure she didn't appear. Mr Toner knew he would get it in the neck if the judge so much as laid eyes on her. She was approaching the porter's desk.

'Excuse me. I need to leave a message for David Shield-Knox, my solicitor. He is appearing for me today.'

'Mr Shield-Knox is in court number four, miss.'

'Is it all right to go in?'

'What's your name, miss?'

'Shantell O'Doherty.'

The porter checked his lists. 'Here you are miss. The state versus O'Doherty, Judge Moore, room four, ten forty-five.'

'Will we go in, Rosie? We could stay at the back. No one would notice.'

'I don't think we should, Shantell. David would have said if he'd wanted you there.'

'Could we go in?' Shantell asked the porter.

'Jimmy.' Mr Toner was at the desk. 'A word, Jimmy.'

'It's that nice Mr Toner,' Shantell said. 'Judge Moore's aide. Hello Mr Toner. Do you remember us?'

Mr Toner had his back to her and was having a hurried, whispered, conversation with the porter.

'I think we should go, Shantell,' Rosie said. 'This doesn't feel right.'

'Nonsense. Mr Toner is probably clearing the way for us. Smile at him, Rosie, be friendly.'

Mr Toner turned abruptly, nodded to Shantell and Rosie, and strode back to the courtroom.

'Well?' Shantell asked the porter. 'What did he say? Is it okay for us to go in?'

'I'm afraid you can't go in, ladies. Judge Moore's cases are being held in camera this morning.'

'In camera?' Shantell said. 'Oh but that's wonderful. There is no problem then. I know all the reporters and cameramen intimately. They will be delighted to see us.'

'There are no reporters, miss, or cameramen.'

'You mean it's being televised with one of those hidden cameras?'

'No, miss. I mean it's private. The public are excluded.'

'What sort of idiots do you take us for? Honestly, Rosie, he is trying to tell us it's in camera but it's private.'

'It's a legal term, Shantell.'

'What is your name, sir?'

'Why do you want my name?'

'I intend to write a letter protesting about your legal terms. I had my suspicions before but now I am convinced that legalese is specially designed to confuse the public.'

'I will have to ask you to leave, miss.'

'Let's go, Shantell, before we get into trouble. How long do you think the case will take?' Rosie asked.

'There's no saying, miss.'

'We'll go, Rosie, but we will be back.' Shantell glanced at the porter as they left the building.

'You shouldn't get so upset, Shantell.'

'I know, Rosie, I know. But we must be on our toes at all times. We must fight injustice everywhere.'

'Where are we going, Shantell? We have to leave a message for David.'

'In the heat of the moment I forgot about him. I don't know, Rosie, it could be a long wait. What do you suggest?'

'We could go to Tower Heights. I still have a key for Gran's flat.'

'That's a wonderful idea. I'll jot down the address for David.'

Ivy Simpson had stepped out on to the balcony to throw the fire rug over the rail for a freshen-up. She nearly went over with it when she saw Rosie and Shantell approaching the flats. 'Martin. Martin,' she roared, thumping on his window. 'Get out here quick, Martin. You're not going to believe this.' Squinting in through the glass, she could just make him out, dozing in his chair in front of the telly. 'Martin come here.' She scuttled across to Dolores's flat. 'Open up.

They're coming up to the flats.' She ran up and down the balcony alerting all the neighbours.

Martin opened his door. 'What the hell is going on, Ivy? Have you finally flipped?'

'It's her,' Ivy said, gasping for breath from her exertions. 'She's coming up in the lift.'

'Who?'

Ivy, hand clutching chest, could only gesture. She waved towards the lift.

'Do you need a doctor?'

'Ivy. What's the matter?'

'What is it, Ivy?'

One by one the pensioners came out of their flats. 'Are you all right, girl?'

'Shantell is coming. I saw her downstairs.'

'Don't be daft, woman.'

'It's true. She's with Rosie. They're in the lift.'

'Quick. Inside everyone. Close your doors and don't make a sound.'

'What are they doing here?'

'Rosie might be collecting some of her gran's things.'

'Why would she bring that one with her?'

'Stop speculating and get in. The lift is nearly here.'

'Come in with me, Dolores,' Ivy said. 'We can see better from my flat.'

'I'm coming too,' Lily said. 'I'm not staying on my own.'

'And me.'

'And me,' the rest of the ladies chorused, as they all crept into Ivy's flat.

Shantell and Rosie emerged from the lift on the fourth floor.

'This was such a good idea of yours, Rosie. I almost feel at home here.'

'It feels very strange, Shantell, coming here knowing that Gran is . . . that she is gone.'

'She is not gone, Rosie. No one is ever gone, Rosie. They are always with us.'

'That's creepy, Shantell.'

'No, Rosie, you are wrong. I read the most wonderful book on the subject. It said that a part of everyone remains behind, that if we reach out we can touch that part. Why I can feel your granny now. Her presence is all around us.'

'Stop, Shantell. You are making me nervous.'

'It is very quiet,' Shantell said, as Rosie opened the door to the flat. 'I seem to remember this place as bustling with people. Where is everyone?'

The flat was spare and spotless. 'It feels a bit damp, Shantell. I suppose because no one's been here for a while.' Rosie moved around lifting sheets that were draped around the furniture and folding them away. She opened the windows and then plugged in an electric fire that was sitting in the grate. 'All Gran's bits and pieces are gone. They're packed away. It doesn't feel like her place any more.'

'What about some tea? That would cheer us up a bit. I'll put the kettle on.' Shantell bustled into the kitchen. 'There is no milk, Rosie,' she called out from the kitchen. 'Can you get some milk?'

'I'll get some from Ivy.'

'Ivy. Are you in there?' Rosie knocked lightly at Ivy's flat. 'I want to borrow some milk.'

'Shush. Someone's at the door.' Lily, who had been sitting near the door was the first to hear the knock.

'Don't say a word.'

The ladies froze in their seats.

'What'll we do?'

'Don't answer it.'

'Ivy,' Rosie called again. 'It's Rosie. I need to borrow some milk.'

'We can't leave her out there. She only wants milk.'

Ivy opened the door a few inches. 'Hello, Rosie.'

'Ivy. Could I borrow some milk? There is tea in Gran's, but no milk. Is there something the matter, Ivy? Aren't you well?'

'Wait here,' Ivy hissed and shut the door tight. 'Get some milk from the fridge, quick,' she ordered Dolores. 'I'll pass it out to her.'

She opened the door again and pushed a small jug through the crack.

'Here you are.'

'Thanks, Ivy. I'll pop the jug back in a few minutes.'

'No don't. Keep it. I have loads of them.'

'Ivy? Are you sure you are all right? You look pale as a ghost.'

'What are you doing here, Rosie?'

'We, Shantell and I – Shantell is waiting for the result from the court. David is there now. I couldn't let her wait on her own, Ivy, it wouldn't be right. I didn't think it was a good idea to wait around in town so we came here. Would you like to come into Gran's and have some tea?'

'No thanks, love. I have the kettle on here.'

'Who's in there with you?'

'No one.'

'I can hear something.'

'It's the cat.'

'I thought you didn't like cats?'

'I'm minding it for a friend. I have to close the door, Rosie. She might get out.'

'I'm worried about Ivy, Shantell. She's acting very strange.'

'Did you tell her I was here? Is she coming in for tea?'

'No. She's minding a cat.'

'Tell her to bring it in. We can help her mind it.'

'I don't think she will.'

'Of course she will. You pour while I go and get her.'

'She's gone,' Ivy said. 'I won't be the better of that for ages.'

'What's going on? What did she say?'

'They're waiting for the result of the court case. Rosie didn't want your woman to be on her own so she brought her here.'

'She's too kind for her own good, young Rosie. Just like her granny.'

'I feel very bad closing the door on her like that.'

'We have to protect ourselves, Ivy.'

'How will I face Rose Deignan when I meet her in Heaven if I closed the door on her granddaughter?'

'Don't worry, Ivy. You won't be meeting her.'

'Why not?'

'They don't let the likes of you into Heaven.'

'Very funny, Dolores.' Ivy thought for a moment. 'I'll have to go in. I'll bring a few biscuits in with me and have a quick cup of tea. Wait here for me. I won't stay a minute.'

Ivy opened her door to find Shantell standing there, fist raised, about to knock.

'Jesus Mary and Joseph.' Ivy jumped back in fright.

'Hello, Ivy. It's me. Shantell. May I come in?' Shantell waved into the room. 'Hello. How nice. You're all here. Rosie's made tea next door. Do come and have some. Come along, I won't take no for an answer. Quickly now before it gets cold. Oh and Ivy, bring your cat.'

'Cat?' Dolores looked at Ivy.

'Come on everyone.' Shantell held the door open and the ladies meekly followed each other out.

'Look what I found, Rosie. Come in, come in. Don't stand on ceremony. We know each other too well for that. More cups, Rosie, it's a party.'

Martin Duffy peeped out his sitting room window. 'What the—?' He saw the ladies file one by one into Rose Deignan's flat. What were they doing? What the hell were they up to now? He lifted the phone but then thought better of it. He'd keep out of it. None of his business. He turned up the volume on the telly to stop himself from trying to listen through the wall of the flat. Stupid. That's what they were, getting involved with that woman again. Well, he was having no part of it. They needn't come to him when things got out of hand. He pressed his remote control and lowered the sound. Nothing. Good. Keep it that way. No shrieks or moans coming from next door. He settled back to watch the telly.

'Are you cold, Lily?' Rosie asked. 'I saw you shivering.'

'No, love. It's probably someone walking over my grave.'

The ladies sipped their tea while Shantell beamed from one to the other. No one said a word.

'Do you still go to bingo, Dolores?' Rosie asked in an effort to break the silence.

'The odd time, Rosie. It's not as much fun as it used to be.'

'Gran used to like bingo. I went with her once or twice.'

'You'd miss her, wouldn't you, sitting here like this. It's like she only went to the shops and she'll be back any minute.'

'We all have to go sometime.'

'Don't start getting morbid, Lily. You know what you are like once you start.'

'It feels like I was only talking to her yesterday.'

'Lily.'

'No, Dolores. There's times, I swear to God, I feel she's still here.'

'But she is,' Shantell said. 'She is still here. I was only saying the same to Rosie, the dead are never gone. I read this wonderful book on the subject. It explains how, if we really concentrate, we can communicate with our departed loved ones.'

'You mean they're not dead?'

'No, Lily. I mean we can talk to their spirits. The spirits never leave.'

Martin couldn't relax. He got up from his chair and put his ear to the wall adjoining his and Rose Deignan's flat. Nothing. Not a word. Normally, when the cronies gathered in the flat, he could hear them. The cackling and the chattering came through the wall. He went into his kitchen, got a tumbler from the cupboard, and brought it back to the sitting room.

This is stupid, he told himself. What do I care what they are doing? He pressed one end of the tumbler against the wall and put his ear to the other end but he still couldn't hear a thing. Bloody movies, he muttered to himself. I knew this trick never worked. He put the glass down and phoned Mick O'Toole.

'Mick. It's Martin.'

'How's it going, Martin?'

'Shut up and listen to me. I want you to walk past Rose Deignan's flat, see if you can hear anything, and then come on into me.'

'What am I to hear?'

'For the love of Christ, Mick. I don't know what you are going to hear, that's why I want you to listen. There's something funny going on in there.'

'Funny like what?'

'If I knew like what would I ask you to listen?'

'Okay, okay. Keep your hair on. Let me get this straight. I'm to walk down the balcony, stop and listen at Rose's, and then go into you.'

'Right.'

'When? When do you want me to do it?'

'Now. Do it now, and Mick, be discreet. Don't make yourself obvious.'


'If we perform this correctly I am sure we can contact the other side.' The ladies were all sitting in a circle around Rose Deignan's table, listening to Shantell's instructions. 'On the count of three I want everyone to lift their arms and hold the hand of the person on either side of them. Then, slowly, bring the hands forward on to the table. Do not for a moment lose touch. This is absolutely vital. I will chant and you must repeat the word, "incantare", at every pause.

Has anyone any questions before we begin? Yes, Ivy?'

'Why do you have a tablecloth over your head and we don't?'

'In order to retain my electricity, Ivy. According to the book, the medium, that's me, must cover her head to retain the electricity. When the beings arrive we must let them know that we are friendly. A shock of any sort would be detrimental. All your electricity will be channelled through to me and I will retain it under the tablecloth. That way we can control it. We need the energy to summon the beings but it must not come out in spurts or shock waves which might be frightening to our departed friends. Are we ready to begin?'

'I need to go to the toilet,' Lily said apologetically. 'I always have to go before I start anything.'

'Very well, Lily, but do hurry on. Does anyone else need to go? We cannot interrupt the session once we have made contact.'

All the ladies, apart from Rosie and Shantell, got up from the table and headed for the tiny bathroom.

'Shove over, Dolores. I can't get in.'

'We won't all fit.'

'I'm not staying out here on my own.'

'Put the lid down and sit on it. That'll make more room. I'll stand in the shower.'

'Shush. She'll hear you.'

'That was very clever of you, Lily. Giving us a chance for a powwow.'

'But I do really have to go.'

'What are we going to do?' Dolores wondered. 'I only went along with the seance business thinking she was joking, but now, listen to her, she's taking it serious.'

'Maybe she is a medium,' Peggy said. 'You never know with those people.'

'My backside, Peggy. Like she was an undertaker?'

'All the same, Dolores, I still think she might be. She has some strange ways about her. I'd hate to think I was passing up a chance to talk to my Eugene.'

'You didn't talk much to your Eugene when he was alive. Why wait twenty odd years for a chat?'

'That's not very kind, Dolores.'

'Peggy. She is not a medium. She's not even a minimum. Now give over. Has anyone any suggestions?'

'We could get out the door. Make a run for it.'

'I'm not leaving Rosie alone with that woman,' Lily said. 'I owe it to Rose Deignan. Young Rosie is far too susceptible. What if she thinks she hears her granny, what'll that do to her?'

'The best thing to do is play along with it for a while. Make a laugh out of it. If Shantell thinks we're laughing at her she'll soon stop. You lot distract Shantell for a few moments and I'll have a quick word with Rosie. Put her in the picture. She's a sensible girl. I don't think she would fall for too much nonsense out of your woman. I nearly got a fit of the giggles when she put the tablecloth over her head. Keeping in her electricity, did you ever. Come on. We'll go back in. Don't forget, play along with whatever she says, and it'll be over in no time.'

'I'll follow you in,' Lily said. 'I still have to go.'

Mick O'Toole opened his hall door and looked up and down the balcony. All clear. He was wearing a dark overcoat, a cap and sunglasses, and he had kept on his slippers to minimise the noise. He whistled as he stepped out and sidled along to number 147. When he reached the flat he stooped down, under the window, and craned his neck upwards. He could hear some sort of noise coming from inside but he couldn't make out what it was. It wasn't the sound of people talking, or a television or radio. He strained up a little more. No good. He would have to get nearer. He stood up at the side of the window and leaned inwards towards the glass. He could make out figures sitting around a table. They were all holding hands. The one at the end looked a bit peculiar with some sort of turban on its head. A foreigner? The foreigner started some sort of low chant and then the others joined in. What were they doing? He pressed his nose to the glass.

'My friends, we will begin.' Shantell signalled for quiet. 'Heads down and eyes closed everyone. Concentrate. Remember, on the count of three, start with the arms. One. Two. Three. Hmmmmm . . .' She emitted a low humming sound which she kept up until all the hands were joined on the table. Waiting a moment or two, she opened her eyes wide, threw her head up facing the ceiling, and began to chant. 'Spirits of our dear departed loved ones, come to us.'

The ladies looked up in surprise.

'Response,' Shantell hissed, keeping her head in the air. 'Response.'

'Incantare,' the ladies warbled.

'Spirits of our dear departed loved ones, appear before us.'

'Incantare.'

'Spirits of our dear departed loved ones, manifest yourselves.'

'Incantare.'

Dolores let go of Ivy's hand and reached for a book that was on a shelf behind her. She began waving it under the table.

'Spirits of our dear departed . . . I can feel something. I can feel a presence. Come, we are your friends.'

'Incantare.'

Peggy opened one of her eyes and peeked out. She saw Mick O'Toole against the window.

'Look. At the window,' Peggy screamed. 'It's the devil. I saw the devil.'

'Calm down, Peggy. Take it easy. It was only a shadow.'

'It wasn't a shadow. I saw it. It had big black holes for eyes and the nostrils were flaring.'

'Ladies. Ladies. We mustn't break the spell. That was probably an Indian come to show the others the path.'

'It was no Indian,' said Peggy. 'It was the devil.'

'Peggy get a grip. If Shantell says it was an Indian, it was an Indian.'

'But, Dolores, I did—' Peggy caught Dolores's wink.

'Oh. Oh I see,' Peggy said, thinking Dolores had set something up. 'Well now you say it maybe there was a – feather?'

Mick O'Toole charged down to Martin's flat.

'Let me in. Let me in quick.' Martin was at the door waiting for him. 'Jesus, Martin. They nearly had me. Lucky I wore my disguise.'

'That's a disguise? What are you supposed to be? Never mind, don't tell me, I don't want to know. What did you find out? What are they up to?'

'It's some sort of seance. They're all sitting round a table, holding hands, and chanting some sort of gobbledegook.'

'I can smell trouble brewing, Mick. We'll have no peace until we get that Shantell out of the flat and off the estate entirely.' Martin got out the telephone book, looked up public houses. 'We're nipping this in the bud, Mick. The people who brought her here in the first place can be responsible for removing her, or the next thing you know she'll be moved in, lock, stock, and the whole fruit and nut.' He found the number he wanted and dialled it. 'Hello, is that Matt? This is Martin Duffy here from Tower Heights. Is Tom O'Gorman there by any chance?'

'He's here beside me, Martin. Hold on a second, I'll put him on. Mr O'Gorman,' Matt called over the counter. 'Telephone call for you. It's Martin.'

'Martin. Thank God it's you. I thought for a minute it was the missis. How are you doing? Are you coming in for a pint?'

'I need you to get over here right away, Tom.'

'Why? What's up?'

'It's Shantell. She's holding a seance in Rose Deignan's flat. You'll have to come and get her out.'

'What?'

'You know how this will end, Tom, I don't have to spell it out. Those old ones will go bananas and start seeing their dead husbands and before you know it the place will be in uproar. We'll have the police on our hands again, not to mention the parish priest.'

'What do you want me to do?'

'I don't care what you do. Just get her out of here.' Martin hung up.

'Matt. Give me change for the phone, quick. Where

did I put that . . .' Mr O'Gorman rooted through his
pockets. '. . . Here it is.' He took out a card with a taxi
number on it. 'Is that Ace cabs? I need a taxi. I'm
going to Orchardstown. Could you get me Malachy
Conway. Yes. He's a mate. I'd rather have him, he
knows the area. How long? That's okay. I'll wait for
him.'

'Oh spirit of the departed loved ones. Who do you
wish to talk to?'

'Incantare. What's that noise?'

'My mobile. My mobile phone is ringing. Where's
my bag? It's there beside you, Ivy. Quickly, pass it to
me before it rings off.'

'I thought we weren't supposed to let go our hands.'

'Never mind that now, Ivy.' Shantell grabbed her
handbag and got out the mobile. 'Hello, Shantell
O'Doherty here . . . David, it's you. It's David.'
Shantell cupped the phone to speak to the ladies. 'I'd
almost forgotten about you. What a long time you've
been. The judge must have been very interested in my
case to take so long. How did it go? Am I to be
reassessed? . . . No. I am not alone. I'm with my
friends here in Tower Heights. We are in the middle
of a seance, actually . . . No, don't ring back, you are
not disturbing anything, the departed are not going
anywhere. I must know what the judge said . . . But
why can't you tell me on the phone? What do you
mean, delicate?' Shantell cupped the phone again. 'He
says it's too delicate to discuss over the phone. He
wants to meet me. Yes, David I know it, but wouldn't
it be nice to pick that pub we had our reunion in . . .
Of course I shall be guided by you. The Liffey Crest,
four thirty, this afternoon. Yes I have that. I'll see you

there. Goodbye, goodbye, David.' Shantell pressed the off-key and put down the mobile. 'Isn't this exciting. I can't wait to hear what the judge had to say. I have to go. I am sorry but, you do understand, this is so important. You will have to continue without me.'

'What about the spirits?' Dolores said. 'We can't leave them hanging around.'

'We don't know what to do.'

'When you make contact explain the situation. Tell them I had to cancel. Tell them something urgent came up which compelled me to leave, and say that I will return as soon as possible. Who would like to take the mantle in my absence? Ivy? Dolores?' Shantell looked round the table. 'Peggy. I am drawn to you. I can feel you are at one with the spirits. Take the cloth and place it over your head.'

'You have plenty of time yet,' Peggy stalled. 'You're not meeting David until half past four. Could you not go on a bit more?'

'My spirit would be restless, Peggy. They would not appear to a restless spirit. Take the cloth, Peggy. Do not be nervous. It is a noble call.'

'Mick. There's a taxi on the way to collect Shantell. I'll wait here for it, you go into Rose Deignan's and break up that session before it gets out of hand.'

'I will not.'

'You have to, Mick. The only way to get her out is to have her driven off. Do you want her in there permanently? I know her sort. She'll get round those women with her seance and persuade them to get the council to give her the flat. That's what this is all about.'

'She wouldn't be entitled to it.'

'No, but Rosie would. The flat can pass to a relation. Rosie could get it and the next thing, Bob's your uncle, she'll have a flatmate. Then Rosie goes off and marries Fionn and who gets left in the flat?'

'What'll I say?'

'You were never lost for words, Mick O'Toole. You'll think of something. Now go on. Don't worry. I'll be here and, as soon as the cab arrives, I'll come and get you.'

'Why don't you go in, Martin? I can stay here and wait for the taxi.'

'They'd be suspicious if I went in. They'd know something was up.'

'And what about me? Don't think they won't be suspicious about me.'

'You often drop in, Mick. It won't be unusual for you.'

'I dropped in to Rose Deignan's flat when she was alive. Do you not think it might be odd that I'm dropping in now that she's dead?'

'Will you stop making difficulties, Mick.'

'I'll go. I know I'm going to regret it, but I'll go.'

'You'll regret it more if you don't. Keep thinking of having Shantell as a neighbour. Half an hour, at the most, Mick. Stall them for half an hour.'

'Hello, ladies. Good afternoon, ladies.' Mick rehearsed his entrance. 'I thought I'd drop in.'

'That's the spirit, Mick.'

'What about a nice cup of tea?' Martin opened the hall door for him. 'Nice day for a neighbourly visit.'

'Mick. Take off the sunglasses. You don't want them getting the wrong idea.'

Malachy Conway pulled up outside the pub and went

in to collect Mr O'Gorman. He was none too pleased to be on this job but he couldn't refuse it. The boss himself had given him the run. 'Good PR, Malachy, when customers ask for a driver by name. Means you're doing a good job.'

'There better be no messing,' Malachy said aloud as he went in.

'Malachy, the man.' Mr O'Gorman spotted him immediately. 'Have you time for a pint?'

'I have not and if you want the cab you'll have to come straight away.'

'I'm ready, I'm ready. Two swallows. and I am yours.'

'Why did you have to ask for me? There's twenty drivers in the fleet. Any of them could have done as well as me.'

'I needed someone who knows the situation.'

'What situation?'

'I'll fill you in on the way.' The two men left the pub. 'Don't look like that, Malachy. It's straightforward enough. We zap around to Tower Heights, collect Shantell, drop her off at her home.'

'Where does she live?'

'I've no idea.'

'It had better be that simple. I nearly lost my licence over you lot. I'm not taking that chance again.'

'Don't worry, Malachy, there's nothing to it. It's a fare, nothing more, I promise.'

Mick O'Toole stood outside Rose's flat looking at the front door. It wasn't that he was superstitious, it was more a case of keeping his options open. If they were having a seance in there, meeting the dead, well, anyone would hesitate, wouldn't they. Martin was out on the balcony. He was shaking his fist, demonstrating knocking on the door, and mouthing at Mick to go in. All very well for him, big know-all that he is, thought Mick, he isn't risking anything. Mick shrugged at Martin and tapped lightly on the door.

'It's Mick O'Toole,' Peggy said. 'I can see him through the curtains.'

'What does he want?'

'You might as well let him in, Peggy. We're finished with our seance now.'

'Well, Mick. What do you want? Who sent you?'

'Thank you, Peggy. May I say that that table cloth on your head really becomes you. Good afternoon, ladies. I thought I'd drop in. It's a nice day for a neighbourly visit. What about a cup of tea?'

'Are you drunk or what, Mick O'Toole? You never paid a neighbourly visit in your life.'

'Excuse me, Dolores. I was a frequent visitor to this flat. Rosie will tell you. Tell them, Rosie. Didn't I used to call on your granny on a regular basis.'

'Probably to scrounge something,' said Dolores. 'We know you.'

'Come and sit down, Mick,' Rosie said. 'He did used to call,' she said to the ladies. 'He often popped in to keep Gran company.'

'There, you see, I told you. So what's going on here? Is it a month's mind or what?'

'We're having a seance,' Peggy said. 'That's why I'm wearing the mantle. The spirits were drawn to me. Ouch. What did you dig me for, Ivy?'

'A seance, eh? Very interesting. And where's your medium?'

'She's in the toilet. She's getting ready to go and meet David.'

'Peggy. Will you keep your big trap shut.'

'It's not a secret, Dolores. There's nothing wrong in having a seance. I've been chosen to take over as the medium while she is gone, Mick. Would you like to join in?'

'No thanks. Maybe another time. So Shantell is leaving?'

'We just told you she was. Why do you want to know anyway? What's it to you?'

'Nothing. I'm only making conversation.'

'Oh no you are not. You're fishing. I can smell it.'

'If that's what you think, I'm off. I'm not staying where I'm not wanted.'

'You are going nowhere, Mick O'Toole. You wanted tea and tea you are going to get. We'll find out the real reason you came snooping around here.'

'I have to go.'

'Stay where you are.'

Shantell emerged from the bathroom. 'Mr O'Toole. How nice to see you. Have you come to join our little coven? It's always good to have a man in the circle, it creates a different sort of vibe. Unfortunately I have to go but I am sure the ladies here are more than capable of continuing without me. We did reach an Indian. Well, to be honest Peggy did, that's why the mantle has passed to her. It takes a very special kind of person to open the way. How do I look?' Shantell gave Mick a dazzling smile, wrinkling the layers of foundation and eyeliner she had applied in the bathroom. 'I'm going to meet David and I want to look well. Men do like make-up on a woman don't they, Mr O'Toole. Be honest. Tell me the truth. How do I look?'

'You look, eh, stunning, miss. A real eye-catcher.'

'"Miss"? Heavens, Mr O'Toole, call me Shantell.

You mustn't be so formal. I must tell you I think David has taken rather a shine to me. He insisted on us meeting when he could have given me the news over the phone. He thinks I don't know. You men are all alike when it comes to matters of the heart. Silly young rascal. I'm far too old for him.' Shantell paused, waiting for denials from the group.

'You're as young as you feel,' Mick stammered gallantly. 'Isn't that right.'

'Dolores. I do believe I have time for a quick cuppa before I go. I would hate Mr O'Toole to think I had no manners at all, especially as he went out of his way to join us.' Shantell sat herself down, wriggling into the sofa beside him.

'How is your young man, Rosie?' Mick turned to Rosie, shifting his seat as far away from Shantell as he could. 'Made any plans yet?'

'Fionn has asked me down to Kerry to meet his mother. I don't want to go but I suppose I'll have to.'

'I don't envy you that, Rosie. She sounds like a bit of a tartar.'

'Fionn warned me. He said she wouldn't be too happy about us. She wants him to marry a country girl.'

'Does she now,' Dolores said. 'City girls not good enough for her.'

'He says to give her time to get used to the idea and she'll come round.'

'I could come with you, Martin,' Shantell said. 'After all, Fionn and I did have a special relationship for a bit.'

'What sort of a special relationship?'

'More tea, anyone?' Dolores hovered with the teapot. 'You'd be better off going on your own, love.

The woman would only get the wind up if you brought people with you.'

'And would you go to live in Kerry, Rosie?'

'I don't know. We haven't got as far as planning anything yet.'

'I wouldn't fancy living in Kerry,' Lily said. 'You can't see where you're going.'

'What are you on about, Lily?'

'They've no street lights. Can you imagine, no street lights?'

'What difference would that make to you? You never go out after dark as it is.'

'It's the principle, Ivy.'

'There's the door again,' Peggy said. 'There's someone else outside.'

'It's like Hueston Station in this place. Open up, Peggy. Let's see who we've got this time.'

Peggy opened the door wide to reveal Martin, Malachy and Mr O'Gorman standing in line on the threshold wearing ridiculous false smiles.

'Look what our seance threw up,' Ivy said. 'It's the three wise men.'

'Good afternoon, everyone. May we come in?'

'You knew they were coming, didn't you, Mick O'Toole,' Dolores said. 'What's going on? Why are they here?'

'Don't disturb yourselves, ladies,' said Mr O'Gorman. 'This is a flying visit. Malachy and myself were out for a bit of a spin and the car headed this way. We dropped into Martin here and, when he told us you were having a gathering, we thought it might be rude not to put our heads in and wish you the time of day. Correct me if I am wrong, but did I hear someone mention the word seance?'

'You did, Mr O'Gorman, and I am the stand-in medium,' Peggy said proudly. 'I am the one who saw the Indian.'

'An Indian, Peggy?'

'Yes. You see, when the spirits are coming they send an Indian angel on ahead to warn people to be ready. Shantell told us. I was picked by him. I'm the only one who saw him.'

'Shut up, Peggy. Do you want the man thinking you are daft?'

'But, Dolores, you said—'

'This is so disappointing,' Shantell said. 'You have just arrived and I have to go. I'm going to miss all the fun.'

'You're leaving?'

'I must. I have an appointment in town.'

Martin stood behind Mick and whispered, 'Why didn't you tell me she was leaving?'

'I couldn't. They wouldn't let me out.'

'This is your lucky day, Shantell. Malachy and I are heading back to town. We can drop you off. Save you waiting for a bus.'

'Would you? That would be wonderful. I said you were my heroes.'

'The meter's running, Mr O'Gorman,' Malachy said. 'We should get going.'

'Madam. Your chariot awaits.'

'Rosie. Are you coming with me?'

'Rosie's staying here,' Ivy said. 'We don't see enough of her. You will stay a bit, Rosie, won't you. We can go into my place and have a bit to eat. You can tell me more about Fionn and his ma.'

'Thanks, Ivy. I'd love to.'

'We'll be off then, ladies, if you've no objection.'

Mr O'Gorman winked at Martin as he whisked Shantell out the door. 'Talk to you soon, Martin. Goodbye everyone. Goodbye.' The door closed behind them.

'Well,' Ivy said to Martin. 'What was all that about?'

'I was doing my best, Ivy. I wasn't to know she was going anyway.'

'I can hardly believe it. Martin Duffy going out of his way to help us. This calls for more tea. Dolores, come out to the kitchen with me and give us a hand before his halo falls off,' Ivy said as she collected up all the dirty cups and brought them into the kitchen.

'Mick. Come on. Make a run for it while they are busy. If we stay here they'll have their claws into us for good.'

'Where are you two going?' Lily said. 'The girls are making something for you.'

'Tell them we had to go, Lily. We have to see a man about a horse.'

# Chapter Twenty

David Shield-Knox sat, waiting for Shantell, in the Liffey Crest. His plan had been to arrive early, sort out his paperwork and have everything prepared before he met her. There wasn't much to sort. Shantell's case had been over in minutes. Judge Moore had summed it up in several terse sentences. David took the file out of his briefcase and reread the transcript. 'In the case of Shantell O'Doherty. Having studied the report of Doctors Walpole and Pilkerton. It is my opinion that nothing will be served by a custodial sentence. However. Breaches of the peace as grave as Ms O'Doherty's must not go unpunished. I therefore recommend two hundred hours of community service to commence immediately. I suggest to you, Mr Shield-Knox, when you discuss this with your client, you will point out the court's leniency in the matter and issue a stern warning of the consequences to Ms O'Doherty if she should appear before me in the future.'

David had been ready for a battle. He had spent several hours the previous night preparing his case,

studying and dissecting the doctors' report, research-
ing cases which had involved assessments, and
bringing himself up to date with the judge's various
findings. He had allowed himself to daydream,
imagining the accolades of his fellows when they read
the banner headlines in the morning papers, 'Brilliant
Young Solicitor Saves Client.' His work had all been
for nothing. He never got a chance to speak. He
blushed as he remembered his only contribution to the
whole affair: 'Might I say, Your Honour—'

'You might not, Mr Shield-Knox. The case is
closed.'

His employer would want to see the transcript.
How was it going to look when all he said was,
'Might I say, Your Honour'? No stunning defence.
No lengthy reasoning or summing up. He felt he
might as well not have been there at all. And now he
had to face Shantell. David ordered himself a stiff
whiskey and sat gloomily over it. It wasn't too late for
a change of career. He was still young enough to take
up something else, go back to college, start again. He
wasn't cut out for this solicitor business. He glanced
at his watch. Shantell would be along in twenty
minutes.

As he drove back into town Malachy listened to
Shantell chattering away to Mr O'Gorman in the back
of the taxi. She was full of the court case and her
meeting with David. She tried to anticipate what the
judge might, or might not, have said, adding that she
was sure he would prolong her assessments once
David had explained how beneficial they had been to
her. She talked about her novels, her new found
powers as a medium, her friend Carmel and someone

called Miss Titchmarch. As she moved, effortlessly, from one subject to another, she appeared to have no conception of the fact that she could be facing a prison sentence.

Malachy glanced at her every now and then through his rear-view mirror, trying to fathom what made the woman tick. She wasn't mad. Odd perhaps. Eccentric might be the kinder word. She certainly had a way of stirring things up. Malachy had to admit if it had been someone else in the court, instead of himself, he would have found the whole thing very funny. When he told his mates at the rank about it they had thought it hysterical. He had been expecting sympathy, but he was wasting his time. Taxi drivers had their fair share of funny stories. His was voted the best.

As they neared the river, Malachy watched out for the Liffey Crest where he could deposit his passengers and make his escape. No way was he going to be drawn in again. He presumed Mr O'Gorman would go in with Shantell to meet David and that would be the end of his involvement. The trip to town had been uneventful and Malachy wanted to keep it that way.

'Here we are, folks. The Liffey Crest.'

'Well done, Malachy. What's the damage? What do we owe you?'

'It's on the house, Mr O'Gorman. My pleasure.'

'We must pay you something,' Shantell said. 'It wouldn't be fair.'

'Don't worry about it.'

'You are all so good to me. I will never forget it.' Shantell stepped out of the taxi, followed by Mr O'Gorman. 'Are you getting out here, Mr O'Gorman?'

'I'll come in with you, girl. Can't have you facing the music alone.'

'That's terribly sweet of you, Mr O'Gorman, but David wanted to meet me alone. I think he has something very personal to say to me and, well, you know how shy he is.'

'Enough said. I understand.'

'He told me it was a delicate matter. A matter he could only discuss with me in private.'

'Say no more, Shantell. We'll be off.'

'You're not hurt, Mr O'Gorman? Malachy?'

'Not at all,' Mr O'Gorman said as he sat in the front seat beside Malachy.

'I wasn't coming in anyway,' Malachy said. 'I am on duty for another while yet.'

'Goodbye dear friends. Don't worry. I will let you know how things are as soon as I can.'

'Where to, Mr O'Gorman? Where do you want me to drop you?'

'Where you picked me up, Malachy. Where you picked me up.'


Shantell stood on the pavement outside the Liffey Crest. She checked the time. Four twenty. She was early. This would not do at all. It would appear too eager. Shantell wanted to make an entrance and find David waiting anxiously for her. Men thought more of you if you were late. She knew that from experience. They would jump to their feet, brushing aside your apologies, grateful that you had arrived at all. She spotted a café further down the road. It would be a good idea to pop in there, have a coffee, and check her make-up. That way she would avoid the risk of bumping into David on the street. She got a window seat where she could watch the passers-by unobserved. As she sat down she felt a little tingling of excitement. There was no doubt about it, she thought, life had become so full since she started novelling. She got out her notebooks to record the tinglings. Shantell kept an alphabetical section at the back of one of them for emotions. It was an extremely useful index: when any of her heroines needed to display an emotion, she only had to look up her notebook and find the appropriate one. She opened it at 'T' and made an entry.

Shantell flicked through some pages but she couldn't settle down. She was too excited. Normally she wouldn't waste a moment – as soon as the notebooks came out, ideas flashed through her head immediately. No fear of writer's block for her. Quite the opposite. She took out her mobile phone. She really should ring Carmel. So many amazing things were happening it would be wrong to leave Carmel out.

'Hi, Carmel. It's Shantell. I thought I'd bring you up to date. When you get this message . . .'


'What do you think of her chances with David then?' Mr O'Gorman said to Malachy as they drove down towards O'Connell Street.

'She's barking up the wrong tree there. She'd have more chance with the judge.'

'I can't see her surviving in a prison.'

'It won't come to that. There's no room for the real criminals as it is. She'll get a reprimand, that's all. They'll hardly put her inside for a misdemeanour and, when you think of it, there was no real crime committed.'

'That judge will want revenge. You can't go upsetting a judge without it coming back on you.'

'He has to be impartial, Mr O'Gorman. That's his job.'

'Yea. And I'm Santa Claus.'

'I wouldn't worry too much. Shantell has a way of landing on her feet.'

'I hope you are right, Malachy. You can't help feeling . . . you know what I mean?'

'God's chosen, Mr O'Gorman, God's chosen. The Indians used to cherish people like that.'

'I hope they weren't from the same tribe as Peggy's Indians. Did you ever see the like, them and their seance? I'd love to have been a fly on the wall during that little to-do. Not that I'd have the courage. There is nothing more dangerous than a bunch of old ladies with a cause. They'd eat you alive.'

'Would you mind if I dropped you off here, Mr O'Gorman? You've only to walk down the lane. It'll save me trying to turn in this traffic.'

'Pull down the lane, Malachy, please. I don't want to be seen so near O'Connell Street in daylight. The wife's in town doing her bits of shopping and it'd be just my luck to walk straight into her.'

'You're a bloody nuisance, Mr O'Gorman, do you know that?' Malachy turned off the main road and stopped outside Hart's pub.

'Door to door. Now that's what I call service. I suppose you'll be busy now that it's coming up to rush hour.'

'Not really, Mr O'G. There is so much snarled up traffic, you'd have three city runs done, the time it takes you to get down O'Connell Street.'

'What time does your shift finish?'

'Six o'clock. I do six to six most days.'

'So if you were to knock off now you wouldn't be losing much business?'

'Oh no you don't. I know what you're at. You are not inveigling me into that pub.'

'Did I say a word? Did I say anything of the sort?'

'You are as bad as Shantell in your own way.'

'It would be frustrating though, not to hear how she got on, wouldn't it?'

'No.'

'Fair enough. I wouldn't press-gang a man into doing something he didn't want to do.'

'And I don't want to.'

'I was going to give her a ring on her mobile. If there is one thing I hate it's loose ends. I imagine you are the same yourself?'

'Damn it.'

'Does that mean what I think it means?'

'One pint. That's the limit.'

'I'll be the first man to hold you to that.'


'You're back, Mr O'Gorman,' Matt said as the two men entered the pub. 'You are a popular man today. There was another call for you.'

'Who was it?'

'Fionn O'Fiachra. He said to tell you he's on his way up from Kerry. He wants to see you to ask your advice about something. I told him you would probably be back so he's coming straight here off the train.'

'By the hokey,' Mr O'Gorman said. 'This is turning into an interesting day.'


The ladies of Tower Heights had regrouped in Ivy's

258

flat and were pumping Rosie for details of her engagement.

'But you hardly know him, Rosie.'

'I know he is the one, Ivy. I knew it the moment I saw him.'

'Isn't that so romantic,' Lily cried. 'It's like a fairy tale.'

'You don't know anything about him.'

'He could have filthy habits,' Dolores said. 'You never know until it's too late. My fellow had filthy habits. He used to—'

'That's enough of that, Dolores, thank you very much. He seems like a nice polite young man, Rosie.'

'I never felt this way about anyone before, Ivy. Does it always feel like this?'

'Dolores,' Ivy threatened, seeing Dolores about to speak. 'It's a wonderful thing, Rosie. If you feel that strongly about it, if you are sure, you have to follow your heart.'

'Oh, Ivy.' Lily got out her hankie and sobbed into it.

'Love is one thing, ladies,' Peggy said. 'But you have to be practical about it. You'll have to sit your young man down and talk everything through, Rosie. In our day we never talked. We groped in the back of the cinema. Went to each other's houses for tea on Sundays and walked down the aisle two years later. It was expected of you. Unless you had a bun in the oven. Then things got speeded up.'

'It's different now, Peggy, they're all living together first. Right and proper in my view. You're not trapped into marrying the first man who puts his hand up your frock.'

'Ivy.' Rosie reddened with embarrassment. It was

hard for her to imagine her gran's friends knowing anything about sex, let alone talking about it.

'She's right, love,' Dolores said. 'If I knew the things I found out about my man before we married I'd have stayed single.'

'Shut up, Dolores. We don't want to hear what you found out. We've enough memories of our own, thank you.'

'We better be coming to the wedding, Rosie.'

'If she doesn't invite us we'll gatecrash.'

'Ivy. What did Shantell mean when she said she had a special relationship with Fionn?'

'The Lord only knows, Rosie love. I wouldn't put any pass on it. You know yourself. The woman is away with the fairies.'


Shantell had delayed for what she felt was a fitting length, in the café. The all important moment had arrived. It was time to go and meet David. She finished her drink and went to check her make-up in the ladies' room. The mirror in the tiny cubicle was distorted. Perhaps a little more lipstick. She got out her new, anti-smear, Flower of the Jungle, and added an extra dash. Smack, smack, smack, her lips hit the mirror. It really did work. *Mr & Mrs David Shield-Knox*. Shantell could feel her heart fluttering as she spoke to her reflection. *Shantell Shield-Knox*. What a wonderful name for a book cover. David would be sure to ask her to dinner, and then? Shantell knew what might lead on from that. His place or hers. She had seen it so often in the movies she had lived for the moment it would happen to her. Her thoughts were interrupted by a knock on the toilet door.

'Are you going to be much longer in there?'

'I'm finished,' Shantell said, opening the door. 'Sorry to have kept you.' She squeezed past the woman waiting to go in, flashing her a bright, Flower-of-the-Jungle smile.

Shantell kept her smile all the way to the Liffey Crest. She wanted to dazzle David. To bowl him over. She would pause in the doorway, he would see her smile, and the stage would be set. David would be overwhelmed.

He missed her entrance. His head was down, looking through some papers, and he didn't see her come in. He looked up, suddenly, to find her standing over him.

'Shantell,' he said in surprise as if he had forgotten he had arranged to meet her. 'How nice to see you.'

'May I sit down?' Shantell deepened her voice.

'Please.' David waved, indicating the empty chair beside him.

Shantell was a bit piqued. David hadn't jumped up and held the chair for her and she had to struggle out of her coat unaided. It wasn't a good start.

'I have very good news for you, Shantell. The judge . . . Would you like a drink before we start? What will you have?'

'Something new, David. Something different and dangerous.'

David called the waiter over. 'Another whiskey for me, please, and the lady will have a . . . she wants something . . .'

'Tempt me with something, waiter, something exotic. What would you recommend?'

'We do a Manhattan, a Bloody Mary, a Tequila Sunrise, a Margarita.' The waiter rattled off his list of cocktails.

'Tequila Sunrise. The spirit of the Mexicans, distilled from tequilana, the dark brooding plant harvested round the pueblos by handsome swarthy men in their colourful blankets and their bandannas –' David and the waiter, gaped, open-mouthed. '– toiling under the hot Mexican skies.'

'A Tequila Sunrise then, miss?'

'Yes. Most definitely. Won't you join me, David? Throw caution to the wind and taste the sun-ripened nectar on this special day?'

'No thanks, Shantell. I'll have the whiskey.'

The waiter went back to the counter. 'A whiskey for the gent and a Tequila Sunrise for the bird at table four, Joe, please.'

'Odd looking bird.'

'She must work in advertising.'

'Shantell.'

'Yes, David.' Shantell gazed with such intensity into David's face that he didn't know where to look. He fidgeted with his briefcase, cleared his throat, and tried to begin.

'Let me relieve you of any anxieties first, Shantell, and tell you you are not going to prison. Judge Moore, very fairly in my opinion, applied leniency in your case.'

'Prison, David. There was never any question of prison. Poor darling, you are so addled by my presence you are mixing me up with one of your other clients.'

'Please, let me continue. You are not going to prison. The judge, after lengthy and deep consideration of your case, suggested a short term of community service would be more beneficial. It was difficult, Shantell. Judge Moore seemed determined to send you down but, with the support of your case assessment, my defence finally won the day. I have kept you a free woman, Shantell.'

'I don't want to be a free woman. No woman wants to be free.'

'Tequila Sunrise.' The waiter appeared at Shantell's elbow. 'And a whiskey for yourself, sir.'

'Women want to be chained by love, David. To feel the shackles of ardour to . . . I don't want you to keep me free.'

'That'll be five pounds twenty-nine, if you please, sir.'

'Shantell. I don't think you have been listening to me.'

'If you don't mind, sir. The five twenty-nine?'

'I have kept you out of prison, Shantell. You only have to do some community service and then the whole thing is forgotten. Judge Moore wanted me to stress—'

'Judge Moore, Judge Moore. Stop talking about Judge Moore. Don't you understand, David? I don't want to talk about Judge Moore or the silly court case. I only want to talk about us.'

'Us?' David gulped.

'You and I and our future together.'

'I won't have a future if you don't pay me,' the waiter said. 'I'm only on a week's trial here.'

'Trials, judges, what is this to me?' Shantell said. 'David. Make your declaration. Tell me the delicate matter you wished to discuss with me. Don't leave me dangling like this.'

'You're not the only one dangling, miss. I hate to interrupt but I have to have the money for the drinks.

I'm not allowed to leave the table without it, being as how I'm on trial and all.'

'Would you please pay this person, David. It's too much to have him here listening to us.'

'I'm so sorry.' David handed the waiter a ten-pound note which he promptly took to the bar. 'I didn't mean to keep you waiting,' David called after him.

'At last we are alone, David. We can talk in private.'

'That was a tough one, Joe. I thought they weren't going to pay me.'

'He doesn't look that type.'

'It's not him, it's her. She's not in advertising, she's been on trial. He got her off. Do you think she is a brasser?'

'No.'

'Well, she's done something. She has to do community work.'

'Amazing isn't it. They get off going to prison and then some poor unsuspecting community has to have them.'

'Shantell.' David gave her a nervous grin, reached for his whiskey, and took a large swallow. They had been warned about this in law school. Clients becoming infatuated with their counsel. He desperately tried to remember what had been said. It was something to do with dependency. 'A classic case of dependency,' the lecturer had droned. No one had listened or taken it seriously. 'It must be handled with sensitivity and kindness. Never let a situation occur where the client can claim they were led on. This can lead to complications and bring the profession into disrepute.

There is always a solution. A gentle way to extricate oneself. The correct wording at the right time can usually solve the problem.'

'Shantell. I asked you here, I wanted to meet you privately, because I, there is something I have to tell you.'

'Yes, David?'

'I'm gay.' David had no idea why he said it. He was desperate. He couldn't think of anything else. He let his disclosure sink in before continuing. 'You are the only one I can confide in.'

'Gay?'

'Yes, Shantell.'

David blinked a few times as if trying to contain his tears. He glanced across, slyly watching her expressions as she tried to grasp the significance of what he had told her. He waited a few moments and then slowly, when he felt the timing was right, he buried his face in his hands. Shantell was silent. She made no movement. She sat, stock-still, staring straight ahead of her. David felt he should add a little more. He let out a long sigh and, keeping one hand over his eyes, rooted out a handkerchief and blew his nose vigorously. The noise woke Shantell from her trance.

'I will have to go away. Away somewhere, where nobody knows me.'

'No, David. You must not do that. You must not give way to despair. I am here to help you. The fact that you have confided in me is a great honour. I will never betray your trust. Forgive me for misunderstanding. I should have been aware. As a writer I should have know how you were suffering. Suffer no more. From now on we shall be the closest of friends. Perhaps more than friends. David. I have just had the most marvellous idea. We could marry. Your secret would be for ever protected by that blessed sacrament.' David's nose-blowing got louder. 'We could live away from prying eyes. Brother and sister under one roof. No one need ever know. I could keep house for you while you are soliciting and help you entertain. We could have evenings for your colleagues, parties for your friends, I have quite a way with gays, it would be the perfect solution. Don't worry about children. We could adopt.'

'Would you excuse me, Shantell. I have to go to the men's room.'

'It's probably too much for you to take in right now, David dear. Go to the men's room. Calm yourself. I shall be waiting.'

David fled from his seat to the Gents, bolted himself into one of the cubicles, and sank down on the toilet seat. He had made things worse. What had possessed him to come up with such a story? He should have known better. What was he going to do? He couldn't stay in the Gents, Shantell would most probably come in after him, or send the waiter to get him. He had to get to a phone. Get help from someone. Who could he turn to for help? David's head started to throb. He didn't normally drink whiskey and it was beginning to have its usual effect on him. He groaned aloud as he realised he hadn't even explained the community service to Shantell. It was his responsibility. He was supposed to inform her and get her sent on to the relevant department without delay. He was due back at the office. It was all too much, it wasn't fair, everything seemed to happen to him. David blinked hard. This time he wasn't shamming. His tears were real.

*

'Excuse me, miss. Your friend's change.' The waiter put the money on the table.

'Young man. My friend is a little upset and has gone to the men's room. Would you follow him in and make sure he is all right?'

'No problem, miss.'

'Thank you. He is going through a difficult time.'

'You don't say.' The waiter feigned surprise although he had been listening to every word of the conversation.

'Don't let him know I asked you to go in.'

'Mum's the word, miss.'

'And, young man.' The waiter stopped in his tracks as Shantell called out to him across the floor. 'Please be kind to him. He's gay.'

David stepped out of the Gents in time to hear Shantell. He stood there, trapped, as every head in the Liffey Crest turned and looked at him. There was no going back. He stumbled back to his place at the table, picked up his briefcase, and went straight out the door.

'David, wait.' Shantell picked up her coat and her handbag. 'Don't rush away like this. David.' She ran out after him. 'David. Come back.' Shantell followed him down the street.

'Oy!' the waiter cried, carried away with the drama. 'You forgot your change.' He stopped short. 'What am I doing?' He picked up the four pounds seventy-one pence, and put it in his pocket.

David ran down the quays. He didn't know where he was going. He didn't care. The whole world was going to think he was gay. Word would get around. The Liffey Crest was a regular haunt for members of the

Bar. His mother would hear. He wouldn't care if it was true. That would be different. But this. He crossed three intersections without even seeing the traffic lights. He heard cars hooting at him but he didn't take any notice. He wanted to put as much distance as he could between himself and Shantell. He was convinced he could still hear her voice calling his name.

David began to slow down. His lungs were bursting and he could hardly breathe. He was conscious of the fact that people were staring at him. When he reached O'Connell Street Bridge he stopped and looked back up the quays. No sign of her. He had shaken her off. As he stood there, trying to catch his breath, a hand tapped him on the shoulder making him jump sky high. He couldn't turn round. He couldn't move. He contemplated a leap into the river but it flashed across his mind that she might jump in after him. How had she run so fast?

'Is it yourself, David. What ails you man?'

It wasn't her voice. It wasn't any voice he knew. David turned slowly keeping his head down. A pair of shiny brown boots. He looked up a bit further. Brown corduroy trousers. It wasn't her. He turned round fully and looked at the face.

'Don't tell me you've forgotten me already, David. It's Fionn. Fionn O'Fiachra. Is it a ghost you've seen or what?'

'Fionn. Fionn, Fionn.' David threw his arms around the startled man and held him to his chest. 'Forgive me. I've had a terrible experience. I'm not the better of it yet.'

'Don't tell me you were going to—' Fionn indicated the river.

'No. Oh no, Fionn. Nothing like that. I am so

pleased to see you. What are you doing here? I thought you were in Kerry.'

'I've only just arrived. I'm fresh off the train. I'm meeting Mr O'Gorman, to have a talk with him, and then I'm going to find Rosie. I've been having awful rows with the mother. She won't have a word said about Rosie in the house and she hasn't even met her. I made up my mind to come to Dublin. I am going to marry Rosie and the mother will just have to get over it. That's why I want to talk to Mr O'Gorman. I want to get married here, in the capital, and take Rosie home with me.'

'I don't think it is as simple as that, Fionn.'

'Why wouldn't it be? I'm a grown man. I don't have to listen to my mother any more. She'll soon come round when she has no one to run the farm.'

'It wasn't your mother I was thinking of, Fionn.'

'Sure there's no other obstacle than the mother.'

'I'll say nothing, Fionn. You are probably right. I'm not the best person to be giving out advice at the moment.'

'Here I am going on about myself and you so upset. Why don't you come with me to meet Mr O'Gorman? When I've finished my talk with him you could have a word. He seems to know a lot, Mr O'Gorman. It's good to be able to talk to an older man. I've no one at home, you see, I can tell about it. They'd all be on Mammy's side. I keep telling them they have to look further afield. We're in the EC now, I say to them, you have to modernise your thinking. You might as well be talking to the walls for all the notice they take of that in my part of the world.'

'I don't think so, Fionn. Thank you all the same.'

'Sure you might as well. You'll catch your death

hanging over this bridge. Have you somewhere else you have to go?'

'No, Fionn. I don't.'

'Well then. We haven't to go far. It's only round the corner.'

Shantell gave chase for a few minutes. She could see David ahead of her ducking and weaving through the crowds. She held her breath in fright as she saw him dash straight across the road, paying no attention to the heavy flow of traffic. After that she lost sight of him. Let him go, poor dear. It was a mark of his faith in her that he had revealed his secret and she must respect his need for privacy. She would always respect that privacy. She felt that tingling again as she strolled on down the quays. 'Mrs David Shield-Knox,' she said aloud to a startled passer-by. 'Shantell O'Doherty Shield-Knox.' When they got their own place David could have a study to himself. All she needed was a little den she could call her own where she could continue with her writing.

It was going to be such fun setting up home with David. A perfect partnership. It had come to her like a flash. She could use this in one of her novels. Naturally she would be discreet. No one would ever know it was first-hand knowledge. She could make one of her heroines gay. Germaine perhaps. She was still a little bit stuck with Germaine. Germaine could attempt suicide, be rescued, and slowly, through therapy, come to terms with her sexuality. It would be difficult but Shantell was not going to shy away from difficult topics. It was the measure of a good writer to be able to deal with sensitive issues and she knew, with her own assessments behind her, she was quite capable of dealing with the subject of therapy.

Her mind was whirling with ideas. Had Germaine's lover forced her into this terrible action? Perhaps she hadn't always been gay, but had turned gay because as a child she came across her father, naked, in the bathroom and she felt repulsed by manly parts. There were so many ways to take this. So many theories to work out. She reached O'Connell Street Bridge and stopped to check the time. The library would be closed. It was too late to pop in and get out some books on gays. She would need those for background information. Shantell knew there were bars frequented by gays, where she might get some tips, but she wasn't sure which ones were 'in' and she didn't want to end up in the wrong place. She could find out from the library tomorrow. The ladies who ran the library seemed to know absolutely everything that was going on in the city.

She didn't feel like going home. She never felt inspired at home. She could follow up on things there but she had to be sitting somewhere, a café or a bar, tucked into a corner watching people and listening to their conversations, to be truly inspired. She looked around trying to decide what she wanted to do, when she realised she was in the vicinity of Hart's pub. The meeting place that had set her on this miraculous course. Her first funeral had been planned there. It was where she met her new friends. Even the prospect of her forthcoming wedding was, indirectly, a result of Mr O'Gorman's local. Everything that had happened there served to enrich her life and extend her reach as a novelist. Shantell smiled to herself. Her feet had taken her exactly where she wanted to go. She turned off O'Connell Street and went down the side road. Wouldn't it complete everything if Carmel could meet her?

'Hello. Joe. Thank goodness you are in. It's Shantell. I have to speak to Carmel. I have the most wonderful news for her . . . Oh dear, will she be long? I was hoping she would come and meet me. Can you give her a message? . . . Yes I do know I only phoned this morning but there have been so many changes. Tell her I met my solicitor, the one I told her about who was interested in me and, I don't know how to explain this to you Joe, but we may marry to protect his reputation . . . No, Joe. His reputation . . . I don't find that the least bit amusing, Joe . . . It's too hard to explain over the phone. Perhaps I could come over later and . . . all evening? You shouldn't allow her to work so hard, Joe. It's not good for her. Oh, I nearly forgot another piece of news. Could you tell her I'll be doing some social work? Judge Moore recommended me. I'm not sure of the details yet but it's bound to be something really interesting. Judge Moore is a most complicated man. He saw something in me, something I didn't even realise I had myself. Naturally I was surprised and not a little proud that he had plans for me. A man of his exceptional qualities . . . Joe? Are you there Joe? I think you've gone out of range, Joe. If you can hear me tell Carmel I will phone her tonight.'

# Chapter Twenty-one

T he men listened to David in silence. They could see he was too upset for any jovial remarks or comments to be thrown about. He left nothing out. He related his whole miserable experience, from the court session that morning to his unmanly dash down the quays to O'Connell Street Bridge.

'And that's where I found him,' Fionn said. 'On the bridge.'

'Gay, David? Why gay?'

'I don't know. I couldn't think of anything else. I wasn't prepared. I thought somehow, if there was something she knew about me that would put her off . . .' David shook his head. '. . . It didn't work.'

The men bear-hugged David in sympathy and Matt, the barman, was so moved by his plight that he set up a round of drinks on the house.

'She won't follow you in here will she, David?' Malachy said, keeping one eye on the door.

'She doesn't know I'm here. I didn't know I was coming myself until I met Fionn. I don't know what to do. What if she makes me marry her?'

'You're taking this too hard, son. She only said that to give you a bit of comfort in your dilemma.'

'I don't have a dilemma, Mr O'Gorman.'

'But you told her you did. Once a woman gets hold of a man with a bit of a problem, bang, you are sunk. They're in there, clutching and clawing, thinking they are the only ones who can do something about it.'

'I don't have a problem, Mr O'Gorman, except for Shantell.'

'If she wanted to marry me,' Malachy said, 'I'd emigrate.'

'Don't worry, David. Shantell was going to marry me at one time,' Fionn said. 'I think we got engaged. I don't remember properly because Mr O'Gorman gave me a drink—'

'Well now,' Mr O'Gorman butted in quickly. 'There you are. She gets engaged to every bachelor she meets. She will have forgotten about it by morning.'

'Do you think so?'

'I know so. Drink up there and don't be worrying yourself over nothing while we have a little chat with Fionn here. He's the marrying man of the moment. All the way up from Kerry, eh, Fionn? Can't get enough of our salubrious company. Set up another round there, Matt. We have serious business to attend to. This young man is about to embark on the adventure of his life. We can't have him sailing under a dry sheet. The floor is yours, Fionn. A problem shared is a problem halved. Isn't that right, David?'

'It's my mother. She's so all against me courting she is ruining my life. I was wondering, Mr O'Gorman, if, when I have finished talking to Rosie, you would venture down to Kerry with me and have a word with her.'

'What?'

'She'd listen to you, Mr O'Gorman.'

'What would I be talking to your mother for, Fionn? Why would she listen to me?'

'I'll come out straight and give you the bare bones of it. I was telling my mother about all the things that happened the last time I was up. She couldn't keep up with me, she kept losing the thread of it, so the gist of it is, to make things simpler for her, I told her you were Rosie's granddad.'

'Come again?'

'I told her you were Rosie's granddad.'

'That's what I thought you said.'

'I'm going home,' Malachy said. 'Life is too short as it is.'

'You can't go, Malachy. Not yet.'

'And why not?'

'In the telling of the story, to make things easier for her to remember, I made out a list of the names and I have you down as Rosie's uncle. She always remembers cousins and uncles and the like. I have you all listed as family members. We are very big on kin down below and if something happens in a family she understands the way they'll pull together.'

'Gosh,' David said drunkenly. 'Am I down, Fionn?'

'You are a second cousin, David.'

'I've heard enough of this baloney. The whole thing is preposterous, Fionn. I'm going home to sanity and my wife.'

'I told her about your wife, Malachy, and about her love of Feng Shui, and how remarkable a coincidence it was with me interested in the same thing. She was amazed at that one.'

'Is there anything you didn't tell her, Fionn?'

'No. I think I gave her the lot. I went easy, mind, on the coffin-stealing, out of respect for Rosie. I didn't tell her how the ladies shifted it. I thought I'd save that for a bit until she got used to everyone. I warned her though that Rosie's Auntie Ivy was a bit of a ticket.'

'Fionn. She can't get used to everyone. We are not Rosie's relations.'

'She's not going to know that.'

'I give up, Fionn. You are as daft as Shantell.'

'That's very hurtful, Malachy. I want to marry Rosie and I don't want the mother upsetting her. This is the only way to do it.' Fionn turned to Mr O'Gorman. 'So you see how it is, Mr O'Gorman. You have to help me out. As her granddad you could speak for Rosie.'

'I've had a lot of strange things put to me in my lifetime but I have to admit this one beats them all.'

'Will you do it, Mr O'Gorman?'

'You are not seriously considering it, Mr O'Gorman,' Malachy said. 'There are laws about impersonating people. You'll end up back in the courts. Tell him, David.'

'I wish you were *my* granddad,' David slurred. 'Then you could tell Shantell she can't have me.'

'Don't you fret, David. No one's going to have you.'

'Thank you, Mr O'Gorman. Thank you. Mr O'Gorman's going to save me from Shantell, everyone. He's a wonderful man.'

'Steady, lad,' Matt said as David wobbled on his stool. 'We don't want you falling over and suing us now, do we?'

'I wozzensue you.' David slid off the stool and down to the floor. 'I love you. I love you all.' David smiled all round and promptly passed out.

'God Almighty. He's gone. He's out for the count.'

'Leave him, Matt. Let him sleep. He'll be the better for a nap. It's the fright that's done that. A fright can take the steam out of a man.'

'You don't think, Mr O'Gorman, that the drink might have had something to do with it?'

'It's the combination, Malachy. In my opinion drink on its own never harmed a man. Combine it with a problem, especially a female problem, that's where the damage comes in. Matt here will verify my theory. Am I right or wrong, Matt? Haven't we had many a discourse on the very same subject? How often have we said—'

'Will you do it, Mr O'Gorman?' Fionn butted in. 'Will you and Malachy help me the way you helped David?'

Mr O'Gorman paused before picking up his pint and taking a long slow swallow. He looked from the earnest, pleading expression on Fionn's face, across to Malachy, and then to the sleeping form of David on the floor. 'What's to be done, Matt? What's to be done? We have two young men here. One desperately wants to marry and the other . . .' Mr O'Gorman laughed. 'Well we all know what young David wants. We cannot turn our backs on them. We were young ourselves once. A long time ago mind, but nevertheless, not so long that we can't remember the agonies of youth.' He turned to Fionn with a grin. 'As Rosie's new-found granddad . . .'

'You'll do it.'

'. . . I'll take on the task. There are conditions, mind.'

'Anything. Anything you say, Mr O'Gorman.'

'This gentleman here has to accompany me.' Mr

O'Gorman indicated Malachy. 'I won't go into unchartered territory alone. He has to agree to back me up or the deal is off.'

'You must be joking!' Malachy said. 'You *are* joking? It's not fair to Fionn to be going on like that.'

'I gave you my condition, Fionn. It is up to you to talk this fellow round.'

'You'll come, Malachy. I know you'll come. I'm going to call Rosie straight away. I have to tell her the news. I don't know what to say except you are the nicest people that ever lived on the planet.'

'Hold on, Fionn, wait,' Malachy called after him. 'This is ludicrous. I can't go to Kerry. Tell him, Mr O'Gorman, stop him.'

'Fionn,' Mr O'Gorman called. 'Rosie is at her granny's.'

'It's getting late, Ivy. I better be going.' Ivy, Dolores and Rosie were sitting in Ivy's flat. The rest of the company had gone and they were chatting quietly round the fire.

'Do you have to go, Rosie? You could stay over.'

'I'd love to, Ivy, really I would. It's so cosy here it's hard to leave, but Fionn is going to phone me later and I don't want to miss his call.'

'We understand, Rosie. But you will let us know how things go.'

'If that Kerry woman gives you any trouble,' Dolores stirred up again, 'we'll soon put manners on her.'

'I don't think it will come to that, Dolores. Fionn is going to find a way to get round her. It's only natural his mother would be worried. He is her only son.'

'They're the worst,' Dolores said. 'Mothers with

only sons. Especially when the father is deceased. The whole countryside is littered with sons who can't get away from their mothers. They end up old bachelor farmers. You read about it every day. You'd be better to grab him and go.'

'Don't say that, Dolores. I couldn't come between Fionn and his mother. He'd only resent it in the end. We'll find a way.'

'Be sure and call us tomorrow, Rosie,' Ivy said as she and Dolores walked out on to the balcony to wave Rosie off.

'I will. I promise.'

'Correct me if I'm wrong but I swear I can hear a phone ringing in your gran's flat. Who would be phoning a dead woman's flat?'

'I better get it.' Rosie got out her key and ran to the door. 'Hold my bag for me Ivy.'

'I hope it's not left over from the seance.' Ivy clutched at Rosie's bag. 'Maybe we did reach someone.'

'I don't think there are telephones on the other side, Ivy,' said Dolores.

'Very funny. I don't see you going in after her.' They waited outside until Rosie reappeared. 'Who was it, Rosie?' Ivy asked.

'It's Fionn. He's in Dublin. He's in the pub with Mr O'Gorman, Malachy and David.'

'Would you credit that.'

'He made no sense at all, Ivy. He said Mr O'Gorman and Malachy are going to Kerry to be my granddad and my uncle, and that Shantell is going to marry David, who is asleep on the floor. What do you make of it?'

'He must be drunk.'

'He didn't sound drunk. I'm going to meet him. I have to find out what is going on.'

'Wait, Rosie. Don't rush off. Wait till I get my coat.' Ivy dashed back into her flat.

'There's no need for you to come with me, Ivy,' Rosie said, following her in. 'I'll contact you if I need help.'

'If you are going, Ivy Simpson, so am I,' Dolores shouted from outside. 'My coat is in your place, Ivy. Bring it out with you and get my bag and don't forget your travel pass.'

'What is all the commotion about?' Martin Duffy appeared at his door. 'Is there to be no peace in this place at all?'

'We're going into town,' Dolores told him.

'At this hour?'

'There's trouble in the pub. Tom O'Gorman has got it into his head he's Rose Deignan's late husband. Shantell is marrying David who is asleep on the floor, and Malachy, the taxi fellow, is calling himself Rosie's uncle.'

'You can't marry in a pub.'

'If you go to Hawaii and marry under a palm tree you can marry in a pub. She's probably got one of those free love sect ministers under her belt. I wouldn't put it past her.'

'And what is it to you? Why are you interfering?'

'If she can't wake David up she'll marry Fionn. He said as much on the phone to Rosie.'

'That's crazy.'

'You said it, Martin. Remember who you are dealing with. It'll break that young girl's heart if she loses Fionn.'

'I'll get my coat.' Martin went back indoors.

One by one the doors on the balcony opened and the pensioners came out to investigate the noises.

'What's happening? What's going on?'

'Shantell's getting married to Fionn. She snatched him from under Rosie's nose.'

'Get your coats everyone. We are going to town.'

Rosie and Ivy came out of the flat to find a crowd on the balcony.

'What's everyone doing? Where are they all going, Ivy?'

'We're coming with you, Rosie.'

'I don't want . . . You don't have to—'

'Not another word, girl. You don't have to say anything.'

'But—'

'You are not putting us out at all.'

'We are all with you, Rosie. Has everyone got their bus passes? Good. Then off we go.'


Malachy and Mr O'Gorman were arguing while Fionn made his phone calls. First he called his mother, and several neighbours and friends, arranging bed and breakfast accommodation for the trip to Kerry. Then he took a deep breath and called Rosie. David was still on the floor, sleeping like a baby, giving out the odd sigh and turning occasionally to find more comfortable positions to lie in while Matt, the barman, sat down to his late afternoon cup of tea.

'We are not going in my car.'

'It makes more sense to drive, Malachy. We'll all chip in for the petrol. It would give us a bit more freedom. We wouldn't be trapped, sitting in someone's kitchen, not able to get out.'

'And what do I say to my wife? "By the way,

darling, I'm driving to Kerry for the weekend. I'm going to impersonate someone's uncle." She will really go for that.'

'Tell her you are working the weekend.'

'Oh yes. And what do I do when she asks for more housekeeping money from my overtime?'

'Tell her it's a funeral. You are driving some colleagues down to the west for a funeral. I'll phone your house and talk to her. I'll leave a message about the arrangements. By the time I've finished my spiel she'll have your overnight bag packed and ready to go.'

'You have it all at your fingertips haven't you, Mr O'Gorman. A master of excuses.'

'I have to admit,' Mr O'Gorman laughed, 'I've a fair bit of expertise in that line.'

Fionn finished his calls and returned to join his friends. 'It's all set,' he said. 'I talked to them down below. There's beds waiting whenever we want. I thought you might prefer not to stay with the mother so I am having you put up in the village.'

'It is not that simple,' Malachy said. 'I can't down tools and run off to Kerry at a moment's notice.'

'Tomorrow, Fionn. We'll go tomorrow,' Mr O'Gorman said. 'There is no point in delaying. If we leave in the afternoon we'll be down in plenty of time for a few pints before the pubs close.'

Before Malachy could reply a loud groan came from the floor. David was stirring. He made several attempts to get up but his legs buckled under him and he immediately sank to the floor again.

'We better get this lad on his feet. We don't want him down there when the regular punters come in after work. Fionn. Take hold of his other arm while I

282

get this one. On the count of three. One. Two. Three. Lift.' They got David to his feet.

'I'm terribly sorry. Did I fall? I don't remember.'

'You're grand, David. You had forty winks you badly needed after the day you put in. Sit up there now and I'll get you a drink. You must be parched.'

'Mr O'Gorman—'

'The best cure of all. Give him a large brandy, Matt, and put a drop of port in it. Very good for the stomach, a brandy and port.'

'I don't think I can handle—'

'Get it down. You'll feel the better for it.'

David hung off his stool trying to clear his head. His vision wasn't great. He could vaguely make out the doors of the pub opening and someone familiar walking in. He tried to focus.

'What a surprise. Hello everyone. It's me, Shantell. I didn't expect to see you all here. Silly me, I should have known. David. I was so worried about you. David?'

David was back on the floor. He had passed out in a dead faint.

The number 78B bus from Orchardstown to the city centre was packed, but the only fare picked up by the driver was Rosie's. Normally, at that time of the evening, the bus going into town would be empty and the driver could take it easy before the commuter exodus from the city. Although it was past the free travel hour he couldn't stop them boarding the bus. The inspector wouldn't be too pleased, but what could he do? There were too many of them. He knew the abuse he'd get if he tried to make them pay. Senior citizens, he muttered to himself. They can be the worst of the lot.

Rosie gripped the rail in front of her trying to calm herself. The situation was ridiculous. She was going to meet her boyfriend flanked by the entire fourth floor balcony of Tower Heights. He would think she was mad. No wonder his mother was anxious. There had been no dissuading them. No matter how she protested she hadn't managed to shake them off. She loved them dearly but she felt as if they were taking over her life. Her plans – to meet Fionn, maybe have a meal and go to the pictures, or take him to her brother's house and introduce him properly to the family – were never going to happen. It was too complicated. She couldn't ditch them. They were doing this for her. What a mess.

She should never have told them about Shantell and David. That's what started it. Why did they keep squeezing her hand and telling her Shantell would never get Fionn? Shantell didn't want Fionn, she wanted David. Rosie didn't think that David wanted Shantell but it was none of her business. He was a grown man. A solicitor. He could sort himself out. She had to admit that there was something about Shantell that made it impossible to refuse her, and things did get a little hectic when she was around. On the other hand, if it hadn't been for Shantell, she would never have met Fionn. Rosie would never forget that. She would always keep that in mind.

'City centre, folks,' the bus driver called out. 'Hot spot for our fair Isle. Night clubs, restaurants. Pin up your elastic stockings – this could be the night.'

'Cheeky bugger,' Dolores said as she went down the steps past him. 'I've a good mind to report you.'

'For what, missis? Letting you all on the bus at this hour?'

'Leave it out, Dolores,' Martin said. 'Thanks, driver. It was very good of you.'

'Isn't this exciting,' Lily said. 'I haven't been in town at night for years.'

'Steady on, Lily. It's only five thirty. You know what happens when you get overexcited.'

'Keep together, everyone. Don't straggle. We're going straight to the pub.'

'It's not a school tour, Martin Duffy. He'll have us holding hands next.'

The pensioners walked determinedly towards the pub and only hesitated when they got to the front door. They grouped together outside.

'You head in first, Rosie,' Martin said. 'We'll be right behind you.'

They pushed Rosie to the front and waited, expectantly, for her to open the door. There was no escaping. The pensioners had lined up behind her.

'What is Fionn going to think of me. He'll probably call the whole thing off when he sees this. My life is ruined.' Rosie pushed the door open and went in.

The first thing Shantell saw when she entered the pub was David, on the floor, with Malachy, Mr O'Gorman and Fionn standing over him.

'What have you done to him?' she cried, dropping to her knees beside the prostrate figure. She knelt there, cradling David's head in her arms and rocking back and forth for, what seemed to Mr O'Gorman and Malachy, an age.

Moments later the pub doors opened again. It was Rosie with the pensioners.

'Fionn,' Rosie called out to him. 'It's Rosie, Fionn.'

'Rosie?' Fionn turned and saw her. 'Rosie.' He ran

to her, threw his arms around her and, oblivious of everything else, held her to him.

'What the hell?' Matt the barman spluttered into his tea as, one after another, the pensioners stumbled in and stood around the couple, cheering and whooping their congratulations. The unexpected arrival of the pensioners left Mr O'Gorman temporarily at a loss for words while Malachy, resigned now to his fate, quietly ordered himself a chaser.

'David, my darling, speak to me. Barman. Quickly. Call an ambulance.'

'You don't need an ambulance, Shantell. He will be right as rain when he comes round. He's had a little too much to drink. That's all.'

'You have done this, Mr O'Gorman. You and your . . . your, taxi-driving friend. How could you?'

'Hold on there, Shantell,' Malachy said. 'We are not the ones who got him in this state.'

'Rosie. I love you.'

'Oh, Fionn.'

The pensioners gave out a loud delighted 'Oooooh.'

'Order. Order here please,' Matt said. 'This is a public house. Not a high wire three ringed bloody circus act.'

'And what are we if we are not the public?' Dolores enquired. 'Unless, by that remark, you mean to insinuate something else?'

'David. Can you hear me? It's Shantell.'

'I love you too, Fionn.'

'Oh, Rosie.'

'Oooooh,' the pensioners sang out once more.

'Ooh.' David was coming round. 'Ooh,' he whimpered as he opened his eyes and saw Shantell kneeling over him.

'Let the lad have some air, Shantell,' said Mr O'Gorman. 'Malachy. Help me move him over there by one of the tables.'

'Any more of this carry on,' Matt said, 'and I'm going to have to ask you all to leave—' The ladies of Tower Heights advanced together towards him. 'Unless,' he hastily added, 'that is, you are ordering something.'

'Martin. For once in your life do something useful and give this man an order.'

'Pints, and glasses of Guinness all round, if you please, sir.'

Matt started to pull the Guinness and Lily sidled up closer to him.

'Excuse me. I wonder if I could have a cup of tea. Only I saw you with a cup in your hand.'

Shantell had been so wrapped up in her concern for David that it wasn't until the second round of *ooooohs* that she became aware of what was happening around her. She jumped up and, momentarily forgetting David, whose head bounced off the floor as he fell back down, threw her arms out in greeting.

'Where are my manners? You must think I am awful ignoring you like that. But you can see how David needs my attention. The poor dear is suffering. Did you manage without me? Have you followed me here for my advice? The seance, did you finish it?'

'We did, Shantell,' Dolores said. 'Not a bother in the world. Peggy's got a whole tribe of Indians wanting to visit. How did you get on, Shantell? What did the judge say? Are you going to prison?'

'Dolores! What a thing to say.'

'Ladies, ladies,' Martin cut in. 'Let's keep things civilised.'

'What on earth gave you the idea I would be going to prison? On the contrary, Judge Moore singled me out for community work. It's a great honour. I was telling my friend, Carmel, only a short time ago what a great honour it was to be chosen.'

'Shantell. You don't choose to do community service.'

'I know, and I don't want to blow my own trumpet, but the fact that the judge selected me, when you think of the wide range of people at his disposal, is so wonderfully humbling. Why don't I get the details, right now, from David? Then I can tell you all about it.'

'There is no answer to that,' Martin said. 'What can you say? The woman doesn't even know she got a sentence.'

'Do you know I was nearly going to congratulate her, she has me that off balance,' Ivy said.

'When Mrs Delaney's youngest got forty hours community service there was uproar. Do you remember, Ivy? "No son of mine is clearing ditches. Put him inside where no one can see him." She should have met Shantell. She'd have found a whole new meaning to community service.'

'David, dear. Can you speak? Our friends are dying to know about Judge Moore's decision. Can you tell me exactly what I will be doing?'

# Chapter Twenty-two

Word spread through the library like wildfire. Miss Conlon was taking early retirement. Even Doreen, who had been Miss Conlon's assistant for so long, had had no inkling of her plans and was taken by complete surprise. Rumours abounded. An illness, an elderly parent to take care of, even a secret romance, were hinted at, but seemed unlikely. Miss Conlon was a woman dedicated to her work. Her literacy schemes, her language courses, and all the other extra activities she had introduced were so successful as to be models for other libraries. She had earned a recommendation for her last, and possibly most noteworthy, project when she had liaised with the courts and the probation officers, and agreed to take on first-time offenders. A pilot scheme was introduced and was currently under way whereby those selected would undertake to stack shelves, chase overdue books and repair the covers on paperbacks which, for the library staff, was an ongoing and time-consuming problem. This project, as well as benefiting those offenders on whom the probation officers felt a prison sentence would have an adverse effect, would free up her regular staff and allow them more time to deal with requests and enquiries from the public.

'My decision is final,' she had told Mr Scott, the head librarian and, being a woman of her word she was unlikely to recant.

Shantell was on her sixth week of community service at the time of Miss Conlon's resignation.

Six weeks earlier, in Mr O'Gorman's local, the evening had ended peacefully enough. All the arrangements had been made. Fuelled with pints and chasers, Malachy had agreed to drive to Kerry the following day. Rosie would travel down on the train later in the day, by which time Mr O'Gorman would have worked his charms on Mrs O'Fiachra. Ivy and Dolores had taken on the mantle of wedding organisers and, with the other ladies, they discussed wedding cakes, invitations and points of etiquette as befitting a country wedding, while the gents, glad to be unexpectedly in the pub whatever the occasion, talked horses and point-to-points. Shantell, fluttering from one group to the other, took notes and dispensed advice. She was so excited that she had forgotten about David, who had recovered his wits sufficiently enough to keep himself semi-hidden, behind Mr O'Gorman's back, from her line of fire.

'This is all so useful,' Shantell told them. 'Not just for my own nuptials but for my work. I will definitely have a country wedding. There seems to be so much more to it in the country.'

The pensioners, seeing no danger to Rosie's prospects, were happy to give her details of their own big days, and had no objections when Shantell begged permission to use their experiences in her novels.

'Humour her,' Dolores said to the others. 'She'll have forgotten it all by tomorrow.'

The Tower Heights contingent drifted home. Malachy called his fellow taxi drivers and ordered three cabs. One to pick up Fionn and Rosie, one for Mr O'Gorman, David, and himself, and the third to collect Shantell and deposit her at her home. For David's sake he arranged for Shantell to leave first.

'I know I have been ignoring you, David,' she said as the driver came into the pub to collect her. 'Don't be angry with me. Artistes can never truly belong to one person. They belong to everyone.' Handing the driver her bag and her coat she swept out the door after him.

'I handled that quite well, don't you think?'

'I hope, Mr O'Gorman, that that's the last of your gatherings.'

'Come, Matt. Think of all that money in your till, and don't forget, you might appear in one of Shantell's books.'

'Very droll, Mr O'Gorman. Very droll.'

'I want to go to Kerry with you,' David said. 'I don't want to be left alone. You know what might happen if you leave me behind.'

'What about your job?'

'My job!' David laughed hysterically. 'What chance do you think I would have if the news got out? *Gay solicitor marries first client.*'

'Steady lad. Steady. You are overwrought. Things will look different in the morning. They always do. Anyway, we need you here. We need a sensible back-up in town. Supposing, for instance, we had to find some information we don't have. Who else could we turn to, eh? No one but yourself. Another thing. Once you have Shantell started on her community service she'll be off your back. Wouldn't you be better off seeing that through and finished with? We're only going for the one day and we'll be back the following morning. It's not worth jeopardising your job for a day now is it?'

'I suppose you're right.'

'There. That's all settled. Don't worry. We'll keep you informed and we'll meet you when you get back.'

'She'll really be off my back, won't she?'

'To be sure, David lad.'

Every stitch that Shantell possessed was laid out on the bed. She was due to attend, at eleven thirty sharp, the offices of the Probation and Welfare Service to meet a Mr William Lawlor, and she wanted to look her best. What would be most appropriate for a community servant, she asked herself. It is so difficult to know. She must approach this interview as an actress going for a role. A good appearance is vital, she concluded. It could make all the difference to Mr Lawlor's decision. She sat down at her little table and made a list of choices.

1. Smart casual day wear.
2. Smart formal wear. (Shoes would be a problem.)
3. Manual type, i.e. dungarees and check blouse? Yes. It could be of a horticultural nature.
4. Early evening wear? Possibility. Night-work.
5. Mix and match. Formal top/casual bottom and vice versa.
6. Check radio for weather. Look out window as extra precaution.

It was eight a.m. Shantell allotted herself one hour for getting ready, half an hour for travel time plus half an hour for transport delays or other mishaps. She checked her watch. Time in hand for another cup of coffee. Get dressed, have coffee? No have coffee, get dressed, in case of drips. She thought of phoning Carmel but she was a little miffed with her. Carmel had not returned any of her calls. She did understand about Joe but you can't drop all your friends because of a man. No. It was up to Carmel to call her.

Smart casual day wear won the toss. Definitely the right choice. Amazing. Every time she made a list for anything important she inevitably went with her first choice. It had to be a natural instinct for the right thing. She put her smart casual outfit to one side and returned the rest to the wardrobe. Make-up next. Not too much. She had the feeling that Judge Moore would not approve of too much make-up and, as he had been the one to put her forward she didn't want to let him down. A light foundation and a hint of lipstick would be sufficient. Handbag contents: she would bring her notebooks. That was bound to impress Mr William Lawlor. Men were always impressed by women who were bookish. Purse, keys, pen, make-up bag, tissues, hairbrush, Sellotape, mobile, address book, extra pen. Everything was in order.

Shantell took a last, long, objective look in the mirror and could find no fault. Good morning, she practised, smiling at her reflection. You must be Mr Lawlor. I'm Shantell O'Doherty. I'm so pleased to meet you. She was at the door, about to leave her flat, when a thought struck her. She returned to her wardrobe. Took out her non-iron black top and folded it into her bag. No point in being caught out. She could always nip into the ladies' loo and change.

'Good morning. You must be Mr Lawlor. So pleased to meet you. I was afraid I was in the wrong place when I saw those people queuing outside. Oh please, don't misunderstand me, I have no prejudices whatsoever, but I have to admit some of them do look a little on the rough side.'

'Shantell O'Doherty?' Mr Lawlor didn't look up from the file he was studying and missed Shantell's vigorous nodding. 'Take a seat.'

'I see you have my notes, Mr Lawlor. Judge Moore was very anxious that we should meet. I'm sure he mentioned that in his report.'

'Are you in current employment?'

'Do you mean by somebody else?'

Mr Lawlor looked at Shantell. Was this another smart alec?

'When was your last employment?'

'I work for myself at present. Mental work that is.' Mr Lawlor's expression darkened. 'Oh. I see what you mean,' continued Shantell. 'I was employed once. But it was a long time ago. My supervisor thought the world of me. She recognised my value to the artistic side of things and she advised me to leave commerce and try my hand at something creative. She even wrote a reference in which she asserted that my capabilities were such as to render me unsuitable for the field I was in.'

'How do you support yourself?'

'I sign on, Mr Lawlor. A temporary situation but one of enormous value. It affords me time for my work and there is a great opportunity to study other aspects of human existence. I expect to publish some books very soon and naturally, when that happens, my circumstances will change dramatically. Mr Lawlor. Are you listening to me?'

William Lawlor had stopped listening a long time ago. He had heard all the stories. The felons, the delinquents, the local hoods, everybody who had passed through his hands, they all had a story. They came to him with one tale or another, claiming that their circumstances were going to change, but in Mr Lawlor's long experience, that never happened. He took out the list of schemes available and cross-checked it with Shantell's file.

'Mr Lawlor, might I suggest—'

'Can you read and write?'

'Of course I can read and write! What a question to ask me. I am here on the behest of Judge Moore. He will not be pleased when I tell him how you have conducted this interview.'

'Interview? This is not an interview, Miss O'Doherty. This is a placement office. You go where I tell you to go. You attend each day on time. You leave each day on time. Once a week you report in here. Any trouble, any complaint from your bosses and you are in the nick. Do you understand?'

'But I am here to serve the community. I shall honour any commitment, provided it is reasonable, to the best of my abilities. Judge Moore—'

'This is not a holiday camp, Miss O'Doherty. You are not going to perform redcoat duties for the kiddies. You are here for rehabilitation. One more word and I will refer you back to the courts. Now, I will read out the list of available places. Nod if you have any experience in any of the following.'

'I love lists. I make them all the—'

'Painter, bricklayer, face-worker, fitter, plumber, welder.' Mr Lawlor paused, looking at Shantell. 'Farm labourer, machine operator, platelayer, porter, stores man, machinist, packer, stacker. Stacker.' He stopped there and scanned the information supplied. 'Shelf stacker: "Willing to take on first-time offenders for shelf-stacking and book repairing. No specific requirements needed as training will be given but ability to work deftly and in silence essential. Contact Miss Conlon at 7633935." Have you ever stacked shelves before, Miss O'Doherty?'

'Certainly not.'

'There is nothing to it.'

'I cannot stack, Mr Lawlor.'

'You can, Miss O'Doherty. I will make the necessary arrangements this afternoon. Report to this office tomorrow morning at nine thirty sharp. Be prepared to go straight on to your placement from here. The sooner you start the better.'

'But where is it? What will I stack?'

'What does it matter what you stack or where you stack it? Stacking is stacking.'

'But I must know.'

'You, Miss O'Doherty, are an offender. You do not need to know anything.' Mr Lawlor got up and went to the door. 'Out, Miss O'Doherty. Remember. Nine thirty sharp.'

Shantell went straight home after her interview in the probation office. She had planned to do a few things in town but she was too upset to go anywhere else. That odious little man. How dare he speak to her like that. To think of all the trouble she went to and he hadn't even looked at her. She sat down at her desk and recorded the interview in her notebook. The world must know there were nasty people like Mr William Lawlor about. That was it. It came to her as she wrote in her notebook. Gillian Turner. Mr Lawlor was the perfect foil for poor Gillian. He would be the type of man to ditch a woman without a backward glance. She had been having a few problems and difficulties with some of her male characters. All the men she knew were so nice it had been hard to conjure up a nasty male villain.

She wrote furiously all afternoon and well into the night, adding Mr Lawlor to every one of her novels. He appeared as Tom Lynch who ditched Gillian Turner; Felicity's married Lothario, Bill Lally; Billy Lavin, the neurotic and dangerous brother of Germaine, and finally, W.L. Lambe and Laurence Lewis, the prison officer and death row keeper of Amy and Doris respectively. Shantell was pleased with her efforts. That would put Mr William Lawlor in his place.

At nine twenty-five the following morning Shantell stood in the waiting room of the Probation and Welfare Service office. This time she had not bothered about her appearance. She put on whatever came to hand. She would not lower herself to try and make an effort. Not after Mr Lawlor's treatment of her the previous day. She stood to one side, by the wall, keeping herself aloof from the rest of the group, all of whom seemed to be on the most friendly terms. The men greeted each other with back slaps and thumps while the women puffed on cigarettes ignoring the no-smoking sign on the wall. Mr Lawlor appeared at nine thirty on the dot. He checked his watch and instructed the duty officer, who had accompanied him, that anyone who tried to enter late was to be turned away. In one hand he held a bundle of duplicate slips and in the other a long list of names and addresses.

'When your name is called step up and receive your slip. On it you will find the name and address of your assignments, your hours, and conditions. No discussion will be entered into. Anyone failing to present themselves at their appointed place of assignment will be issued with a warrant. Do I make myself clear?'

'Mr Lawlor.' One of the offenders spoke up. 'I have a sick cert from the doctor. He says I'm not fit to work.'

Mr Lawlor looked at the speaker, a young man with a shaven head and a forest of rings in his nose.

'A cert,' Mr Lawlor repeated.

'That's right, Mr Lawlor.' The young man grinned. 'You can't make me go now.'

'Officer. Take this gentleman downstairs and make out a warrant.'

'You can't do that.'

'You will get all the medical treatment you require inside.' The young man was frogmarched out of the waiting room. 'Has anyone else got a cert?' Mr Lawlor glared around the room daring anyone to speak. 'Ramsey, Scott, Bourke.' As the names were called each person went forward to receive their slip and sign Mr Lawlor's book. Muted whispering broke out as they read their assignments. 'O'Casey, Dunne, O'Doherty. Aren't you O'Doherty?' Mr Lawlor shouted at Shantell. 'What are you waiting for? A special invitation?'

'I'm so sorry. I was miles away.'

'I bet you wish you were, missis,' a voice murmured from the group.

Shantell got her slip, signed for it, and returned to her spot by the wall. She was trembling so much the woman standing next to her gave her a nudge.

'Is this your first time? Don't worry, love. You'll get used to it.'

'How could anyone get used to this?' Shantell said. 'I can't bear even to read it.' She forced herself to look at the piece of paper, staring blankly at the jumble of words in front of her. The jumble began to clear:

Assignment to commence immediately. Five mornings per week. Three hours per morning, 10 a.m. to 1 p.m., until the allocated time of 200 hours has been completed.

Shantell did a calculation. Thirteen weeks, she thought, despairingly. How could anyone stack for thirteen weeks? She continued reading:

The assignee will be eligible for unemployment payments and should continue to collect payment at his or her regular post office.

| | |
|---|---|
| Placement address: | The Central Library |
| | Henry Street, Dublin 1 |
| Position: | Shelf stacking and book repairing |
| Contact: | Miss Conlon |

Shantell gasped and held her breath. She looked again at her slip. It was true. The address and the position were detailed in neat handwriting.

'That bad is it, love?' the woman said. 'I got the bloody laundry again. I'm sick of that laundry. Nothing but sheets, sheets, and more sheets. The only thing is I can sneak some of my own in and get them done. Christ. What was that?'

Shantell had let out a cry that rocked the entire waiting room. She ran to Mr Lawlor.

'I have been so wrong about you. I totally misjudged you.' She held the startled man against her chest. 'How can I ever thank you? Anything. Ask me anything and I will do my utmost to carry it out.'

'Wow. Right on, Mr Lawlor. You're on to a good thing there.'

'We won't tell if you don't tell.'

'Some people will do anything,' sniffed the woman who had tried to be nice. 'I thought she was respectable. Goes to show. You can never tell can you.'

'Miss O'Doherty,' spluttered Mr Lawlor. 'Control yourself. Officer. Get this woman off me.'

# Chapter Twenty-three

'Full house I see, Matt.' Mr O'Gorman walked into Hart's and looked around the empty pub. 'This place would close only for me.'

'It's yourself back is it, Mr O'Gorman?' Matt, unperturbed, continued to polish his glasses. 'You were gone that long I thought you'd emigrated. The usual?' Matt put on a pint without waiting for an answer.

'I've said it once, Matt, and I'm not ashamed to say it again. That shower down below in Kerry could teach us all how to suck eggs.'

'Is that right, Mr O'Gorman?'

'I'm telling you. We're in the wrong place. No wonder they call us jackeens. That's what we are.'

'I'm not a jackeen, Mr O'Gorman. I'm from Wicklow.'

'That's only a tuppence-ha'penny place, Matt.'

'I'll have you know it's called the Garden of Ireland.'

'They only tell you that to keep you content. "Garden of Ireland" my arse. Hectares of bungalows,

Matt. That's what you've let it become. Now our cousins further down, they have it all sewn up.'

'Is that so?'

'They've got grants for farming. Grants for not farming. Tourist grants, fishing grants. They've even got grants for keeping fields. Fields! Once a child is born in Kerry, his or her name is on a grant, paid for, let me tell you, by whom? Us! The idiot jackeens.'

'One visit to Kerry and you're an expert.'

'I saw it with my own eyes.'

'And through which end of the glass, Mr O'Gorman?'

'Bitter words, Matt, bitter words. Do you know what else I'm going to tell you? The pint is twenty pence cheaper. Even the drink is subsidised.'

'Do I take it from this conversation, that I can remove your name from that stool?'

'Good God no. I'm not a man that can sit around all day watching grass grow. Don't get me wrong, Matt. I'm all for organics, thought what the missis spends on those free-range eggs is enough to make a grown man cry, but I couldn't be doing with it.'

'Was your mission successful, Mr O'Gorman?'

'Was it what? We had them eating out of our hands. If I was to tell you the ins and outs and the doings, I'd be here all day. Suffice to say the banns are to be read this very Sunday in the local church.'

'You probably will, Mr O'Gorman.'

'Will what?'

'Be here all day.'

'The journey down was pleasant enough. We stopped, for a few refreshments don't you know, in Naas, and a very pleasant watering-hole it was too.'

'That's only fifteen miles out.'

302

'So it is, Matt. So it is. On then to that grand stretch of land, the Curragh, training ground of our armed forces, not to mention some of our best racehorses. You know you have left the city behind when you see that green pasture. Traversing the countryside, you go through the towns of Portloise, Roscrea and Nenagh, before you hit the side of the city of Limerick—'

'You stopped in them all I take it.'

'We had to. Sure you couldn't favour one above the other. Anywhere, where was I? Yes, so we bypassed Limerick, due to the enormous expansion of its centre . . .'

Matt put the kettle on. He didn't usually take tea at this hour but he had a feeling he was going to need a cup.


Shantell ran through the town towards the library. The doors opened to the public at ten and she wanted to get there before that. Why, oh why had she not dressed with more care? There was nothing she could do about it now. If she went home to change she would be late and that would create a very bad impression on her first day. She flew past a pharmacy and then stopped. She'd had an idea. She dived into the shop, picked up a pair of spectacle frames and took them to the sales desk.

'I'll take these please, and a packet of hairpins.'

'Would you like to see our optician? He can insert your lenses for you. We don't guarantee a proper fit unless the optician checks them.'

'I don't need an optician, thank you. I have perfect eyesight. I just want the frames.'

'Twenty-seven pounds, fifty, please.'

'What? For empty frames? That's outrageous.'

'Do you want them or not?'

'Yes I want them. But it's daylight robbery.'

'It works out cheaper if you buy two pairs.'

'Why would I buy two pairs when I don't need glasses in the first place?'

'Shall I just give you the hairpins then?'

'Give me the frames.'

'But if you don't need them?'

'I want the frames. I want the frames and the hairpins and I want them now!'

'Certainly, madam.'

Ten minutes. Ten minutes wasted with that wretched girl. Now the public doors would definitely be open. Shantell stood in a shop doorway, dropped her bag on the ground, and got out the hairpins. Twisting this way and that, she tried to make out her reflection in the shop window, but it was no use. She couldn't get a proper image. She would have to go by feel. She coiled her hair up and fastened it tight to her head and then donned the glasses. A bit heavy on her nose, but worth it for the studious look she was seeking. If only she had more time. She took the library steps two at a time and arrived, a little out of breath, at the information desk.

'Miss Conlon,' Doreen called into Miss Conlon's office.

'Yes, Doreen. What is it?'

'Could you come out to the front desk please. There is someone here to see you.'

'I'm on the telephone, Doreen. Ask the person to wait a moment.'

Miss Conlon was on the telephone to the probation office confirming the fax she had received from them earlier that morning. It appeared satisfactory. Mr Lawlor, the gentleman she dealt with, knew there were certain offenders she would not take on. She was very willing to assist in the project but she had her readers to think of and she couldn't afford to upset them.

'Impersonation and inciting,' she read. That, she agreed, didn't warrant a prison sentence. She herself had been an ardent ban-the-bomb marcher in her youth and had been accused of being a rioter. There was no such thing as community service in her day and a number of the march leaders had actually gone to prison.

'Miss Conlon,' Doreen called again.

'Coming, Doreen.'

Miss Conlon walked out to the front desk where she saw Doreen, open-mouthed, staring at a customer.

'You.'

Shantell gave her a smile. At least Miss Conlon thought it was a smile. It was difficult to make out as her lipstick extended the corners of her mouth. Her hair was chain-mailed above her head and she was wearing dark, heavy spectacles, with no glass.

'Can I help you?' Miss Conlon asked.

'Miss Conlon. I believe you are expecting me.' Shantell handed over her duplicate slip. 'I'm Shantell O'Doherty and I am here to assist you.'

Miss Conlon felt her legs weaken. She recovered, took the slip in silence, and returned to her office.

'Doreen. A moment of your time please,' she called from her sanctuary.

'Excuse me,' Doreen managed to say before fleeing after her employer and closing the door.

'Miss Conlon,' Doreen said, once in the privacy of her superior's office. 'Isn't that the woman who keeps coming in here with strange requests? Perhaps this is another one of her—'

'I'm afraid not, Doreen. Her name is on the slip. She is our probationer. She is here to do two hundred hours of community service.'

'Can we not cancel her?'

'It's not that simple. We can't turn her away. I'll get on to Mr Lawlor right away. In the meantime, she will have to stay. Take her out the back and find something to keep her occupied. Stay with her if you have to but, whatever you do, don't let her near the public area.' Miss Conlon waved Doreen out while she picked up the phone. 'Do your best, Doreen. It won't be for long.'

Doreen sidled out of the office and approached the desk. Before she could say anything Shantell leaned forward and grasped her hand. 'Hello, Doreen. I'm Shantell. I feel we are going to become the best of friends. I've seen you so often, from the other side of the counter of course, and now, here I am, a bona fide member of the staff. I can't begin to tell you how wonderful it feels. Where would you like me to start?'

# Chapter Twenty-four

Ms Shantell O'Doherty
c/o The Central Library
Henry Street

Mr David Shield-Knox
Via Interflora

My dear dear David
  There is no easy way to tell you this but I must
sever our engagement. From the moment I took up
my position in the library I realised I must devote
myself to books. Do not be broken-hearted.
Remember, hearts recover, and one day you will
find the man of your dreams. I know you
wouldn't want to stand in the way of my career.
Yes, David, I can say it aloud, my career. And I
have you, and Judge Moore, to thank for it.
  You wouldn't believe how well I am getting on.
I'm getting on so well that Miss Conlon, the
librarian, has to practically beg me to leave. In the
mornings I do official library work. Dealing with
readers, sorting books, all kinds of things. The
afternoons I sit in the reading area and get on with

my novels. That way I'm always on hand in case Miss Conlon or Doreen need me. The works are progressing so well it's all I can do to keep up with them. My heroines lead me on through their lives page by page. There are times when I have no say, no voice, I am merely the recorder.

I know I have been very remiss in keeping up with everybody but I intend to remedy this. Miss Conlon insists I take two days off at the end of the week. She is so funny, David. One day I heard her ask 'would they have to carry me out to get rid of me?' She also hinted that some of the readers had spoken to her about me. I feel bad because she never gives Doreen, or the other staff, time off and it might be showing them up a little. What can I do? It occurs to me that whatever I turn my hand to I always get preferential treatment. People always talk to me. As you know, David, I never seek this. I seem to fall into it. Anyway. I have arranged to meet Rosie on Friday afternoon, in Mr O'Gorman's pub. I hope you can come along. If this doesn't suit you, don't worry. I can call to your office and we can go to lunch before I meet the others. We are not allowed to take phone calls in the library but if you ring my mobile and leave a message I will know which arrangement suits you.

Accept this token of red roses as a symbol of my affection for you.

Yours truly,

Shantell x x x

p.s. When you see Judge Moore please tell him how grateful I am for my community service. I tried to phone him but I never get put through. I have asked for an appointment and I hope to see him soon.

*

'You will have to talk to her, Miss Conlon. She won't listen to me.'

'Am I never to have any peace?' Miss Conlon was on her tea break in the staff room when Doreen burst in. She put her cup down and gave a long, low, sigh. There was no need to ask who Doreen was referring to. It was Shantell. It was always Shantell. Every day some member of staff came to her with the same request. 'What is it this time, Doreen?'

'She has restacked all the books.'

'That's what she is supposed to do, Doreen.'

'You don't understand. She is restacking them by colour.'

'What? Doreen, calm down and take your time. You are not making any sense.'

'She has all the 940s down on the ground, and she is restacking them by colour. I tried to stop her but she kept saying that it was much prettier that way and that people would find it more agreeable. I don't know what to do, Miss Conlon. She told me not to tell you. But I had to tell you. What will Mr Scott say? He'll probably blame me. That section is my responsibility. And what will our readers think? You'll have to do something.'

'You better sit down, Doreen. I'll handle this.'

Miss Conlon left the staff room and walked, through the library, to the history section while Doreen slumped down in the empty chair.


'Miss O'Doherty. What on earth do you think you are doing?'

'Miss Conlon. What a fright you gave me.' Shantell was kneeling on the floor surrounded by towers of history books. 'Did Doreen tell you? She must have told you. Now she has spoiled my surprise. I was hoping to be all finished before you knew anything about it. It's going to be really great, Miss Conlon. I am colour coordinating the whole history section. We start with a blue shelf on the top, then a red one, then green, then brown, right down to the sort of mottled ones on the bottom. Do you like it?'

'Like it? Like it?' Miss Conlon repeated herself. 'Have you even the slightest conception of the shambles you are creating? This is the Central Library. How do you expect our readers to find what they want?'

'I've thought of that already, Miss Conlon. I am going to make a long list with all the names and pin it down the side of the bookcase. Then, when anyone takes a book, they tick the list. Simple.'

'Simple,' Miss Conlon croaked.

'Yes. And we can tie a pencil on to the list so no one steals it. What do you think?'

'Think.'

'It will take a little while to sink in but I know when everyone gets the hang of it they'll be delighted.'

'Simple think. Think simple. I cannot think. I have not been able to think for some time. I don't think I will ever be able to think again.'

'Miss Conlon, are you okay? You seem upset.'

'Upset.'

'Don't move, Miss Conlon. Stay where you are. I'll get someone.' Shantell ran to the staff room. 'Doreen. You better come quick. There is something the matter with Miss Conlon. She's stuck on her words and she is turning a very funny colour.'

*

'Hello. This is David Shield-Knox. Would Mr O'Gorman be there?'

'He would. Do you wish to speak to him or are you just establishing his whereabouts?'

'Let me speak to him. Please.'

Matt held the phone aloft and spoke across the bar to Mr O'Gorman. 'David Shield-Knox is on the line. Are you available for consultation or will I take a message?'

'What's got into you, Matt? Am I available? I'm here aren't I, with only you for company. Give me over the phone.'

'I'm not running a bureau you know. All these calls, I should be putting in for secretarial fees.'

'One call a week, if that, hardly constitutes abuse of the telephone. Hand it over.' Mr O'Gorman snatched the phone. 'David, my boy. How are you?'

'I'm sorry, Mr O'Gorman. Is it awkward for you to talk? I couldn't help overhearing.'

'Not a bit of it. Pay no attention. Matt's in a funny mood today. What can I do for you?' Mr O'Gorman twisted away a little to prevent Matt overhearing the conversation. 'Aha . . . Yep . . . Is that so? . . . Friday. What time Friday? . . . I'm sure you will find me here . . . And did she say who else was coming in? . . . I see . . . I don't think you've anything to worry about. From what you tell me she's preoccupied elsewhere . . . Okey-dokey. I'll see you Friday then. Bye for now, David.'

'What's all that about Friday?' Matt asked.

'Young David is coming in to see me.'

'I hope it's not another one of your gatherings, Mr O'Gorman because, I'm telling you now, if it is I'm closing up shop.'

'No it's not a gathering, Matt. And since when does a pub close because a few friends are getting together?'

'It better not be.'

'Would I lie to you?'

Shantell was hovering around the library door waiting for Miss Conlon to arrive. She was bursting to tell everybody her news but she felt it only proper that Miss Conlon should be the first to hear it. It was Miss Conlon she had to thank for her position in the library. She almost let it slip to Doreen but managed to stop herself in time.

'What are you doing here, Shantell? You should be on overdues. Miss Conlon won't be pleased if she catches you hanging around the door like this.'

'*Au contraire*, Doreen. Miss Conlon is going to be more than pleased, even positively stunned, with my news. You could be looking for someone else to do your overdues.'

'Are you leaving?'

'No, I'm not leaving, but there is a strong possibility that I may be moved up the ladder.'

'What do you mean, Shantell?'

'Please, please, Doreen, don't try to squeeze it out of me. You can be there when I tell her but Miss Conlon has to be the first to know.'

'Doreen? Miss O'Doherty? Is there no work to be done? Why are you both standing here?'

'Good morning, Miss Conlon. We were waiting for you. Shantell has something to tell you. It's a surprise.'

'A surprise?' Miss Conlon repeated the words slowly trying to interpret what Doreen was implying. Was it possible Shantell was being posted elsewhere?

Could her community service have been commuted? Miss Conlon felt in her pocket for the draft letter of resignation she had worked on the previous evening. Perhaps she wouldn't present it to Mr Scott. Maybe she was overreacting, letting unimportant things get to her.

'It's the most amazing, wonderful thing, Miss Conlon. You will never guess.'

'I don't have time for guessing games, Shantell.'

'It's almost too wonderful.' Shantell took hold of Miss Conlon's arm and half dragged, half walked her towards the staff room. 'I want you to be sitting down when you hear my news. Doreen, aren't you coming?'

'Let go my arm, Miss O'Doherty.'

'You will be delighted, Miss Conlon. I promise you.' Shantell pushed open the door and jerked the librarian to a chair. 'Miss Conlon. You know I have been working on my novels?' Shantell hesitated for a second, mistaking an uninvoluntary cringe from Miss Conlon as a sign of assent. 'Well. A few days ago I made a big decision. I sent samples of my work to several prominent publishing companies. Naturally, I didn't tell anyone about it. Miss Titchmarch, my mentor, advises this on page one hundred and thirty nine of her creative writing manual. "Send it off and get on with the next one," she says, and that's exactly what I did. Except, of course, I do have more than one on the go. It makes it so much simpler. If you have words that don't fit in one novel you can always find a use for them in one of the others. "Nothing is waste to the writer," Miss Titchmarch says.' Shantell stopped suddenly and gave a deep sigh of admiration, oblivious of the shocked expressions on the faces of

Doreen and Miss Conlon. 'Forgive me,' she went on. 'I am getting away from my news. Once I get on to the subject of my beloved Miss Titchmarch there is no stopping me. Where was I?'

'Publishing companies,' Doreen said.

'Oh yes, thank you, Doreen. I sent two chapters each of *Waiting for Tom* and *Felicity's Story* plus a brief synopsis of *Doris on Death Row* and . . .' Shantell waited, savouring the moment, '. . . this very morning I got replies.'

'Replies,' Miss Conlon and Doreen said in unison.

'Yes, replies.' Shantell beamed across from Miss Conlon to Doreen. 'I can appreciate your astonishment. I was astonished myself. Now for the best part. They want more. As much as I can send them.' Miss Conlon sucked hard for air. 'I can see you are stunned, Miss Conlon. I did say to Doreen you would be stunned by my news. Didn't I, Doreen?' Shantell's eyes fixed on Doreen waiting for affirmation. 'Didn't I say that Miss Conlon would be surprised by my news?' Doreen could only nod helplessly. 'Shall I make tea? I could run out for cakes, by way of celebration or, better still, we could all go for drinks later on. It's not every day one hears such news.'

'No.' Miss Conlon shook her head. 'No, no, no. This cannot happen.'

'Goodness me, Miss Conlon. Don't think that making tea is below me now that I am about to be published. I shall never change. I am too well aware of your good influences on me for that to happen. And you too, Doreen. Working here, with both of you, has changed my life. Did you ever expect to nurture an up-and-coming writer among your staff, Miss Conlon? Imagine. One day a person will hand out a book from the library and my name will be on it. Think how thrilled you will be.'

'Would you be so kind as to get me a glass of water, Doreen?'

'Certainly, Miss Conlon.'

'If you will both excuse me.' Miss Conlon took the water and left the staff room.

'Poor Miss Conlon. She is so overwhelmed she can't speak. I can understand. This is not something that happens every day. I didn't get a chance to tell her I would be dedicating one of my works to her. Never mind. I'll save that for another day. She has enough to think about at the moment. I have to tell you, Doreen, it's going to be hard to concentrate on overdues when my mind is reeling with ideas.'

Miss Conlon sat at her desk, took out the draft copy of her resignation letter and made adjustments to it. She then typed it, signed it, and addressed it: 'Personal. For the attention of Mr Scott.' Early retirement. A prospect she had never considered, never made plans or provision for. The library had been her life. Could it be for the best? Perhaps it was better to get out while there was still time to do things. See the world. Go to all those places she had only read about. In ten years' time she might not be able to travel. She might have lost her health or her enthusiasm and be left with questions. A lifelong service and nothing at the end except a small flat, a cat, and shelves of dusty books.

Shantell sat on the edge of her bed and smiled at her mobile phone. It was a specific smile, oozing confidence and self-assurance. She had practised it in front of the mirror until she had had it down pat and could summon it at will. It was for her publishers. She was expecting a call from them and she wanted to be able to reflect these feelings when she spoke to them. 'You can always tell a confident person from a smiling voice,' was one of her favourite quotes from *Developing your Telephone Technique*, a book she had read in the library. She was satisfied that it worked. She had been able to test it when she called Carmel and Rosie to tell them about her news and to invite them to join herself and David the following Friday for a celebration drink.

It hadn't seemed worth the effort, smiling confidently into Carmel's answering machine, but she did it anyway. It was good discipline. A chance to try out her smiling-voice spontaneity. Rosie was next. Rosie knew immediately that there was something different about her. She said she could tell by Shantell's voice. It was gratifying that she was so surprised and excited. She promised to contact Tower Heights and tell everyone and she was going to persuade Fionn to come up from Kerry for the day. David was out but she left a message, using a particularly strong smile, with his mother. How impressed she had been to learn that her son knew an author, and what a refined accent she had.

'Will there be a launch?'

'I'm afraid not, Mrs Shield-Knox. Lunch would not be appropriate at this time.'

'How disappointing. When will you launch?'

'I'll have something before I go.' Poor dear, no wonder David worries about her.

'What are you talking about, Miss O'Doherty?'

'Lunch, Mrs Shield-Knox. You were asking me

about lunch.' Shantell strained to retain her smile. 'Have you forgotten?'

'Forgotten? Forgotten what? I never mentioned lunch. Why should I have the slightest interest in your lunch?'

'Don't worry, Mrs Shield-Knox. We all get confused at times. It's nothing to be ashamed of. Where would we be if we didn't recognise that none of us is perfect?' She really is bad, Shantell said to herself. 'Are you on medication?' The silence on the other end of the phone made Shantell uneasy. 'Would you like me to come over and keep you company until David gets back?'

'I certainly would not. I do not know you.'

'But if I came over you would.'

'I do not wish to know you and I am perfectly happy with my own company.'

'I understand, Mrs Shield-Knox.' Brave old thing. One of the old stock. You can't beat them. 'Let me give you my number in case you change your mind.'

'I never change my mind.'

'Have you got a pencil? Wait. I have a better idea. When you hang up I will phone again. Don't answer it and the number will go into your answering machine. I can be with you immediately.'

'If you come here I shall call the guards.'

'Goodbye for now, Mrs Shield-Knox. Goodbye.' Phew, she really is a handful, thought Shantell. Poor David. After the call, Shantell made a note to try and get David later. She had the distinct impression that Mrs Shield-Knox hadn't fully understood the message.

It was frustrating not having a number for Miss Titchmarch. Not listed. Like as if Miss Titchmarch had no phone. That girl didn't even try to get it. How many Titchmarches can there be in England? Especially famous Titchmarches. If she had the time she would write a letter of complaint to the telephone company. Best to wait. She would get her publisher to contact Miss Titchmarch's publisher. Shantell only hoped it wouldn't be too late. It would be so perfect if Miss Titchmarch could fly over for the celebration. There were so many things to organise. Things to be done. It was wonderful.

# Chapter Twenty-five

'Tom-toms reverberating round Tower Heights,' was how Mick O'Toole described it to Martin. 'Bell might as well not have invented the telephone. All those women need is an old army blanket and a packet of firelighters.'

Martin, who was sitting in front of his telly watching the races from Fairyhouse, looked up when Mick burst in. 'Either tell me what you are talking about, Mick, or get out.'

'There's another meeting in town. Rosie Deignan phoned Ivy who told Dolores who informed Peggy and Lily and the whole lot of them that they're all meeting in town.'

'What's that got to do with me?'

'What's that got to do with you? Do you want those women in there unsupervised? Spreading the Lord only knows what rubbish about us. Not me, Martin. If they are going to town so am I.'

'What are they going for? Nothing but a girls' night out, theoretically speaking.'

'That's exactly it. That's the danger. Ivy heard it

from Rosie. Your woman's books are going to be published. I need evidence so I can pursue the libel case.'

'The what?'

'The libel case. She's bound to have us in the books. What else would she have to write about? I want to be ready to sue. We get a sneak preview and then we know what we are up against.'

'Published. Are you sure?'

'Certain sure. That's what the trip is all about. We are invited into town to celebrate.'

'How come nobody told me?' Mick's gesture, raising his hands and eyes to the heavens, reminded Martin he had told everyone never to mention Shantell's name in his presence again. 'For once, Mick, you have a point. She could have something in about the flats.'

'That's what I'm worried about, Martin.'

'Mobilise the men. Find out what time the women are meeting and where. I'm going to try and borrow one of those tape recorders.'

'You'll have to shave your chest. You see it on the telly all the time. They always shave their chests when they're going undercover.'

'You are daft as a brush, Mick O'Toole. Now get over to Ivy's and see what they are up to.'


'Shush,' Dolores said. 'Keep it down. Mick O'Toole is snooping around outside.' Dolores was looking out the window of Ivy's flat where the ladies had gathered to prepare for their trip to town.

'He was probably sent to see if we were ready, Dolores. The men will want to escort us into town. I'll tell him to give us a few more minutes.' Ivy opened her door and had a quick chat with Mick.

'That shower couldn't escort a chip out of a paper bag,' Dolores sniffed. 'Why do we need them? We are perfectly capable of going to town by ourselves.'

'It's nicer to be escorted, Dolores. Men don't take advantage of a woman if she is escorted.'

'I don't think you need have any worries on that score, Peggy. There's no danger of white slavers coming for you.'

'Isn't this living, girls,' Lily butted in. Dolores was getting on her high horse and Lily could sense a row brewing. 'In and out of town like elastic. I've never had the good coat on so often. It makes a change from going to funerals. The only occasions I get to wear it is to go to funerals. That's all we ever seemed to do before we got involved with an author. Do you think we're in it? The book I mean.'

'I don't doubt it, Lily,' Peggy said. 'Why else would she be asking us?'

'Is everybody ready?' Dolores asked. 'Check your bags. Keys, purse, bus pass, pension book—'

'Why do we need our pension books?'

'For identification purposes, Ivy. You never know when you are going to need identification.'

'She'll be asking if we have clean underwear on next,' Ivy whispered to Peggy.

'She can't help it,' Peggy whispered back. 'She used to be in charge of the Girl Guides over in Clanbrassil Street.'

The ladies left the flat and, in two shifts, took the lift to the ground floor. They linked, arm in arm, as they made their way to the bus-stop outside Tower Heights. The gentlemen followed, keeping a comfortable distance behind. Martin didn't want the women catching sight of the tape recorder he had hidden underneath his coat.

'Are they behind us, Peggy?'

'Yes.' Peggy looked back at the men. 'They're straggling after us.'

Dolores took a quick glance round. 'The state of them. Wouldn't you think they'd have got dressed up a bit for the occasion.'

'They have no sense of style, Dolores. At least we're not letting the side down.'

Mrs Shield-Knox waited anxiously for her son, David, to contact her. 'Out with a client,' the secretary had told her when she had called his office. She'd left several messages for him to get in touch with her but had no way of knowing if he got them or not. She didn't want to keep calling. It might arouse suspicion, give food for idle speculation, in his place of work. She had forgotten all about that strange telephone call. It had completely slipped her mind. She had been listening to a book programme on the radio when it suddenly came back to her. The programme, dealing with the oddities and eccentricities of certain writers, reminded her of the woman who had phoned for David. At the time Mrs Shield-Knox had presumed it must have been a crank call but now, listening to the programme, she was not at all sure. David's behaviour had been so odd recently. As a mother she knew something was wrong. She couldn't question him of course. Young men took such exception to being questioned by their mothers. Was it possible that this author woman was the reason? She might have got her claws into the poor boy. The more she thought about it the more convinced she became that this was the root of David's troubles. She checked through her telephone message book. There it was. *David. Friday – Launch. S. O'Doherty*. Today was the day he was expected to attend, but he didn't know about it, because she hadn't given him the message.

It became very clear to Mrs Shield-Knox that this woman had designs on her son. What woman wouldn't? He was handsome and charming with a lucrative career ahead of him. Not to mention the legacy left to him by his father. An ideal figure for some scheming authoress to have draped over her arm. That was why she wanted David in attendance as an accessory. Her son, David, an accessory! She must act. Do something. But what? What could she do? An idea came into her head. It was an audacious idea, and there were a few flaws, but the more she thought about it the better it seemed. There was nothing else for it. She would attend this event herself. It would be a perfect way to discover more about this woman. No one would notice an extra guest. There were always extra guests at these functions. If questioned she would say she had been invited. She even had the woman's phone number as proof.

Mrs Shield-Knox went to her bedroom and looked through her wardrobe. She needed something that would blend in, slightly arty, but not overdone. She didn't want to draw attention to herself. David, she knew, would worry if she was out when he got home – it had been so long since she had been out alone – but it had to be done. It was her duty. She would leave him a note.

'However you feel about it, Miss Conlon, I do think it

is imperative that there is a representative from the library at this impromptu gathering for Miss O'Doherty.' Mr Scott, the library manager, was talking to Miss Conlon and Doreen in the staff room during their coffee break. 'It's not often that a member of staff gets published and we are, after all, in the business.'

'She is not a member of staff, Mr Scott.'

'Technically no, Miss Conlon, but the fact that she was doing her community service here, during which time she wrote her novel, is all the more reason someone should attend. It shows us up in a very good light and presents a great opportunity for publicity. As you are very well aware, Miss Conlon, we are badly in need of funds. This could be the boost we're looking for.'

'I do not think that Miss O'Doherty's novel is the sort of literature we would want to promote, Mr Scott.'

'Have you read it, Miss Conlon?'

'No. I haven't. But I do feel, knowing Miss O'Doherty—'

'Feelings do not come into this. I will not have the public thinking we are in any way prejudiced. Someone will attend. I insist on this. What if the media were present? Who would be there to tell them how we, against all opposition, involve ourselves in rehabilitation? How our programmes, aimed at bringing offenders out of their life of crime, can add a new dimension to their lives? Increase their skills, help them to achieve ambitions that they would not otherwise realise.'

'But you were always against the programmes, Mr Scott,' Doreen blurted out.

'Don't nit-pick, Doreen. I do admit to having had certain reservations. As head of this library, naturally, the safety and welfare of my staff was my first concern. However, this success has proved we are second to none in our contribution to society as a whole. I would happily volunteer but, unfortunately, Mrs Scott and I are committed elsewhere. I will leave the decision as to who attends in your capable hands, Miss Conlon. Ladies.' Mr Scott left the staff room.

'Of all the nerve. He is trying to take the credit, Miss Conlon. Everyone knows you set up those programmes.'

'Would you like to go, Doreen?'

'Oh, Miss Conlon. I couldn't.'

'And why not?'

'You should be the one to go. You are the head librarian.'

'I am definitely not going, Doreen. Wild horses couldn't drag me there.'

'Are you sure?'

'Absolutely sure. That's settled then. I shall inform Mr Scott you will go after work.'

'After work. But I'm not dressed properly, I'd have to go as I am. I couldn't go looking like this.'

'You look perfectly respectable to me, Doreen.' Miss Conlon caught Doreen's crestfallen expression. 'Out with it, Doreen. What's on your mind?'

'If I could leave now, Miss Conlon, I could get my hair done on the way home, change my clothes, and still make it back to town in time. I'll make up the hours, Miss Conlon. I can come in on Saturday and—'

'Go, Doreen.'

'I wouldn't want you to think—'

'Go before I change my mind.'

Doreen scooted off and Miss Conlon returned to her office. There was work to be done. The sooner this nonsense was over the better. She was determined to put the whole thing out of her mind.

David was enjoying himself as he ambled round town. His meeting with his client had been brief and he found himself with time on his hands. He wasn't expected back at the office, and if he went back now he would have to spend the afternoon sitting at his desk, trying to look busy. He took advantage of the situation to indulge in one of his favourite pastimes, browsing round bookshops. He'd have a browse and go for a coffee. Pop into one of those haunts he used to frequent in his student days. He might even phone one of his old university friends and arrange to meet later that evening. It would be a good idea to have something lined up for the evening. Stop him thinking about Shantell. He refused to think about Shantell. He wasn't going to meet her and that was that. What could she do to him? Nothing. He smiled, thinking of the dreadful state he had got himself into, and over what? One woman. A client.

He bought some reference books he needed for work and then wandered through the shop to the new publications section where he found himself facing a large promotional poster of smiling Irish writers. As he stood there, happily studying the faces, trying to distinguish each one of them, something happened. Every face turned into Shantell. A terrifying wave of dizziness came over him. Was he going crazy? He shut his eyes tight, struggling to control his heart which was promising to burst through every vein, and started to count.

When he got to ten, and the pounding had subsided a little, he ventured a blink. He blinked a couple more times before he found the courage to open his eyes fully. She was gone. The authors were back, their smiles unchanged. Bizarre. Quite bizarre. He dismissed the experience as a hallucination brought on by the lack of lunch, and looked back at the poster, picking out authors whose work he knew when, without any warning, it happened again. This time she wouldn't go away. He made for the exit, mumbling apologies as he jostled through the crowd, and stood, trembling, outside the shop. Crushed and powerless, he eventually turned and walked in the direction of O'Connell Street.

Mrs Shield-Knox, sporting a strange feathered hat as her contribution to the world of art, stood at the bay window watching for her taxi. She had spent her afternoon leafing through the literary section of the previous Sunday papers, bringing herself up to date with titles. One couldn't go to these literary parties without being able to drop a name or two into the conversation. When her taxi arrived she gave directions to the driver. 'It's one of those literary public houses, driver. Something to do with Joyce.'

'Whatever you say, missis.' The taxi driver had heard it all. These old dears would say anything to keep their drinking respectable. He looked at her in his rear-view mirror. Funny hat, he thought to himself. She probably thinks no one will recognise her.

'Do you know the public house, driver?'

'Don't worry, missis. I know where we are going.

I'll get you there safely.' He knew the pub all right. 'Literary' was not a name he would put on it.

'Hello. Hello. Is that Ace Taxis?' Mr O'Gorman was calling from the public phone in the pub. 'I'd like to book a cab please . . . Around four thirty. Could I have Malachy Conway? Yes, Malachy. I've a few runs to do and Malachy has taken me before so he knows the route. The name is Tom O'Gorman. Tell him to pick me up at the usual place. He'll know where I mean.' Mr O'Gorman hung up and went back to his pint. 'We can't leave Malachy out,' he said to Matt, 'he's been in on it since the start.'

'Leave Malachy out of what, Mr O'Gorman? What's going on? Is there something you are not telling me?'

'Relax, Matt. Nothing's going on. I'm meeting David here later and I thought it would be nice if Malachy joined us.'

'Why the deception? Why can you not ring him, like any normal person, and ask him to join you? Always have to play mystery man, don't you? Booking a taxi. You'll get that man fired by the time you're finished.'

'Where's your sense of drama, Matt?'

'At home. Where it belongs.'

'Do you know your trouble, Matt? You work too hard. You never lighten up. You work here all the hours God gives and the boss still doesn't make you manager.'

'It's not as simple as that.'

'Don't tell me, I know. The turnover doesn't warrant the extra manager's pay he'd have to give you. Am I right? Isn't that the line he gives you?'

'You only know that because I told you.'

'I have eyes, Matt. I can see for myself.'

'It's none of your concern, Mr O'Gorman. Keep your business on the public side of the counter and leave me to mine.'

'No offence, Matt, you know that. I just don't like to see people being taken advantage of.'


The train from Kerry was late. Rosie kept looking at the station clock, willing the train to arrive. She had hoped that she and Fionn would have a little time together before meeting the others but now, because it was so late, they would have to go directly to the pub. At least this time Fionn would be in town for a few days. Not an up-and-down day return, like he usually did. They were going to stay together in her granny's flat. Rosie was really looking forward to it. It would be their longest time together. A real couple at last. Fionn had been a bit dubious about it at first. Thought it wasn't quite proper. He relented when she quoted some of the local bed and breakfast charges to him. She decided not to say anything to Ivy about staying in the flat. She didn't want the neighbours popping in and out all the time.

When she saw the train approach she jumped into a taxi. No point waiting for the taxi stampede as everyone poured off the train. She opened the cab window and watched for Fionn at the station exit.

She spotted him among the crowds and shouted to him, 'Fionn. Over here. At the taxi rank.'

'Rosie, my love.' Fionn ran over to embrace her. 'It's so good to see you.'

'Get in, Fionn. We have to go straight away or we'll be late. You look very smart, Fionn. Is that a new suit?'

'The mother got it for me. She said if I was coming to Dublin to meet writers and the like, she wasn't having me letting Kerry down.'

'Oh,' Rosie said disappointedly. 'I thought you had got it for me.'

'Where to, miss?'

'Into town, please driver. We are going to a pub near O'Connell Street Bridge. I don't know the name of the street but I'll recognise it when we get there.'

'Don't be angry, Rosie,' Fionn said. 'I only let her get it to keep the peace.'

Rosie stayed silent for a few moments, thinking about Fionn's mother. 'I'll be the one picking your suits after we are married, Fionn,' was all she would say to him.


Three taxis turned down the small side street and pulled up outside Hart's pub. Rosie and Fionn, and Mrs Shield-Knox, were in the first two, followed almost immediately by Malachy. As all the passengers alighted, the band of pensioners turned into the street from the opposite end, and came galloping towards them. Mrs Shield-Knox shrank back in her seat.

The ladies of the Tower Heights contingent, arriving in town too early for the meeting, had stopped in Adam and Eve's Church to light candles. They stayed in the church longer than they'd intended, and ended up rushing down the quays. The gentlemen, who had taken refuge in a turf accountant's near the pub, kept a sharp lookout. They didn't want the ladies getting in before them. When they saw the women heading down the side street, they stepped out from the bookie's and joined the group, bringing up the rear.

'What's going on, driver? Is it a demonstration?'

'Joyceans, missis.' The driver decided to play Mrs Shield-Knox at her own game. 'You know yourself. They're everywhere. They pop up all over the city. Scholars and the like. You'd be surprised how many Japanese would be among them.'

'Japanese?' Mrs Shield-Knox exclaimed.

Doreen, changed and coiffured, had walked into town. It would be awful to be the first to arrive. Better to slip in when everyone was there. That way she wouldn't be noticed. She could mingle with the crowd, listen to what was going on, and report back to Mrs Scott. When she turned the corner and saw the crowd, she froze. She didn't want to go in. What was she doing there anyway? She was no good in crowds – she didn't know anyone, and she was hopeless at striking up conversations with strangers. Shantell would be too preoccupied with important people even to notice her. She thought of running away, but how could she go to work on Monday and tell Mr Scott and Miss Conlon she had had a half day for nothing. She crouched down behind Malachy's taxi and waited for everyone to go in.

Stress, David told himself, as he shuffled on towards the rendezvous. It had to be down to stress. There was no other explanation. The papers these days were full of articles dealing with modern day stress. What he needed was a break. Get away for a few days. No big plans. Simply point his Mini in one direction and take off. As he fantasised, seeing himself zooming through the countryside, the same old thorny question loomed. His mother. What could he do with his mother? She hated being left alone. He had two choices. He could take her with him or get someone in to stay with her. At a push, there was always Aunt Mollie. His mother, he knew, wouldn't be too happy about Aunt Mollie but, what the hell, it would only be for a few days. He began to cheer up a little. He spotted Malachy's taxi, parked beside the wall outside the pub, and gave a sigh of relief. 'Thank goodness. If Malachy is there as well it will take a bit of pressure off. I'll give it half an hour. That's enough time to show my face, say my hellos, and go. What I need is an exorcism. What way does that thing work, I wonder? Is it me that needs to be exorcised, or is it her?' He started to laugh aloud. 'Get a grip on yourself David. You, my son, are losing it. In fact, you are becoming hysterical. You are supposed to be a man, not a mouse.' He stopped short, suddenly aware that he had been talking out loud, when he heard a noise coming from behind the taxi. Oh, God, he muttered to himself, as he realised someone had been listening to him.

'Who's there? Shantell. Is that you?'

Doreen crept out from behind the cab. She didn't want to be found, crouched down, as if she were having a pee.

'Hello,' she said. 'Sorry to disturb you. I was just going.'

'What were you doing there?'

'I dropped something.' Doreen was bright red with embarrassment. She had heard David's ranting and didn't know what to make of it.

'Are you going into the pub?'

'No. Yes. I mean, I was going to go in but I think I've changed my mind.'

'Are you meeting someone in there?'

'I was supposed to be meeting a woman I work with, but—'

'Look. I hope you don't take this the wrong way, but would you come in with me? I would really appreciate if it you say yes. I would rather not face it on my own.'

'Well . . .' Doreen hesitated. She would much prefer to be accompanied by this nice looking young man than go into the pub on her own, but would he think she was brazen? 'It doesn't seem right. I don't even know you.'

'We can soon change that. My name is David. David Shield-Knox.' David thrust out his hand. 'Very pleased to meet you.'

'I'm Doreen. Doreen Brown.' Doreen took his hand and shook it, giggling a little, to hide her confusion.

'Allow me.' David took Doreen's arm and escorted her into the pub. 'Don't worry. This pub is always very quiet in the afternoon.'

Doreen looked at him in surprise.

'Hello, Mr O'Gorman. Hello, Matt.' Rosie greeted them as she entered with Fionn and Malachy.

'Well, well, well. This is a pleasant surprise. I didn't know you were in town, Fionn. And there's Malachy. Bang on time as usual, Malachy. Matt. Put down that cup of tea and serve these good friends of mine a drink.'

'Afternoon, folks,' Matt said. 'What can I get you?'

Before they had a chance to order, the door opened again, and the pensioners swarmed in.

'Here we are,' Dolores cried. 'I bet you never thought you'd be lucky enough to see us again so

soon. Come on girls, let's get our seats before the
place fills up. Rosie, darling. How are you? You have
your young man in tow. We'll be over to talk to you
when we get settled. Aren't you the terrible man, Mr
O'Gorman? Getting us girls into pubs in the middle of
the afternoon.' She went over to the other ladies who
were pulling tables and chairs out from the walls, and
placing them together. 'Martin,' she called out.
'Order the drinks will you. You know what we're
having.'

'Mr O'Gorman.' Matt called him to one side. 'Can
I have a word?'

'You needn't look at me like that, Matt. I don't
know what's going on. I swear to God I don't. I was
meeting Shantell and David. That's all. That's why I
phoned Malachy. A bit of support for young David.
You know how terrified he is of Shantell. Martin.' Mr
O'Gorman beckoned across to him. 'Martin, come
here a minute will you. Would you ever tell us what
the hell is going on?'

'Didn't you know, Mr O'Gorman? It's Shantell.
She is going to be published.'

'You're having me on.'

'True as God. I didn't know it myself until Mick
here told me, and even then I could hardly believe it.
That's the reason I'm here. I want to find out what's
in the book.'

'Put on the pints, Matt. I can feel a strong weakness
coming over me.'

Mrs Shield-Knox stood in the centre of the room and
looked around her. Tables and chairs were being
moved about and there seemed to be a considerable
amount of confusion. She had obviously arrived too

soon. 'I'm here to see Miss Shantell O'Doherty,' her deep voice boomed round the room. 'I understand there is a launch.'

'We're all here to see Shantell, missis,' Ivy said. 'Why don't you take the weight off your feet and sit down? You can sit over there beside Lily.'

'Thank you. That's very kind of you. I shall order a drink from the counter first.'

'Martin,' Lily roared. 'There's another one for a drink. Martin will call it for you, missis, and you can pay him later. We always go Dutch when we're out together.'

'Is that Joycean? I believe you are all Joyceans.'

'No. I'm Ivy and that's Dolores, and there's a Lily, and a Peggy and a—'

'What are you on missis?' Martin shouted over, interrupting Ivy. 'Is it a glass?'

'As you are kind enough to ask, I will have a gin and tonic with plenty of ice and lemon. I believe I am to sit with the lady over there.' She pointed across to Lily.

'They don't do lunch,' Lily said to Mrs Shield-Knox as she sat down beside her. 'I heard you asking Ivy. I tried before. He will give you tea though.' She nodded over to Matt. 'He makes a song and dance about it mind. That's a lovely hat. With a hat like that you could go anywhere.'

'Thank you. I thought it would be suitable for the occasion.'

'I know what you mean. That's why I wore my good coat.'

'Mother!' David, with Doreen in tow, got the shock of his life when he entered the pub and saw his mother sitting at the pensioners' table. 'What are you doing here, Mother?'

'I am here for the launch, David.'

'I don't understand. What launch?'

'Don't be tiresome, David. I know all about it.'

'I didn't know she was your mother, David,' Lily said. 'I told her they don't do lunch. Still, the bit of lemon will keep her going for a bit.'

'Who is that woman?' Mrs Shield-Knox pointed her finger at Doreen.

'Forgive me.' He turned to Doreen. 'I am being rude. This is my mother, Mrs Shield-Knox. Mother, this is—'

'Are you the woman who phoned my son?'

'Oh no, Mrs Shieldknox,' Doreen said immediately, wilting under the scrutiny. 'We only met outside.'

'Outside? What do you mean you met outside?'

'We've known each other a long time, Mother. In fact I've been meaning to introduce you. This is Doreen, Doreen Brown.'

'Are you related to the Brown-Thomas Browns?'

'Mother!'

'And what does Doreen do, David dear?'

'Mother, please,' David said helplessly, mortified by the inquisition.

Doreen rushed to his rescue. 'I work in the library, Mrs Shieldknox. The Central Library.'

'How clever of you. Then you must know my new acquaintances.' She gestured up and down the table. 'The Joyceans.'

Ivy leaned back behind Mrs Shield-Knox and shrugged at Dolores. 'Joyceans,' she mouthed. 'What is she talking about, God bless her?' She straightened up quickly in case she was caught.

'I'm afraid I don't, Mrs Shieldknox.'

'There is a hyphen, dear. It's *Shield-Knox*. David. Did you not tell her there is a hyphen?'

'Your G and T, missis.' Martin came over with the drink. 'You can sort me out later. I've organised a tab at the bar. David, me old segotia, leave the women to themselves and come and join us men at the bar.'

'You are not leaving me here, David,' Doreen said in a panic.

'Don't worry, Doreen. I won't leave you anywhere within range of my mother's clutches.'

Shantell made her way through the streets. It was nearly five. She knew she was late but she wanted to be sure everyone was there before her. She wanted to make an entrance. She had taken great care with her appearance, trying to imagine what Miss Titchmarch would wear for such an event, and was thrilled with the results. Bright and flowing was how she had envisioned Miss Titchmarch. Bright and flowing with a harmonious mix of scarlets and purples. Shantell was aware – although pretending to be impervious – of the glances of passers-by. These glances served to confirm her opinion that her outfit had succeeded. She exuded confidence. Confidence and grooming. You couldn't beat it.

As she walked, her stride responded to the swish of her full length nylon skirt, which was electrified by its continued rubbing against her tights. She knew the purple skirt went so well with the bright red tunic-style top, and the red and gold trimmed bolero she had found in a thrift shop. The final touch was a scarf. Multicoloured, with gold and black tassels on the ends. It was a nuisance having to wear her overcoat which covered up most of her ensemble. In spite of the cold, Shantell left it open.

She paused to empathise with everything she passed. The city streets, the noise, the buildings, the people. She stopped, lingering on O'Connell Street Bridge, savouring the river smells, the squawk of the seagulls, the lapping of the water. How was it she had never noticed all this before? She had taken it all for granted. The bridge had been something to walk over. Now, being an artiste, she was learning to appreciate even the small things. Shantell gave a deep sigh of pleasure as she walked on to the pub. To think. They were all waiting for her. Destiny had arrived. She went in.

Shantell surveyed the room. The seating had been rearranged. Six tables, joined together, were lined up across the floor of the pub and a group of ladies, almost all of whom she recognised, sat behind them, facing the bar. At the centre table, in a striking feathered hat, one woman she didn't know sat talking to Lily. Shantell stared at this woman, noting her every move. There was definitely something different about her. Something cosmopolitan. Shantell gave a knowing smile as she continued her scan. The gentlemen had collected in small circles beside the counter. A little way off David and Doreen were engrossed in intimate conversation. There was quite a din. Everyone seemed to be talking at once. Shantell slipped off her coat, threw it on a nearby chair and lingered, expectantly, by the door. She donned a radiant smile, followed by a demure, modest dropping of the head. Humility and gratitude all in one movement. She had practised this stance in front of the mirror before she left home, and she would be ready with her performance the moment she was spotted. Time ticked by. Shantell was beginning to get very cross. If no one noticed her soon – she couldn't just stand there.

Matt was the first to see her. Being the professional barman that he was, he looked around, ready to take the next orders, and saw her. He nudged Mr O'Gorman across the counter, letting him know she was there.

'If it isn't the authoress,' Mr O'Gorman said. 'It's Shantell everyone. She's arrived at last.' He went over to her, gave her a big bear-hug, and dragged her back to his position at the counter, giving her no opportunity to use her head movement.

'Give this lady a large brandy, Matt. The first time we met I was privileged to be able to buy her a brandy and now, here she is, about to be published.'

'Thank you, Mr O'Gorman.'

'Now then. We all want to know about the book. Is it fiction? Autobiographical? What is it about?'

'Please. Please, Mr O'Gorman. You must give me a moment. I must talk to my guests.'

'Of course, Shantell. You do the rounds and then you can tell us about it.' Mr O'Gorman handed Shantell her drink and led her, with a grandiose gesture reminiscent of a variety-show speciality act, to the centre of the room. He was rewarded by a trickle of applause initiated by Ivy. 'Here she is, folks. The woman we've all been waiting for.'

Shantell reversed her prepared routine: dropping her head, she did gratitude and humility first, then modest and demure, and ended with radiant smile. 'Thank you. Thank you everyone. You will never know how much this means to me. I am deeply touched. When we first met I was a humble undertaker . . .'

'An undertaker?' Mrs Shield-Knox clutched Ivy's arm.

'That's right,' Ivy whispered. 'She was booked to bury our friend Rose Deignan. She never did though.'

'. . . and now I am to have my work published . . .'

'Quick, Mick. She's going to talk about the book. Look for a socket while I get the tape recorder.'

'I thought you had it strapped to your chest?'

'I'm not bloody MI5. It's over there under my coat.'

'. . . Deep down, for as long as I can remember, I knew I was destined for something special.' Shantell allowed a moment for this disclosure to sink in. 'I have so many people to thank . . .'

'It's just like the Oscars.' Lily reached for her hankie.

'. . . For helping me achieve this. You, my friends.' Shantell blew kisses in all directions. 'My colleagues in the library, represented here by Doreen.' She blew a special kiss to Doreen. 'But most of all.' Shantell moved closer to the centre table. 'To this lady here.' Shantell flung her arms out to Mrs Shield-Knox. 'This is the lady to whom I have dedicated my first work . . .'

'Mother?' David said in surprise.

'. . . Her book entitled *Getting Started: The Essential Guide to Writing a Good Novel* has been my inspiration and my revelation. Without it, there were times, I felt I couldn't go on. Miss Titchmarch. Would you do me a great honour and step up here beside me? A round of applause, everyone, for Miss Titchmarch.' Shantell led a slow hand clap of appreciation. 'Bring her up, ladies. She is too modest to come forward herself.'

As Dolores, Peggy and Ivy pounced on Mrs Shield-Knox and tried to drag her from her seat, the feathered hat was the first casualty.

'Stop it. Stop it at once. Unhand me,' Mrs Shield-Knox cried. 'David, do something.'

'Order. Order,' Matt shouted from behind the counter. 'You'll all be barred. Mr O'Gorman. Malachy. Don't just stand there.'

'Bring her up,' Shantell continued to cry.

'I'll give you one minute to restore order or I'm calling the guards.'

Mr O'Gorman and Malachy rushed to rescue Mrs Shield-Knox while David and Doreen, and Rosie and Fionn, could only stand by and watch hopelessly.

'Are you getting all this on tape, Martin?' Mick asked.

'What would be the point?' Martin responded. He and the other male members of Tower Heights continued, unperturbed, to drink their pints. 'Do you know what I'm going to tell you? The foreigners have it right. Women shouldn't be allowed out at all, let alone in pubs drinking. They should bring suttee into this country. There'd be a lot less trouble if they introduced suttee.'

# Chapter Twenty-six

Calm had been restored in the pub. Matt's hammering on the counter and threats to call the guards had had their effect. Mrs Shield-Knox was put back in her seat and placated with more drink. Shantell, a little disconcerted that Miss Titchmarch had turned out to be David's mother, apologised for her mistake.

'Forgive me, Mrs Shield-Knox. I was deceived by your distinguished manner and that charming hat.'

'No harm done,' Mr O'Gorman said, picking up the hat and trying to fluff the feathers. 'A straightforward case of mistaken identity. It happens in the best of circles. Why, only recently the Aga Khan, while here on a visit for the Dublin Horse Show, was mistaken, in a prominent restaurant I'll have you know, for a boxer by the name of Al-Hizar Huful. The Aga, I am delighted to say, handled the situation like a true gentleman.'

Mrs Shield-Knox was at a loss. She was completely dumbfounded. To be mistaken for Miss Titchmarch, and manhandled because of that, was one thing. Now this gentleman beside her, who was plucking the feathers out of her hat, seemed to be making comparisons between herself, the Aga Khan, and a pugilist with a name which was unpronounceable to the English-speaking tongue.

'Don't pay any attention to him, Mrs Shield-Knox,' Ivy said kindly. 'Men are all the same. Any excuse to talk about sport and they're off.'

'David! Where is my son, David?'

'He's over there. Talking to that nice young girl from the library.'

'Thank goodness. I must confess to you, Ivy, I am here because I thought that woman, Shantell, had designs on my boy.'

'I wouldn't worry on that score. Between ourselves, I don't think she ever got past the design stage. First it was Fionn, the young man over there with our Rosie, then it was David. Who knows where her eye is going to fall next? The funny thing is that as soon as she takes her eye off them they usually fall in love.' Ivy looked across to David and Doreen. 'Don't they make a lovely couple.'

'When are we going to hear about the book?' Mick said to Martin. 'If nothing happens soon it'll be time to go home. We can't wait until it's out. It'll be too late to do anything about it then.'

'Give things a minute to settle down, Mick, and I'll bring it up. Better still. I'll get Mr O'Gorman or Malachy to get her talking about it. That way we won't be suspected of having an ulterior motive.'

'What does that mean when it's at home?'

'It means we didn't force her to reveal the contents of the book. If we use our evidence in court, i.e. the tape recording, to prevent the publication, we didn't coerce her into giving it to us.'

'You are a genius, Martin. A bloody genius.'

Martin, Malachy and Mr O'Gorman were huddled together in deep conversation.

'And we want to know the contents, Mr O'Gorman. We don't want anything incriminating to be out there in the public arena.'

'I absolutely agree, Martin,' Malachy said. 'I have my job to think of. If she wrote anything about the events at Tower Heights, or the trial, I could get my marching orders. Taxi drivers have to be very careful of their reputation. We should get everyone in on this. We're not the only ones who have to worry.' Malachy indicated David and Fionn. 'They have a stake in this as well. It wouldn't do David's career any good and Fionn would probably be run out of Kerry. We have met the mother, don't forget.'

'What about you, Mr O'Gorman?' Martin asked. 'Would it matter to you?'

'Matter to me? Suffice to say I might never see the inside of a hostelry again if herself got wind of the true nature of the story. She knows what I told her and that is all.'

'That's settled, then,' Malachy said. 'You go and talk to Fionn and David. I'll get organised here.'

'Mick,' Martin called. 'We're on, Mick. Plug in that tape machine as near as you can to Shantell.'

'The lead doesn't stretch very far, Martin.'

'We'll have to rearrange the tables then. Make some excuse to get the tables nearer the wall.'

'How the hell do you expect me to do that? They're all sitting at them.'

'I don't know, Mick. Think of something – anything – just do it.'

'Mr O'Gorman.' Matt called him over. 'A word, Mr O'Gorman. There is something afoot. I can smell it. I trust you are not going to stir things up again?'

'It's disappointing how little faith you have in me, Matt. No. I am not stirring anything. I am trying to save my job.'

'What do you mean?'

'Have you any idea of the contents of Shantell's book?'

'You know I haven't.'

'Think about it. How would it look if you got a mention? An unfavourable mention. Do you imagine your boss would be jumping for joy? The pub named. You named.'

'Christ. I never thought about that.'

'Well you better start thinking about it. We are going to try and persuade Shantell to give us a synopsis of the story. Get her to read us a bit. I'm sure she'd have those notes of hers in her handbag. She never goes anywhere without them. Martin has a tape recorder hidden over there. We can record her and, if there is anything damaging, at least we have something to take action with.'

'What do you want me to do?'

'Back me up. Whatever I say, back me up.'

Rosie and Doreen pulled up some chairs and sat down opposite the other ladies. They were chatting about Rosie's forthcoming wedding. Doreen was both delighted and relieved to be included in the chat. It kept her out of Mrs Shield-Knox's line of fire. Shantell had squeezed herself in between Ivy and Mrs Shield-Knox, neither of whom could get a word in edgeways, and was regaling them with choice paragraphs from

Miss Titchmarch's book. Mr O'Gorman approached the group cautiously.

'Well, Shantell. Are we not going to hear more about your book? We – the other gentlemen and myself – were only saying it would be wonderful to hear a few extracts.'

'How very flattering, Mr O'Gorman. I would be delighted. Would you excuse me, ladies. My public awaits.' Shantell jumped up and walked round the tables to the centre of the room.

Martin plugged the tape recorder into the wall and was ready to switch on. He signalled to Mick to try and get Shantell closer to him. In desperation Mick started pulling at the tables, forcing the ladies to grab up their drinks to avoid them spilling.

'What are you at, Mick O'Toole? You'll have the drinks all over us,' Dolores scolded.

'I thought you would like to be closer, Dolores. I was only trying to help you.'

'Leave those tables alone. We're grand as we are.'

Matt, who had been watching Mick's efforts, appraised the situation and came out from behind the counter. 'I'll have to ask you ladies to move,' he said.

'Move? Why do we have to move? Shantell is going to tell us about her book.'

'Fire hazard,' Matt said quickly. 'I can't have the tables in a row like that for a reading.'

'What's he talking about?'

'If you ladies would just lift your drinks we can have the tables rearranged in a jiffy. Gentlemen. Would you care to assist me? I don't want to inconvenience the ladies for longer than I have to. If we just move these tables into a semicircle near that wall. That's the way.' The men shifted the tables, chairs and stools to where

Martin was. 'It's all right, Martin.' Martin had panicked and was trying to shove the recorder further under his coat. 'You stay where you are. You're not in the way. Now then, ladies. Isn't that cosier for you? You can group around your speaker and you are nearer the fire exit door.'

The ladies bustled round the tables. 'Fire hazard. Did you ever hear the like?'

'Shush. A bit of silence now for our authoress.' Ivy said, as they sat down at the tables and waited for Shantell to begin.

'This is truly an honour,' Shantell said. 'If you would grant me a moment, I have some notes in my bag I would like to consult.'

'I knew it,' Mr O'Gorman hissed. 'I'd love to get my hands on those notes.'

Everyone shushed. They spoke in whispers as Shantell flicked through her notes.

'I know I'm going to love it,' Lily said. 'I love stories.'

No one noticed the man who entered the pub and walked behind the counter. Matt was busy collecting glasses and everyone else was looking at Shantell. The stranger opened the till and started to count the day's takings.

'Oh my God,' Lily called out. 'Look!' She had turned around to find her bag in case she needed a fresh hankie. 'The pub is being robbed.'

Every head turned to where Lily was pointing.

'It's all right, missis, it's Mr Costello. He owns the pub.' Matt knew immediately who it was. He didn't even need to look. He should have guessed Costello would be in. What would happen now? 'I'm done for,

Mr O'Gorman,' he said under his breath. 'He'll be sure to give me my walking papers.' The bar tables and chairs were all over the place and hardly a glass had been washed because he hadn't had the time. That wouldn't impress Costello. No excuses with Costello. 'Afternoon, Mr Costello. I wasn't expecting you in so early.'

'I can see that, Matt. It's obvious you weren't expecting me at all.'

'I can explain—'

'We're having a reading, Mr Costello,' Mr O'Gorman piped up. 'A literary session. Miss O'Doherty here is about to read from one of her own works.'

'Does this happen often, Matt?'

'Not often enough, Mr Costello,' Mr O'Gorman said, before Matt could speak. 'The place is crying out for this sort of thing. It would go down a treat. It's a perfect spot. With all the original fixtures and fittings intact, this pub could be on the literary trail.'

'The literary trail. Up the Joyceans,' Mrs Shield-Knox shouted out. Her fifth, or was it sixth, gin and tonic was beginning to kick in.

The atmosphere was tense as Mr Costello checked the takings again. He didn't say anything. He stood there looking from the money to Matt as if trying to decide what to do. Finally, he poured a drink and placed it in front of Matt. 'Pick it up, Matt.'

'I told you, Mr Costello. I can explain. I can explain everything.'

'Pick up the glass, Matt.' Matt slowly lifted the glass. 'Now drink it.'

'Steady on, Mr Costello,' Malachy said. 'You've already been told that this is not Matt's fault.'

'Mr O'Gorman.' Mr Costello turned to him. 'I dare say you are a man who knows how to pour a drink. You've certainly watched it often enough. Why don't you come around behind here and pour a drink for every man jack, woman and child in the place? I need to talk to Matt.'

'If you've something to say, Mr Costello,' replied Mr O'Gorman, 'say it here and say it now.'

'I do indeed have something to say. You are all very welcome to what is about to become Dublin's newest literary pub. A literary pub with Matt here as manager.'

'Mr Costello. I don't know what to say.'

'Yes. That's all you need to say, Matt. Drink up, everyone. It's a celebration.'

'Three cheers for Matt.' Mr O'Gorman led the chorus. 'That's great news. The best I've heard yet.'

'Excuse me. Excuse me, everyone.' Shantell felt her day was being taken away from her. 'I don't want to spoil your celebration, but I haven't finished my own yet.'

'Shantell,' Mr O'Gorman said. 'In the heat of the moment I forgot all about you. You were going to do your reading. Sit down everyone. Let Shantell give her reading. A new reading in a new literary pub. What could be more fitting?'

'Ready with the tape, Martin?' Mick asked in a whisper.

'You bet. She's completely off her guard. That interruption was great for us. I'm all set up and ready to go.'

'Righto, Shantell. You have the floor.'

'Thank you, Mr O'Gorman.' Shantell cleared her throat before beginning.

'Chapter one.
'Gillian Turner sighed deeply, crumbling the tissue in her hand, and looked out the window purposefully. She had watched for Tom, her special Tom, for over a week now but to no avail. Her hand languished on the back of the sofa, her eyes filled up with tears, she dropped her tissue and leafed through his last long letter which she also dropped. Thinking of him, and him only, her hands went to her breasts. She felt a tingling between her legs and she knew what she must do. Tearing herself from the window she slumped upstairs and threw herself upon the bed. She hated herself for this. For the low despicable figure she had become. But without Tom she was nothing. She stripped off her dressing gown, dived in between the sheets, and proceeded to masturbate.'

'That's the first paragraph. What do you think? Isn't it wonderful.'